Titles by Jennifer Estep

KARMA GIRL
HOT MAMA
JINX

continued . . .

JINX

Jennifer Estep

BERKLEY SENSATION, NEW YORK

THE BERKLEY PUBLISHING GROUP
Published by the Penguin Group
Penguin Group (USA) Inc.
375 Hudson Street, New York, New York 10014, USA
Penguin Group (Canada), 90 Eglinton Avenue East, Suite 700, Toronto, Ontario M4P 2Y3, Canada
(a division of Pearson Penguin Canada Inc.)
Penguin Books Ltd., 80 Strand, London WC2R 0RL, England
Penguin Group Ireland, 25 St. Stephen's Green, Dublin 2, Ireland (a division of Penguin Books Ltd.)
Penguin Group (Australia), 250 Camberwell Road, Camberwell, Victoria 3124, Australia
(a division of Pearson Australia Group Pty. Ltd.)
Penguin Books India Pvt. Ltd., 11 Community Centre, Panchsheel Park, New Delhi—110 017, India
Penguin Group (NZ), 67 Apollo Drive, Rosedale, North Shore 0632, New Zealand
(a division of Pearson New Zealand Ltd.)
Penguin Books (South Africa) (Pty.) Ltd., 24 Sturdee Avenue, Rosebank, Johannesburg 2196, South Africa

Penguin Books Ltd., Registered Offices: 80 Strand, London WC2R 0RL, England

This is a work of fiction. Names, characters, places, and incidents either are the product of the author's imagination or are used fictitiously, and any resemblance to actual persons, living or dead, business establishments, events, or locales is entirely coincidental. The publisher does not have any control over and does not assume any responsibility for author or third-party websites or their content.

JINX

A Berkley Sensation Book / published by arrangement with the author

PRINTING HISTORY
Berkley Sensation mass-market edition / September 2008

Copyright © 2008 by Jennifer Estep.
Cover illustration by Aleta Rafton.
Cover design by Judith Lagerman.
Interior text design by Kristin del Rosario.
Text composition by ReadSmart® from Language Technologies, Inc.

ISBN: 978-0-425-22062-7

BERKLEY® SENSATION
Berkley Sensation Books are published by The Berkley Publishing Group,
a division of Penguin Group (USA) Inc.,
375 Hudson Street, New York, New York 10014.
BERKLEY SENSATION and the "B" design are trademarks of Penguin Group (USA) Inc.

PRINTED IN THE UNITED STATES OF AMERICA

10 9 8 7 6 5 4 3 2 1

To my mother and grandmother,
for always taking care of me.

ACKNOWLEDGMENTS

As always, this book would not have been possible without the help of many people.

Thanks go to my super agent, Kelly Harms, and editor, Cindy Hwang, who always help me make my books the absolute best they can be.

To Andre, who always finds time to patiently listen to me talk about my books, even when all I'm saying is "And then stuff happens."

And especially to all the readers out there. Your letters, e-mails, reviews, and blog comments mean more to me than you will ever know. To know that people read, enjoy, and look forward to my work is truly wonderful and humbling. This one's for you.

Happy reading!

PART ONE

I
Hate
Superheroes

Dinner with superheroes.

It's an interesting experience—and one that I rather hate.

The empty wineglass floated past me, sailing along as though carried by a steady, invisible hand. I tried to pretend it wasn't there. That I didn't see it. That the glass was as invisible as the force propelling it forward. But that was hard to do since it landed on the table next to me.

I further tried to pretend I didn't see the crystal carafe beside my elbow rise up, tip itself over, and pour ruby red sangria into the waiting glass. I even tried to convince myself I didn't *really* see the glass float back across the table.

I failed miserably at all three.

The other people gathered round didn't pay any attention to the floating glass. Didn't slow their conversation or ignore their food for an instant.

Unfortunately, floating glasses had become a normal sight around the Bulluci household these days—no matter how I wished otherwise.

"Is that really necessary?" I asked, my voice a little snappish. "I would have been happy to pour you some more wine."

Chief Sean Newman held out his hand, and the glass drifted over to him. "There was no need to bother you, Bella, when I could do it for myself."

"But you could have just asked," I persisted. "You didn't have to use your powers like that."

"Please," Fiona Fine cut in, turning her blue eyes to me. "What's the point of having superpowers if you don't use them?"

Fiona grabbed the bread basket and waved her hand over the top. A few red-hot sparks shot off the ends of her fingertips, and the delicious smell of warm cheese bread filled the air.

"Lighten up, Bella," Fiona continued, putting the entire loaf on one of the dozen plates in front of her. "We all know each other here—alter egos and otherwise. It's not like there are other people around to catch us in the act."

No, there weren't any other people around. No *normal* people anyway. Just me, Fiona, Chief Newman, my brother, Johnny, and my grandfather, Bobby.

I'd barely touched my whole wheat ravioli, but I put my fork down. I wasn't hungry anymore. I never was when there were superheroes around.

But Fiona and Chief Newman weren't just *any* superheroes. There were plenty of those in Bigtime, New York. No, they were Fiera and Mr. Sage, members of the Fearless Five—the most powerful, elite team of heroes in the city. In addition to being stronger than five people put together, Fiera could also form fireballs with her bare hands, while Mr. Sage had all sorts of psychic powers, including telekinesis, or the ability to move objects with his mind.

And now, they were part of my family.

Fiona had gotten engaged to my brother, Johnny, a couple of months ago after she'd saved him from two ubervillains who were trying to enslave the city. During all the commotion, Fiona had revealed her secret identity as Fiera to my grandfather and me and got us to help her rescue Johnny. And Chief Newman was Fiona's father, as well as her teammate.

But they weren't the only superheroes in the family these days.

The Fearless Five were a package deal. In addition to Fiera and Mr. Sage, we also got Karma Girl, Striker, and Hermit. Or Carmen Cole, Sam Sloane, and Henry Harris. That's how I thought of them. As nice, regular people who were mostly normal. Never as their alter egos. I tried to pretend those other people didn't exist.

I tried to pretend a lot of things didn't exist.

Especially my own supposed superpower.

My grandfather, Bobby Bulluci, clapped his hands together. "Come! Let's talk of other things." He turned to Fiona and Johnny. "Are the two of you packed for your trip?"

Johnny had some business to take care of in the overseas divisions of Bulluci Industries, so he and Fiona had decided to make a working vacation out of it. The two were leaving tomorrow on a month-long trip to explore the Mediterranean.

"Of course," Johnny answered, flashing Fiona a grin. "Although I don't know how we're going to get all of Fiona's clothes onto the plane."

Fiona reached over and punched my brother. Johnny flexed his biceps, which took on a hard look—like his skin had suddenly morphed into metal. Fiona's fist smacked into his arm, and she frowned and shook her hand. Even with her great strength, it hurt to punch my brother when he was concentrating on forming his superhard, supertough exoskeleton. It made Johnny immune to just about everything. Kicks, punches, explosions, Fiona's flare-ups. That was good, since my brother had an annoying tendency to dress up in tacky, formfitting black leather, zoom around town on his motorcycle, and fight ubervillains.

Instead of an exoskeleton, I'd gotten something far less useful from the mutated family gene pool—luck. As if that was any kind of superpower. Superannoying was more like it.

Fiona sniffed and tossed her blond hair over her shoulder. "I've told you a million times you can never have too many clothes, especially when you're going on vacation. Besides, we're taking Sam's private jet. There'll be more than enough room for my things."

Johnny gave Fiona another wicked smile. "But, baby, you know I think you look fine in whatever you're wearing—especially when it's nothing at all."

Fiona rolled her eyes. "Please. There's nothing sexier than a well-dressed woman. Right, Bella?"

"Of course," I murmured.

Fiona and I knew a few things about well-dressed women, since we both worked as fashion designers. Fiona was the head of Fiona Fine Fashions, while I ran the design portion of Bulluci Industries. Fiona and I had completely different styles, and we'd been friendly rivals for years. She created garments that screamed *Here I am! Look at me! I'm fabulous!* with their bright colors, wild patterns, and mounds of sequins and feathers. I preferred simpler styles, with muted hues, clean lines, and absolutely, positively no sequins. Ever.

Don't get me wrong. I liked Fiona just fine. Her father too. And I was glad Johnny had found someone he wanted to spend the rest of his life with.

But there was nothing I hated more than superheroes and ubervillains. Dressing up in those silly costumes. Calling themselves absurd names. Plotting and scheming and planning elaborate ways to take over the city and rule the world. It was all so dramatically ridiculous.

C'mon. Who would want to rule the world, really? It'd be nothing but a giant headache, with everyone constantly whining and crying at you. Not to mention all the paperwork and demands on your free time. But the ubervillains always tried to reign supreme, and the superheroes always stopped them. The cycle was endless.

Unfortunately, I had lots of experience with superheroes. Or rather pseudoheroes. All the men in my family masqueraded as Johnny Angel in their youth, riding around Bigtime on a tricked-out motorcycle, getting into trouble, and taking on ubervillains when the mood hit them. Masquerading as Johnny Angel was how my brother had met Fiona a few months ago.

And how my father, James, had died.

I was happy for Johnny, but I couldn't help shuddering at the fact that he'd added another superhero to the family tree. Five of them. Six, actually, if you counted Lulu Lo, the computer hacker who was engaged to Henry Harris.

Oh, I liked Fiona, Carmen, Sam, Henry, and Chief Newman just fine when they were themselves. It was their nightly habit of turning into Fiera, Karma Girl, Striker, Hermit, and Mr. Sage that had me concerned.

Knowing the Fearless Five's secret identities was sort of like being in a Mob family—once you were in, you were *all* the way in whether you wanted to be or not. And you couldn't get out, no matter how hard you tried. Whenever we had any of the heroes over for dinner, all they talked about were their latest epic battles and daring escapes. Or the new equipment Henry Hermit Harris had purchased for their underground lair.

Or the current ubervillains populating Bigtime. Or a dozen other superhero-related things that made me grind my teeth. Last week, Fiona had even asked me if I thought her costume needed a redesign. Sheesh.

But I was just going to have to live with my extended superhero family, like I did all the other cursed heroes in my life.

My power flared up at my dark thoughts. I didn't know how the other superheroes felt their power, but mine was sort of like standing in a ball of static electricity. My skin hummed. My fingertips itched. And worst of all, my caramel-colored hair frizzed out to alarming proportions. There wasn't a conditioner on the market that could tame it. Believe me, I'd tried them all. Together. At the same time.

The overall sensation wasn't uncomfortable so much as it was aggravating. Because the static, the power, the energy, built and built and built until it had to be discharged. And when it did, well, watch out. More often than not, whatever was around me either exploded, shattered, fell from the sky, or spontaneously combusted. Sometimes all at once. My luck was like some sort of supercharged telekinesis I couldn't control. Stuff just happened, whether I wanted it to or not. And here's the really annoying thing about having luck as a superpower— it can be good or bad.

Sometimes, if I thought about something, wanted it to happen, willed it to be, I'd get my heart's desire. I'd catch the subway a second before the doors closed. Snag the last seat in a crowded movie theater. Find the only dress in my size. I even won five hundred dollars in a sweepstakes as a kid just by staring at my entry form before I sent it in and wishing I would win.

But just as often, my luck turned on me. I'd catch the subway, but rip my jacket on the doors. Get the last seat, but sit down in a puddle of sticky soda. Find the perfect dress, but forget my credit cards. Win the lottery, but lose my ticket.

Luck, the most capricious thing in the world. That was my supposed power. My curse was more like it.

My jinx.

I always felt the static energy around me and did my best to keep it clamped down and under control. But the sudden surge told me it was time for it to let loose—and for something to happen. I could never tell whether that something would be good or bad, but I wasn't taking any chances.

I slowly, carefully, calmly pushed my chair back from the table, making sure I was clear of the tablecloth, candles, bread basket, wineglasses, plates, silverware, and anything else I could drag down or knock off or upset in any way. Then, I stood.

With small, thoughtful steps, I backed around the chair until I was standing five feet away from the table—and out of range of everyone and everything. Now, nobody else would get caught in the cross fire if something crazy happened, like the chandelier above my head plummeting from the ceiling, despite the ten or so bolts that held it in place.

"Bella? Are you all right?" Chief Newman asked, his eyes flashing a brilliant green. "Is your power bothering you again?"

Chief Newman had offered to work with me, to try to find some way to help me learn to control my power. I'd refused. There was no controlling luck. I'd long ago given up hope of ever taming it, along with my hair.

The doorbell rang, saving me from an explanation.

"I'll get it," I said. "It's probably more trick-or-treaters."

It was late October and still several days before Halloween, but little ghosts and ghouls and goblins had already started showing up asking for candy. Or else. Halloween was a two-week-long event in Bigtime that wouldn't wrap up until the night of the thirty-first. The extended holiday gave everybody, kids and adults alike, a chance to go around town all dressed up, instead of just the heroes and villains.

"What are you giving them?" Fiona asked, her eyes gleaming at the thought of Halloween candy. "Snickers? M&M's? Chocolate Twinkies?"

The only thing Fiona loved as much as Johnny was food. With her fire-based superpowers and high metabolism, Fiona could eat whatever she wanted to, whenever she wanted to, and never gain a pound. Besides her nighttime gig as a superhero, that was the only other thing I really hated about her. Well, that and her sky-high legs. I was just a couple inches over five feet. And her perfectly smooth blond hair and gorgeous baby blues.

My tawny locks resembled a bush more often than not, while my hazel eyes just sort of faded into my bronze skin. All right, so I really hated a lot of things about Fiona.

"Hardly. I'm giving them apples, fat-free trail mix, boxes of raisins, and bags of unpopped, butter-free microwave popcorn." I pointed to the far end of the long table, where I'd put the plastic bowls of goodies.

"What's the fun in that?" Fiona said.

"Not contributing to the American epidemic of childhood obesity, for one," I snapped.

Fiona rolled her eyes. "Your house is *so* going to be covered in toilet paper in the morning."

Bobby cleared his throat. "Actually, Bella, I took the liberty of buying some candy bars on my way home today. Just in case you ran out of apples."

"Chocolate? Where?" Fiona demanded.

I put my hands on my hips and glared at my grandfather. There was a devilish twinkle in his green eyes I knew all too well.

"And how many did you eat before you put them away?"

His lips twitched. "Bella, you've told me many times I shouldn't eat candy. I didn't have a single one."

Right. And I looked good in a thong.

"Grandfather," I warned.

Bobby's heart, cholesterol, and blood pressure weren't the best in the world, something I was trying to change. With little success. My grandfather still ate like he was twenty-three, instead of seventy-three, despite doctor's orders and my constant nagging. And don't even get me started on his other bad habit—motorcycle riding. Bobby had broken his leg two years ago gallivanting around town, and I'd moved back home to take care of and keep an eye on him.

Bobby ignored me. "They're in the kitchen, Fiona, if you want to hand them out."

Fiona snapped to her feet. "Count me in."

Bobby's eyes sparkled. "Try to leave some for the kids."

Fiona sniffed and tossed her hair over her shoulder again before disappearing into the kitchen.

I grabbed the bowls of apples, raisins, and popcorn, and carried them to the front door. The static still crackled around me like an invisible force field, but it seemed to be holding steady. For the moment. Fiona came out of the kitchen and fell in step beside me, candy bars in hand. She opened the door, and I smiled, ready to greet our visitors.

"Trick or treat!" the kids shouted, holding out plastic orange pumpkins.

There were five of them, of course. Each one dressed like a member of the Fearless Five. There was a girl in reddish-orange spandex who was supposed to be Fiera, and one in silver for Karma Girl. One of the little boys wore an Irish green cape as Mr. Sage, while the other had on black leather and two long swords made out of aluminum foil for Striker. The man with them was dressed in black and white, representing Hermit.

Superheroes. More stupid superheroes. What happened to the good old days when kids dressed up as princesses and cowboys and monsters?

My smile faltered, but I held out the bowls. "Who wants some apples?"

Silence. Dead silence. I didn't even hear crickets chirping in the front yard.

The kids looked at me, then at each other, then at the man. No one said anything.

My power surged again. The static discharged.

And the plastic bowls in my hands shattered.

You would have thought I had some explodium in the containers instead of just healthy snacks. Raisins and popcorn showered us all, while bits of pulverized apple pelted my thick, curly hair and my face. The few apples that survived the explosion intact bounced down the long driveway and out of sight. The pieces of the splintered bowls zipped through the air, embedding themselves in the stone steps like daggers around my feet. In a perfect circle, no less.

I sighed and wiped a bit of apple juice off my nose. I'd long ago grown used to my power—and the embarrassment that went along with it.

"I'm so sorry," I said, scooping raisins and popcorn into my hands. "I have more inside. Let me get that."

I'd been prepared for such a disaster. In fact, I always bought five of everything, whether it was candy or jewelry or clothes. Years of bad luck had taught me that my jinxed power would find a way to trash even the safest, sturdiest object. In the last six months, I'd gone through seven purses, dozens of shirts, and more shoes than I cared to admit. And two cars.

"Um, I think we'll just try the next house," the man replied, drawing the kids close to him.

Fiona not-so-gently shouldered past me. "Don't worry. I've got some Hershey bars right here. They're a little melted, but they're still good."

"Yeah!"

The kids stepped forward, and Fiona gave them each a chocolate bar. The girl in the Fiera costume got two. Naturally.

Satisfied, the kids headed back down the driveway in search of more Halloween goodies to rot their teeth and drive their sugar levels through the roof.

Fiona smirked. "See? I told you the kids would want candy."

I sighed again. I should have known better. After all, it was almost Halloween.

And the perfect time of year for my power to play tricks on me.

After cleaning up my unwanted goodies and picking most of the apple bits out of my hair, I went back to the dining room, where I said my goodnights to everyone and wished Johnny and Fiona a safe trip.

"Call me when you land, and remember to check in every other day," I said. "I want to know how you're doing and what you've seen."

Johnny gave me a tight hug. "Don't worry, Bella. Nothing's going to happen. We'll be fine."

"Of course we will," Fiona added, unwrapping her third candy bar in as many minutes. "No work, no ubervillains, no city to save. Just fun, sun, and food. *Lots* of food. We're going to have a fabulous time, and that's all there is to it. Relax, Bella. I'll bring Johnny home in one piece. Don't I always?"

I started to remind her about the incident two weeks ago, when the two of them had run into Yeti Girl, who'd almost removed Johnny's head from his body. But Grandfather cut me off.

"Of course you will," Bobby said, winking at her.

I bit my lip. Everyone thought I was a silly worrywart who saw danger lurking around every corner. Well, it did. You could never be too vigilant or too careful. Not only did you have to worry about superheroes and ubervillains in this city, but there were ordinary things to be cautious of too—muggers, car accidents, paper cuts, carbs. Add all that to my capricious luck, and you had a recipe for disaster.

Chief Newman's eyes flashed. "Yes, I think you'll have a wonderful time. And I think I'll have some more of that delicious sangria."

The older superhero waved his hand, and his wineglass started back across the table toward me.

I headed upstairs and went to bed. I'd had enough super heroes—pint-sized and otherwise—for one evening.

Early the next morning, I plodded down to the gym in the basement of the Bulluci mansion. I started every day by huffing and puffing on the elliptical trainer for at least thirty minutes. Unlike Fiona, I had to work out like a fiend to stay in reasonably good shape.

In addition to my sun-kissed skin, my mother, Lucia, had also passed down her curvy form to me. While it had looked good on her, I was all hips and thighs. Just staring at food was enough to make me gain three pounds. It didn't help that I had an unhealthy weakness for carbs—namely mounds of pasta and piles of French fries.

I let myself daydream about a plate of cheese fries from Quicke's for two whole minutes. Then, I flipped on my favorite James Taylor CD, climbed onto the machine, and went to work. I pushed myself hard, staying on the elliptical trainer for the better part of an hour, until my legs burned and screamed for mercy.

Grandfather and Johnny didn't understand my need to live healthy. They didn't know why I worked out so much or tried to get them to eat things that weren't drenched in oil and butter and salt. I couldn't control my supposed superpower, but I could control the rest of my body and what I put into it. I had enough things to worry about. My health wasn't going to be one of them.

I finished my workout with a little yoga and some slow stretches. The static gathered round my body, ready to lash out. My skin almost hummed with energy, but I ignored the sensation. Sometimes, if I pretended I couldn't feel the static, I could delay the chaos. For a few minutes.

I headed to the kitchen to grab a quick breakfast. My grandfather had built our villa-style house when he came to the States some fifty years ago, and the kitchen was one of my favorite rooms. White cabinets with angel outlines carved into the wood hovered above a tile counter that ran along one wall. A round, maple-colored table sat in the middle of the open area, underneath a wing-shaped crystal light fixture. A sliding glass door led out to a stone patio, where you could view the orange, fig, olive, and other trees in the orchard in the backyard. More angels decorated the refrigerator magnets, the fresco on one wall, and even the dish towels hanging above the stainless steel sink.

Grandfather sat at the table reading the morning editions of the *Chronicle* and the *Exposé*, the city's two major newspapers. The remains of a bagel and some fresh fruit littered a plate in front of him. I looked around, but I didn't see or smell any telltale signs of steak, bacon, eggs, and hash browns—Bobby's breakfast of choice.

"Anything exciting going on?" I moved over to one of the refrigerators and poured myself some calcium-fortified, low-calorie, low-sugar orange juice.

The kitchen was one of the biggest rooms in the mansion. It needed to be to house all our appliances. There were two of everything in here—stoves, refrigerators, microwaves, coffeepots, juicers, blenders, food processors. Not to mention the drawers full of silverware, plates, and glasses. We needed all the backups, since I had a nasty habit of destroying them. You'd be surprised how easy it is to blow up a microwave or snap the handle off a stainless steel pot.

Plus, the extra refrigerator helped feed Fiona and her enormous appetite. Although, when I zapped one of them, she was more than happy to eat everything inside before it spoiled, including some of the condiments. Fiona had a particular fondness for chocolate-flavored whipped cream, a craving I didn't really understand. She was always grabbing a can of it and rushing off to find Johnny.

"Not much," Bobby said, rustling the tall pages. "A pileup on the interstate, a purse snatching downtown, a home invasion. Some guy got beat up pretty badly in that one, but Swifte came along and broke it up. He rushed the guy to the hospital."

Swifte was another one of Bigtime's superheroes, famous for his speed, public relations skills, and shimmering white costume. He zoomed around town fighting evil and getting every bit of press coverage he could. Unlike the Fearless Five, who tried to keep a low profile, Swifte loved the spotlight.

I helped myself to some more orange juice, along with a bowl of apple-cinnamon-flavored oatmeal and a banana.

"I'm going to see Joanne James and the rest of the committee about the museum benefit," I said between sweet, steaming bites. "It's our last major planning session, so I probably won't be home until late. What do you have planned for today? Going to have lunch with your lady friend again?"

Lady friend was Bobby's term for the woman he'd been seeing for the last month. I didn't know where he'd met her or even who she was, but Bobby had been spending a lot of time with her. Having lunch and dinner together. Walking through Paradise Park. Going dancing at some of the jazz clubs. He'd even stayed overnight at her place a few times.

My grandmother had died years ago, and Bobby had dated plenty since then. But there was a smile on his face and a pep in his step whenever he talked about his lady friend that made me think she might be more than just another casual flirtation.

I was thrilled for Grandfather, but a little concerned that I didn't know who she was. I wanted to make sure Bobby found someone who loved him for him, and not for his money or the Bulluci name. I was also a tiny bit jealous. Johnny had Fiona, and now Bobby had a lady friend. I wanted someone special in my life too.

"No, we're not having lunch today," Bobby said. "But I'm sure I'll find something to do."

"So when are you going to introduce her?" I asked. "I'm dying to meet the woman who's captivated you."

Bobby waggled his finger. "Soon, Bella. Soon. She's busy with her work right now, but once that's done, I promise we'll have her over for dinner, and you can grill her to your heart's content."

Just because I'd asked Fiona what her intentions were toward Johnny, I'd gotten a reputation for being overprotective when it came to my brother and grandfather's love lives. I just wanted to keep them safe from everything, including broken hearts.

"Has Johnny called yet?" I asked, scooping up the last of my oatmeal. "Did they get to the hotel all right?"

"He called this morning before you were up."

"Why didn't you wake me?"

"Because everything was fine, and they were on their way out to do some sightseeing. Johnny said he'll call back in a couple of days. You can talk to your brother then."

Grandfather stuck his nose in the sports section, reading the latest European soccer news. Unlike me, he didn't feel the need to know where the members of his family were every single hour of the day. Maybe it was his age or all that he'd seen in his seventy-three years, but Bobby had a very casual, relaxed attitude about life. He could always find something to laugh at or smile about, no matter how bad things were. I envied his carefree nature.

Bobby kept reading his papers, so I finished my breakfast and went upstairs. I took a quick shower, then put on a crisp, tailored white shirt, fitted black pants, and sensible black pumps. Fiona could wear jungle prints and leopard spots and zebra stripes all she wanted, but there was nothing classier and more elegant than basic black with a refreshing splash of white.

I rummaged through my jewelry box until I came up with a short, thin silver chain. I fastened it around my neck, and a small pair of diamond-cut angel wings settled into the hollow of my throat.

Given my male relatives' propensity for morphing into Johnny Angel, we Bullucis have become collectors and connoisseurs of all things angel-related. From furniture to carpets to light fixtures, if it has an angel or cherub or pair of wings on it, we probably have one. Or thirteen.

In my set of rooms alone, angel and wing and halo carvings decorated the headboard on my bed, the coffee table in the sitting room, and the desk where I kept my sketch pads and art supplies. Clouds splashed across the walls and ceiling in the bathroom, and instead of claw feet, four small angel heads supported my oversized bathtub.

I looked into the full-length mirror standing in the corner of the bedroom. My eyes lingered on my necklace. The chain and winged charm had been a present from my father, James, on my sixteenth birthday. I'd started wearing them more often since he'd been murdered. It made me feel a little closer to him, even though he was gone. I fingered the small charm, and my father's face flashed through my mind.

Sandy hair, dark skin, blue eyes, strong, sure hands. James Bulluci had been a wonderful father. Kind, caring, and never too busy to read me a story or tuck me into bed. After my mother died in a car accident, he'd doubled his efforts to be a good father. He took Johnny and me out at least once a week to spend some quality time together. We'd go to Paradise Park to ride the Ferris wheel, or to the library to listen to tall tales, or even to the art museum to look at all the wonderful paintings and sculptures.

I'd loved my father dearly. Except for one thing—his alter ego, Johnny Angel. It was a tradition he'd inherited from my grandfather, the original Angel. I'd never understood why the two of them had felt the need to dress up in black leather. They weren't superheroes. At least, not traditional heroes like the Fearless Five. Neither one had a power. But for years, they'd both ridden around Bigtime on custom-made motorcycles, hanging out with the local biker gangs and getting into trouble.

And fighting ubervillains.

At least once a week, my father would come home bloody and bruised from some battle. And I'd be waiting to patch him up. I'd help him out of his torn, ripped costume, wipe the blood off his face, assess the damage, and go to work with my needle and thread. I knew as much about cuts and stitches and setting broken bones as any ER doc did. Maybe more, given all the ones I'd treated over the years.

But the wounds weren't the worst part.

It was the waiting. The wondering. The heavy, crushing fear that my father wouldn't come home. Ever again. That some ubervillain would kill him. Or that he'd get beaten to death in a bar fight. Or the more pedestrian worry that he'd have a motorcycle accident.

Just about every night, I'd sit up with my mother and wait for my father to come home. After she died, I did it by myself.

Sometimes, Grandfather and Johnny would wait with me, but most nights, I was alone. They didn't worry like I did. They always thought my father would come home safe and more or less sound.

Until one night, he didn't.

Two ubervillains, Siren and Intelligal, had muscled in on territory controlled by some bikers my father was friendly with. They'd asked him to help get rid of the ubervillains. My father confronted them, and Intelligal had launched a couple of explodium missiles at him. He'd tried to outrun the missiles on his motorcycle, but he'd never had a chance. All we'd found of my father had been his watch—without his hand attached—and a few of his teeth.

My brother, Johnny, had become Angel then, determined to bring my father's killers to justice. That's when he'd crossed paths with Fiera and the rest of the Fearless Five. The superheroes had been after Siren and Intelligal as well, and Fiera had convinced Johnny to join forces with them. But Johnny had still almost died when the ubervillains had kidnapped him and held him hostage.

My power pulsed, and my wavy, shoulder-length hair started to frizz, despite the bottle of extra-strength conditioner I'd just used. My luck always got more unstable when I was upset. I closed my eyes and took deep breaths, pulling the air down into the pit of my stomach.

I pushed away my troubled thoughts and fastened a silver watch onto my wrist. At least I tried to. Bright, blue, static-charged sparks shot out as soon as I touched the metal, and they sent the watch flying across the room. It landed with a soft thump on the far side of the sofa.

I sighed, walked over, and picked up the watch, which was embossed with angel wings. Luckily, it hadn't broken, and I looked at the time. Almost noon. I needed to get going. A chairperson should always be on time for her own called meeting.

Besides, Joanne James would eat me alive if I was late. In her own way, the Bigtime society queen was scarier than even the most feared ubervillain.

* * *

I grabbed my black leather shoulder bag and headed outside. It was a beautiful October day, and I breathed in, enjoying the rich, earthy aroma of the changing seasons. Fall was my favorite time of year. The sun seared my eyes with its brilliance, but the air still felt damp and cool. Puffy clouds zoomed across the sky, pushed on by a steady breeze. The wind stirred the scarlet leaves on the maple trees lining the curved driveway, and a few fluttered down to the burnished brown of the lawn. I made a mental note to do some sketches of the trees before they lost all their magnificent leaves. Everything was showing off a last bit of color before the gray winter took hold, and I wanted to capture the city in all its autumn glory.

Joanne lived only three houses down, but on Lucky Way, the street where we lived, that was more like three miles. So I got in my car, a nice, safe, reliable Benz, and steered down the driveway and through the iron gate that bordered our property.

I saw Brilliance, the Berkley Brighton estate, two miles before I actually got to it. Unlike our house, no trees surrounded Berkley's mansion to hide it from sight. It would take a whole mountain range to do that. The house sat on a tall rise that afforded the whiskey billionaire a spectacular view of Bigtime Bay from his seventh-story windows. That story was glassed in on all sides, along with the first, third, and fifth floors. The rest of the mansion was constructed of steel and chrome, giving it a very chic, sleek feel. You would never run out of things to do at Brilliance, which featured an Olympic-sized hot tub, three tennis courts, and two helicopter pads. And that was just on the roof.

The Bulluci manor was large, but Berkley's sprawling, modern-day behemoth made it look like a doll's house. The only other residence in all of Bigtime that exceeded the size of Brilliance was Sublime, the enormous estate owned by Sam Sloane.

I drove up the mile-long drive and stopped the car at the

front door. A tuxedo-clad valet greeted me and whisked my vehicle away to Berkley's private garage. Another valet scurried to open the front door for me, while still another waited inside to take my black pea coat, brush it, steam it, and hang it in a spotless, empty closet.

Berkley wasn't into antiques and suits of armor like Sam Sloane was. Instead, his house featured lots of open space with modern, deco-style furniture done mostly in whites, silvers, and grays, with a few black pinstripes. Very minimalist, very modern, very sophisticated. I loved it.

A butler led me to one of the libraries on the second floor. Books and globes and maps galore populated the room, along with a white marble fireplace, several tables, and five sets of cream-colored chairs. Gray rugs covered the marble floor, and the heavy black drapes on the windows were open, offering a wonderful view of the dark, dense woods that lined the back of the mansion.

Joanne James waited in the library, with her husband, Berkley, by her side. Joanne was a tall, skinny, almost anorexic-looking woman with black curls that cascaded halfway down her back. Her eyes were a vivid blue, almost violet, and her skin was as smooth and flawless as porcelain. Even though it was a bit chilly in the library, Joanne wore a sleeveless, powder blue suit with square white buttons. A Fiona Fine original, given the amount of leg and cleavage it showed.

Berkley was a short, square, fiftysomething man with a mane of blondish hair. He was also the richest person in Bigtime, having turned his family's secret whiskey recipe into a multibillion-dollar empire. Brighton's Best whiskey was legendary for its smooth flavor and hefty price tag.

At the moment, though, Joanne and Berkley didn't look like the obscenely rich, high-powered couple they were. Berkley leaned over the back of a chair, kissing Joanne's throat while his hand caressed her exposed breast. Joanne's chin was up, her eyes closed, her lips parted. She was thoroughly enjoying her husband's, um, attention.

Joanne and Berkley had gotten married three months ago during a late-summer ceremony in Paradise Park. They'd pulled out all the stops for the wedding, renting out the whole park for three days. Food. Flowers. Oceans of champagne. Mountains of presents. All that was just for the two thousand invited guests. I could only imagine what Berkley and Joanne had treated each other to in private.

Like Berkley, Joanne had plenty of money of her own. She'd just gotten it a different way. Joanne wasn't a superhero, but she had a superhero-like nickname—the Black Widow. That's what Fiona and some of the other society folks called her. Joanne had married and divorced several men over the years, adding to her bank balance every time.

But she truly seemed to care about Berkley, and he about her. It never ceased to amaze me. A pang of loneliness stabbed my heart at the sight of them bonding so, um, vigorously. I hadn't even been out on a date since before my father was murdered.

But first things first. I had a meeting to attend and a benefit to plan. If I could break up the happy couple.

"Ahem." I cleared my throat. "Ahem."

Joanne opened her eyes, but Berkley kept kissing her throat and stroking her chest.

"Oh, hello, Bella," Joanne said, her voice low and husky. "I didn't hear you come in."

I doubted she would have heard a marching band, the way she was purring under Berkley's touch.

"Hello, Joanne," I replied, staring at the Oriental rug under my pumps instead of at her breasts.

"Hello, Bella." Berkley straightened, took his hand out of Joanne's top, and quit kissing her. "It's so nice to see you again."

"You too, Berkley." Normally, I would have shaken his hand. Not today.

"How's Bobby doing?" Berkley asked, a smile creasing his face. "I haven't seen him in a few weeks."

"He's fine."

Berkley had been friends with my father and grandfather for years. The three shared a love of motorcycles, and Berkley had convinced my father to build several for him. Berkley had spent many nights in the Bulluci manor, drinking wine and talking about paint jobs and chrome pipes and everything else related to motorcycles. But he was never too busy to speak to me, and he'd brought me all sorts of dolls and stuffed animals and art supplies when I was a kid. I thought of him as an uncle of sorts.

"Well, I'm afraid I have a conference call to sit in on. I'll leave you girls to finish your planning," Berkley said, pressing a kiss to the top of Joanne's head.

She grabbed his hand. "I'm not sure what time we'll be done. We've got a lot of ground to cover today."

"Don't worry. I'll wait up for you. In more ways than one." Berkley winked at his new bride.

"Just like always?" Joanne asked in a teasing tone.

"Just like always."

Berkley touched Joanne's cheek. She put her hand over his and gave it a gentle squeeze. Berkley squeezed back and left the library, whistling a cheery tune.

I sank into a chair on the opposite side of the table from Joanne. I pulled my notes and files out of my shoulder bag, pretending not to notice the other woman buttoning up her blouse. Evidently, Joanne hadn't felt the need to wear a bra today. I couldn't help hoping my breasts looked that good when I was her age. Whatever it was. Joanne's face was so smooth and unlined it was hard to tell exactly how old she was, although I would guess she had to be at least forty.

"Sorry if we shocked you, Bella," Joanne said, fluffing out her mass of raven-colored curls. "Newlyweds, you know. We just can't seem to get enough of each other."

"Of course," I murmured. "Think nothing of it."

I didn't really mind Joanne and Berkley's open display of affection. After all, it was better than watching superhero-propelled glasses float past me.

★ 3 ★

While Joanne applied a fresh coat of lavender lipstick and powdered her nose, the rest of the committee trickled into the library—Grace Caleb, Abby Appleby, and Hannah Harmon.

I greeted each in turn, shaking hands with them. "Grace. Abby. Hannah. So glad you could make it."

Grace Caleb was a seventysomething widow and one of the bastions of Bigtime society. She came from money so old no one could remember how she'd gotten it in the first place. Grace was the sort of genteel lady who grew roses and drank tea and played bridge. She wore a sedate flowered dress topped off with a knit mauve sweater set with pearls. Grace never went anywhere without a sweater or shawl of some kind.

Where Grace was sweet, pink softness, Hannah Harmon was all bright, hard lines. Her glossy auburn hair, cut in a razor-sharp bob, ended at her chin, highlighting her killer cheekbones. Her thin lips were a red slash in her face, and her brown eyes slightly pointed, like a cat's. A heavy gold chain flashed around her neck, contrasting with the coffee color of her silk blouse and skirt. Gold rings set with rubies sparkled on her fingers, and a gold filigree bracelet encircled her wrist. Hannah was from new money, and she liked showing it off.

Abby Appleby was somewhere in between, although much farther down on the income ladder. Her brown hair was pulled back into a sensible ponytail, and clear gloss covered her lips. She wore olive-colored cargo pants and a white, lacy camisole topped with a green plaid, button-up shirt. A thick, wide watch clamped across her wrist and looked like it could tell you what time it was in New Zealand, Thailand, and Madagascar—all at once. My attention went to the bag slung over Abby's shoulder. It resembled a large suitcase and had more zippers and pockets and hidey-holes than a box full of purses.

The three women took seats around the table, murmuring hellos to me and each other.

I took my own chair across from Joanne and flipped through the files I'd brought. "I thought we'd start with a quick recap of what we decided on last time."

Given my rabid love of art, I'd been elected chairperson of the Friends of the Bigtime Museum of Modern Art a couple months ago. My main duty as madam chairperson was to plan and organize the museum's annual fall fund-raiser. The museum, which relied heavily on public donations, had opened up a new wing and needed money to finish paying for it.

Joanne and Grace were also involved in the Friends group. Joanne, because she was the richest woman in the city and that's what rich women did, and Grace, because she was one of the best-loved society matrons and actually liked art. They'd both volunteered to help with the benefit.

Abby was *the* professional event planner in Bigtime. Whether you were having a wedding, a funeral, or a convention, you called Abby to plan it. She'd built her reputation and her business, A+ Events, on her ability to pull off complicated events in a matter of weeks, or sometimes, days. Abby fronted just about every fund-raising committee in the city, and I'd drafted her for this one too.

Hannah had also offered her services. The businesswoman had lots of connections and knew how to get things done, which was why I'd been happy to let her help.

The five of us had been meeting for the last two months. The benefit was less than a week away, and it was crunch time.

I scanned my papers. "We agreed to have the Bigtime Bachelors event at Quicke's, starting two hours before the official benefit at the museum. We've sent out invitations to all the eligible bachelors and bachelorettes. Abby, how are we coming on that?"

Abby unzipped a pocket on her enormous bag and pulled out some laminated, color-coded pages, along with an itemized list and three highlighters. "We signed the contract with Quicke's to supply food and space for the bachelor auction, as well as food and drinks at the museum. Kyle Quicke haggled with me, but I got him down into our price range. Most of the bachelors and bachelorettes we approached have agreed to participate. I'm still tracking down a few stragglers, but we'll have more than enough people."

"Good," I replied. "What else?"

"We also approved my costume ball idea for the overall theme," Grace added in her soft voice.

I grimaced. I'd been horrified when Grace had brought up the idea of a masquerade ball. There were more than enough people running around Bigtime in costumes already. But the others had agreed with Grace, and I'd been outvoted. Joanne, in particular, thought it sounded like marvelous fun, especially since the benefit was scheduled for Halloween night. Evidently, Joanne was tired of dressing up in the finest clothes money could buy, and she wanted to slum it in spandex. Designer-made, of course.

"Right. That." I tried to muster up some semblance of enthusiasm. "Are the invitations done yet?"

Grace nodded, her coifed silver hair bobbing up and down. "I okayed the final proof a week ago, and they went out in the mail that same afternoon."

We'd been announcing the date of the benefit for weeks to drum up interest and solicit early donations. But I wanted to make sure all the bigwigs got a personal invitation to attend, as well as a follow-up phone call to confirm their RSVPs. Such specialized attention made them more agreeable to parting with some of their cash. You had to suck up a lot to get a whole lot more. That was the way the game was played in Bigtime.

"And the decorations?" I asked.

"We can't put up much in the museum because of the security and climate-control issues, but I've arranged for the usual greenery and lights," Grace replied. "They'll arrive at the museum the day before the benefit."

"Good." I turned to Joanne and Hannah, who were handling the most delicate part of the event. "And how are the other donations coming?"

"Fine," Joanne said. "For the most part."

There were lots of wealthy art lovers and collectors in the

city, who had more than a few priceless pieces tucked away in their mansions. My idea had been to get the Bigtime high-society members to donate art from their private collections. The pieces would be housed in the museum's new wing as part of a special exhibit that would open the night of the benefit. My plan was for the pieces to remain on display through the end of the year, so everyone in Bigtime could come and see them. Public interest alone, along with a small admission fee, should raise over two million, more than enough to pay off the new wing.

"*For the most part?* What does that mean?" I asked. "If it's the security they're worried about—"

"It's not the security," Joanne said. "We've gotten verbal commitments from everyone to donate something."

"Verbal commitments? That's all? The benefit's in six days. Stuff should already be arriving at the museum."

My hair frizzed, and my fingertips itched with static. My luck always acted up when I was emotional or stressed out. The thought of the benefit being a miserable failure put me on the edge of panic.

"No one wants to commit until they know what everyone else is donating. They all feel the need to outdo each other." Hannah sniffed.

"But the point of this was to donate different things, fun things, not the same old Picassos and Rembrandts and Renoirs," I said. "Our theme is *Whimsical Wonders*. Who cares how much a statue cost?"

Abby gave me an amused look. "Why, they do, of course. Everything's a competition in this town. You should know that, Bella, given how you and Fiona go at it."

I grimaced. Fiona and I didn't really *go at it*. We'd never romped around in fountains or pulled out each other's hair, but we were the top two designers in the city. With our radically different styles, people just assumed we hated each other, especially since Fiona had gotten engaged to Johnny.

"It really doesn't matter, though," Joanne said in a proud voice. "Naturally, Berkley will have *the* most expensive item on display."

That small item Joanne was so casually referring to was the Star Sapphire. Weighing in at a couple hundred carats, the sapphire was one of the most expensive gemstones in the world. Berkley had graciously agreed to put the sapphire on display. After I'd more or less begged him and agreed to design a whole new wardrobe for Joanne. At cost.

I'd do anything to ensure the benefit was a success, even sew until my fingers fell off for Joanne James. It was all going to be worth it in the end. The Star Sapphire was the centerpiece of the *Whimsical Wonders*, and we'd used pictures of the enormous stone in all our promotional materials. Ticket sales to see the gem had already exceeded everyone's loftiest expectations. Even Arthur Anders, the quiet, reserved curator of the museum, was salivating about the prospect of it going on display.

Joanne waved her hand. "Don't worry, Bella. I'll put the word out Berkley is donating several more items no one can hope to top, and everyone else will fall in line. They always do."

It was true. Whatever Berkley Brighton did, people hurried to hop on the bandwagon.

"Are you sure?" I asked.

Joanne nodded. "Honey, I'm always sure."

Several hours later, I slumped back in my chair and rubbed my aching head. We'd gone over every possible thing three times. The food. Auction. Bachelors. RSVPs. Decorations. Donated art. I knew all the details by heart. I could recite the menu forward and backward. Spit out the exact number of cream puffs we'd ordered. Rattle off the names of all the bachelors we'd signed up. Remember the exact cost of the potted plants. Conjure up obscure facts about the art exhibit.

And I still felt like I was forgetting something.

We decided to take a break before wrapping up for the evening. One of the cooks brought in a silver tray full of star-shaped cucumber sandwiches, three kinds of cheese, crackers, fresh fruit, and steaming tea.

Grace and Joanne chatted about some event they'd attended

last night. Abby shuffled her papers, pens, and files back into the proper slots in her shoulder bag, while Hannah sipped some cinnamon-flavored tea. I desperately wanted something to eat, but I scooted my chair away from the table. I didn't want my luck to flare up and cause me to upset the whole tray. The way my fingers itched, it was only a matter of time before something bad happened.

"What did you think of Nate Norris's barbecue, Hannah?" Grace asked, turning her blue eyes to the other woman.

"I don't know. I wasn't invited." Hannah said, her voice frosty.

"Careful, honey," Joanne said in a glib tone, her violet eyes sparkling. "The chip on your shoulder's showing again."

Hannah's red lips puckered. Like most women on the society circuit, Hannah was a millionaire in her own right. It was how she'd gotten her money that some people had problems with. Hannah's specialty was hostile takeovers. She took bankrupt corporations, bought up all the stock to get a controlling interest, made the businesses profitable again, then sold off the pieces for far more than she'd invested in the first place. The whole process resulted in a lot of hurt feelings all the way around.

Of course, there was some other talk about Hannah as well. That she used less-than-legal methods to divide and conquer. Some folks even whispered that she had ties to ubervillains and employed them on occasion to get what she wanted. But nothing had ever been proven. In addition to being a ruthless businesswoman, Hannah had enough money to make just about any problem disappear, including society gossip.

But she couldn't quite break through the thin pink wall put up by the older matrons, no matter how hard she tried. And Hannah tried. Taking people to lunch, sending them presents and hard-to-get items, throwing lavish parties herself. For some reason, being rich wasn't enough for Hannah. She wanted to be one of the in-crowd too.

"That was probably just an oversight on Nate's part. Next time, dear, I'm sure you'll get an invitation. It was nothing, really. Just a simple barbecue," Grace said.

She let out a sympathetic cluck and leaned over, like she was going to pat the other woman's hand, but Hannah jerked hers away, almost spilling her tea. Joanne smiled and poured herself a cup of the steaming beverage. Abby kept on shuffling her things, ignoring the drama.

I decided to follow suit and reached for one of the star-shaped sandwiches. Surely, a few carbs wouldn't hurt. I could pretend the bread was whole wheat—

My power surged the moment I picked up the soft mound. I immediately dropped the sandwich back onto the silver platter.

Too late.

The sandwich was featherlight, but it hit the edge of the platter with the force of an anvil. The dish flew into the air, flipping end over end six—no, seven—times before landing right side up in the exact spot where it had been a moment before. The sandwiches that had been on the platter also rose into the air before stacking themselves neatly back onto the silver surface—one on top of the other until they formed a perfect little pyramid. The final sandwich plunged point first into the others, creating a star shape atop the mound of bread. There wasn't a chef alive who could have created a more perfect display.

Mouths agape, everyone stared at the now-immaculate platter. I sat perfectly still, scarcely daring to breathe.

"Well, you certainly don't see that every day," Joanne said in a wry tone.

"No," Hannah replied. "You certainly don't."

Hannah put her teacup down on the platter. She did it gently, with caution, given the weirdness of a moment ago. But that one small act was enough to upset the delicate balance my luck had achieved between platter and bread.

And send the pyramid of sandwiches tumbling into my lap.

Bread and cucumbers and cheese and mayonnaise splattered onto the front of my shirt and dripped off my lap onto the thick rugs below. But that wasn't the worst part. The cup tipped over too, sending a spray of tea at me. The brown liquid hit my chest before dribbling down my torso, making one enormous, soupy mess.

At least the tea had cooled down. Otherwise, I would have

been badly burned. That was the weird thing about my luck. It made bad things happen to me, but they were never terribly serious or life-threatening. Just horribly embarrassing. Like this particular moment.

The other women stared at me. Shocked and disgusted.

"Well," I said, trying to laugh as I picked a bit of cucumber off my cheek, "I guess I won't be needing a facial anytime soon. Mayonnaise is supposed to be great for your skin, right?"

Nobody answered me.

⋆ 4 ⋆

The meeting broke up after that. Grace, Hannah, and Abby said their goodbyes to Joanne and me. I echoed their sentiments from the floor, where I was on my hands and knees picking up soggy pieces of tea-soaked bread.

Joanne lounged in her chair and surveyed the mess. A small smile played across her lavender lips. "You certainly know how to clear a room, Bella."

"Don't worry," I said, trying to ignore the slick, greasy feel of mayonnaise on my hands. "I'll clean it up and pay for the rug. I know it must be expensive."

Joanne waved her hand. "Don't worry about it. I've been dying to get a new one anyway. Now, I have the perfect excuse. There's a bathroom down the hall. Go get yourself cleaned up. And try to do something with your hair, will you? It looks all nappy and frizzy. I'll get one of the housekeepers to take care of this."

"Are you sure? About the rug, I mean—"

"Go!" Joanne pointed her manicured nail toward the door. "Berkley has a hundred rugs like this one. He won't miss it, I promise."

Well, I'd offered. That was all I could do. This wasn't the first rug I'd ruined, and it wouldn't be the last. In fact, there were several locations in the greater Bigtime area where I was no longer welcome because I'd caused so many catastrophes. Just last week, I'd been barred for life from Jewel's Jewel Emporium. I'd obliterated not one, not two, but three diamond-solitaire pendants. It is very, *very* hard to break diamonds, but somehow, I'd found a way to reduce them all to powder. With my bare hands.

I followed Joanne's directions as best I could. *Down the hall* might as well have been in another state as big as the mansion was. It took me ten minutes to find the bathroom, which could have housed a whale. Everything sparkled. It was so clean and white and sterile I doubted anything in the room had ever been used. I ran the tub-sized sink full of hot, soapy water, stripped off my white shirt, and scrubbed it. Despite the soaked-in globs of mayonnaise, the fabric came clean almost immediately. That was another strange thing about my luck. Sometimes, it was actually good, a blessing instead of just a jinx.

As for my hair, well, until Berkley or some other tycoon started making super—and I mean really, really *super*—strength conditioner, I'd just have to live with it. And so would Joanne.

I rummaged around in the tall cabinets until I found a hair dryer. I plugged it in one of the wall outlets, far, *far* from the sink and bathtub so I wouldn't tempt fate and electrocute myself. Or blow every fuse in the mansion. Using the hot, steady blast from the hair dryer, I got most of the moisture out of my shirt. Fifteen minutes later, I was ready to face the world again.

I headed back toward the library, admiring the rooms and furnishings I passed. Many of them were familiar to me. Johnny and I used to have a ball playing hide-and-seek in the mansion, while Berkley entertained Bobby and James. Sometimes, it took us hours to find each other. Once, Johnny hid so well Berkley had to get his staff to help me look for him so we could go home. We finally found Johnny asleep in a bedroom closet—

POP!

I stopped, wondering at the strange sound. It reminded me of cereal snapping when you poured cold milk on it. For a moment, I wondered if I'd imagined the noise. And why. I didn't particularly like cereal.

POP!
POP!
POP!

The sound came again and again, louder every time, and I knew I wasn't daydreaming. The *pops!* emanated from a salon a few feet ahead. I crept up to the doorway and peered inside. It was one of Berkley's viewing rooms, where he kept his paintings and statues and other expensive, important works of art. Cushioned chairs and low couches scattered throughout the area invited people to sit and stare at everything. Night had already fallen outside, but white footlights highlighted the art against the dark walls. I'd spent many hours in this room and others like it, trying to draw and paint and sketch as well as the masters.

POP!

A man appeared in front of a particularly abstract Picasso, where there had only been empty space a moment before. He wore a formfitting leather suit so blue it was almost black. The insignia of a scarlet rose intertwined with a silver thorn flashed on his chest. Dark hair curled around his face and silver mask, which had jagged edges that matched the thorn insignia. Although I tried to listen to as little superhero and ubervillain gossip as possible, I still recognized him.

Debonair.

One of the most notorious rakes—superhero, ubervillain, or otherwise—in Bigtime. He seduced women of all ages like other men breathed—with supreme, unconscious ease. He had a body even the other male superheroes envied—totally, perfectly chiseled. Michelangelo's *David* come to life. He wasn't too tall or too short and had a dazzling smile that could make a blind woman see. The gallant teleporter oozed sex appeal from head to toe, and billed himself as the ultimate lover and seducer. Debonair even had his own aptly named hideaway—the Lair of Seduction. Any woman who spent any time with Debonair there couldn't help falling under his charming spell. At least, that's what they said on SNN, the Superhero News Network. I'd never found blue-black leather to be any sort of turn-on, no matter how impressive the body underneath it was.

Debonair wasn't a superhero, but he wasn't quite an ubervillain either. He didn't care about taking over the city or world domination. Instead, he was a master thief. Of sorts. Several priceless works of art had gone missing from various homes and galleries in Bigtime over the years after Debonair had paid them a visit. But just as many had later turned up in museums and other public places around town. Debonair had his own shady agenda no one had ever really been able to figure out. The only thing you could really count on was for him to *pop!* in using his teleportation superpower, make some witty, charming quip, and *pop!* back out. He was rather like Swifte that way.

Debonair snapped his gloved fingers. A painting depicting a field of irises left its frame and appeared in his hand a second later. Berkley had more security than Fort Knox, and I waited for an alarm to start blaring. Sirens to sound. Bars to crash down over the doors and windows.

Nothing. Not even a whisper.

Debonair snapped his fingers again. A long, hollow tube appeared in his other hand. He carefully rolled up the painting and stuffed it inside. He snapped his fingers a third time, and the tube disappeared. My eyes darted around the room, wondering where the container had gone, but I didn't see it anywhere. Only an empty frame remained where the painting had been hanging on the wall.

I looked up at the ceiling. The mansion's security cameras swiveled left and right and up and down as though everything was fine and dandy. Debonair must have done something to them, obscured them in some way. Or maybe he was teleporting around too fast for them to follow. Either way, it was up to me to stop him.

"Hey!" I said. "What do you think you're doing?"

Debonair turned at the sound of my voice. He didn't seem alarmed by the fact I'd caught him stealing the painting. Didn't seem worried or bothered in the slightest. Instead, the thief tilted his head and gave me a thorough once-over. I crossed my arms over my chest and tried to look taller and scarier than I really was. Of course, that's rather hard to do when you're just over five feet. But still, I tried.

POP!

He appeared at my elbow, and I stifled a surprised scream. I would have stepped back, but he grabbed my hand and pulled me toward him. I put my other hand out to brace myself against his chest and immediately realized that Debonair didn't wear a sculpted breastplate like some of the other superheroes and ubervillains did to improve their looks or hold in a less-than-flat midsection. Those tight, taut muscles under that slick leather were all him.

My fingers spread out. Oh my. I couldn't help being impressed, despite my hatred of all things superhero.

"Bella Bulluci. What a delightful surprise." His voice was low and throaty.

"You know my name?"

I stared at his broad chest, the rose insignia just even with my eyes. He smelled sweet but manly, like rose petals mixed with a rich musk. The heady scent made my head fuzzy.

Debonair put a finger under my chin and tipped it up. His eyes slammed into my hazel ones. They were blue—as blue as blue could possibly be and then some. A ring of silver and black shimmered around the edges of his bright irises, adding to the intensity of his gaze.

"Of course I know your name. You make some of the finest clothes in all of Bigtime. And as you may know, I'm a purveyor of fine things." His gaze raked over me in a slow, sensual way that made my breath catch in my throat. "All sorts of fine things. In fact, I think it's time for me to sample one right now."

Debonair leaned in and lowered his lips to mine.

And I got angry. Really, *really* angry. Yeti Girl angry. Debonair might be attractive—okay, sexy with a capital *S*—but that didn't give him the right to just *pop!* over here and manhandle me. Lots of sexy heroes and villains called Bigtime home. They were a dime a dozen, really.

But Debonair thought he was going to kiss me just because he could? Without any encouragement whatsoever from me? After he'd stolen from my friends? I didn't think so.

I might be short, but I can take care of myself. Johnny's supertough exoskeleton had given him an unfair advantage when we were kids. As a result, I'd learned lots of dirty tricks to ward off unwanted noogie and tickle attacks. Like the one I was about to use right now.

I ducked Debonair's looming lips, turned my body into his broad chest, grabbed his left arm, and flipped him over my shoulder.

POP!

He teleported away a second before he slammed into the floor. My eyes flicked around, wondering where he'd poof to next.

POP!

He appeared in the hallway in front of me. "That wasn't very nice, Bella. All I wanted to do was kiss you."

"Well, I didn't want *you* to kiss *me*."

"But I'm Debonair," he said.

His tone was smug and self-assured, like the very mention of his name should be enough to make any woman his willing slave. And get her to take off her panties. Sexy and arrogant. A dangerous combination. One I had to work very hard not to find attractive. Maybe the Casanova routine worked on other women, but it wasn't going to on me.

"Oh, get over yourself," I snapped. "You're not all that."

He smiled. That too was perfect, just like the rest of him. White teeth. Nice lips. A tiny dimple in his chin.

"I think the folks in SSS would disagree with you. I've been their Man of the Year three times in a row now."

"Slaves for Superhero Sex? The cult group full of crazies who worship heroes?" I snorted. "They're hardly an appropriate judge of character. They'll do anything in spandex."

That was an understatement. Slaves for Superhero Sex was a group of men and women whose sole purpose in life was to get up close and personal with superheroes. SSS members deliberately did stupid, life-endangering things—like handcuff themselves to railroad tracks and swallow the key or climb to the top of the Skyline Bridge—in hopes that some superhero would come along and rescue them. Not only that, they usually tried to make time with their superhero savior after they were out of danger. In recent months, some of the more enthusiastic, morally challenged members had gone over to the dark side and started volunteering to be flunkies for various villains. At least, that's what had been reported on SNN.

"And what about you, Bella? Do you like spandex? Or are you more of a whips-and-chains kind of girl?" Debonair asked.

"That's none of your business!"

I couldn't stop myself from blushing. Whips and chains? I'd never dream of doing such a thing. Why, I hadn't even been much of a regular-sex girl lately. Not since before my father died, really.

Debonair gave me another sexy, knowing smirk, but I'd had enough of the witty banter. I was damp and tired and I smelled like moldy bread. So, I skirted around him, careful to stay at least six feet away at all times, and headed down the hall.

"Where are you going?" he called out. "We were just starting to warm up to each other."

"You want warm?" I asked, stopping in front of a small red knob. "Think how warm you'll be when the police show up and toss you in the slammer. Stealing from Berkley Brighton? Now, that was dumb. But pissing me off? That's what's really going to get you into trouble."

I yanked down the fire alarm. Loud bells and sirens blared to life throughout the massive house. *Please exit the building,* a man's voice intoned over the commotion. *Please exit the building.*

Debonair smiled and bowed his head to me. "Well, it seems you've bested me. I'm afraid I'll have to take my leave of you now. Until we meet again, Bella Bulluci."

"Which will hopefully be never."

Debonair gave me another long look. "We'll see."

POP!

He appeared in front of me again. Before I could stop him, the thief grabbed my hand and pressed a quick kiss to the inside of my wrist. Then, he gave me a sly wink and teleported away.

I leaned against the wall and let out a long breath. I suddenly felt weak and shaky. And for some strange reason, my pulse pounded in time to the fire alarm.

"I'm sorry he got away, Berkley," I said. *"Maybe if I'd* pulled the alarm sooner, the police would have been able to catch him."

An hour had passed since I'd set off the fire alarm. Now, Berkley, Joanne, and I stood in the salon, along with a couple of Bigtime Police detectives, Chief Sean Newman, and Berkley's personal insurance adjuster. My eyes scanned the room, taking in the damage. There really wasn't any. Unless you considered the loss of a priceless painting to be a catastrophe. I did.

"It's not your fault, Bella. I knew this would happen, sooner or later." Berkley stared at the empty frame.

"What do you mean?"

"Someone's been trying to get into the mansion," he replied, running a hand through his wavy hair. "The alarms have been going off all week. It must have been Debonair. I guess tonight he found a way to succeed."

"Well, he's certainly bold—I'll give him that," Joanne said.

"And effective," Berkley added. "According to my security chief, he managed to bypass all the alarms. The heat sensors, the motion detectors, the tripwires, the lasers, everything."

"Well, most alarms aren't designed to deal with someone with teleporting superpowers," I said. "Is there anything I can do for you? Anything at all? I feel like this is all my fault."

It was, given how terrible my luck was. Even now, I could feel the static building up around me, waiting to lash out yet again. And I should have pulled the alarm right away, instead of confronting the thief. I knew better than that.

Berkley shook his head. "Thank you, Bella. But no."

After giving my statement to the detectives and Chief Newman, I drove back home. It was almost midnight now, and the street was dark and empty. I found myself thinking of Debonair. Wondering where he was. What he was doing.

Why he'd wanted to kiss me.

Had he just wanted to distract me? Or was there some other reason?

I shook my head. Debonair was just another guy who dressed up in leather and went around Bigtime doing whatever to whomever he pleased. I wasn't going to give him another thought. Not a second more of my time or attention.

Easier said than done.

Ten minutes later, I parked the car in the driveway. My stomach rumbled, letting out a sound that would have made Fiona proud. So, I headed for the kitchen, determined to get something, anything, to eat before going to bed, even if I had to scoop it up off the floor.

Bobby sat at the kitchen table, sipping a glass of red wine. "Ah, Bella. There you are."

"Waiting up for me?" I asked. "That's not like you. I said I was fine."

I'd called Grandfather and told him what happened at Berkley's. The robbery would be big news, and I didn't want him to worry.

Bobby shrugged. "I couldn't sleep. I thought a nice glass of wine might help me relax. Do you want some?"

"Please." I wanted the whole bottle, maybe two, but unlike Fiona, I had some restraint when it came to food. I had to, given my thunder thighs.

Bobby poured me a glass, which I carefully picked up. I swirled the wine around and took a deep drink. The fruity liquid coated my tongue with its sweet-and-sour taste. I swallowed, and a pleasant warmth spread through me, melting my tension.

"Do you want some food?" Bobby said. "Let me make you a sandwich, and you can tell me about the robbery. I want all the details. What he took. What he said. What his costume looked like."

Like many older folks, Grandfather was a news hound. He read several papers every day to learn about the latest goings-on in Bigtime and around the world. Given his time as Johnny Angel, Grandfather was also obsessed with heroes and villains, which was why SNN was his favorite TV channel.

"Not a sandwich," I said, remembering what had happened to Joanne's rug. "How about a salad?"

"Done."

Grandfather pulled lettuce, cheese, carrots, tomatoes, oil, vinegar, and more out of one of the refrigerators. I told him about finding Debonair and how I'd pulled the fire alarm to summon help. The only part I omitted was when the thief tried to kiss me—and the whole whips-and-chains comment. I just couldn't talk to my grandfather about some things. Sex was definitely one of them.

"Well, I'm just glad you're all right," Bobby said, sliding a bowl full of salad across the counter to me. "From what I've read, Debonair isn't too terrible a fellow, but you never know what someone will do when he's cornered."

I made a noncommittal sound. After tonight, I thought Debonair was the worst of the worst. With other heroes and villains, all you had to contend with was them trying to save or kill you with their superpowers. But kissing people's wrists? Seducing unsuspecting women? That was just weird. In a sexy kind of way.

I reached for the bowl, and my power flared. The round container scooted off the island. It was plastic, like all the other dishes I used, so it didn't break. At least, not this time. Instead, it zoomed along the floor like a bowling ball. Rolling, rolling, rolling. I stared at the container, wishing it would somehow stop without spewing my salad everywhere. I really wanted to eat *something* tonight.

I felt the energy gather round me again, but I kept looking at the bowl. The container slowed and tipped itself upright, contents intact. I relaxed my concentration, smiled, and looked at Bobby.

And that was when the bowl began to spin.

Round and round it turned, like a washing machine out of control. Pieces of cheese and lettuce and tomato whirled out of the spinning container one after another, splattering onto the floor and ceiling and cabinets. A particularly buoyant carrot bounced up onto the sliding glass door on the opposite side of the room, a good thirty feet away. Oil and vinegar also arced out of the bowl, splashing around and creating even more of a mess. By the time the container stopped spinning, the kitchen looked like a vegetable cart had exploded inside.

I surveyed the damage for a moment, then opened a drawer and plucked out a fork. Utensil in hand, I sat down cross-legged in the middle of the kitchen floor and stabbed the first cherry tomato within easy reach. I bit down and sighed with pleasure as the tart juices filled my mouth. I was so hungry I didn't even care if it had a little dirt on it.

"What are you doing?" Bobby asked.

"Eating dinner," I replied, spearing a carrot. "While I still can."

5

The next morning, I went down to the gym for my daily workout and flipped the TV mounted on the wall to SNN. Sure enough, the major news story was Debonair robbing Berkley. The tanned anchor sent the continuing coverage out to Kelly Caleb, SNN's star reporter and Grace's granddaughter. Kelly stood outside the closed gates to Berkley's mansion. She flashed the camera her trademark toothy smile and launched into a recap of last night's events.

"Well, Jim, it seems even the richest man in Bigtime isn't safe from crime. Bigtime police were called out to the home of whiskey billionaire Berkley Brighton around nine o'clock last night. Debonair, one of the city's most notorious thieves, broke into Berkley's home and removed a Pandora painting worth almost three million dollars. Brighton's home is one of several Debonair has allegedly robbed in recent years . . ."

While Kelly recapped Debonair's life of crime, SNN showed a photo montage of the thief. There were still shots from his video game, *Debonair Deluxe*. A panoramic scan of his action figures sitting on the shelves at the department store Oodles o' Stuff. Even some footage of him accepting an award from the Slaves for Superhero Sex group. He looked the same in every single photo. Black hair. Blue eyes. Self-confident smirk.

I listened to the report with half an ear, my thoughts turning back to Debonair. I didn't know why I was thinking about him again. He was just another super-something-or-other. Strong. Devious. Sexy.

I sighed. So sexy. Too bad he felt the need to go prancing around in head-to-toe leather. Because if there was one thing I would never, *ever* do, it was date a superhero. Or a pseudo-superhero. Or whatever Debonair thought he was, other than a lousy thief.

Kelly pitched her segment back to the anchor sitting in the SNN studio.

". . . So, Kelly, how will this affect plans for the *Whimsical Wonders* benefit, set for Saturday night at the Bigtime Museum of Modern Art? I understand Berkley Brighton was going to donate several items to be displayed as part of a special exhibition. Is he worried about security at the museum? Especially since his own house was victimized?"

My hair frizzed out to I-stuck-my-finger-in-a-light-socket proportions. Static electricity gathered around me. And my fingers itched so badly I felt like there were bugs crawling on them. I tightened my grip on the handles of the elliptical trainer.

But my jinx wouldn't let me be.

Blue and white sparks flew out from my palms, and a few of them landed on the control panel of the elliptical trainer. The machine started shrieking. Gears whined. Lights flashed. Smoke spewed up from the top. And then the device abruptly stopped, almost throwing me off.

I stumbled away, but the destruction continued. Bolts flew out of their joints. Screws popped loose. Even the paint flaked off the handlebars. Thirty seconds later, the once shiny elliptical trainer collapsed in on itself, reduced to the sum of its parts, as it were.

I put my hands on my hips, slumped over, and tried to get my emotions in check. Breathe. Breathe. I needed to just breathe . . .

I exhaled, grimacing all the while, and not because I'd just reduced another thousand-dollar piece of gym equipment to scrap metal. We didn't need this sort of bad publicity, especially this close to the benefit. If people thought the museum wasn't safe, they wouldn't loan out their items. The special exhibition would be canceled, and the museum would have to return the money it had made from advance ticket sales. The benefit would flop, and it would be all my fault. Sometimes, it just didn't pay to get out of bed in the morning.

On the TV screen, Kelly nodded to the anchor and gripped her microphone a little tighter. "Well, Jim, I spoke with

Berkley's wife, Joanne James. She said Berkley isn't worried about security at his home or at the museum. He considers this to be a fluke and nothing more. In fact, he's decided to donate even more items to the museum to show his good faith."

I could have wept. "Bless you, Joanne. Bless you."

Eventually, SNN moved on to the other stories of the day, including a brief blurb about the man Swifte had taken to the hospital. He was expected to make a full recovery. Good for him.

"And speaking of Swifte, we go back out live to Kelly Caleb, who's managed to catch up with the speedy superhero. Or rather, he's caught up with her," Jim said.

Kelly popped back up on the screen. A white, almost silver blur ran circles around her before abruptly stopping. The cameraman swung his lens to the right and zoomed in on Swifte, who leaned one arm on Kelly's shoulder and smiled.

I flipped off the TV. I didn't want to hear the superhero blather on about his latest rescue. I didn't want to think about any superheroes or ubervillains.

Especially not Debonair.

My hair poofed out again. Somehow, my extra-arch-support, nonskid sneakers slid out from under me, and I tumbled to the ground, almost whacking my head on the side of the ruined elliptical trainer.

Even though pain flooded my body, I knew nothing was broken. I never broke anything when I fell or stumbled or slipped, except dishes. Heck, I didn't even get a concussion when a piano rolled off its dais and slammed me into the makeup counter at Oodles o' Stuff two months ago. What I would have tomorrow, though, would be lots of nasty-colored bruises. They'd replace the ones from last week that were just fading away.

I sighed into the carpet. First, dinner with Fiona and Chief Newman. Spilling my goodies in front of the trick-or-treaters. My run-in with Debonair. The bad press about the upcoming benefit. Dropping every bit of food I tried to put in my mouth. It was only Monday, but I'd already had enough bad luck to last most people for an entire year.

Unfortunately, I had a feeling it was only going to get worse. My jinx was rather predictable that way.

I spent the next few days working nonstop on the Whimsical Wonders *benefit.* The committee had made a lot of progress during our last meeting, but there were still a thousand little details to see to in order to make sure the event went off without a hitch. Not to mention the fact I had to repair the damage done by Debonair and his visit to Berkley's mansion. Why, oh why, couldn't he have waited until *after* the benefit to rob Berkley? It would have made my life so much easier.

Speaking of Debonair, I had the strangest feeling the super-thief was following me around. More than once, I thought I heard that distinctive *pop!* that signaled his arrival, or smelled his sexy, sweet scent. But whenever I looked for him, he was nowhere to be seen.

In the end, I decided it was just my imagination playing tricks on me. Debonair wasn't interested in me. I certainly had no interest at him. None at all. At least, that's what I kept telling myself. Surely, if I repeated it enough times, I could pretend it was really true.

So, I carried on with the benefit work. I met with the staff at Quicke's to review seating arrangements. Locked down the bachelor lineup. Double-checked the security setup at the museum. Called all the bigwigs and assured them their priceless art objects would be perfectly safe. The list went on and on.

I had plenty of time to devote to the benefit, since I was taking a two-month sabbatical from Bulluci Industries, where I oversaw our fashion and housewear lines. With my father's death and Johnny's engagement and all the other changes in my life, I needed a break. Some time off to figure things out. That was the perk of working for the family company—I could hand things off to Johnny and Grandfather for a few weeks. It wasn't that I was unhappy with work, but I felt there was more I could be doing with my life than designing dresses for the rich and infamous. Like maybe be a different kind of artist.

A museum-quality artist.

I'd loved drawing and painting from the first time I picked up a brush, but sketching portraits was my specialty. Over the years, I'd drawn countless pictures of Bobby, Johnny, and James. Movie stars. My favorite authors. People I passed on the street. I even used to do superheroes, back in my younger, more foolish days.

Secretly, I longed to have my works hang next to the other masterpieces inside the Bigtime Museum of Modern Art. But it was a dream I kept to myself. I didn't know if I had the talent to be a real artist. It was a completely different sort of skill set than designing clothes. Fiona would disagree with me, of course, but anybody with a needle and thread could sew, however poorly. Not everybody who picked up a pencil could draw with it.

Besides, the one time I'd attempted to break into the art world, I hadn't exactly been greeted with open arms. Heartbreak was more like it.

"Do *not* drop that unless you want me to use your head as a bowling ball."

Abby's sharp voice pulled me back to reality. It was Friday, the day before the benefit, and we stood in the new wing of the Bigtime Museum of Modern Art. The two of us, along with Hannah, were overseeing the installation of the pieces for the *Whimsical Wonders* exhibit, while Grace and Joanne had headed over to Quicke's to make sure everything was coming together at the restaurant.

The burly guy that Abby had just admonished wrapped his whole beefy hand around the Ming vase he'd been carrying, instead of just sticking his fingers in the top of it. Abby nodded her approval and checked off something on her enormous clipboard. The event planner was in her usual getup today—cargo pants, a camisole, and a flannel shirt.

And the vest.

No matter how fancy or simple the party, Abby always wore a khaki mesh vest to any event she planned. It reminded me of something a fisherman would wear, although with more pockets and zippers and hidden compartments. Pens, highlighters, note pads, a water bottle, a stun gun. That was just the stuff I could see hanging off the front. Abby had more supplies hidden in the inner pockets, and the vest had to weigh ten pounds if it weighed an ounce. She could probably survive in the wilderness for a month with all the gear she had crammed into that thing.

I'd dressed down today, wearing my favorite pair of jeans and a blue-striped oxford shirt. Hannah was a different story. Instead of jeans or khakis, she sported a wraparound silk top and pencil skirt in a deep burgundy color. Gold sparkled around her neck and her fingers, and she looked as put together and polished as ever. She stood off in a corner, shooting looks at all the art and murmuring into her cell phone.

My eyes drifted over the rest of the wing, which had opened a month ago. The area, done in white flecked marble like the rest of the building, rose seven stories into the air and was three times as wide. The first floor featured a vast, open space with black granite benches set in front of particularly significant or popular pieces. Greek-style columns marked recesses in the walls that people could wander through and examine rotating exhibits. Three scalloped archways allowed access to the other, older parts of the museum, while stairs set in the corners led to the upper floors. Each story sported a wraparound balcony that overlooked the main exhibition space. Diamond-shaped panes of glass crisscrossed with silver solidium beams comprised the pointed ceiling far above. Natural light filtered in through the glass and let people see the art as it really was. Clean white. Bits of color in the marble. Smooth curves. Round, soft edges. No matter how many times I visited the museum, I never tired of it. The architecture itself was a work of art, along with all the paintings on the walls.

"Will you look at that?"

Abby stabbed her pen at two guys up on ladders in one corner of the room. A large, rather gaudy picture of Elvis hung between them. Painted on velvet, of course. That had been one of Joanne's donations. If it had been anyone else, I would have told them to keep Elvis away from the light of day, where he belonged. Forever.

But I couldn't exactly inform Joanne that velvet Elvis wasn't whimsical or wonderful. After all, she was sort of an aunt to me. Not to mention the richest woman in the city.

"I've told those guys at least five times the painting of Elvis goes on the left wall, not the right. Idiots. I'm surrounded by idiots," Abby muttered.

The event planner stomped off to go make some more of the movers cry. I shook my head, glad I wasn't in the line of fire. And Fiona thought I was wound too tight. She needed to spend some quality time with Abby, who morphed into Ms. Hyde the second she stepped into the museum. I didn't know what was wrong with the event planner, but every single thing had annoyed her today, from the smell of the cleaning supplies used in the museum to the glare of the lights overhead. Abby even complained the movers made too much noise walking around—though they wore thick coveralls that just barely whispered together.

Footsteps sounded on the smooth marble floor, and Arthur Anders appeared in one of the wide arches. He was a thin man who always wore a brown plaid jacket and corduroy pants. Half-moon glasses perched on the end of his nose, and he sported a small ponytail. Arthur was the museum curator and sort of a mentor to me. He also worked as a professor at Bigtime University, and I'd taken many of his classes. The man knew more about art than anyone else in the city. Even now, several years removed from college, his discerning eye and expertise still awed me.

"It's coming along nicely, Bella. Very nicely," Arthur said, taking in the items already on display.

People had donated a little bit of everything, from elaborate crystal candlesticks and animal figurines to antique miniature cars to old-fashioned Barbie dolls to Fabergé eggs to tea sets. The gleam of gold. The red fabric of the dolls' dresses. The luster of the dishes. The objects decorated the room with a rainbow of colors and shapes. Everything was classy, but fun, just the way I'd intended it to be. Art wasn't just about O'Keeffes and Whistlers and Pollocks. To me, anything well crafted with loving care was art.

Well, anything except velvet Elvises.

"Thank you. But I couldn't have done it all without the others, especially Hannah and Joanne. They're the ones who convinced people to donate such wonderful, interesting items."

"I still can't believe you got Berkley Brighton to show the Star Sapphire," Arthur said, his eyes going to the gem. "That was quite a coup, Bella."

I shrugged. "Berkley is a family friend and Joanne's husband. It really wasn't that difficult."

The sapphire was the first thing we'd put into the room this morning—in the very center, of course. The gem, cut into an oval bigger than my fist, rested on three curved silver tines. Thanks to the maintenance workers positioning the lights just so, the sapphire cast out hundreds of rays of cool blue light that reached into the farthest corners of the open area. The display dazzled me, even if the stone rested behind four inches of bulletproof, shatterproof glass rigged with more alarms than a fire truck. Berkley hadn't gotten to be one of the wealthiest men in the world by taking chances with his treasures, and I wasn't about to take any with his most prized possession.

"Still, we've had more excitement about this exhibit than any we've had in a long time," Arthur said. "You've done a wonderful job."

"Don't congratulate me just yet," I warned. "There's still plenty that could go wrong."

Like Debonair or someone else breaking in and stealing Berkley's sapphire. That was my main, paranoid fear, although the museum staff and I had done everything in our power to prevent that from happening. Added more patrolling guards. Increased the number of cameras in the room. Blanketed the entire wing with alarms and lasers and every other conceivable security device. Arthur had even called upon the Fearless Five to be on standby during the exhibit to apprehend any would-be thieves.

Then, of course, there was my other fear—I'd have a colossal bout of bad luck during the benefit and bring every single display tumbling down like dominoes. Even now, I felt the static gathering around me, ready to strike.

"Oh, nonsense, Bella. What's the worst that could happen?" Arthur asked.

My hair began its daily climb upward. I just grimaced.

* * *

We didn't finish installing the exhibition until almost midnight. We would have been done a lot sooner, but my power kept flaring up at the most inopportune times. Like when one of the heavy overhead light fixtures I was staring at decided to break free from the wall and plummet to the ground—missing my head by about six inches.

Or when we ordered dinner from Quicke's. I'd taken the box of food from the delivery guy and started up the museum steps. I got all the way to the top before my power pulsed. The box exploded, and its contents slid through my hands, tumbling down the stairs like a Slinky. Every single one of the lids popped off the takeout containers. Salads, pasta, burgers, fries, sodas, milkshakes. It wasn't pretty.

But on the bright side, as I was scrambling around trying to clean up the mess, a gust of wind blew by—and plastered a pair of hundred-dollar bills to my forehead. It wasn't the first time this had happened, and I snagged the money before it could blow away again. The C-notes were more than enough to pay for another order of food from Quicke's. I even got fifteen bucks back in change—until I managed to drop it down the subway vent outside the museum.

But my luck didn't bother me too much. Well, no more than usual. I was just grateful nobody dropped or broke any of the exhibit pieces.

And I'd actually had another bit of good luck today, besides the money. No matter how hard the museum staff tried, they just couldn't seem to hang Joanne's hideous painting of Elvis. Something untoward happened every time they attempted it. One of the workers would lose his grip on the side of the painting and drop it. Or it would fall off the wall by itself. Or one of the strings anchoring it to the ceiling would snap. Finally, even Arthur gave up and put Elvis back in storage for safekeeping.

Now, after hours of work, everything was finally finished, which meant I could mostly relax tomorrow night. At least until the bachelor auction. As chairperson of the benefit and a somewhat noteworthy citizen, I'd put myself on the auction block at Abby's insistence. According to her estimates and the fancy calculator she kept in one of her vest pockets, I should bring in a couple thousand dollars at least. I just hoped someone bid on me. It would be rather embarrassing to be passed over at my own event.

Abby and I said our goodnights to Arthur and the rest of the staff. Hannah had left hours ago, claiming she had an important business meeting. Grace and Joanne had called to tell me that everything was a go at Quicke's, and they'd packed up shop too. Abby had stayed to the bitter end, although I'd had things more or less under control. But she was a perfectionist that way.

We stepped outside, and a cool, crisp, fall breeze kissed my face. I shivered and stuck my hands in my pockets, wishing I'd brought my wool pea coat.

"I'm heading for the subway. Want to walk together?" Abby offered.

"No, thanks," I said. "My car's right there."

Abby frowned and looked at my car parked at the bottom of the museum steps. "How did you manage to snag that spot? There's never any parking on this street during the day."

"Oh, a car was pulling out right when I drove by."

Despite my hatred of my supposed superpower, I could always find a parking space, no matter how crowded the street was. It was one of the few things I was consistently lucky at. Sometimes, I could even put an extra hour on the meter just by focusing on it. When I didn't make it crumple into a metal heap.

Abby and I went our separate ways. I got into my silver Benz, locked the doors, turned on the heater, and headed for home. The downtown streets were mostly deserted, except for the occasional homeless person huddled over a steaming subway grate. The wind picked up, and a rain of dry, brown leaves splattered against my windshield and off into the night.

The usual nighttime sights greeted me as I headed for home. A few shoppers walking out of Oodles o' Stuff, their arms full of shopping bags. The three-story-high *F* that marked the entrance to Fiona Fine Fashions. Reporters huddled in the doorway at the *Exposé* offices puffing at cigarettes, while the skyscraper loomed over them with its winking blue lights. The same scene over at the *Chronicle*. Muted shrieks of childish glee and calliope music drifting out of Paradise Park.

The light in front of me flashed to red, and I cruised to a stop. I never ran traffic signals, not even this late at night. With my luck, there'd be a cop waiting just around the corner who'd be more than happy to write me a three-hundred-dollar ticket. And impound my car when my taillights and windshield spontaneously shattered. It had happened before.

I sat at the intersection, waiting for the light to change, and a strange sort of *thump-thump-thumping* sound caught my attention. A man in black flew through the air, across my windshield, and smacked into the pavement. I winced. Definitely not the most graceful landing.

The man struggled to get up, but a seventysomething woman sprinted into view and brought a diamond-topped cane down on the man's most sensitive area. He howled, curled up into a tight ball, and grabbed himself. The woman smacked her cane in her hand, ready to dish out another whollop if the guy did anything but whimper. A large white pocketbook dangled from her arm, while gravel-sized pearls hung around her throat. A purple angora sweater fluttered like a minicape around her shoulders, and a flower-shaped mask covered most of her face.

Granny Cane. She was one of Bigtime's older and most respected superheroes. She didn't have any powers I knew of— just a diamond-topped walking stick she used to beat muggers and purse snatchers into submission. Granny claimed she kept the streets safe for the elderly. I thought she liked dressing up and showing off, just like all the other heroes and villains. C'mon. A stun gun would have been much more effective for subduing bad guys than a wooden stick.

Granny hauled the injured man to his feet, grabbed his ear, and stepped into the crosswalk. She yanked him along after her, evidently not caring he now had a pronounced limp and would probably never be able to have children. I averted my eyes, pretending she was just another little old lady crossing the street—albeit one with a weeping, masked man in tow.

Granny Cane made it to the other side and kept walking. She

was probably heading toward the Bigtime Police Station to turn in her latest capture. It was only a couple blocks away.

I shook my head and kept on driving, hoping she'd be the only superhero I'd see.

No such luck.

Even though it was after midnight, it was a hot time in the old town tonight because the superheroes were out in full force. Swifte sped by me a couple of times, followed by police cars and an SNN news truck. Pistol Pete, a superhero who dressed like a cowboy, pulled out his six-shooters and performed some quick-draw tricks for a crowd of onlookers near Laurel Park, while the Fearless Five van cruised around the downtown area.

I also drove by more than a few villains trying to get the upper hand on their archrivals. Big, brawny Yeti Girl duked it out with Black Samba on top of one of the city buses. But Black Samba danced away from her every time, while the snakes on the superhero's arms and in her headdress hissed their displeasure at the ubervillain.

Hot Stuff, an ubervillain who thought she was, well, hot stuff, threw Molotov cocktails at Wynter from her perch on top of the Bigtime Public Library. But the superhero used her ice-based powers to shield herself from the worst of the explosions.

And finally, there was the Mintilator, the villain devoted to making the world a germ-free, minty-fresh place. He was trying rather unsuccessfully to fend off Halitosis Hal and his horrid breath over next to the entrance to the marina.

Sheesh. Didn't these people have real lives? Wives and husbands to go home to? Kids to take care of? Elderly parents to visit? Apparently not.

After a few more unwanted hero and villain sightings, I reached the house. The light above the front door burned, but the rest of the mansion was dark. I'd called Grandfather hours ago and told him not to wait up. Looked like he'd taken my advice. That, or he hadn't come home yet. He'd told me he had a date with his lady friend and might be late.

I'd asked him once again who he was going out with, but Grandfather had been his usual cagey self. He still hadn't introduced me to his lady friend, something I was going to rectify, even if I had to start following him when he left the house. Maybe I could get Lulu Lu to put some sort of tracking device in his silver angel cuff links. She was good at that sort of thing. The best, actually. With her computer skills and shady contacts, Lulu could find out anything about anyone. Lulu was like a sixth member of the Fearless Five, even though she didn't have any official superpowers. She'd been let in on the group's secret identities when she'd started dating Henry Harris.

I fished my keys out of my purse and got out of my Benz. It had been a hectic, stressful day, and I was completely exhausted. I needed a hot shower before climbing into bed—

POP!

Debonair puffed into view on the hood of my car. Surprised, I screamed and stepped back, slamming my butt into the driver's side door. Despite my love of pasta and potatoes, my ass wasn't that big, but the metal still caved in with a screech, forming a dent about two feet wide and a foot deep.

"Well, that wasn't exactly the reaction I was hoping for," Debonair said in his low, seductive voice.

I rubbed my butt until it quit throbbing. Then, I balled up my fist, focused on the car door, and smacked my hand against it. The massive imprint popped right back out. This wasn't the first time I'd put a dent in my car—or taken one out. Things like this were rather routine in my life, along with odd items like air conditioners falling from the sky and almost hitting me in the head. I didn't even flinch anymore when that happened. I just kept walking.

"How are you tonight, Bella?" Debonair asked, lounging on the hood like some lingerie model.

"I was fine, until you showed up," I muttered, trying to pretend the thief didn't look as sexy as ever in his leather costume. Blue-black leather was *not* attractive. The same color in cashmere? Maybe. Leather? No. Definitely not.

"Well, I didn't want to teleport into your car. That's how accidents happen."

I crossed my arms over my chest. "What are you saying? That you've been following me around town tonight? Why?"

So, I hadn't been imagining him lurking around these past

few days. I wondered why he was following me. And how many times he'd seen me explode or shatter or destroy something. I might have been cursed with bad luck, but what I really *hated* was for other people to see the messes I made. I couldn't stand the thought of other people laughing at me. If Debonair had been following me around, he would have seen and done both. Many, many times.

"Well, I couldn't exactly talk to you at the museum. Arthur Anders tends to get a little upset whenever he sees me. Did you know the even-tempered curator actually has a shotgun in his office with my name engraved on it?"

"I can't imagine why," I sniped. "Oh, wait. Yes, I can. Perhaps it's because you go around town *stealing art.*"

Debonair gave a not-so-modest shrug. "Everyone should have a hobby."

"And stealing is yours?"

He smirked. A horrifying thought struck me, and my hair began to morph into a bush around my head.

"You didn't steal anything, did you? Tonight? At the museum?"

"Would I do something like that?" he asked, his blue eyes wide and innocent.

"Absolutely."

Debonair held his arms out, giving me an unobstructed view of his chest. His very broad, very solid chest. "Well, why don't you come here and frisk me? And see if I took anything from the museum?"

I couldn't tell if he was serious or just being kinky. I stared at him, and he looked at me. His lips twitched. A slight little quiver that somehow made him more attractive. Making fun of me. He was making fun of me.

Pushing my buttons, yet again.

Somehow, he seemed to know every single one, even though we'd only spoken a few dozen sentences to each other.

My power surged, my hair frizzed, and I just lost it.

I threw my shoulder bag at him. The black missile hit Debonair in the chest and exploded.

Literally.

The straps snapped. The pockets sprang open. And the zipper ripped off the top. Pens and papers and lipstick and loose change went everywhere, plinking away into the dark, cool night. I sighed, knowing I'd never find everything. I was still picking up apples from the trick-or-treating fiasco, and they were a lot easier to spot.

Debonair chuckled, amused by my humiliation. Red-faced, I curled my hands into fists, wishing I had the strength to pummel him. Where was Fiera when you really needed her?

"Well, that was something," Debonair said. "Do your purses always do that?"

"Just when I'm around you," I snarled.

Debonair put his arms behind his head and leaned back on the windshield like it was a recliner. I could see him striking that same pose in bed, after a night of long, slow lovemaking—

"I rather like you, Bella Bulluci. You're spunky."

"Spunky?" I said, pulling my thoughts back to the here and now. "You think I'm spunky? Wonderful."

"What's wrong with spunky?"

"Kids are spunky. Old ladies who speak their minds are spunky. Lots of things are spunky. I'm not one of them."

"What are you then?" Debonair asked. His blue eyes flashed like the Star Sapphire in the darkness.

I ignored the suggestive tone in his voice. "Listen, I don't know what sort of game you're playing, why you decided to *visit*—and I use that word loosely—me tonight, but I've had a long day. I'm tired, and I want to go to bed."

"I told you why I'm here. I like you."

"You like me? Like me how? Like a cold sore on prom night? Because that's exactly how I like you."

Debonair smiled. "That's how you like me *now*. But you'll warm up to me once you get to know me. Everybody does. So, how about dinner? Say, Monday night?"

My mouth fell open. "Are you asking me out?"

"Yes, on a thing called a date. I'm sure you've had at least one before."

"Of course I've been out on a date before," I snapped. "But why would you want to go out with me?"

"Have you looked in a mirror lately?" Debonair asked, giving me an appreciative leer. "Those big hazel eyes, that mane of hair, those killer curves. You're gorgeous, Bella. Not to mention that wild, passionate personality, just waiting to get out from under all this buttoned-up repression."

He thought I was gorgeous? A little thrill of excitement surged through me, along with my usual wave of static electricity. It lasted about three seconds. Then, I snapped back to reality.

"Forget it," I said. "I don't date superheroes or ubervillains or anyone in between."

"Why not?" Debonair asked, looking puzzled.

"Let's be clear. I don't like thieves, I despise ubervillains, and I hate superheroes. You're a bit of all three. You and me? Never going to happen. So, go pop off to one of your Slaves for Superhero Sex groupies, and let them fawn all over you, because I'm not interested."

It was the truth. I'd made a vow a long time ago never to get involved with superheroes and ubervillains. In any way, shape, or form. I'd been successful at keeping it too, until my brother had decided to become Johnny Angel in order to track down our father's killers. Then, he'd gone and fallen for Fiona, who'd brought not only herself, but the other members of the Fearless Five into our lives. Now, I couldn't take two steps in my own house without running into a hero or listening to one talk about how hard it was to avoid a panty line under their spandex suits.

"Are you sure? Because I think the two of us could have a good time together," Debonair said, his voice husky, his eyes flashing. "A *very* good time."

I let myself fantasize. With his hard body and suave ways, and my general loneliness, we could have more than a good time. Much, much more. If Debonair was as good as everyone claimed, the sex would be amazing. I got a little out of breath just thinking about it.

After about a minute, I put the fantasy aside, just like the smushed fries I'd refused for dinner. They might taste good going down, but I'd regret eating them later. Just like I'd regret doing anything with Debonair.

"Sorry, I'm not interested. Besides, if you really wanted to show me a good time, you'd help me pick up everything that was in my purse."

Debonair gave me a small, slightly sad smile. "All you had to do was ask, Bella. Your wish is my command—whatever it might be."

Anticipation pulsed through me, despite my pretending I was completely indifferent to his suggestive proposal.

Debonair snapped his fingers in rapid succession. The bag appeared in my hands and began to fill. A minute later, I stared down at it in awe. I didn't know how he did it, but everything was in there. My compact, cell phone, wallet, keys, lipstick, quarters. Even certain feminine products I wished he hadn't seen.

"Um, thanks," I said, not sure what to make of it. "That was actually kind of nice of you."

Debonair slid off the car hood and sauntered over to me. I clutched my purse to my chest, as if that would protect me from him. And all my conflicting emotions.

"Think nothing of it, Bella. Until we meet again."

Debonair grabbed my wrist and kissed it, just as he had before. His lips lingered on my skin, and I knew he could feel my roaring pulse. Then, Debonair straightened, gave a little flourish with his hand, and—

POP!

He teleported away into the starry night.

6

An hour later, I sat on my bed, combing out my tangled mane of hair. After Debonair popped away, I'd taken my much-longed-for shower. I was almost ready for bed, but I wasn't tired anymore. In fact, I doubted I'd be able to sleep much tonight.

And it was all *his* fault.

I kept replaying my meeting with Debonair. I didn't understand the handsome thief. Why had he come back to see me? I'd made it perfectly clear I had no interest in him. Hell, I'd given the police a statement about the robbery, which had led to a warrant being issued for his arrest, one of many already on file. Maybe he was one of those guys who pursued you that much harder if you rejected him. Or turned him in to the cops.

Since I couldn't sleep, I grabbed one of my sketch pads and went out into the hall. The house was quiet and still, the night air chilly on my bare feet. From the carpet to the crown molding to the light fixtures, angel eyes followed me from the floors and walls and ceilings, tracking my every move. Some people would have found them creepy, but they comforted me. I always thought of them as my own guardian angels, watching over me.

I turned into a hallway filled with portraits of my ancestors. Generations of Bullucis stared back at me. Some smiled, some didn't. Some were old, some young. But there was something in their eyes, an intensity, a look, that told you they had a zest, a passion for life that couldn't be denied. I'd spent many hours here, going from portrait to portrait, trying to capture that elusive sparkle on paper—and wondering if I had it too.

I stopped in front of the painting of my father, James. Tan skin. Blue eyes. Slightly bushy chestnut hair. He looked the same as always—and I felt the familiar ache gather in my heart at his loss. I ran my fingers over the nameplate on the bottom of the painting, then moved on.

A large, cushioned window seat lay at the end of the hall. Besides the kitchen, it was my favorite place in the entire house. The window seat looked out into the backyard, with its exotic trees and shrubs and flowers. I'd spent many hours here, day-dreaming and sketching. I sank onto the cushion and curled my feet up under the hem of my thick, cloud-covered, terrycloth robe.

I stared into the backyard, admiring the way the moonlight frosted everything, from the leaves and branches of the trees to the tiny blades of grass. Then, I flipped to a new page in my pad and started doodling nothing in particular. As my charcoal pencil moved over the blank paper, my thoughts turned back to Debonair.

I couldn't get him out of my mind, which wasn't like me at all. I prided myself on being extremely sensible, especially when it came to my love life. I liked nice, normal men who brought me flowers, could carry on an intelligent conversation, and didn't wish I had bigger boobs, smaller hips, and smoother hair.

Debonair was not a nice man. And it would not be at all sen-sible to get involved with him. He'd propositioned me twice in less than a week. He was a thief. A lout. And he wore blue-black leather. Three big turn-offs. I couldn't possibly like him.

The grandfather clock down the hall chimed out the hour. Two in the morning. It was time to go to bed, whether I thought I could sleep or not. It wouldn't do to be auctioned off with bags under my eyes.

I sighed and glanced down at my sketch. My pencil froze in midstroke.

Debonair's masked face smiled up at me.

"Let's start the bidding at one thousand dollars. Do I hear one thousand dollars? One thousand from the gentleman in the back."

I squinted into the bright lights, but I couldn't tell who'd bid to go to dinner with me. The night of the benefit had arrived, and the bachelor auction was in full swing at Quicke's. As the chairperson, Joanne and the others insisted I should be the first person auctioned off. So here I was, standing on a stage next to the long bar, trying to look nice and friendly, instead of scrunching my face up against the hot glare of the spotlights.

"Two thousand? Do I hear two thousand dollars?"

The auctioneer's loud voice spurred the crowd on to further action. A flurry of bids filled the air, and my worth quickly increased to just under five thousand dollars. Not too bad. More than I'd hoped for, actually. I didn't have a rep for being a boozy party girl, like some of the other fashion designers in town.

"Ten thousand dollars. I bid ten thousand dollars." Bobby's booming voice cut through the murmurs of conversation and clink of glasses and silverware.

I hid a smile. Trust Grandfather to drive up my price, even if he had to do the bidding himself.

"Twenty thousand dollars," a male voice called out.

"Twenty thousand!" the auctioneer crowed. "A very lovely offer for this very lovely lady. Do I hear twenty-one? Anyone? Anyone? No? All right, twenty thousand dollars. Going once . . . going twice . . . sold! To the gentleman in the front."

I squinted through the lights to see Devlin Dash holding up a numbered placard. Devlin was another one of Bigtime's wealthy businessmen, having half a dozen companies under his command. But Devlin didn't quite look or act the part. His ink black hair had more cowlicks than a little boy's, while thick, silver-rimmed glasses obscured his eyes. Devlin also had a habit of pulling at his tie, as if it was always just a bit too tight. He wasn't nearly as suave as the other billionaire playboys. In fact, he sort of reminded me of Henry Harris, the technological whiz for the Fearless Five. Henry had a nasty habit of wearing polka-dot bow ties with plaid sweater vests, something Fiona and I were trying to change, with a little help from Lulu.

Devlin also happened to be Grace Caleb's grandson, along with Kyle Quicke, the restaurant owner. She'd probably told him to bid on me. During our time working together, Grace had dropped more than a few hints to Abby and me about what a nice young man Devlin was and what a good family he came from. She'd also gone through all the bachelor files, looking for someone for Kelly. At the moment, Kyle was dating Piper Perez, Fiona's chief financial officer, so he was off the market. Still, it was pretty clear Grace wanted some grandchildren. The sooner, the better.

I actually liked Devlin. We'd chaired an art auction together earlier this year and had dinner once. He was a sweet guy, very quiet and almost painfully shy. Devlin was also a real old-fashioned gentleman, the kind who hurried to open doors and asked before he even thought about kissing you. I wouldn't have to worry about him trying to paw me at the end of the night. Twenty-thousand dollars could buy a lot of things, but it did not get you an all-expenses-paid trip around the world with Bella Bulluci.

I left the stage to polite applause and stopped to let my eyes adjust to the light. Abby Appleby stood just to the right of the stage. In keeping with the costume ball theme, she'd come dressed as a rock 'n' roll queen and wore tight black leather pants, spiked heels, and a shredded, paint-splattered white T-shirt with a lacy black camisole underneath. At least, I thought that's what she had on. It was tough to tell with the khaki vest covering most of her torso. Not to mention the massive clipboard she held in her hands and the many pens stuck in her teased hair. I'd told Abby to just relax tonight and enjoy the benefit, but obviously, she hadn't listened to me.

Abby nodded her head. "Way to start things off, Bella. Let's hope everybody goes for as much as you did." She ticked something off on her board and started doing some calculations, probably trying to guess the final tally already.

I shook my head and moved off into the crowded restaurant. Quicke's had some of the best food in the city, and their cheese fries were to die for, but I didn't really like coming to the restaurant for one reason—it was a shrine to all things superhero.

During normal business hours, framed posters, newspaper clippings, and autographed pictures of heroes and villains covered the red brick walls from floor to ceiling. Plastic action figures posed in mock battle positions lined the shelves behind the bar, along with liquor bottles. Board games, miniature cars, die-cast models, and every other merchandising tie-in you could dream of peeked out from windowsills and the rest of the available space. Superheroes might be dedicated to saving the city and the world, but most of them weren't above making a few bucks doing it. Along with Oodles o' Stuff, Quicke's was a great place to have their products showcased.

Several menu items were even named after Bigtime's various heroes and villains, like the Caveman Stan Steak or the Wynter Cosmopolitan. When I was in the mood for Quicke's, I always got takeout. I couldn't stomach actually eating inside the building. Especially since there were more than a few Johnny Angel posters on the walls—and they included depictions of my grandfather, father, and brother.

But everybody else loved Quicke's, even ubervillains, which was why we'd decided to have the bachelor auction here, along with its close proximity to the museum. Tonight, the restaurant had packed up its superhero stuff and been transformed into a fairyland. Ropes of glossy ivy, white roses, and baby's breath crisscrossed overhead, creating a green canopy that contrasted with the rust-colored walls. More greenery curled around the edges of the bar, partially obscuring the brassy railing. White lights entwined with the ivy twinkled like small stars, while Chinese-style lanterns perched on every table, adding more illumination to the scene. Jazz music played in the background, softening the harsh buzz of conversations and the clink and rattle of dishes. Grace had really done a wonderful job on the decorations.

"Bella! Bella! Over here!"

Speaking of Grace Caleb, the old woman fluttered her hand, and I walked over to her table.

"Devlin, Grace. You're both looking wonderful tonight," I said.

Grace had dressed like a flapper from the Roaring Twenties. She wore a knee-length silver dress, ropes of fake pearls, and chunky heels. Her silver hair lay in waves against her head, held back with a pearl-studded headband, while a lacy white shawl covered her arms. Devlin was dressed in a gray jumpsuit with matching boots and gloves. I think he was supposed to be a race car driver. Either that or an astronaut, but I didn't want to be rude and ask.

"So do you, Bella," Grace replied. "Even if you're not wearing a proper costume."

There was no way I was dressing up in costume—especially one that involved spandex or leather. Instead, I'd opted for a long-sleeved, powder blue dress with a flowing skirt that reached to my ankles. The scooped-out neck showed off my angel charm and silver chain. My only concession to tonight's party theme had been the silver-tinsel halo I'd placed on top of my head. I'd gotten it out of the very first box of Christmas decorations I'd looked in out of the dozens that gathered dust in the attic.

"Bella is so lovely she doesn't need a costume, Grams," Devlin said, shooting me a shy smile.

"Why, thank you, Devlin. What a sweet thing to say."

I smiled back, and Devlin's cheeks exploded with color. He took a long swig of his champagne, but it must have gone down the wrong way, because he started coughing. Grace whacked him on the back a few times, and Devlin managed to catch his breath.

I couldn't help but compare his awkward behavior with Debonair's smooth surety. The thief wouldn't be flustered by giving or getting such a simple compliment. He'd probably start talking about all the *sweet things* we could do together. With handcuffs. More than once tonight, I'd scanned the crowd, wondering if the handsome thief was here—and whom he might be masquerading as.

Grace cleared her throat, and I realized she and Devlin were staring at me.

"I'm sorry, what did you say?"

Devlin looked at me. "I asked when you might want to have dinner. How about Monday?"

"Oh, just about any night is fine with me. Give me a call tomorrow, and we'll set it up." My social calendar wasn't exactly full these days. Unlike Debonair, who probably had a different woman penciled in every night of the week. Maybe two or three.

"Oh. Okay."

Through the crowd, I saw Joanne James crook her finger at me in a clear *come-here-right-now* gesture.

"Please excuse me."

I flashed Devlin and Grace another smile and headed for Joanne. Unlike me, she'd gone all out for the costume part of the evening. Joanne wore a bustier, miniskirt, and four-inch leather boots that reached up to her thighs. All of which were a bright lavender. The material was shiny, almost like vinyl, and clung to her body like wet cotton. Joanne was either going for Catwoman or a dominatrix. Maybe both. With a heavy S&M vibe thrown in for flavor. All she needed was a whip and some chains, and she'd be Debonair's dream woman.

"What's up?" I asked, trying to pretend I couldn't see Joanne's pale cleavage yet again. What was it with this woman flashing her chest at me?

Joanne jerked her head toward the stage. "I think we're going to have a problem. No one's bidding on Hannah, and she seems to be getting rather upset about it."

Hannah Harmon stood in the middle of the stage, her hands on her hips. She'd come dressed as a she-devil, with a long, flowing red cape and a headband topped with tiny horns.

"Do I hear one thousand dollars? One thousand? Anyone?" the auctioneer asked. "Anyone at all?"

Hannah glared at him, and he edged away from her.

"What's wrong?" I asked. "Hannah's attractive and rich. What's the problem?"

"Haven't you heard?" Joanne asked.

"Heard what?"

She shook her head, her black curls spilling over her bare shoulder. "Bella, sometimes, you're so sweet and naive you make my teeth hurt. Hannah made an offer on DCQ Enterprises yesterday. She went before the board and pretty much demanded they accept the bid, or she'd take over the company, split it up, and sell off the pieces just like she always does."

"DCQ? But that's—"

"Devlin Dash's company. Dash-Caleb-Quicke. Grace is on the board too, along with Kyle Quicke and Kelly Caleb. None of them were pleased with Hannah's tirade."

"Oh." I looked at her. "How do you know this?"

"Berkley's on the board, of course. And so am I."

"So Grace decided to have Hannah blackballed because of the takeover? She told people not to bid on Hannah tonight?"

That didn't seem like Grace. If anything, the society matron would kill you with kindness, no matter how rude you were to her.

Joanne laughed. "Of course not. Grace would never do anything like that. She's far too nice and generous." She smiled. "But I would."

"Why?"

Joanne looked toward the stage, where Hannah glared at the auctioneer. "Because Hannah Harmon is nothing but a bully in a short skirt and high heels. She thinks just because she has a little money she can do whatever she wants—and that everyone should love her."

I wanted to point out Joanne was wearing a shorter skirt and higher heels than Hannah. And that she had more money. And that she pretty much did whatever she wanted to, whenever she wanted to. But Joanne wasn't through with her rant.

"The woman's an egotistical ass. I know. I've been married to a few." Joanne turned her violet eyes to me. "Did you know she made a play for Berkley while we were engaged? She practically took off her clothes and danced around naked in front of him. She still hits on him every time she sees him, and she's always calling and asking for his advice on business deals or wanting to see his art collection. Like I don't know what *that* means."

Ah, now we'd gotten to the real reason Joanne had sabotaged Hannah—she'd tried to horn in on Joanne's man. Her prize possession, as it were, just like the Star Sapphire was Berkley's. I rubbed my temple and tried to talk some sense into Joanne.

"So, Hannah's not the nicest person around. So, she made a couple of passes at Berkley. That's not a crime. Besides, it's not like he reciprocated. Everyone knows he's crazy about you, Joanne. So, why did you have to do this tonight of all nights? You know how important the benefit is to the museum. Pissing off Hannah won't help our cause one bit."

"Don't worry. I'm going to write the museum a check that will cover whatever pitiful amount Hannah might have raised tonight."

I sighed. "Joanne—"

"Oh, there's Berkley. Gotta run, Bella. See you later."

I tried to grab Joanne's arm, to stop her and demand she find a way to fix this. But my power flared, and a waiter chose that exact moment to step between us. I just barely managed not to slam into him. Joanne darted through the swirling crowd.

". . . sold! To the gentlemen at the bar for one thousand dollars!"

The auctioneer brought down his gavel. Hannah clomped off the stage, grabbed a drink from the closest server, and downed it in one gulp. Her fingers tightened around the empty glass, and she looked like she wanted to throw it at somebody. Joanne was right. Hannah looked pissed. I'd never liked dealing with angry people, but I, being the diplomat, decided to go over and see if I could cheer her up.

"Hi, Hannah." I plastered a smile on face. "Are you having a good time? I love your costume."

Hannah looked down at me over the rim of her champagne flute. "A good time? Of course I'm having a good time, Bella. I was just humiliated in front of five hundred of Bigtime's wealthiest citizens. And now I have to go have dinner with Milton Moore for a measly thousand bucks."

"What's wrong with Milton?"

My eyes flicked to the man in question. Milton Moore sat at the bar, a nurse on either side of him. They were real-life nurses, dressed in flowered scrubs and sensible, thick-soled shoes. Milton never went anywhere without at least two of them by his side. It cut down on his trips to the emergency room. Sensing our stares, Milton took a hit off his oxygen tank and waved his aged hand in our direction. A glass of Scotch trembled in his fingers.

"The man's ninety-five years old, and he smells like mothballs," Hannah snapped. "That's what's wrong with him."

She grabbed another drink from a passing waiter and chugged it down too. "I'm so sick of the people in this town. They think they're so special just because they've had money for a couple of generations. They try to pretend like they never had to work. Or if they did, that everything was always by the

book and perfectly legal. They're nothing but a bunch of phonies. Fakes. Liars. They've all got skeletons and secrets in their
closets. They're no better than me. Not a single one of them.
One day, they'll realize it."

Hannah wasn't the easiest person to get along with, but I'd
never heard her talk this way before. Her voice was so harsh, so
angry, that I took a step back.

"It just takes time," I said. "They'll come around eventually.
I think most people—"

"Oh, I don't care what you think, Bulluci. You're just as bad
as the rest of them."

Hannah turned on her heel, leaving me to stare at her retreating back. The businesswoman stormed through the crowd, right
past Joanne.

Joanne watched her go, a smile playing across her lips. She
spied me staring at her and raised a glass, as though she'd just
won some great victory.

All I could do was sigh.

7

Thankfully, the rest of the bachelors and bachelorettes were auctioned off without incident. SNN news reporter Kelly Caleb, Grace's granddaughter, raised the most money, bringing in a bid of just over forty thousand dollars for a night of drinks, dinner, and dancing.

Once the crowd had exhausted the food and liquor at Quicke's, everyone made the trek to the museum a block away, hurrying up the wide, flat steps. Spotlights at the bottom of the stairs pointed upward and highlighted the *Whimsical Wonders* banner that stretched over the massive columns framing the entrance. More lights picked up the pink and blue and green flecks in the white marble, which shimmered in the dark night.

The crowd stampeded into the new wing. Several squeals of delight rippled through the room as people saw what everyone else had donated and where all the items had been positioned. Folks rushed from one side of the room to the other, trying to look at everything at once, and people clustered three-deep around the Star Sapphire, which looked even more dazzling tonight. I stood to one side of the wing, watching the scene unfold. Everyone seemed impressed by the exhibit, and Arthur Anders flashed me a discreet thumbs-up.

I hadn't thought it possible, given all the catastrophes of yesterday, but the exhibit looked marvelous. Round white globes hung from the high glass ceiling, while potted palms twined with lights perched in the corners. The soft light made the colors in the cars and dolls and crystal figurines that much more vibrant. Everything gleamed and glistened and glowed from the items on display to the sequin-covered costumes of the people surrounding them. Classical music trilled in the background, adding a finishing note to the festivities.

It was all very clean, very classy, very Bella Bulluci.

Everything was going so smoothly I decided to allow myself a treat, carbs and calories be damned. I flagged down a waiter and took a glass of champagne off his silver tray. But as soon as I grabbed the crystal flute, my power flared. My fingers twitched. My hair frizzed. And my body hummed with static energy.

I sighed. And things had been going so well. I hadn't exploded food or shattered diamonds or been almost brained by a falling anvil the entire day. I'd hoped to get through the rest of the evening without incident.

But my itchy fingers told me one thing—that I would spill the drink before the night was over. Probably in the loudest, most embarrassing, attention-getting way possible. My fingers tightened around the crystal flute, as if they could keep the golden liquid in my grasp and stave off my impending doom. But in the end, that small action wouldn't save me.

I was just jinxed, and I always would be.

"Why are you frowning, Bella?" a thick, familiar voice rumbled in my ear.

"I wasn't frowning, Grandfather."

Bobby waggled his white eyebrows. "My dear, I know a frown when I see one, especially on your beautiful face. Why are you unhappy? Tonight is your big night, and it's gone off wonderfully."

"So far," I muttered, clutching the glass to my chest.

"It's too bad Johnny couldn't be here," my grandfather said. "I'm sure he and Fiona would have been very proud of you."

"Actually, Johnny called to congratulate me this morning and tell me what a wonderful time they're having in Greece." I took a cautious sip of my champagne. Perhaps if I drank it quickly, it would be gone before I spilled it. Then, I'd only have the glass to worry about. Not that that would be much better. I could do things to glasses that would make Martha Stewart weep. "I'm actually glad Fiona isn't here."

"Why's that?"

"If she'd come tonight, I would have been forced to add another ten thousand dollars to the food budget just to keep her modestly fed. You know how she eats."

My grandfather threw back his head and laughed. "That she does, with gusto. It's one of the things I like about her."

Fiona did just about everything *with gusto*, from eating like she had four stomachs instead of just one to designing clothes to battling ubervillains. She could afford to. She had a useful power, one she could control, instead of it controlling her, like mine always did.

"You're frowning again," Bobby accused. "What's wrong?"

I plastered a smile on my face. "It's nothing, Grandfather. I just feel some bad luck coming on."

"Maybe you're wrong this time."

"I'm never wrong. Something bad will happen before the night is through. You'll see."

"Well, everyone is having a marvelous time, and the museum has received several large donations already, including one from this old man." Bobby winked. "What's a little bad luck compared to all that?"

I smiled, despite my sour mood. Grandfather was so cheerfully exasperating he always took my mind off my troubles.

"Come," Bobby said, offering his arm to me. "I want to take another look at Berkley's sapphire before he hides it back in his vault."

"Why? Are you thinking of stealing it?"

Bobby's green eyes were sly and bright. "Perhaps. If my Angel wings hadn't been clipped long ago."

My grandfather led me through the room, making sure to greet each and every woman we passed. He kissed hands and flirted and laughed, in keeping with his costume. Grandfather had chosen to come dressed as a pirate, a Johnny Depp for the senior set. He wore a white shirt with flowing cuffs, along with black boots and breeches. A red sash added a bit of color around his waist, while a black eye patch gave him a dashing, slightly dangerous air.

I kept a close eye on all the women he talked to, seeing if one had a certain reaction to my grandfather. A soft look on her face. A shy smile. A particular sparkle in her eyes. But I couldn't tell who Bobby's mysterious lady friend might be.

After a good twenty minutes of small talk, we reached the

center of the room, where the Star Sapphire rested on top of its white pedestal. It looked as dazzling as ever, throwing out endless rays of cool, blue light. The gem's deep, brilliant color reminded me of Debonair's eyes.

Grandfather wandered off to talk to some of his old cronies. I kept staring at the sapphire, mesmerized by the way each one of its thousands of facets caught and reflected the gleaming light. I bit my lip, wishing I'd brought along a sketch pad tonight so I could try to capture its beauty.

"It's fantastic, isn't it?" a voice murmured.

I started. I'd been so deep into my admiration of the gem I hadn't even heard Devlin Dash walk up beside me.

"It is impressive," I admitted.

"What do you like best about it?" Devlin asked.

I cocked my head to one side, studying the glistening jewel. "I love the way it catches the light and glows, as if it has an inner fire."

"Why, Bella, I didn't realize you were quite so passionate about the arts," Devlin said.

If I didn't know better, I would have thought he was teasing me. But I'd never known Devlin Dash to tell a joke. At least, not without stumbling over the punch line.

"The arts are one of my main delights in life," I said. "What about you, Mr. Dash? Are you passionate enough to give the museum another hefty contribution this year?"

Normally, I would never be this blunt and aggressive, but the museum deserved all the funds it could get. And it was my job as chairperson to make sure I squeezed every penny out of every person I could, even shy, awkward businessmen.

Devlin tugged at his tie. "Of course. I'll be more than happy to write you and the museum a check."

I smiled. "That would be wonderful. Anything you could do to support the museum would be most appreciated."

Devlin opened his mouth to respond, but Joanne James walked up to us, still wearing her outrageous lavender leather getup. Devlin's mouth fell open a little more. The businessman was right at six feet tall, giving him a perfect, bird's-eye view down Joanne's low-cut bustier. But to his credit, Devlin took a nervous swallow of his champagne and moved off to stare at some Fabergé miniatures instead of at Joanne.

"It really is something, isn't it?" Joanne said, referring to the sapphire and not her costume. I hoped. "It's just a shame it's too big to wear. And that Berkley won't have it cut just a little bit."

Her eyes dropped to the enormous diamond ring on her finger. It wasn't much smaller than the sapphire. I took another cautious sip of my champagne and shook my head. You could always count on Joanne to be openly avaricious.

"I rather like it the way it is," I said. "I don't think it would be nearly as beautiful cut up into rings."

"I agree," a cold feminine voice cut in. "Something that exquisite shouldn't be divided into shallow pieces. It should stay just the way it is."

Hannah Harmon joined us. She looked remarkably calm, given her rant against everyone in attendance less than an hour ago. She tipped her head to me, then turned and gave Joanne a look that would have caused a lesser woman to spontaneously combust. Evidently, Hannah had figured out exactly who'd sabotaged her at the auction.

"That's a rather ironic thing for *you* to say, Hannah, since you make your living selling off bits and pieces of other people's companies," Joanne replied.

Hannah gave Joanne a dismissive glance. "That's just business. This—this is art."

"Are you enjoying the benefit, Hannah?" I asked in a sympathetic tone.

Despite her earlier outburst, I felt rather sorry for Hannah and about what Joanne had done to ruin her evening. I'd never understood why people felt the need to be nasty to each other. Or call themselves weird names. Or dress up in spandex. Sometimes, I didn't understand very much at all about life in Bigtime.

"Of course, Bella," Hannah murmured, her eyes fixed on the sapphire. "I never stay down for long. No matter how much some people might wish otherwise."

Joanne snorted, but Hannah pretended not to notice.

"Well, I just want to tell you again how much I appreciate your hard work. The exhibit wouldn't be nearly the success it is without you," I said, trying to smooth things over.

Hannah didn't respond. Instead, she admired the sapphire another moment before drifting off into the crowd. She strolled over to a guy sitting in a wheelchair, leaned down, and started whispering in his ear. Nathan Nichols was his name, I believed. He did something for one of Hannah's many companies, although I couldn't recall exactly what at the moment.

"I can't stand that woman," Joanne declared, tossing her black hair over her thin shoulder. "She's such a fake. Everyone knows what a complete bitch she is, no matter how hard she tries to hide it."

I eyed Joanne, looking at her fortysomething face, which was curiously free of wrinkles, and her full chest that didn't quite seem to match her stick-thin body. But I didn't say anything. We'd already had enough catfights for one night. I was just glad the two of them weren't grappling on the floor, kicking and clawing and screaming.

Joanne and I started talking about other things, mainly when I was going to get started on the clothes I'd promised her. Eventually, she wandered off to see what Berkley was up to. I stayed in front of the sapphire, admiring its many depths and committing them to memory so I could draw the jewel later. It truly was stunning.

While I was not-so-discreetly gawking, Carmen Cole came up to me.

"Bella! It's so nice to see you," Carmen said. A soft Southern twang colored her voice.

I smiled at the taller woman, grateful to see that someone else had decided not to dress up. Carmen had forgone the costume theme in favor of a little black dress. Then again, your typical little black dress was Carmen's costume of choice for functions like these. Despite being married to billionaire Sam Sloane, Carmen still kept her day job as a society reporter for the *Exposé*. I also thought the simple black dresses were Carmen's way of compensating for her superhero suit. Her silver spandex Karma Girl costume had plenty of flash to it.

"Where's Sam?" I asked, scanning the crowd for the handsome billionaire.

"He couldn't make it, unfortunately. Since Johnny and Fiona are taking their vacation, he had to stay at the manor and be on call tonight. Work. You know how it is."

I grimaced. In other words, Sam was sitting in the secret underground library that functioned as the headquarters of the Fearless Five, listening to the police scanner, ready to go out and battle evil. I could have thought of a thousand ways I would rather have spent an evening, but that was superheroes for you. Putting their powers and responsibilities above everything else—their jobs, their lives, their families.

My father's face flashed before my eyes, and I felt the familiar pain of his loss. He should have been here tonight. Enjoying the exhibit. Laughing and talking and drinking with Berkley and his other friends. Encouraging me about my art. He should have been here.

He *would* have been here if he hadn't gone out as Johnny Angel. If he hadn't tried to take on Siren and Intelligal by himself. But no. He'd been hooked on the adrenaline high and spandex fumes, and he'd paid the ultimate price for it. A spurt of anger replaced my sadness. Sometimes, I was so mad at my father for getting himself killed I couldn't think straight.

Sensing my thoughts, Carmen placed a gentle hand on my arm, but I shook it off. I liked Carmen just fine, but I didn't want her superpowered sympathy. Not now.

"Can I get a few quotes from the woman of the hour?" Carmen asked in a kind voice, pulling a digital tape recorder out of her purse.

I let out a long breath and nodded. It wasn't Carmen's fault my father was dead. Besides, as chairperson of the benefit, I still had a job to do. Hopefully, Carmen's story would encourage people to come see the exhibit and donate even more money to the museum.

Once I gave Carmen all the inside scoop she wanted, I wandered through the museum, accepting everyone's praise and reminding them to open up their wallets, checkbooks, and trust funds. But I couldn't quite shake off my anger at my father or my melancholy at missing him.

Once I'd worked the room for the umpteenth time, I turned to take one more look at the sapphire, hoping the sight would cheer me up. The instant my foot pivoted, I knew I was in trouble. My hair went windblown wild. My fingers sparked. And I felt the static around me snap tight for an instant, like a rubber band stretched to its breaking point. I was about to have my bad luck. In spades.

SMACK!

I crashed into someone behind me. The champagne flew up out of my glass, splattering all over Devlin Dash. He took a step back at the jarring impact, his silver glasses teetering on the end of his nose. A golden drop of champagne rolled down one of the lenses and splashed onto my hand. That little plop of pressure was enough to send the glass sliding from my fingers. It hit the marble floor and splintered into at least a hundred pieces.

Every eye in the room turned to the two of us. All conversation stopped. Even the music quit playing.

For a long, horrified moment, I stared at Devlin. I'd just soaked one of the wealthiest men in Bigtime with champagne in front of five hundred people. At my own benefit. Before he could write me a check.

I truly was jinxed.

8

To my credit, I didn't sputter or stammer or spew out endless apologies. Didn't cry or scream or run away in horror. Didn't even blush. Well, not much. I'd long ago grown used to my jinx. Resigned myself to it, actually.

"Wait here," I told Devlin. "I'll get you some napkins. Try not to step in the glass."

I grabbed some white linen cloths from a passing waiter and handed them to Devlin, so he could wipe the alcohol off his smeared lenses. Everyone watched us a minute longer. When they realized Devlin wasn't going to blow up at me, they returned to their drinks and conversation.

"I really am sorry," I said. "I'm such a klutz sometimes. I hope this accident won't change your mind about donating to the museum."

Devlin pulled a wet sheet of paper out of the inside of his gray space suit costume. He didn't even have to say anything. I took the check from him, and the soggy mess fell apart in my hands.

Devlin went to the bathroom to wash the champagne off his face, while one of the waiters rushed forward to clean up the shattered glass.

The party wound down soon after that. Joanne was right. I really did know how to clear a room. Despite my earlier embarrassment, I stationed myself by the exit and thanked all the society patrons for their time and generous donations.

My grandfather was among the last to leave. "It was a wonderful evening, Bella. You should be proud of yourself."

I grimaced, thinking of Devlin Dash and his waterlogged check.

Bobby didn't notice my sour expression. "Do you want to ride home with me in the limo?"

"No, I'll catch a cab. I have to stay and take care of a few more things. I'll see you at home."

Bobby's eyes twinkled. "Maybe, maybe not. I have a date tonight."

"Now?" I checked my silver watch. It was after two in the morning. "With whom?"

"Why, my lady friend, of course."

"So, are you finally going to tell me who she is?" I asked, scanning the remaining stragglers for a likely suspect. "Or do I have to guess?"

"Now, you know a true gentleman never kisses and tells. She's a lovely lady and that's all you need to know. We'll have dinner one night this week, I promise. Don't wait up for me, Bella." Grandfather leaned over and kissed my cheek. "Go home and get some rest. You've earned it."

"Call me later!" I shouted to his retreating back.

Bobby waved his hand at me and walked outside. I sighed. He wouldn't call me, and I'd spend the rest of the night sitting up and waiting for him to get home. Sometimes, watching after my grandfather was worse than trying to deal with a hormonal teenager.

Even though I was bone-tired, I spent the next hour helping the other volunteers count donations and tally up contributions. In the end, it was worth it. The benefit had raised over five million dollars for the museum, more than enough to pay off the new wing and far beyond my cautious estimates. Grandfather was right. The benefit had been a smashing success, despite my bad-luck run-in with Devlin Dash.

"This is wonderful, Bella. Just wonderful." Arthur Anders beamed. "The benefit has exceeded all my expectations. We've gotten enough donations to keep the museum in tip-top shape for the next three years. I even think we'll be able to add some pieces I've had my eye on."

"I'm glad I could help," I said. "You know the museum has always been one of my favorite places—and favorite causes."

We were in Arthur's office, and he'd just put the last of the checks into his personal safe. Arthur spun the dial around on the metal door, locking it, and moved over to his executive-style chair. I sat across from him in a similar seat, sipping some bottled water. Hopefully, I could finish it without soaking the papers on Arthur's antique desk. I sat six feet away from them. Just in case.

"I know, and I appreciate it, now more than ever." Arthur leaned back in his chair and laced his fingers over his stomach. "So tell me, how is your own art going, Bella? Are you still sketching?"

Of all the things we could talk about, he had to bring up my art. I sank a little lower into my chair. Once, in college, I'd shown Arthur some portraits I'd drawn. Although they were well-done from a mechanics standpoint, he said they didn't have any real passion or life or enthusiasm in them. Arthur's comments had been thoughtful and constructive and helpful, but I'd still been devastated. Completely, utterly devastated. My mentor, the man I admired, the person whose opinion mattered the most, had told me my work was adequate. Merely adequate, not spectacular or noteworthy or amazing at all.

That was ego-crushing enough, but that hadn't been the worst part. I'd foolishly submitted the portraits for inclusion in the senior art show, which was run by Arthur's teaching assistant, an odious little toad named Terence Torres. I'd thought Terence might have a different opinion of my work, especially since I was sleeping with him at the time. But no. Terence had totally trashed every single piece I'd given him. He'd called my work amateurish and flat and boring and lacking any semblance of artistic merit. Then, he'd put my portraits in the senior show—as an example of what not to do. Terence might as well have just burned the pieces in front of me. Oh, and he dumped me too, claiming that our artistic visions were just too different. I didn't find out until later that he'd been cheating on me with another student, one with a more suitable vision—and a C cup.

Between Arthur and Terence, I'd never had the heart to show anything else I'd done to anyone outside my family, no matter how good I thought it was.

"Sometimes," I murmured, answering Arthur's question. "Not so much since my father died."

My father had been the one who'd encouraged me the most, the one who thought I had real talent. He was the one who kept telling me not to give up, to keep on drawing and painting and sketching, no matter what. He was also the one who'd threatened to run over Terence and Arthur with his motorcycle. It was one of the many things I missed about him.

Arthur nodded. "Well, I can understand that. But you should keep working. After all, a true artist never gives up, no matter how long it takes to find success."

What a sugar-coated platitude. I grimaced. "Of course not."

Arthur got to his feet. "I don't know about you, but I'm ready to lock up and call it a night."

"Just let me grab my purse and I'll be ready to go."

"I'll be waiting here to let you out."

I headed down the hall to the small office where I'd stashed my things this afternoon before the benefit. I put my purse strap across my chest and made sure my pepper spray lay in the top of the bag. Granny Cane might be a superhero, but even she couldn't stop all the muggers out there. It would be just my luck to run into the one guy she hadn't carted off to the police station tonight.

I flipped off the lights in the office and headed back to the new wing. I wanted to check on things one more time before I left.

I stopped in the archway and peered inside. The benefit had been over barely an hour, but all the glasses and food and trash had already been cleared away. Kyle Quicke and the rest of Quicke's staff, along with the museum's, were nothing if not efficient. All the items seemed to be in their proper places, with the Star Sapphire in the middle of the room, standing guard over everything.

I turned to go back to Arthur's office, when I felt my luck flare up. I froze.

What was I going to do now? Fall on the slick floor? Knock over one of the statues and shatter it? Get one of the paintings on the wall to burst into flames? But instead of pulling me down or sideways or causing the art to fly around, my power quieted, returning to its usual, steady hum.

I shook my head and took a step forward

POP!

Debonair puffed in front of me. I managed not to scream or fall or otherwise do something stupid. I'd sort of been expecting him to show up. Looking forward to it, actually. Which wasn't like me at all.

"What are you doing here?" I asked. "Come to steal something else?"

Debonair bowed his head. "Of course not. I came to congratulate you on your success. Your hard work really paid off. Everything went smoothly tonight."

I thought of Devlin Dash again and grimaced. "Not everything."

"I take it you're referring to the champagne you spilled on Mr. Dash? I wouldn't worry about that. Although, the man did look like a deer blinded by headlights. The whole scene was rather amusing." Debonair smirked.

"I like Devlin," I said, defending the awkward businessman. "He's a nice guy. Unlike you."

"Don't you know nice guys finish last?" Debonair flashed me a sexy smile. "And that women, real women, like bad boys better?"

"Bad boys?" I snorted. "Oh, give me a break. Women like to fantasize about bad boys, but no one in her right mind would actually want to have a *real* relationship with one."

Debonair looked amused. "Really? Why not?"

"One, they're probably going to cheat on you. Bad boys tend to think rather highly of themselves. Two, the surly attitude and skintight leather get really old after a while. Three, most of them don't know anything about art or poetry or music or books. All they want to talk about is their car or their motorcycle or their perfectly ripped abs." I ticked off the points on my fingers. "I want a nice guy. A nice, normal, stable guy who doesn't think he's God's gift to women and that it's his sworn duty to spread himself around to anyone who'll have him."

"You want a nice guy?" Debonair asked.

He stepped closer to me, and my senses kicked into overdrive. I could smell the sweet, musky scent that clung to his skin. See the silver and black rimming his blue eyes. Imagine his hot mouth pressed against mine. My pulse started to throb—along with other parts of my anatomy.

"Of course that's what I want," I snapped, pretending I wasn't the least bit attracted to the sexy thief. "That's what every woman really wants, deep down inside."

"And you think I'm a bad boy?"

I eyed his leather costume and perfect body. "In every sense of the word."

Debonair smiled. "Well, then, I guess I should play the part, shouldn't I?"

Before I could stop him, Debonair pulled me toward him and lowered his lips to mine.

He smelled sweet, like rose petals. The heady aroma seemed to permeate his skin, his lips, his tongue. I found myself lost in a sensual haze, swept away in a fog of sultry emotions.

And I did something I would never, ever do. At least not before the end of a first date that included dinner *and* a movie. I kissed him back. I wanted to taste him the way he was tasting me. Wanted to lose myself in this moment, this feeling, this bright flare of attraction.

Being on the short side, I had to stand on my tiptoes to weave my fingers through his thick hair. But I did that too, pulling him even closer. Electricity that had nothing to do with my luck rippled against my skin in a most pleasant way.

The kiss went on for quite a while. I enjoyed every second of it. Every playful nip. Every sure flick. Every thrust of our tongues against each other.

Debonair drew away and pressed a kiss to the inside of my shaking wrist. My pulse roared under his lips. He dropped my hand.

"See? I told you bad boys have more fun. But darling, delicious, delectable Bella, I'm afraid I must be on my way." His voice was as smooth and suave as ever, but his eyes were dim, as if he were troubled by our kiss.

Had I not measured up to his Slaves for Superhero Sex

standards? The thought disappointed me, even as I tried not to stagger around like a drunk. The man was intoxicating in every sense of the word, and he could kiss like nobody's business. No wonder women threw themselves at him.

"I've enjoyed our time together, and I bid you a very fond goodnight." Debonair tipped his head to me, turned toward the door, and walked away.

I admired the view for a moment. Then, my head cleared. He enjoyed our time together? What was I? A hooker he'd paid for an evening's amusing?

Like hell.

Debonair wasn't leaving that easily. He wasn't going to kiss me and walk away like I was another one of the countless women he'd loved and left without a backward glance.

My eyes narrowed, and I ran after him, focused on his retreating form. "Stop right there!"

For once, luck was on my side. Static pulsed around my body, and Debonair's boots slid out from under him, as if he'd stepped on a patch of ice. His arms flailed about. Then—

POP!

He disappeared. I sprinted forward to the spot where he'd been, right in front of the Star Sapphire. It reminded me of Debonair's eyes—only not quite as blue.

My power hummed around my body, almost in warning. I turned. Debonair stood behind me. I hadn't even heard him teleport back into the room.

He stared at the floor, then raised his gaze to me. His eyes were dark now, almost black. "Did you make me do that, Bella? Did you make me fall?"

"Of course not. How could I make you fall?"

We might have just shared a hair-raising kiss, but my power or lack thereof was none of his business.

"I'm not sure, but I find the possibility very interesting," Debonair said in a smooth voice, moving closer to me.

I backed up against the display case that housed the sapphire. My fingers itched. My hair frizzed. Static gathered around my body once more.

And then, the roof shattered.

9

For a moment, I thought my luck had gone completely haywire. That I'd somehow, some way shattered the glass roof hundreds of feet above our heads. That was quite an accomplishment, even for me. Then, luck or not, my sense of self-preservation kicked in. I screamed and dove out of the way of the falling shards, sliding across the smooth floor. My power kicked in of its own accord, as it so often did, and the static field propelled me farther than I could have ever gotten on my own.

Of course, I couldn't get clear of all of it. I was lucky, not indestructible. I threw my arms over my head, even as bits and pieces of glass sliced into my skin. My blood spattered scarlet against the white floor, reminding me of the red rose on Debonair's costume.

Thinking of Debonair, I didn't hear him *pop!* out of the way, but he must have, because the sweet smell of roses filled my nose, making my head swim. Well, that and the blood loss.

The tinkling rain of glass stopped, replaced by the museum's ringing alarms and a faint, *whooshing* sound, like I had water in my ears. I looked up. A shadow fell over the sapphire, and a muscular man in a gray spandex suit glided to a stop in the middle of the museum. He was enormous—seven feet tall and almost as wide with biceps bigger than my waist. A gray cowl covered his hair, while a black mask obscured his face. A variety of odd items, including what looked like grenades, hung off the silver utility belt around his waist. It too was big—larger and thicker than my arm.

This was how I got my first look at Hangman, one of Bigtime's preeminent ubervillains. Unlike the Fearless Five, Hangman didn't hang around with other ubervillains. He didn't have to. With his ability to fly, superstrength, and gadget-filled belt,

Hangman was an army all by himself. Which was why he hired himself out as a contract assassin, enforcer, and all-around bad guy. If you wanted someone dead, mangled, or beaten to a bloody pulp, especially someone with superpowers, Hangman was your guy.

So what was he doing at the museum? What was he after? There were all sorts of paintings and statues here that would tempt even the richest—

The ubervillain drew back his hand and drove his massive fist through the glass case housing the Star Sapphire. I should have guessed. I closed my eyes. Should have known. Hangman stealing Berkley's sapphire and who knew what else from the exhibit. Yep, my jinx was definitely working overtime. Although I supposed I should be grateful he'd at least waited until the opening was over.

Right now, though, I had more important things to worry about. Like getting out of the room alive. My father had died at the hands of an ubervillain. I had no desire to repeat his fate—especially not at the tender age of thirty. Grandfather had already outlived his only child. It would be a shame for him to outlive me too.

I rose to my knees, trying not to dig my hands into the supposedly shatterproof, bulletproof, ubervillainproof glass surrounding me like a glittering crystal carpet. Superhearing must have been another one of Hangman's powers because his head snapped in my direction.

"What the hell are you doing here?" he snarled, reaching for one of the strange-looking grenades on his belt.

I froze. Panic filled my body. If he threw that, there wouldn't be enough of me left to put into a spoon—just like my father. I was about to die exactly the way he had, despite all the precautions I'd taken to stay as far away from ubervillains as possible. The irony wasn't lost on me.

POP!

Debonair teleported in front of me and glanced over his shoulder. Once he saw I was more or less in one piece, he leaned against one of the Greek columns like he didn't have a care in the world.

"Hey, Hangman. How's it hanging?" Debonair's voice was low and smooth, but there was a hard, slightly mocking edge to it. "I haven't seen you flying around the city much these days. Still upset I clipped the wings off that missile launcher Violet Crush paid you to set up?"

"Not as upset as you're going to be when I get through with you, runt," Hangman snarled.

The ubervillain's hands hovered over his grenades like he was some gunslinger from the Old West. Debonair just smirked.

Every hero had his villain, and Hangman was Debonair's. They'd been battling each other for years. In fact, theirs was the preeminent duel in Bigtime, since the Fearless Five had taken out the Terrible Triad. About a month ago, Debonair and Hangman had made news after one of their battles spilled over into Paradise Park. Another ubervillain, Violet Crush, had hired Hangman to set off some sort of horrible device to blackmail the city into naming a street after her. Or some such nonsense. Debonair had intervened, and the usual round of fistfights, explosions, and daring escapes had ensued. I remembered because Grandfather had made me watch it on SNN with him.

Debonair relaxed even more, as though he couldn't care less that he was standing in an angry ubervillain's line of fire. "If you're going to do something, then do it. Because your conversation bores me."

Hangman's fingers fluttered over his grenades, ready to draw down on Debonair.

"Stop right now! Both of you!" another voice rang out.

Striker stormed into the room, followed by Karma Girl, Hermit, and Mr. Sage. Black, silver, more black, green. They formed a colorful line in their costumes, cutting off the front door. The Fearless Five—well, four of them—had finally arrived. For once, I was glad to see them.

Hangman cursed. His hand flew to his waist, and he hurled a grenade at the four superheroes, taking them by surprise.

My eyes widened. We were going to die. In about ten seconds. Not to mention all the priceless works of art around us. If that thing went off, the whole room would go up in flames. All the *Whimsical Wonders* would be reduced to smithereens. Not to mention the Monets, the Renoirs, and the Van Goghs in the upstairs galleries. They'd be destroyed too. I didn't know which was worse—us dying or the art being obliterated.

I shouldn't have worried, though. Mr. Sage used his telekinesis to stop the grenade in midair and launch it back at the ubervillain.

"No! Not at him!" I pointed up to the blasted-out ceiling. "Throw it up there! Now!"

I didn't know if Mr. Sage heard me or not, or if my luck finally decided to cooperate with my will, but the grenade veered upward, sailing toward the massive hole in the ceiling.

Just before the grenade cleared the roof, it exploded. Fire roared out from the small device, filling the room with thick, black smoke. The shock from the explosion tossed me back, thankfully away from most of the broken glass on the floor. I slammed into a life-size statue of Han Solo made out of toothpicks and bounced off. The statue swayed, but it didn't break. The Force really was with Han tonight.

Me too. Everything went dark for a second, before my vision snapped back into focus. I shook my head, trying to clear the fog from my mind. Somehow, I got to my feet and started forward. I couldn't see the door, though. I couldn't see much of anything except the smoke blanketing the room.

Something soft and gooey touched my arm. I screamed and jumped back before I realized it was snowing. Well, not exactly snowing, but white foam flew through the air like tiny flakes. The explosion must have set off the museum's fire alarm system. Although I couldn't see them, I knew sprinklers had popped out from their hiding places in the marble walls. That was where the foam was coming from. It was a special kind of fire-retardant chemical that could be wiped off paintings and other artwork without leaving any stains behind. Practically all the businesses in Bigtime featured some sort of similar system. Most of the homes too. They had to, if they wanted to survive any kind of superhero-ubervillain battle.

The white foam also had the effect of dissipating the smoke. I waved my hand in front of my face, helping it along. After about ten seconds, my eyes adjusted to the dim light, and I spotted the others. Debonair and Hangman stood next to the sapphire, grappling with each other, while Striker, Mr. Sage, and Hermit hovered around them.

A shrill, creaking sound caught my ear, and I looked up.

A chunk of debris broke loose from the ceiling and headed for the pedestal holding the Star Sapphire. My eyes widened, and I felt my power discharge. A second before the debris made impact, the pedestal tipped over, and the gem slid across the floor, landing at the feet of a mermaid statue. Hangman cursed and scrambled toward it.

POP!

Debonair beat him to it. The thief reached for the stone, but Hangman crashed into him just before he picked it up. The two of them rolled around on the floor, bouncing off statues, walls, and anything else in their way.

A hand grabbed my arm. I turned and screamed, right into Karma Girl's face.

"Are you all right, Bella?" Karma Girl asked, her eyes glowing neon blue.

I nodded. "I'm fine. Just a few cuts and bruises. But you guys have to take out Hangman before he gets the gem—and destroys any more of the museum."

"We'll handle it. You need to get out of here." She pointed me toward the door.

I nodded and staggered toward the archway, happy to comply. Unlike my grandfather and brother, I had no desire to trade punches with evildoers. At that moment, all I wanted to do was pretend like tonight had never happened.

Except for my kiss with Debonair. That was definitely worth remembering, even if the man was a thief and a blatant lothario. Who knew? Maybe I'd splurge and buy his video game.

I shook my head and made a mental note to stop at the emergency room on the way home. Because I definitely had to have a concussion to be thinking about how sexy Debonair was at a time like this.

Another explosion ripped through the room, sending rubble and glass everywhere. My power flared, but it didn't throw me forward or backward or sideways. Instead, for some reason, my foot lurched forward.

A moment later, the Star Sapphire skidded across the floor and stopped at my shoe. The shimmering blue facets caught what little light there was, reflecting it into my face. Mesmerized, I picked up the heavy gem.

My power pulsed again, and I ducked. Striker flew past me, slamming into the wall. His head snapped against the hard marble, and he slumped to the ground and didn't get up. I ran over to him and put my finger against his throat. His pulse thumped steady and strong. As I looked at the superhero, a nasty cut over his right eye sewed itself shut. An instant later, you couldn't tell he'd been injured at all. It was a good thing Striker regenerated. He'd be all right in a minute or so.

I squinted, but I couldn't see the other members of the Fearless Five through the blizzard of foam. What I did see was a very tall, very menacing figure. Hangman. Coming right at me. I barely had time to scramble to my feet before he was there.

"Give me that. Now," Hangman snarled, drawing back his fist to punch me.

A blow from him would break my neck like a piñata. Even as I took a step back, I knew I couldn't get out of the way in time. He was going to knock me into next week. Next month. Next year. This was going to hurt. A lot.

I was vaguely aware of Striker, or maybe it was Karma Girl, shouting something to me, but I was more concerned with the fist coming at my face to pay any attention.

Then, an arm wrapped around my waist, and the world disappeared.

10

Well, the world didn't exactly disappear. It just sped by in a jumbled, mishmash of color and light and sound. It was like being in the world's biggest kaleidoscope and roller coaster at the same time. I felt like my body was being pulled apart, even as the sights and sounds of Bigtime flashed before my eyes. The museum steps. Paradise Park. The marina.

Finally, things stayed still for longer than half a second. A cold, fall wind whipped around me, tossing my caramel-colored hair in my face. I clawed the frizzy mess out of my eyes so I could see, and my mouth dropped open. I teetered on a small metal platform. Empty space surrounded me, while cars crawled along a thousand feet beneath my trembling high heels.

The Skyline Bridge. We stood on top of the Skyline Bridge that spanned Bigtime Bay. No matter how unlucky and jinxed and jaded I was, this was not what I'd expected when I'd agreed to chair the museum benefit. So, I did what any sane woman would do under these circumstances.

I screamed.

"Quit struggling and be quiet. I'm teleporting us out of danger," Debonair snapped in my ear. He wrapped his arm around my waist again before I could stop him. "We'll be there in a minute."

That *minute* involved trips to the top of the skyscraper that housed the *Exposé*, the women's wear floor of Oodles o' Stuff, and half a dozen other places. Debonair snapped his fingers, popping certain items off to wherever, before grabbing me and teleporting us on to our next destination. Debonair even poofed into Quicke's long enough to get takeout. Takeout!

I screamed through most of it. I just couldn't help myself. My power kept snapping and pulsing and crackling around my body, as thrown off by all this teleporting as I was. I couldn't even see half the time, we moved so fast. Swifte had nothing on Debonair.

Finally, though, the world slowed into focus.

"Here we are. You're safe now, Bella." Debonair's voice was gentler than it had been before.

"No more teleporting around the city?" I asked, my legs wobbling.

I tried to focus on Debonair's face, but the room wouldn't stop spinning. I felt like I was trapped in a giant hamster wheel. Going round and round with no end in sight.

"No more teleporting. At least not until I decide what to do with you—and the gem."

I looked down. Even though I couldn't see it all that well, I still clutched the Star Sapphire in my fist. I was surprised I'd managed to hold on to it this long. Debonair's gloved hand closed around my wrist. My fingers tightened around the sapphire. I wasn't losing it. Not now. Not after all of this.

Debonair sighed. "What am I going to do with you, Bella Bulluci? You haven't left me with many choices."

That sounded fairly ominous, even for the daughter of a sometime superhero. So, I did what any good damsel in distress would when faced with a strange man who'd just kidnapped her.

I fainted.

Sometime later, I woke. I snuggled my cheek deeper into the pillow under my head. It was large and fluffy and plump, just the way I liked. And the sheets were cool and slick against my skin—

Hold on. My eyes snapped open. I liked cotton sheets. Plain, sensible, sturdy cotton. Flannel in the wintertime. But sheets made of the finest, softest silk imaginable encased my body. I sat up, panicked.

And promptly sank down and rose back up like I was in a boat. I was lying in the middle of the biggest water bed I'd ever seen. One with black-and-scarlet-striped sheets.

I waited for the wave to subside and scooted over to the edge of the bed, determined to get out of the locomotion love nest. Something filmy brushed against my leg. I peeked under the covers and realized I was wearing a lacy scarlet teddy that just barely covered anything at all. Where was I? And why was I wearing something so trashy?

After a few seconds, it all came back to me.

Benefit. Museum. Debonair. Kiss. Hangman. Explosions. Teleporting.

Debonair.

I clutched the sheets up to my chest. My eyes darted around the room. Empty. He wasn't here. Debonair wasn't in here.

I took a deep breath, fought back my panic, and thought about things. Debonair hadn't hurt me. He'd saved me from having my face smashed in by Hangman. Besides, Debonair was more of a lover than a fighter anyway. He probably wouldn't kill me. More than likely, he'd try to seduce me. The teddy and water bed were proof enough of that.

After a few more breaths, I came the rest of the way back to my senses and scanned the area. It was large, sort of like a swanky loft. The bed, where I was, took up a good part of the left side of the room, while a black-and-white-plaid sofa flanked the opposite wall, along with four chairs and a love seat. A large ebony cabinet sitting against another wall looked like it held a television and other entertainment devices. A small, glass-topped table was tucked away in one corner, while watercolors of men and women in the throes of passion adorned the walls. Crimson roses clustered in crystal vases throughout the room, making it smell sweet and inviting. An open door on one side led to a bathroom. Through a glittering, beaded red curtain, I spotted what looked like a black granite tub sunk into the floor. Another door, closed, presumably led out to the real world.

I'd heard about this place. The Lair of Seduction. It had been profiled in countless men's magazines. In addition to being a thief, Debonair also dispensed romance tips to lonely men and women in a variety of Bigtime publications. He was always particularly prominent around Valentine's Day. I thought even SNN had given him his own half-hour show on V-Day this year, but I wasn't sure. I tried to ignore superheroes and ubervillains whenever possible, as if by not thinking about them, they would go away. Now *that* would have been a useful superpower.

I was in Debonair's Lair of Seduction wearing a silk teddy and a grimace. This was not how I wanted to start my day. If it was even day yet. Or still day.

There were no windows or clocks in the room, so I had no sense of time. Or where I could possibly be. In the city, in the country, on another planet. I could have been anywhere.

Another flash of scarlet caught my eye, and I spotted a robe that matched the teddy on one of the chairs near the bed. He'd left me a robe. Thank heavens. I might work out every day, but I definitely didn't have a superhero's hard body. Or even one that could pull off wearing a barely there teddy. I was too curvy in all the wrong places.

I surfed off the water bed, snatched up the robe, and wrapped it around my body. It didn't cover up much more than the teddy did, but at least there wasn't a draft *everywhere* anymore. My eyes fell to the floor, and I spotted a pair of kitten heels that matched the rest of my outrageous ensemble. Naturally.

Oh my. Debonair was certainly serious about keeping up his image. A teddy, a robe, and heels with feathers attached to them. I felt like I was in some cheesy porn movie. The fashion designer and wannabe artist in me shuddered, but I put on the shoes anyway. Debonair had style, all right; too bad it just wasn't current. Or classy. Fiona, no doubt, would have loved this place.

Static surged around me. I stopped, not wanting to fall in the shoes.

POP!

Debonair teleported into the room and settled on the long sofa. Blue-black leather suit. Dark hair. Blue eyes. And a body that was too good to be true. I couldn't take my eyes off him. He really was handsome. Too handsome for his own good. For my own good. Because all I wanted to do at the moment was put my hand on his chest, right over the scarlet rose, and draw his lips down to mine.

Concussed. I was definitely concussed. Or perhaps I'd lost more blood than I'd thought—

"Did you sleep well?" Debonair asked, his voice as husky and sexy as ever.

"I wouldn't call it sleeping. But yes, I feel a little better." Except for this insane attraction that kept sweeping over me.

"Good."

His eyes drifted over my body, taking in the flimsy robe and ridiculous shoes. Realizing how precariously close to naked I was, I clutched the robe tighter around my body. Debonair's eyes flared, and the smell of roses intensified. I felt like a kitten caught high in a tree. One false move, and I'd plummet to my death. Or in this case, be ravished by a notorious rogue. And probably enjoy it a little too much.

He kept staring at me, evidently content to do that and nothing else. I tried not to teeter in the heels.

"Where's the sapphire?" I asked, desperate to focus on something other than the fact that he kept looking at me like he was enjoying the sight very, very much.

Debonair jerked his head, and I spotted the sapphire sitting on the carpet near his feet.

"Why did you just leave it there?"

"For one, I had a hell of a time prying it out of your fingers. Then, when I did that, it kept slipping out of my grasp. That was as far as I got with it before I realized it didn't want to leave your side. Or that you weren't letting it out of your sight." Debonair's eyes held mine. "You'll have to tell me how you do that, especially since you were unconscious at the time. I'm most curious."

"I didn't do anything. Maybe you were just being clumsy."

"Darling Bella, I'm never, ever clumsy. No matter what I do. Or who I do it with."

My breath caught in my throat. Kisses. Caresses. Long, slow strokes. All sorts of sensual things flashed through my head, and I stared at the floor to keep my eyes off the suggestive paintings on the walls.

I bit my lip to bring myself back to my senses. Debonair might dazzle the other women he brought here, but not me. I wasn't going to succumb to his charm. And I sure as hell wasn't going to sleep with him—or any other superhero. There was too much heartache, too much worrying involved in superheroes. Even pseudo-superheroes like Debonair. And my father.

All I wanted to do was go home. Back to the Bulluci mansion, back to Grandfather, and back to my safe, calm, mostly superhero-free life.

"Can I go home now? Please?"

Debonair shook his head. "I'm afraid that's out of the question, Bella. Not until I figure out a few things."

"Like what?"

Debonair gestured at the jewel on the floor. "Like what Hangman wanted with that. He seemed most anxious to get it, taking on me and the Fearless Five at the same time. Usually, he's smarter than that, loath as I am to admit it."

He reached down. My power flared up, and the static arced out, not wanting the handsome thief to pick up the gem. Somehow, I managed to squash it. Debonair didn't need to know about my power—or lack thereof. He might try to make me use it for his benefit. He wasn't taking advantage of me any more than he already had.

Debonair's hand closed around the sapphire, and he straightened. "It really is a beautiful thing, isn't it?"

"You have to give it back to the museum," I protested. "It's not yours. Neither is that painting you stole from Berkley."

"Why should I give back the sapphire? Finders keepers, and all that."

"Because the gem belongs to Berkley, and he loaned it to the museum so everyone could have a chance to enjoy it. Not just you."

Debonair cocked his head to one side, staring at me as though he was seeing me for the very first time. "That's an interesting theory, Bella."

"It's not a theory. It's the truth. By hoarding the art you steal or whatever you do with it, you're denying others the chance to enjoy its beauty. It's criminal. It's worse than whatever Hangman wanted to do with the sapphire."

"Oh, I doubt that. Hangman is much fonder of killing people than I am."

I gulped. That was true too.

Debonair tossed the sapphire in the air and caught it. Then, he turned to me. "So, what do you want, Bella?"

"What do you mean?"

He sauntered toward me. I tried not to notice how his muscles coiled and rippled with every step.

"Well, I like my guests, particularly my female guests, to feel at home. And you're going to be here for a while, Bella. So, tell me, what is it you want right now?"

I want you to kiss me again. Kiss me like I'm the only woman in the world. I must have really, *really* hit my head hard at the museum because, strangely enough, that was the first thing I thought of. But I pushed that silly fancy aside and moved on to more sensible matters. I wasn't going to pass up this opportunity.

"I want some food and water, of course. I'm not picky. I want my dress and purse back. And I want to call my grandfather and tell him that I'm all right."

"I think I can do a little better than just bread and water. But your dress was ruined beyond all repair, which is why you're wearing that robe."

I stared at the scarlet fabric. "You undressed me?" I cringed, thinking of love handles and stretch marks and cellulite, all of which I had in abundance.

"Don't worry. I didn't look." Debonair winked. "Too much."

Which meant he had seen my thunder thighs in all their huge glory. Wonderful.

He ticked off answers to the rest of my demands. "I'll give you back the purse, but calling your grandfather is out of the question. There aren't any phones in this room."

I threw up my hands. "Well, can't you just *pop!* one in like you do everything else?"

"I'm afraid not. Besides, I don't even think they'll work down here."

Down here. That meant I was probably underground or that the walls were excessively thick. It didn't inspire me with a lot of confidence about my chances of escaping.

"You have to let me call him." My panic bubbled back to the surface. "You have to."

"No, I don't."

I shook my head. "You don't understand. My father was . . . he . . . he was killed earlier this year. He didn't come home on time, but I . . . just thought he was wrapped up in a business deal or something. And then, we, um, got the news his body had been found. Or what was left of it. Ever since then, I've made it a point to check in with my grandfather every few hours. He'll be worried sick, especially when he hears about what happened at the museum."

Debonair studied me, his eyes tracing over my face. I didn't want to beg, but I didn't want Grandfather to worry. I didn't want him to experience the same fear I'd had every night for so long.

"Please, please let me call him. I'll do anything you want, and I won't say anything about where I am. I can't anyway because I don't even know where I am. I don't have a clue."

"I'll think about it," Debonair said.

I bit my lip to keep from pleading with him some more.

"Is there anything else you need or require?" he asked in a soft voice.

"Can you find me some other clothes?"

"Why? Aren't you comfortable?"

"You're kidding, right?" I threw my arms out wide. "Look at me. I look ridiculous in this getup. Not to mention it's rather cold in here."

Debonair's eyes dropped to my nipples, which were clearly visible through the thin silk. "Yes, I suppose it is."

Embarrassed beyond belief, I crossed my arms over my chest. Debonair walked closer to me. He stretched out a hand.

For a moment, I thought he was going to pull me to him. My breath caught in my throat in fear and more than a little anticipation. I didn't know what I would do if he kissed me again. Melt in his arms, most likely. What was it about him that had me so worked up?

Instead, he fingered the sleeve of my silk robe. "I think you look quite fetching, Bella. You really should wear red more often. It suits you." Debonair dropped his hand. "But I'll see what I can do about getting you some other clothes."

All I could do was just look at him.

Then—

POP!

Debonair vanished, taking the sapphire with him, and leaving me alone.

And strangely wishing he'd come back.

11

I hadn't taken half a step toward the closed door when things started *popping!* into the room.

First, food appeared on the glass table in the corner. Debonair wasn't boasting. He could do a whole lot better than just bread and water. A veritable feast poofed into being right before my eyes. Cheeses and breads and fresh fruits and chocolates galore, along with a bottle of fine champagne. The spread was even more impressive than what Quicke's had served at the benefit. The sight made my stomach roar, and my mouth water.

Second, my purse teleported in, along with my dress. Both landed at the foot of the enormous water bed. Debonair was right. The dress was beyond saving. Soot and ash and blood dirtied the satin fabric, along with more rips and tears than I could ever hope to sew shut again. Stains also covered the matching purse, but it, at least, was in one piece.

Third, a set of clothes materialized. A pair of hip-hugging, tight-fitting khakis teleported into the room, along with a sleeveless paisley shirt so low cut it wasn't much better than the teddy. A moment later, a matching green leather jacket appeared, along with a pair of low slingback heels. Everything had sequins on it, from the multicolored flowers on the pockets of the khakis to the flashing rhinestones that dotted the shirt to the tiny pearls stitched across the tops of the shoes. Sequins *and* rhinestones *and* pearls. The outfit looked like something Fiona would wear, only more flamboyant. Not my usual style, but I was just going to have to make do. Or keep wearing the silk teddy, which wasn't an option.

Fourth—

There was no fourth.

No phone materialized in the room as I'd requested. So, I dug through my purse until I found my own cell phone. I snapped it open, but a message on the screen told me there was no signal and to seek higher ground or my nearest cell tower.

Disappointed, I shut the phone. Debonair hadn't been lying when he said one wouldn't work down here. I supposed I should be grateful to my captor for what he'd given me. I doubted Hangman would have been so generous. But I found myself listening, waiting for one more *pop!* that would tell me Debonair had returned.

He didn't appear either. I wasn't sure why I was so disappointed.

But I was.

Still, I was too sensible to mope for long. Not if I had any hope of getting out of my orgy-painting-lined prison. Debonair hadn't said anything about letting me go, and I had no reason to think he wouldn't. But I wasn't about to take any chances. Not with the sexy thief. I didn't trust him. Or maybe I didn't trust myself around him.

Either way, I got busy.

I pushed through the beaded curtain, went into the bathroom, and locked the door behind me. Not that a locked door would keep him out, of course. Debonair could probably teleport into any place he wanted. But it made me feel a little bit better.

The first thing I did was examine my various wounds. There were lots of them, especially on my arms and hands and knees. But none was so deep it'd need stitches. In fact, most weren't much more than paper cuts. Any other person would have probably been sliced to ribbons by the shattered glass from the museum roof. I knew it was because of my luck. For every bad thing that happened, something good did too. So, while I'd been in the middle of a superhero-ubervillain battle, I'd escaped it with just a few minor injuries. Not a bad trade-off.

So, I moved on. I had lots of bruises and would be extremely sore in a few hours, but nothing seemed to be sprained or twisted or broken. I also didn't feel any telltale lumps or bumps on my head, and my vision was fine. Which meant I probably didn't have a concussion. I wasn't so sure I was happy about that. Otherwise, how could I explain this intense attraction I felt for someone as inappropriate as Debonair?

I took a quick dip in the oversized bathtub, scrubbing every-thing several times, including my thick hair. Then, I stuffed myself into the clothes, albeit sans underwear. The bra and panties I'd been wearing under my dress were as ruined as it was, and I just couldn't bear to put the bloodstained fabric back against my clean skin. So I went without, even though I didn't particularly like going commando.

The clothes fit, but just barely. And the shirt was practically indecent without the jacket to cover it. Debonair had quite the eye when it came to guessing a woman's size.

I wiped the steam off the mirror over the sink in the bath-room and stared at my reflection. Tawny, curly hair. Hazel eyes. And an outfit so garish it was almost pretty. I looked like me, but different. It wasn't the clothes so much as it was something else. Something I couldn't quite put my finger on. There was a flush in my cheeks and a glint in my eyes that hadn't been there before. Who knew? Maybe being in mortal danger and kidnapped by a handsome uberthief agreed with me. Or was at least good for my skin. Or maybe I really was concussed and just didn't know it.

Once I was more or less properly clothed, I sat down at the table and devoured the food, not even caring about calories and carbs. Fiona would have been proud of me. I ate all the cheese. All the chocolates. All the fruit. And all the bread, except for the crusts. I'd never liked crusts.

I didn't drink the champagne, though, instead getting some water from the bathroom. I wanted a clear head. I would need one, if I had any chance of escaping.

Once I was through with my meal, I tried the door. Locked. So, I ransacked the room, opening the drawers and cabinets, peering under the furniture, checking around the edges of the massive water bed.

Nothing. There was nothing that would help me escape. Not even so much as a rusty nail I could pry out of the wall and stab Debonair with. If I could muster up the courage to do that and not just stare dreamily into his eyes. The man was gorgeous, but why was I acting this way? You'd think I'd never seen a hot superhero or ubervillain before. That I'd never even had sex before. Of course, it had been a while, but that was no excuse. Debonair had kidnapped me and told me in no uncertain terms I was his prisoner. I should hate him.

But for some reason, I didn't.

And he wasn't all bad. He'd saved me from Hangman. He'd given me everything I'd asked for, except a phone. Still, thinking about him didn't help me out of my present situation.

So I got up off the bed and went through the room again, slower and more carefully. Opened all the drawers. Peered under the furniture. Checked around the edges of the water bed.

And I realized that things seemed a little . . . off.

Oh, lots of sexy, slightly pornographic DVDs lay next to the TV inside the entertainment center. But the covers were all slick and shiny, as though they'd never even been opened.

Oh, lots of exotic bath oils and warming lotions and soothing creams lined a shelf in the bathroom. But the lids were screwed on, and the bottles were all full, as though they'd never been used.

Oh, lots of faux sex toys, like fake, fur-lined handcuffs and edible underwear populated the dresser next to the bed. But they looked brand-new, and none of the underwear seemed to be missing from its foil package.

And I didn't find any condoms.

Not a single one.

You'd think a Romeo like Debonair would have had an industrial pack stashed away somewhere in his Lair of Seduction. Maybe even two or three, if he was really the stud he was rumored to be. But I didn't find any.

And I started to wonder—was the whole Lair of Seduction thing even real?

Or was it all for show?

And if so, why?

I wasn't sure I really wanted to know. The whole place gave me a weird vibe. So, I grabbed a pad and pencil I'd found stuffed in one of the drawers in the entertainment center and plopped down on the water bed.

It didn't matter what Debonair did in here or with whom. There was one thing that was real—I wasn't getting out of here by myself. I'd just have to wait for the Fearless Five to come rescue me. Surely, they were on their way by now. Sam and Carmen probably had Henry Harris and Lulu Lo working overtime on their computers trying to find me. If anyone could, it would be the two computer gurus. After all, Lulu had managed to find Johnny earlier this year, when he'd been hypnotized and kidnapped by Siren and Intelligal.

My eyes scanned the room for about the tenth time, and an idea hit me. I started sketching the layout of the Lair of Seduction and made note of all the items inside. Doing this same thing had helped Carmen Cole uncover the real identities of the Terrible Triad last year. Instead of being a superhero, the newspaper reporter had once exposed heroes' and villains' secret identities. Maybe my list would help her puzzle out Debonair's alter ego when they rescued me.

I did a couple of quick drawings of the room and bathroom. Then, I moved on to Debonair. To my surprise, he was easy to draw. Or maybe I was just obsessed. I filled page after page with images of the handsome thief. Him standing in the museum. Him holding the sapphire in his hand. Him staring at me.

But the sketch I was proudest of was a close-up portrait I did of Debonair's face. I drew him in profile, half turned toward me, half hidden by shadows that spilled over the page. A half smile pulled his lips upward, hinting at his roguish, rakish nature, and he peeked at you out of the corner of his eye.

I added a bit more shading to his hair and looked at my drawing, pleased by my effort. I'd majored in art in college and had taken a few classes on my own since then, so I knew good work when I saw it—even if it was my own. I doubted Arthur Anders would have been able to find fault with my sketch. Not that he was ever going to see it.

My art was my private, personal escape—one I didn't share with anyone else, except Johnny and Grandfather. They encouraged me, but I don't think they knew how important my art was to me—and how passionate I was about it. No one had really known, except for my father, and he was gone now.

Tired and spent, I yawned. The fight at the museum had taken a lot out of me, as had the wild teleportation around the city, and waking up to find myself wearing nothing but a silk teddy. But my ordeal was almost over. The Fearless Five would find me soon, and I could go home, where I belonged.

Since there was nothing I could do to escape, I curled up on the water bed, pad beside me, and went to sleep.

★ 12 ★

I knew he was in the room the second I woke up. The smell of roses permeated the air, and there was a stillness I was coming to recognize as the calm after the storm. Or more like the quiet after the *pop!*

I sat up to find him lounging on the sofa, staring at me. His eyes were dark and thoughtful. I wondered how long he'd been sitting there. Watching me. And what he'd thought about while he did it.

"What time is it?" I asked, my voice thick with sleep.

"A little before midnight. You've been asleep all afternoon."

I rubbed my eyes and cleared the rest of the cobwebs from my mind. I'd been gone almost a whole day. Grandfather would be frantic by now. I would have been, in his shoes. I hoped the stress wouldn't be too much for him. And that he wasn't using this as an excuse to eat and smoke and drink whatever he wanted. Just because I'd been in mortal danger was no reason for him to turn to chocolate cannolis for comfort.

A faint rustle broke through my worry. I looked up. Debonair held the pad filled with my drawings in his gloved hands. Horror, pure horror, filled me. I never, *ever* showed my work to anyone but Grandfather and Johnny. I was too afraid of what they'd say. That they'd laugh or scoff or make fun of it like Terence had. That they'd confirm my suspicion I was just wasting my time on a dream that would never come true. It was one thing to think that myself. It was a bit more soul-crushing to have it confirmed by a third party.

Debonair saw me looking at the pages. "The pad was lodged under your arm. It looked like it was making you uncomfortable, so I took the liberty of removing it."

"Give it back." My fingers dug into the silk sheets, twisting them. "Please."

Debonair crossed one leg over the other and flipped through the drawings, studying each one.

"I was just doodling." Panic colored my voice, even though I was trying to be as nonchalant as possible. "It's something I do when I'm bored."

"Well, you can *doodle* quite nicely. I particularly like this one." He pointed to the portrait of his face. "You have some real talent, Bella. Do you draw all the time?"

"I dabble a bit, that's all."

"Well, you should do it more. And you should let people see your work. It's quite good. Your strokes are sure and firm, the proportions are spot-on, and your shading is exquisite."

His praise pleased me. More than I would have thought possible. Johnny and Grandfather both told me repeatedly that I had talent, that I should show my work to others. So had my father, James, when he'd been alive. But it was quite another thing to hear it coming from a complete stranger—well, almost a complete stranger. And one who stole fine art. Maybe my dream of being an artist wasn't so far-fetched—if I could muster up the courage to pursue it.

"Do you really like it? Or are you just being nice?"

Debonair smiled. "I really like it, Bella. Truly, I do."

My heart fluttered, and I didn't know if it was because of his kind words or incredible smile.

"In fact, I like it so much I'm going to give it the official Debonair seal of approval." He snapped his fingers, and a pencil appeared in them. "Do you mind?"

"No. Please. Go ahead."

Debonair scrawled his name across the bottom of the drawing and held it out to me. I scooted off the water bed, took the paper, and squinted.

"You call that a signature? It looks like a big D with some squiggles after it."

Debonair shrugged. "Unfortunately, penmanship is not one of my superpowers. We all have our weaknesses."

He held out his hand. "Come. It's time for dinner. I've brought you something a little more substantial than bread and cheese this time."

I hesitated, then slipped my hand in his gloved one. It felt better than I thought it would. Almost natural.

Debonair led me over to the table in the corner of the room. He'd been busy while I'd been asleep. Covered platters sat on the smooth surface, along with several lit candles and a fresh bouquet of roses. A bucket of white wine chilled next to the table, which had been set with fine china and crystal. A perfect romantic scene, like something out of a book or movie. The sight made me uncomfortable.

Debonair held out a chair. I slid into the seat, while he dropped into the opposite one. The thief took a folded white napkin, whipped it open, and settled it in his lap with an innate grace I envied. If I tried to do that, I'd probably give myself a black eye.

Then, Debonair took off his leather gloves and laid them aside. I stared at his hands. Maybe it was the artist in me, but I'd always had a thing for hands. His were very nice. Strong and capable-looking, with short, neat nails and just a sprinkling of dark hair across the knuckles.

"How about some wine?" he asked, holding up the bottle. "Or would you prefer something stronger?"

I loved wine, but I didn't drink it that often. Or rather, I couldn't. Whenever I tried, my luck usually went helter-skelter, and I ended up wearing more of the liquid than I actually drank. I think it was because of my underlying guilt about all the calories. As a result, I usually stuck to low-calorie, vitamin-enhanced water. It didn't leave as many stains behind on the floor or table or my clothes.

But I couldn't be too picky tonight. Debonair had given me so much already. I hated to ask for more, even if I was here against my will. I'd just have to hope my luck wouldn't decide to make me do something particularly chaotic.

"White wine is fine."

He poured us both some, then snapped his fingers. The covers on the platters disappeared, revealing orange-glazed chicken next to a medley of mixed vegetables, toasted baguettes, and mounds of mashed potatoes covered with butter, sour cream, bacon bits, and cheddar cheese.

Steam rose up from the chicken and vegetables, overpowering the rosy scent in the room. My stomach rumbled, even though I'd eaten a few hours ago. Or had it been longer? I couldn't tell.

"Please. Help yourself. I know you must be hungry after everything you've been through," Debonair said.

I eyed the food like Fiona would look at a bag of candy bars. Heaven on a plate, despite the heavy carb load. But I figured I'd earned the right to splurge. It wasn't every day I survived being in the middle of a superhero-ubervillain battle.

I bit into the tender chicken and sighed as the sweet-and-sour juices filled my mouth. "This is delicious."

Debonair raised his wineglass. "Only the best for you, Bella."

Normally, I would have been nice and polite and merely picked at my meal, avoiding most of the treacherous bread and potatoes. But I was too hungry to care what Debonair thought of my table manners. Or maybe watching Fiona inhale food like there was no tomorrow had affected me more than I'd realized. Either way, I polished off my meal in a matter of minutes without dropping or spilling anything. My luck kept to a low, steady buzz around me, content not to interfere. For a change.

"Do you want some more?" Debonair asked.

"No," I said, dabbing at my lips with a crisp linen napkin. "That was more than enough, and everything was wonderful."

He smiled. "I'm glad you approve. The chicken and vegetables are an old family recipe. My grandmother taught me to make them many years ago."

"Your grandmother, is she here?"

Perhaps if she was, I could appeal to her to help me escape. Or at least get her to let me call my grandfather. Despite Debonair's obvious charms, I couldn't let myself think he was anything but my kidnapper. Albeit the nicest kidnapper anyone had probably ever had.

Debonair shook his head. "She's still alive, if that's what you're asking. But she's not here. She's a wonderful woman."

"What's her name?" I asked, hoping to catch him off guard.

"You know I can't tell you that, Bella."

I didn't really expect it to work, so I tried another tactic. "You love your grandmother very much, don't you?"

He seemed almost insulted by my question. "Of course I love my grandmother. I might be a rake and a thief, but I do have a heart."

"So, you can imagine how worried your grandmother would be if you were, say, kidnapped. You'd want to call her and let her know you were all right, wouldn't you?"

Debonair sighed. "I can't let you call your grandfather, Bella. Anything else you want, I'll freely give to you, but not that."

"Why won't you let me call him? All I want to do is let him know I'm okay."

"Because he's got the whole city looking for you, superheroes included. If I let you call him, odds are he'll trace it back to me. Call me a coward if you want, but I don't want to face your grandfather. Or your brother, Johnny. They're both very powerful men." A sly smile flitted across his face. "They'd tear me limb from limb for kidnapping you, even if I did so with the best of intentions."

I couldn't argue with him. Family and honor and tradition meant everything to my brother and grandfather. They'd do more than just tear Debonair limb from limb. They'd put him back together and repeat the process. Several times. Then, they'd both probably dress up as Johnny Angel and run him over with their motorcycles. I might want to go home, but I didn't want to do it at that cost. I might despise heroes and villains, but I couldn't deny the sexy thief had sort of grown on me. And he'd saved my life. That counted for a lot.

"Well, have you figured out what Hangman wants with the Star Sapphire?"

Debonair shook his head. "Not yet. He could want it just to want it, of course. But Hangman's never been known to be overly greedy, just power hungry. I think someone else hired him to steal the sapphire. What that person plans to do with it, I have no idea. Maybe if I had more resources, I'd be able to discover the answer quicker. But I must confess that I've fallen on hard times recently."

My eyes flicked around the room, taking in all the rich furnishings, as well as the exquisite meal we'd just eaten. This didn't look like hard times to me.

"Well, I can't stay here forever. I can't put my grandfather through that. Surely, you can understand?"

"I do. More than you know. But I can't risk Hangman coming after you to get to me. He will, you know. He saw me teleport you away. He knows I have the sapphire. He'll come to you and demand to know where I am, who I am. And when you can't tell him, he'll hurt you. Terribly."

"I can take care of myself. And I have friends who will help me. Powerful friends." If I could put aside my dislike of the Fearless Five's spandex costumes and alter egos long enough to let them help.

"That won't be enough. Not against Hangman." Debonair stared into my eyes. "I don't want anything to happen to you, Bella. You're far too important to me."

I laughed. "You almost sound like you care about me. Me, a complete stranger!"

"You're not a complete stranger to me, Bella. You're not a stranger at all."

Debonair looked like he wanted to bite his tongue the second the words came out. He dropped his eyes to his half-eaten chicken and fiddled with his fork. I couldn't tell for sure, but I thought I saw a blush creeping up the side of his neck. Debonair? Blushing?

His confession confused me as well.

"Do I— Do I know you? The real you?"

He looked away, and I knew the answer.

"Who are you?"

For a moment, Debonair chewed on his lower lip. He looked lost, unsure, and nothing at all like the suave rake he was. Then, his eyes shuttered, and he came back to himself.

"That's not important," he said in a smooth voice. "What is important is keeping you safe. That's why you're going to stay here until I can figure out what Hangman is up to."

He wasn't going to let me go. Not anytime soon, at least. My thoughts turned to Grandfather. He'd be worried. He was probably sitting up now, just like I'd done so many nights when my father and brother were out prowling the streets as Johnny Angel. Grandfather would be staring at the phone, praying for it to ring. And afraid that when it did, it would be the police or the Fearless Five on the other end of the line with bad news.

Frustrated, I threw down my napkin. My power flared, and the cloth landed on top of one of the candles. It immediately caught fire. The candle tipped over, and the flaming cloth hit my half-drunk glass of wine, spilling it. In an instant, hot, hungry flames engulfed the table.

Not for long, though. Debonair snapped his fingers, and a fire extinguisher popped into his hands. He pulled the pin out of the device and squeezed down on the metal handle. White foam spewed over the table, smothering the red-orange flames, and the fire ended as quickly as it began.

I just sat there, looking at the remains of the ruined table and watching smoke puff away from the mess.

The battle, the kidnapping, the Lair of Seduction, not being able to contact Grandfather, Debonair, my jinx. It was too much. It was just too damn much.

I got to my feet and stalked over to the water bed. I tried to muffle it, but a small sob escaped my lips.

"Bella . . ."

"Please just go." My voice cracked, and I closed my eyes to keep tears from spilling down my face. "Please."

Hands settled on my shoulders and gently turned me around. I opened my eyes and found myself looking at the scarlet rose and silver thorn that decorated Debonair's blue-black leather costume. The thief tipped up my chin so he could see into my face.

"Don't cry," Debonair whispered, wiping away a tear from my cheek. "Please. I can't stand to see you cry. I'll find a way to get a message to your grandfather. Somehow."

"Promise?"

"I promise."

For some reason, I believed him. Debonair wiped another tear off my face. He stared at me, and I at him. I realized how hot his hand felt on my cheek. Realized how close our bodies were. Realized how much I suddenly wanted him to stay.

"Bella, do you know how beautiful you are?" he said.

I forced myself to laugh, even though I trembled inside. "I bet you say that to all the women you bring here."

His eyes flared sapphire blue, and his mouth opened, as if he wanted to say something. But he didn't. Instead, he reached out and rubbed a lock of my frizzy hair between his bare fingers.

"Soft and smooth, just as I imagined it would be." Debonair held the strand up to his nose. "It smells like roses. Sweet and delectable."

"You're the one who smells like roses," I corrected. "That's just your shampoo I used earlier."

Amusement sparkled in his eyes. "You're very practical, do you know that?"

"And you're very impractical, do you know that?" I countered.

"That's what makes me so adorable." He smirked.

I couldn't stop myself from laughing.

"You should do that more often."

"What?"

"Laugh," Debonair said. "I like the sound of it."

I just looked at him. His perfect body. His blue-black suit. His dark, curly hair.

Debonair stared back, a hungry expression in his blue eyes.

"Well, it's been a long day," I said, nervous. "I suppose this is goodnight."

"Goodnight, Bella." His voice was low and husky.

"Thank you for dinner. And for agreeing to contact my grandfather. You don't know how much that means to me."

On an impulse, I leaned up on my tiptoes to give him a quick peck on the cheek, but Debonair turned his head, capturing my lips with his.

Suave. Very, very suave.

He wound his hand in my hair and pulled me to him, so close that our bodies were flush against each other. His thickening erection pressed into my thigh, making me ache as he probed my mouth with his tongue. He smelled of sultry roses and tasted sweet, like the orange sauce we'd just eaten.

I ran my fingers up and down his broad chest, marveling at his smooth muscles, wishing I could touch his bare skin. He seemed pleased by my explorations, growling and cupping my ass in his hands.

Debonair slid the leather jacket from my body, exposing my mostly bare shoulders. He pressed soft kisses to my eyelids and cheeks and nose. Then, his lips moved lower, scorching a path down my chest. His lips closed over my taut nipple, sucking at it through the thin fabric of the shirt. And I was suddenly, extremely, undeniably grateful that underwear hadn't been part of the ensemble he'd given me earlier.

I arched my back. My power pulsed and surged around me, static electricity gathering in my hair and on my fingertips. But it was nothing compared to the sensations snapping and popping and sparking through my body like firecrackers one after the other.

Debonair was on his knees before me. "I've wanted you for so long now. Tell me you want me too, Bella. Tell me."

I traced his face with my fingers, ignoring the mask that obscured most of it, pretending it wasn't really there. Instead, I focused on the curve of his chin. His tiny dimple. His straight nose. His thick, perfect lips.

"I want you too," I whispered, surprised by the truth of it.

"You don't want me to stop?"

His voice was small and timid, as though he was afraid I was going to reject him. Me. Reject Debonair. The sexiest superhero in the city.

Debonair might be a seductive rake, but I somehow knew he wouldn't make me do anything I didn't want to. He was still a gentleman at heart, and his shy uncertainty touched me. So, I did something that I never, ever did.

I gave in.

"No, I don't want you to stop."

A slow smile spread across his face, like he'd just won the lottery. Debonair retraced his path up my body with his lips. He eased me back, and I sank onto the water bed. Debonair joined me a moment later. I reached for him and pulled him on top of me, reveling in the feel of his body on mine. His warmth. His touch. His sweet, seductive scent.

Part of my mind screamed at me to stop, to think, to be sensible.

He was Debonair. A thief, a rake, a notorious playboy, a super-something-or-other.

I was Bella Bulluci. The woman who liked nice guys and hated superheroes above all else.

And yet, I still wanted him. Desperately. Totally. Impossibly.

I didn't want to be sensible tonight.

Tonight, I wanted to be free.

Free of my rules and worries and constant fears.

Tonight, I wanted Debonair.

We kissed and kissed, until I was dizzy from the feel of his tongue on mine. His hands moved up my chest, cupping my breasts through the thin shirt. I couldn't stop the moan that tumbled from my lips.

"Do you like that?" he asked, staring into my eyes.

I nodded.

"So do I. But I think we'll both like this a lot better."

He snapped his fingers, and my shirt disappeared.

I gasped at the rush of cool air on my skin and pressed my hands over my exposed chest. "You can pop people's clothes on and off at will?"

He smiled. "Teleportation has its uses, Bella."

He drew my hands away from my breasts and pressed them against the bed. His eyes roamed over me, devouring me from head to toe. The hunger in his gaze startled me.

"Do you know how beautiful you are, Bella? How much I want you?"

I shook my head.

"Well, let me show you."

Debonair dipped his head to my breast, sucking and scraping the nipple with his teeth. He lavished attention on first one, then the other, over and over again. I cried out from the pleasure of it all, writhing under him. The water bed roiled and heaved with our movements.

He licked his way up my throat. I grabbed his head and

pulled his lips to mine for another heated kiss.

"Take off your clothes," I whispered against his warm, inviting mouth. "I want to touch you too."

Debonair snapped his fingers. His leather suit and boots vanished, along with the rest of my clothes. I propped myself up on my elbow and looked at him. His chest was broad, with firm, defined muscles. More dark hair covered the expanse, trailing downward past his taut stomach. No wonder women threw themselves at him. He truly was perfect. My eyes went lower. In every single way.

I scooted back into his arms, splaying my hand across his chest and planting kisses on his face and neck.

"What are you up to?" Debonair asked, his breath catching in his throat.

"You'll see."

Without warning, I took him in my hand and stroked him, even as I darted my tongue in and out of his mouth. Usually during sex, I let the guy take charge, set the pace of things. Maybe it was the wine I'd had. Or his sweet, intoxicating scent. Or maybe I'd just snapped from all the stress. But for once in my life, I was being bold and daring and adventurous. And loving every second of it.

"Bella . . ." Debonair murmured, closing his eyes. "Bella!"

His release was sudden and swift. I watched the euphoria dance across his face, pleased that I was able to bring him so much pleasure. The last shudder left his body, and he turned to me and smiled.

Then—

POP!

I found myself on my back with Debonair lying on top of me. And his fingers inside me.

"That's not fair!" I squealed.

Debonair moved his fingers in and out of me in a slow motion. "Who said anything about being fair?"

He took my nipple in his mouth even as his fingers continued their delicate work. My power flared as bright as a star as I writhed and thrashed with passion. I was hot, aching, desperate for him to stop, eager for him to go on.

I felt him harden against my thigh again, and Debonair rose up above me, ready to take the final step.

"Wait . . . Wait," I panted. I wasn't so far gone I didn't remember to be safe about this. Well, physically safe at least. "Protection . . . must . . . use protection. Do you have . . . any?"

He snapped his fingers, and a foil packet appeared. "I do now."

Debonair covered himself with the condom. He eased my legs apart and sank into me.

My breath caught in my throat.

"Am I hurting you?" he asked, stilling.

I clutched at his back, wanting him to go further. "No. You could never hurt me."

I wrapped my legs around his waist and pulled him closer, deeper into me. He moved slowly at first, sliding in and out with a steady rhythm.

I wasn't nearly so sweet and gentle. I raked my nails up and down his back. My mouth latched on to his, and I drove my tongue inside.

"Bella, I can't concentrate when you do that. I can't hold back," he whispered against my cheek.

"I don't want you to hold back," I rasped. "I want you inside me, now. All of you."

So, he didn't.

Debonair thrust himself at me, and I welcomed him. I marveled at the thick length of him filling me. At his hot, hard body covering my own. At the pleasure building and building inside me. We rode up and down on the bed as the water crested below us.

Then, with a final plunge, we both shuddered and were still.

I woke up sometime later. I breathed in deeply, but there was no lingering smell of roses. I opened my eyes and sat up.

I scanned the room, peering in every corner and even the bathroom. But he wasn't here. The ruined table was gone, and the place looked like it had been tidied up. But Debonair was nowhere to be found. I didn't know whether I was relieved or disappointed.

Without the sexy thief here to distract me, all my fears and doubts and worries roared back to the surface. My sensible nature took over, the way it always did. I flopped back down on the water bed and put my hands over my eyes. I couldn't believe it. I'd broken my own number one rule—never, *ever* get involved with superheroes and ubervillains.

And yet, I'd slept with one.

And thoroughly enjoyed it.

What was wrong with me?

I didn't want any part of superheroes and ubervillains and epic battles. It was all so silly. Spandex, leather, masks, secret identities. Didn't people have better things to do with their time than play dress-up?

Or sleep with people who did?

But the irony was when I was a kid, I'd longed to be a super-hero. I'd dreamed of taking over the family mantle of Johnny Angel, going out into the city, and righting wrongs. But the years of waiting up and wondering if my father was going to come home had taken their toll. Now, all I saw was the absurdity of the whole thing.

My family had gone through too much already. I'd gone through too much already. I wasn't going to sit at home waiting for the phone to ring or some other superhero to knock on the door and tell me that I needed to come down to the city morgue.

I wouldn't put myself through that. Not for Debonair. Not for anyone.

I shook my head. Why was I even thinking about having a relationship with Debonair? Sure, we'd slept together, but it wasn't like the handsome thief cared about me. He couldn't possibly. I was just another woman he'd brought here and seduced with his charm and sharp wit and dark good looks. Dinner, wine, roses, sweet words. It was probably the same tired routine he used every single time.

And I'd fallen for it.

I wallowed in my shame and self-pity for the better part of two minutes. Mentally berated and beat myself up for being such an eager, willing, lonely fool. Then, I thought about things a little more calmly, a little more rationally. At least the sex had been good.

And then some.

But that didn't change the fact I didn't want to be here when Debonair came back. I couldn't face him. I'd fallen under his spell once—I wasn't going to be so stupid a second time.

Today, I was escaping—one way or another.

Luckily, Debonair had just teleported my clothes over to one of the chairs, instead of leaving me with nothing but a silk sheet to wear. I put on my borrowed clothes, wincing a bit as I stuffed my stiff, sore body into the fabric. Funny, but I wasn't hurting from the attack at the museum. It was my other, ah, activities that had left certain parts of me rather sensitive.

As I dressed, I tried not to look at the bed, tried not to think of what had happened in it. How I'd begged him to pleasure me.

Me, begging a superhero.

I'd never thought it would happen. Well, Debonair wasn't exactly a superhero, but he wasn't an ubervillain either.

I tried the door, of course. Rattled it until my arms ached. But the wood was so warped it didn't budge. I doubted even Fiona could have opened it with all her superstrength. I didn't have superstrength—just capricious, whimsical, unpredictable luck. And precious little of it to start with.

So, I did the only thing I could—I reached for my power.

Normally, I did my best to ignore the static electricity crackling around my body. Ignored the sudden pulses of energy. Ignored my itchy fingers and mile-high hair. As if by ignoring it, I could pretend it wasn't there. That it wasn't real. That I wasn't the unluckiest woman in Bigtime.

My power, my luck, my jinx had never brought me anything but grief and misery and embarrassment. But now, I concentrated on it. Imagined the force field around me, gathering strength, gathering power. My fingers twitched in anticipation. So did my hair.

I looked at the door. I couldn't go through it, but maybe I could get around it another way. My eyes went to the hinges that held it to the wall. I focused my attention on them, my energy, my power, my luck. Imagined them popping off as easily as I could crack open a bottle of water. Then, I willed my power, my charged-up luck, all my jumbled emotions at the door.

I didn't really expect it to work.

But somehow it did.

Perhaps it was my desperation. Or maybe my luck just decided to give me a break for being so supremely stupid already. But I pulled on the top hinge. It snapped off like popcorn in the microwave. I repeated the process on the second and third hinges. They too popped off into my waiting hands.

It took me a few minutes to shove aside the heavy door, but when I did, I found myself in a long, carpeted hallway. I quit concentrating on my power, ignoring it as usual, and took a step forward.

And promptly tripped.

My foot caught on a nonexistent wrinkle in the smooth carpet, and I smacked into the wall before falling to my knees. I huddled there in the hallway, grimacing at the pain pulsing through my body. It wasn't serious, wasn't anything I hadn't felt a thousand times before. In the morning, I'd have a few more cuts and bruises to add to the collection Hangman had given me.

So, I ignored the dull throbs in various parts of my body, got back to my feet, and walked forward. I moved as quietly as I could, stopping every few feet to look ahead and back and listen. I didn't want Debonair to find me roaming the halls. He'd teleport us both back into his Lair of Seduction, and then who knew what would happen? He'd be angry at me for trying to escape. And I couldn't help but feel he'd be hurt and disappointed as well.

I bit my lip. Why should I care if he was hurt and disappointed? He was the one who'd kidnapped me. Who wouldn't let me call my grandfather. Who'd started this little game. Not me.

The hallway ended at the bottom of a flight of wooden stairs. I hugged the wall and crept up them. One of the stairs creaked, and I froze, afraid he'd heard me. But Debonair didn't *pop!* into sight, and my power kept to its usual low buzz. I kept climbing.

I stopped a few steps from the top and peeked over them. A large open space lay up ahead, with another long hallway on the far side. A set of doors lay several hundred feet away at the very end. That was my goal. Surely those led outside the house or mansion or wherever I was. If I could get outside, I could get away.

I entered the open room and slithered along the wall, keeping to the shadows as I moved around the perimeter. My eyes flicked over the empty space. It might have been a living room or even a ballroom at one time, but nothing remained inside now but dust. Large outlines of what I assumed used to be furniture sat in the gray film. Thick cobwebs hung in the corners, as though the room hadn't been used or cleaned in a very long time. The air smelled wet and musty.

I eased into the hallway and slid down the wall, stopping every few feet to peer into the rooms that branched off it. They were all curiously empty, just like the area I'd snuck through. I could see outlines on the walls where paintings had hung, as well as scuff marks on the floor where sofas, armoires, and other furnishings had sat. Even the light fixtures had been taken out, bathing the interior in long, murky shadows. Well, at least none of them could plummet from the ceiling and almost bonk me on the head.

It might have been a grand house at one time, but now, everything was empty and barren and rather sad-looking. In fact, the only furniture I'd seen had been the items in the subterranean Lair of Seduction.

I thought back to Debonair's talk of hard times. Perhaps he'd been telling the truth. Or maybe he was one of the superheroes and ubervillains who weren't independently wealthy. But this place, this house, didn't look abandoned, merely run-down. It was the home of a very rich person. At least, it had been at one time.

I stuck my head into another room and stopped. This one was different from the others. For one thing, it had a smattering of furniture. For another, the Star Sapphire rested on a pedestal on top of a table, along with some microscopes and other scientific equipment. I stepped inside and looked at the papers and gadgets, careful not to touch anything. For once, my luck cooperated, and I didn't crack the lens on a five-thousand-dollar microscope just by looking at it as I threaded my way through the area.

I stopped in front of the sapphire. A few papers lay scattered about it. I squinted, but they were written in Debonair's indistinguishable scrawl. I could make out the words *carats* and *reflective properties?* among the mess, but that was about it.

I slid the sapphire and papers into my stained purse and put the long strap over my head so I wouldn't lose it. Debonair might not be able to figure out what Hangman wanted with the sapphire, but the Fearless Five surely would. Besides, he'd taken something from me—my dignity. I wanted to return the favor. Petty, I know. But it was the only thing keeping me going.

I left the room and continued on my prison break. I started to ease by another door when a splash of color caught my eye. I turned my head and gasped. All sorts of paintings and sculptures and drawings crowded inside the room, along with tables full of paint, brushes, and other art supplies. It was sort of like being in a wing at the Bigtime Museum of Modern Art—albeit a run-down version.

My eyes roamed over the jeweler's eyes, paint scrapers, and other art paraphernalia. I walked toward a painting of irises leaning on an easel on one side of the room. I recognized it as the one Debonair had stolen from Berkley's house. Notes covered the wall next to it, pointing out flaws and a small patch of mold on the painting.

I frowned. It almost looked like he was restoring the painting. Debonair? An art lover? Was that why he stole paintings? To restore them? I didn't understand. Then again, I'd never understood what drove a person to make himself a spandex suit, dress up in it, and call himself by another name. It was sheer lunacy.

I turned to go when another drawing caught my eye. The one I'd done of Debonair. The one with his illegible signature. It lay in the middle of a small table, with no brushes or paints anywhere near it. Instead, a heavy silver frame sat next to it, as though he'd planned on keeping it. I stared at the drawing, looking at the face I'd sketched. The face of the man I'd slept with.

I took the drawing, rolled it up, and put it in my purse. I don't know why I did it. Perhaps I wanted something to remind me of my time here. Or maybe I just wanted to take back what was left of my sanity. I didn't know anymore. For once, my calm, rational sensibility had deserted me.

The art room was the last one before the doors. I tried the knob. Unlocked. I slipped through and found myself on a wide stone balcony, as empty as the rest of the house had been. But the emptiness wasn't what made my heart squeeze in on itself. It was what lay beyond it.

Water. It stretched out for miles in front of me, before the dull gray waves faded into the early morning skyline of Bigtime. A horrible suspicion filled my body.

I ran to the other side of the balcony. It had the same view. I sprinted to the third side. More of the same.

Water, water everywhere.

An island.

I was trapped on an island in the middle of Bigtime Bay.

★ 14 ★

I stared at the shimmering water. An island. How the hell was I supposed to get off an island? The shore was miles away, much too far for me to swim. Besides, it was November. I'd get hypothermia if I even tried.

I let myself panic for about thirty seconds. Let my heart pound. My hands shake. And little whimpers of panic tighten my throat.

Then, I took a deep breath and started thinking about my predicament. There had to be a boat here somewhere. That was the only way to reach the islands in Bigtime Bay. Of course, Debonair could just *pop!* over whenever he wanted, but surely he had other people out here sometimes. He'd have to bring them by boat, if he didn't want to risk blowing his real identity to his guests.

I hurried down a set of spiral stairs that wound down one side of the overlook. A carpet of grass rolled out from under the balcony, shaded by rows of pear trees. Their burnished red leaves provided a colorful contrast to the golden grass. It was a beautiful spot, the perfect place to take a long nap or enjoy a picnic. Normally, I would have stopped a few minutes to do some rough sketches of the trees and the way the gathering sunlight brightened the dew drops on the crimson leaves. But I didn't have time for such fancies now.

I had a boat to find.

I walked underneath the trees, keeping to the shortening shadows. It couldn't have been much past six or seven in the morning, because the sun had just crested over the tops of the distant skyscrapers. A wet chill hung over much of the bay, along with a thin, soupy fog. I shivered and put my hands in the pockets of my jacket, grateful Debonair had left it behind. A few birds twittered in the trees, while an occasional frog croaked from a hidden spot in the grass. Everything smelled of salt and brine, and my nose tingled at the rough scent.

I broke free of the trees and headed for the water's edge. The grass gave way to a rocky, pebble-filled beach. The grayish sand reminded me of the color of Hangman's uniform. I put one hand on a rock for support and stuck the other in the lapping water. My hand turned to ice in an instant. I shuddered. Much too cold to swim.

So, I moved on and kept looking for a boat or a canoe or a kayak or something, anything I could use to get off the island. I'd walked about a half mile along the shore when I spotted a dock. It stretched out into the water about thirty feet, a long, pale arrow pointing toward the city. Like the rest of the house, it too looked like it had seen better days. The boards appeared warped and weathered, with more than a few cracked or missing altogether.

But my eyes scanned past the wet wood and latched on to the prize at the very end—a small sailboat. My ticket off this rock and away from Debonair, and all these strange, unwanted feelings he stirred in me.

I stepped onto the dock. The wood moaned, and the board sank down under my weight, but it didn't break. I took another step. Then another, walking slowly and carefully. Putting each foot down before I lifted the last one up. A small slip, and I'd get dumped into the bay. Then, I wouldn't have to worry about getting rescued. I'd freeze to death before anyone found me.

I navigated past the missing boards, but the closer I got to the boat, the more my heart sank. The vessel couldn't be more than twelve feet long and appeared just as ratty and run-down as the rest of the house. The scarlet paint had cracked and peeled so much I couldn't even tell what the boat's name had been. Mold and mildew blackened the sail, and the ropes tying the vessel to the dock looked like they might snap at any moment. Still, it bobbed up and down with the gentle waves and looked seaworthy enough. It was going to have to be.

I didn't know anything about sailing or seafaring, but I stepped down into the boat and untied the flimsy ropes that held the craft to the dock. The boat drifted out into the bay, pulled along by the brisk current. There was little wind, but maybe I could fix that. Loath as I was to do it, I reached for my power again and focused my attention on the limp sail, willing the wind to come along. My power flared, and a breeze whistled down.

I smiled, pleased my luck cooperated for a change. But the breeze didn't last long. After about thirty seconds, it died away altogether.

Still, the boat floated farther out into the bay, pulled on by the occasional gust of wind and growing current. I used the opportunity to dig through my purse and flip open my phone. The signal was clear and strong now, and I dialed 555-5555, the emergency hotline for the Fearless Five.

Carmen Cole picked up on the first ring. "Bella! Where are you?!"

"I'm in a boat in the middle of Bigtime Bay," I said. "I'm fine. For the most part. Didn't Debonair get a message to you guys? Or my grandfather?"

"No, we haven't gotten any message from him. We've been looking for you nonstop. Are you all right? Are you hurt?"

I bit my lip. He'd lied to me. He hadn't sent a message to Grandfather. He hadn't sent a message to anyone. What a fool I was.

I told Carmen about Debonair saving me and holding me in his Lair of Seduction. I left out the part where I'd slept with my captor, though. I didn't want Carmen to think I was one of the nutty people in the Slaves for Superhero Sex club who put themselves in danger on purpose so they could cozy up to heroes. Or that I'd enjoyed being a prisoner, despite the fact part of me had.

"How's Grandfather?" I asked.

"I'm fine, Bella. I'm right here." Bobby's sharp, strong voice came through the line. "Did he hurt you?"

"No, Grandfather. He didn't hurt me. Just scared me a little."

Carmen came back on the phone. "All right, Bella. Stay on the phone. Henry and Lulu are working on pinpointing your location. Sam, Chief Newman, and I are heading out now to come get you. Look for a big black boat."

"You guys have a boat?"

"Of course we have a boat," Carmen replied. "We're the best superheroes in the city. We're prepared for anything, and we have everything, thanks to Sam. Now, here's Bobby again."

"Grandfather?"

"I'm here, Bella."

Now that help was officially on the way, I leaned against the rail and told my grandfather the same story I'd told Carmen. Debonair had teleported me around the city, before taking me to his Lair of Seduction.

"Lair of Seduction? Bah!" My grandfather snorted. "If I was ten years younger, I'd hop on my motorcycle and mow him down for scaring you like that. Johnny Angel could teach him a thing or two about how to treat a lady. These young superheroes just don't have the proper respect for anybody."

"Don't talk like that. Debonair didn't hurt me," I protested. "He saved me from Hangman. In fact, he was very kind and generous."

Especially in bed, but I couldn't tell Grandfather that. I couldn't tell anyone that. Ever.

An odd noise penetrated my conflicted thoughts. Music— wild, happy music with a pulsing, calypso beat.

Calypso music? In the middle of the bay?

"Hold a second, Grandfather. I hear something strange."

I looked around, trying to find the source of the sound. The hum of a powerful motor filled the air, and a moment later, a boat cut through the dissipating fog—the most colorful, buoyant vessel I'd ever seen. The ship was painted in wild, tie-dye colors that ranged from electrified orange to vitriolic violet and every other shocking shade in between. All swirled together. FREE LOVE! FREE BEER! FREE SEAS! screamed a banner hung between two billowing sails. It took me a minute to put it together, but I realized whose ship it was.

Cap'n Freebeard and his Saucy Wenches. Cap'n was another one of Bigtime's shady characters—not quite an ubervillain but definitely not a superhero either. The modern-day pirate and his band of Saucy Wenches sailed out on the bay almost every day on their psychedelic party barge. Sometimes, they'd help lost fishermen get back to shore or tow in a broken-down boat. But they spent most of their time waylaying the big cruise ships and stealing all the liquor and food they could carry. The cruise ships didn't mind so much, though. The pirate was good for business. People flocked to the ships just on the off chance they'd run into Cap'n, be shanghaied, and get taken over to his boat to party with the crew.

The ship sailed by, and I got a good look at Cap'n Freebeard. He was a tall man with sun-kissed skin and hair so blond it was almost white. Tiny silver bells and bits of coral dangled from the ends of his dreadlocks and the bottom of his thick, curly beard. Cap'n stood in front of a shining silver wheel, flanked on all sides by topless—and sometimes bottomless—beauties. They all had rather buoyant personalities, if you know what I mean. Especially since it was so cold this morning.

Cap'n spotted me too. He took off his floppy straw hat and tipped it to me in a respectful fashion, while the wenches hung over the railing and blew me flirty kisses.

I thought about signaling to Cap'n that I needed some assistance, since I knew nothing about sailing or seafaring. But help was already on the way. The Fearless Five would be here any minute. I could wait.

"What's that noise?" Bobby asked.

"Nothing," I replied, trying not to stare at all the bare, naked, oily flesh passing in front of me. "Nothing at all."

Cap'n Freebeard and his merry band sped on by, and I kept talking to Grandfather. But after a few minutes, a weird *whooshing* caught my attention. At first, I thought it was fish, splashing and leaping and playing in the salty water. All sorts of dolphins and whales and other interesting creatures populated Bigtime Bay. But then, my fingers started to itch, and my hair frizzed. The *whooshing* came again, louder this time. My heart started to pound. And not in a good way.

A tall shadow fell over me.

Boots smacked against the deck.

And I turned to find Hangman standing behind me.

15

"Hangman's here. Tell the Fearless Five to hurry!" I screamed into the phone before Hangman smacked it out of my hand.

The phone hit the brass railing. For a moment, I thought it would go overboard and be lost in the depths of the deep blue sea. But the silver phone bounced back toward me and landed on the deck. I hoped it was still on and that Grandfather hadn't been cut off.

"Where is it? Where's the sapphire?" Hangman growled, advancing on me again.

I shrank back, eyes frantic, looking for a place to hide, a weapon, something, anything that would keep me alive until the Fearless Five arrived. But there was nothing, not even a cracked oar, to help me. Hangman stretched his massive hand toward my throat, no doubt to throttle the life from my body. I panicked, and my power flared to life.

Wind screamed into the sail, and the ropes holding it in place snapped like toothpicks. The sail tumbled down, landing right on top of Hangman. The ubervillain cursed and tried to free himself from the heavy canvas. I leaned down, grabbed my phone, and ran all of ten feet to the other end of the boat.

"Grandfather!"

"Hang on, Bella! They're almost there!"

Sure enough, in the distance, I spotted a rapidly moving black speck. *Come on,* I begged. *Come on!*

With a mighty, angry roar, Hangman ripped free of the sail. There was only one thing left to do. I tore off my jacket, kicked off my shoes, and climbed up onto the railing—ready to swim for it. But a hand latched around my ankle and dragged me down before I could leap over the side. That same hand tossed me up in the air like a tennis ball before catching me right side up.

Hangman put his hand around my throat and lifted me up so that my face was level with his. My feet barely reached to his knees. I tried to plant my toes on his utility belt to take some of the pressure off my neck, but my feet kept slipping off the cold, hard metal.

I stared into his face. Hangman's eyes were as light as the sky—colorless really, except for the cold rage burning in the depths.

"Where's the stone? Tell me now, and I'll make your death quick and mostly painless. Otherwise, I'll give you to Prism. She won't be nearly as pleasant as I am."

"I . . . don't . . . know . . ." I wheezed, trying not to black out.

"Fine. Have it your way."

Hangman's grip tightened, and stars exploded before my eyes. Then—

POP!

The smell of roses filled the air. My eyes went over Hangman's shoulder. Debonair stood behind him, hands clenched into tight fists. My heart swelled with relief.

"Let her go," Debonair snarled, his eyes glowing with rage. "I'm the one you want. I've got the sapphire. Not her."

Hangman threw me aside like I was a wadded-up piece of paper. I hit the railing, momentum pushing me overboard. I willed myself to stop, and somehow avoided flipping over into the cold water below. I slumped to the bottom of the boat, dazed by the hard hit I'd taken, but not seriously injured. Despite my dislike of my supposed superpower, sometimes it was good to be lucky. Very, very good. I still would have preferred Johnny's superstrong exoskeleton, though.

Hangman launched himself at Debonair, who teleported out of the way at the very last second. Hangman slipped on the tattered sail and banged his head against the side of the boat. The thief reappeared by my side.

"Are you all right, Bella? Did he hurt you?" Debonair asked, cupping my cheek with his hand.

I jerked my head away from his familiar, comforting touch. "I'm fine. Now leave me alone."

Confusion and hurt flashed across his face. "What's wrong? Why did you run away?"

I glared at him. "Why didn't you get a message to my grandfather?"

He didn't have time to answer. The Fearless Five pulled along beside us in a sleek black vessel. Hermit manned the wheel, while Karma Girl, Striker, and Mr. Sage stood on the deck ready to board the sailboat.

Striker raised a bullhorn to his lips. "This is the Fearless Five! Hangman, Debonair, put up your hands! Both of you! Now!"

Hangman struggled to stand, his feet still tangled in the ripped sail. "To hell with that!"

He grabbed a grenade from the belt around his waist and dropped it on the deck. Then, he held his hands up and zoomed away into the blue sky, the sail flapping around his ankles.

I watched, horrified, as the grenade *tink-tink-tinked* around the sailboat. Finally, it skidded to a stop, and a red light on the top began to blink. I tried to move, to launch myself overboard. But my power pulsed, and my bad luck boomeranged around the way it always did at crucial moments. My feet slid out from under me.

Debonair grabbed my waist.

POP!

The world disappeared as he teleported me over to the Fearless Five's boat. A second later, the grenade exploded, sending fire and smoke and bits of boat hundreds of feet into the air. Debonair forced me to the deck, covering my body with his, as the debris rained down on us. Striker did the same to Karma Girl, while Hermit and Mr. Sage crouched underneath the boat's wheel.

The boat bucked and heaved from the shockwave of the explosion, making me sick. But the seas eventually calmed. The smoke and ash and fire faded away, swallowed up by the cold water. After a few moments, we all got to our shaky feet.

"Are you all right?" Debonair asked, helping me up.

"Fine. Now let go of me," I snarled, pushing him away.

"Bella?" Karma Girl asked, approaching us. Striker followed behind her.

"I'm fine, Karma Girl. Really, I am."

The two superheroes looked at each other, then moved to flank Debonair.

"We need to talk to you, Debonair," Striker said, his eyes going to me. "About a lot of things."

But the thief didn't pay any attention to the two superheroes. He kept staring at me, hurt shimmering in his sapphire eyes. For a moment, I wanted to go to him, to tell him I was sorry for running away, for leaving him behind. Then, I remembered how he'd lied to me about Grandfather. The notion faded.

Debonair leaned forward. "We're not through, you and me. Not by a long shot."

"Yes, we are. Leave me alone. Please."

Debonair stared at me. Then, he leaned forward and pressed his lips to mine in a rough, hard kiss that left me breathless. He stepped back. Debonair gave me a smirk and bowed with a small flourish.

"Stop!" Karma Girl said, her eyes beginning to glow neon blue.

But it was too late.

POP!

Debonair had already teleported away.

PART TWO

An Exception to the Rule?

16

"Anything, Hermit?" Striker growled.

Hermit's fingers glowed a bluish white color over the keys on his laptop as he used his superpower to plug his brain into the computer and sort through billions of data bytes. Mind-melding, Hermit called it. After a moment, the glow disappeared, and the black man shook his head. His eyes were wide and apologetic behind his round goggles.

"Lulu?" Striker asked.

The pretty Asian woman with spiky blue-and-black hair tapped away on another computer. "Nothing. Not a trace of either one of them. Hangman went up, up, and away, and Debonair just went poof. They're both gone."

The six of us sat in the main stateroom in the Fearless Five boat—Striker, Karma Girl, Hermit, Mr. Sage, Lulu, and me. It was a little like being trapped in a color wheel. Hermit wore a black-and-white-checkerboard outfit with matching goggles, while Karma Girl dazzled in her silver spandex. Mr. Sage was clad in green and white, while Striker wore a tight black leather suit that reminded me of Debonair. Lulu and I were the only ones not in costume. Fiona Fine would have been here too, in her reddish orange catsuit, if she and Johnny hadn't been on their vacation.

"How are you feeling, Bella?" Mr. Sage asked, his blue eyes soft and kind as he took my blood pressure.

"A little shaken up," I admitted. "I'm glad you guys showed up when you did."

It was one thing to be the daughter of a murdered sometimes superhero. I could afford to be angry and bitter and bitchy in the safety of my own home. It was quite another to be attacked, kidnapped, attacked again, and rescued all in the space of a day and a half. I was exhausted—physically, emotionally, sexually.

"Are you sure they're gone?" Striker asked.

Lulu nodded. "Unfortunately. We left in such a rush I didn't have time to grab all my gear. This laptop you had on board is a piece of junk, along with the rest of this stuff. There's no way to track them with this."

The computer hacker gestured at the monitors and keyboards that surrounded her. It didn't look like junk to me. The stateroom had almost as many gadgets and maps and computer equipment as the Fearless Five's underground library did. It constantly amazed me how much time and money superheroes spent on their toys. Then again, there was a reason the Fearless Five were the preeminent superhero team in Bigtime. And right now, I was grateful to be among superheroes—instead of sleeping with the fishes in Bigtime Bay.

"All right then, I'll set the course back to the cove," Striker said, punching in some commands on a large control panel.

He took off his black mask, and the others followed suit, revealing their true identities—Sam Sloane, Carmen Cole, Henry Harris, and Chief Sean Newman.

"Your blood pressure and temperature are fine. I'm a bit worried about that bump on your head, though. And I'm afraid you're going to be quite stiff and sore in the morning," Chief Newman rumbled in his Irish brogue. "But other than that, you'll be fine."

In addition to masquerading as a superhero, Chief Newman was also the Fearless Five's resident doctor.

"Thanks," I said, flashing him a weak smile as he took the tight cuff off my right arm. "Where's Grandfather? He didn't come with you?"

Carmen shook her head. "He didn't want to leave the phone. He told us to come on and that he'd wait at Sublime until we brought you back."

Sublime was Sam Sloane's mansion on the outskirts of Bigtime. It was one of the most impressive homes in all of the city, but few people knew that a maze of caverns under the mansion housed the members of the Fearless Five and all their gizmos. I hadn't known about it either, until Fiona had taken Grandfather and me there when we were frantically searching for Johnny when he'd been kidnapped by ubervillains.

"I just sent Bobby a text message telling him that you were safe and sound," Lulu said.

"Grandfather doesn't do so well with computers. Maybe I should just call him."

Lulu smiled. "Don't worry. I programmed it to flash on the big screen in the library. There's no way he can miss it."

While we motored back to the Fearless Five headquarters, I filled the superheroes and Lulu in on everything that happened on the boat, including Hangman's mention of someone named Prism.

"Prism?" Carmen asked. "That's a strange name. I wonder what her power is. Have you ever heard of her, Sam?"

The handsome businessman shook his head. "No. Have you guys?"

Both Henry and the chief shook their heads. Lulu cleared her throat, and all eyes turned to her.

"It's probably nothing," she said.

"Which means that it's definitely something," Carmen replied, picking up a Rubik's Cube and twisting it around in her hands. "Spill it, Lulu."

"Well, you guys know about my other interests outside the Fearless Five, right?"

The chief laced his fingers together and stared at the younger woman. "You mean your network of spies and information traders? Or your friendship with a notorious bomb maker? Or perhaps the corporate espionage you've been dabbling in recently? You have lots of *interests*, Lulu. Not all of which are legal. We've discussed them on many occasions, but apparently with little success."

The computer hacker looked a bit sheepish, despite her mane of multicolored hair. "Yeah, well, this is about Jasper. I talked to him last week, just catching up and stuff, and he mentioned the name *Prism*. Said somebody by that name wanted him to do some work for her, but he turned down the job."

Jasper was one of Lulu's many shady friends. He specialized in blowing up things in Bigtime, but he'd also helped out the Fearless Five on more than one occasion.

"Well, we'll just have to go pay Jasper a visit and see what he knows about the mysterious Prism," Carmen said to Lulu.

"I want to go too," I piped up.

The others stared at me like I'd hit my head a little too hard. Maybe I had.

"I would think you'd want to go back to headquarters or even home," Carmen said in a soft tone. "We all know how you feel about superheroes and ubervillains, Bella."

"I know." I shifted under her curious, probing stare. "But I was the one who got attacked and kidnapped and almost blown to bits. Twice. I want to know what the hell is going on. Besides, maybe if we show Jasper this, it will help."

I pulled the Star Sapphire out of my battered purse and set it on a table in front of me. Somehow, I'd held on to it again through all the commotion. Lulu reached over and picked up the gem.

"Look how big this sucker is." She turned it around so the sapphire caught the light streaming in through the portholes. "You know, Henry, if you wanted to get me something for Christmas, this would make a very nice engagement ring."

Henry pushed his glasses up his nose. "But you already have an engagement ring."

Lulu held up her pale hand. A not-so-small emerald sparkled on her finger. "But just think how much better they'd look together."

Lulu grinned at Henry, and I just had to laugh.

Twenty minutes later, we all stood on deck as Henry steered the boat into a small, secluded cove that branched off the bay. He aimed the vessel right at a sheer rock cliff. I looked at him, then at the cliff, then at the others. Everyone else seemed unconcerned by the fact we were going to get splattered against the sharp rocks in another three seconds.

I closed my eyes, bracing for the hard, jarring impact, but it never came. Instead, I felt something cool slide over my skin, and a white light flared against my eyelids. I opened them and realized we were in some kind of watery cave. I looked back.

The cliff face stood behind us, looking as solid and real as ever.

"It's a 3-D hologram," Henry explained, seeing my confused look. "The cliff's not really there."

"Neat trick."

I shook my head. Despite my aversion to superheroes, the Fearless Five never ceased to amaze me.

The boat sailed on through the cave. Lights set at various intervals in the rocky walls cast a dim, yellow glow on the rocks, highlighting the specks of fool's gold and rose quartz embedded in the grayish stone. A few bats hid in the darker cracks and crevices. The creatures were small, no bigger than my hand, and had their wings wrapped tight over their inverted bodies, sleeping. The air smelled of the salty sea, with just a hint of sulfur. Everything was quiet except for the drone of the boat's engine and the occasional splash from a passing fish.

We rode in silence for another five minutes before coming to a steel door that stretched from the top of the cave down below the waterline. Something told me this door was very real. Henry held out a small clicker that looked like a garage-door opener and punched it five times in rapid succession. The steel door rattled up, revealing a metal dock flanked by all kinds of boats, life jackets, and other sailing equipment. Henry steered the boat into an empty slot. Two more just like it took up the other spaces.

"I didn't know you guys had an underground harbor down here too." I marveled at all the expensive, high-tech equipment. I'd only been in Fearless Five headquarters a few times, but whenever I came down, it always seemed like the superheroes had added a whole new wing of stuff.

"It's a fairly recent addition," Sam said, tying the boat to the wide dock. "I got tired of storing the boat in the marina. People took pictures of it all the time, and we could never get to it when we needed to."

We'd just stepped onto the floating dock when a booming voice called out, "Bella!"

Grandfather appeared at the far end of the room. I ran to him as fast as I could with my various aches and pains. I threw my arms around him and hugged him tight. The static pulsed around me, fueled by my intense relief, but it didn't make me fall or trip or suddenly go sideways. For now, anyway.

"Oh, Bella, I'm so glad you're safe," Grandfather said, stroking my snarled, frizzy hair.

"Me too," I whispered. "Me too."

Despite my protests, Chief Newman ushered me off to the sick bay, while the others trooped to the library to see if they could find Hangman or Debonair. I spent the rest of the afternoon being poked and prodded and pricked in all sorts of uncomfortable, unmentionable places. I also managed to break a thermometer, three plastic syringes, and a heart monitor just by looking at them.

At the end of the torture session, the chief said he'd keep me overnight for observation before letting me go home tomorrow.

Grandfather sat by my bed, holding my hand during the examination and cleaning up the various messes I made. Once the chief left, Grandfather peppered me with questions about the attack at the museum and, more specifically, about how Debonair had treated me. I answered most of them honestly, telling Bobby the sexy thief had shown me the utmost respect— except for the part where he refused to let me go and all the sex we'd had. There were some things you just couldn't tell your grandfather, no matter how hip and cool he was.

"Well, I suppose I can understand his reasoning," Bobby grumbled. "He was trying to keep you safe."

If you considered *safe* sleeping with a notorious playboy and thief, sure, I supposed Debonair had kept me safe enough. At least we'd used protection. That was probably the safest thing we'd done during our time together.

"Did you call Johnny and tell him what happened?" I asked, changing the subject.

Bobby nodded. "He wanted to come home immediately, but I told him there was no reason to now. I hope that's all right with you. He's going to call and check on you in the morning."

"Of course."

I was fine now. There was no need for Johnny and Fiona to cut their vacation short. Unfortunately, the Bulluci family had gone through a lot worse than this before. On a scale of one to ten, one being a minor fender-bender and ten being my father's murder, my ordeal didn't rate more than a four—at least not in Bigtime.

Finally, Bobby ran out of questions. "You should rest, Bella. I know you must be tired. We'll talk more later. Try to get some sleep."

Grandfather pressed a kiss to my forehead, turned off the lights, and left the infirmary.

I settled down and tried to get comfortable. Like everything else in the Fearless Five's headquarters, the hospital bed was the best that money could buy. The thick mattress cushioned my aching body, along with several fluffy pillows and soft, five-hundred-thread-count sheets. Despite the luxuries, I couldn't sleep.

And it was all *his* fault.

Debonair. My thoughts turned back to the handsome thief. I couldn't stop thinking about him. I kept remembering the way he'd kissed me. The way he'd held me. How gentle he'd been.

I even thought about who he might be—who he really was under all that blue-black leather. Try as I might, though, I couldn't figure out his true identity. Maybe Carmen could help me puzzle it out. She had a knack for that sort of thing.

Mostly, though, I replayed last night over and over again in my mind. The dinner, the wine, the great sex.

Although I was as weary as weary could be, it was still several hours before I drifted off to sleep.

"Are you sure you want to come along?" Carmen asked me for about the fifth time. "You don't have to."

It was the next morning. After spending the night in the sick bay, Chief Newman had given me the green light to resume normal activities and rejoin the rest of the world. Grandfather had gone home last night, after I'd insisted I didn't need him to stay.

Besides, Bobby had told me he'd promised his lady friend that he'd check in with her after I was safe and sound. The warm glow in Bobby's green eyes when he talked about this mystery woman told me my hunch was right—she was more than just a casual acquaintance or dinner date to him.

I was happy for my grandfather. I knew how lonely being single could be. Besides, who was I to deny the old man the pleasure of a woman's company? As long as he was responsible about things, of course. But I didn't let Bobby leave until he promised to introduce me to his lady friend at dinner one night this week.

"Bella?" Carmen asked.

"Yes," I said, focusing on the other woman. "I want to go. I need to go."

Carmen, Lulu, and I sat in the library around an enormous wooden table bearing the *F5* insignia. It was just us girls today. Sam, Henry, and Chief Newman were all busy with their day jobs. Sam adding to his billion-dollar business empire, Henry working on his latest technology column for the *Exposé*, and the chief overseeing the Bigtime police department and catching criminals.

"I want to know why Hangman wants the sapphire so badly, and who Prism is." I took a deep breath. "And I want you to help me figure out who Debonair is. I want to know who he really is. I need to know."

"But you hate superheroes," Lulu said, her dark eyes never leaving the computer monitor in front of her. "You only tolerate us because Fiona's marrying your brother. Why do you care who Debonair is? I would think you'd be happy enough to go home and forget about the whole thing."

Carmen looked up from the jigsaw puzzle she was working on and stared at me. Her blue eyes grew cloudy, then cleared. "You slept with him, didn't you?"

I couldn't stop my mouth from dropping open. I knew Carmen was an empath, a sort of psychic who could tap into people's emotions and even their powers, but I'd never expected her to guess my deepest, darkest secret. Especially since it was only twenty-four hours old. My fingers twitched, my hair frizzed, and my power flared up like a neon sign.

It was like something out of a cartoon. Loose puzzle pieces

flew through the air, bouncing off books and walls. A few of the small missiles hit the various globes in the room, making them spin round and round in perfect time. Some pinged off Lulu's laptop, causing her to duck farther down behind the monitor. And, of course, one puzzle piece shot up into the air like a rocket, hitting the enormous film screen that hung down from the wall. Even though it was bolted to the ceiling in six places, the screen wobbled for half a second, then crashed down, frame and all, making a thunderous roar as it slammed into the floor. Carmen and Lulu jumped, startled by the sudden collapse. I just sighed and looked over my shoulder. The screen landed right behind me. If my chair had been back two more inches, I would have gotten brained by the frame. But I'd been just out of range, just like always. Lucky me.

"I'll take that as a yes," Carmen said, moving to pick up the wayward pieces.

I grimaced, ashamed by my sudden outburst and unwanted power display. "How did you know?"

Carmen grinned. "There are some benefits to being a psychic empath. Guessing your friend's secret is definitely one of them. So come on, Bella. Spill it."

"Yeah, I slept with him," I muttered.

I told the two women about Debonair asking me out, kissing me in the museum, how we'd had dinner together in the Lair of Seduction, and what happened afterward.

"And he said the weirdest thing—that I wasn't a stranger to him, that I was important to him. I didn't know what to make of it at the time. I still don't. Do you think I know him? The real him?"

"Probably," Carmen said. "He's probably another one of the rich businessmen on the society circuit. Hell, he might have even written you a fat check at the museum benefit the other night. Either way, I'll help you find out who he is."

"I feel like such a fool," I admitted. "He's probably seduced hundreds of women, and I fell for all his lines, just like everybody else."

"You shouldn't feel too bad, Bella. These things happen. I think it has something to do with all that tight leather, myself."

"What do you mean?" I asked, looking at Carmen.

"Carmen means she did the exact same thing—slept with a superhero," Lulu chimed in.

"You did?"

A sheepish grin spread over Carmen's face, and she nodded. "Yeah, I slept with Sam before I knew who he really was."

My confession was enough to get Lulu's full and undivided attention.

"Speaking of superhero sex, how was it?" she asked, her dark eyes bright with curiosity. "Debonair's supposed to be *very* skillful in all sorts of interesting things. At least, that's what I've heard."

"You're engaged. What does it matter to you?"

Lulu held up her hand. "Just because there's a ring on this finger doesn't mean a girl can't have fantasies."

"Doesn't Henry take care of all your fantasies?" I sniped.

I was being bitchy, but I didn't care. I didn't want to talk about what had happened between Debonair and me. Didn't want to admit how easily I'd fallen under his spell—and how foolish I felt that part of me wanted to see him again, despite the fact he'd lied to me.

Lulu paid no attention to my sharp tone. Her eyes narrowed, and she gave me a sly, satisfied smile. "Henry does just fine in the fantasy department. He can do more with his fingers than just type really, really fast, if you know what I mean. Lots more. But there's always room for improvement."

The three of us got in Lulu's van and headed into the city. Lulu kept questioning me about Debonair and his legendary skills in the bedroom, but I was able to ignore her—for the most part.

Twenty minutes later, Carmen stopped the van in one of the nicer neighborhoods in Bigtime and parked in front of a well-kept brownstone that took up the better part of the block. A wrought iron railing flanked the steps, while a cement, urn-shaped flowerpot beside the front door held a smattering of fall pansies. More flowers bloomed in the window boxes on the upper floors. Just looking at it, you'd expect this upper-class home to be occupied by a wealthy widow and her yippy, teacup-sized dog—instead of by the city's foremost explosives expert.

I'd been to this same brownstone earlier this year when Fiona and Lulu had gotten some bombs to help us battle two ubervillains who'd kidnapped Johnny and the other members of the Fearless Five. Using Jasper's bombs, we'd managed to save the others and obliterate most of the Bigtime Observatory in the process. They were still rebuilding the structure. Like the superheroes, Jasper was also very, very good at what he did.

Carmen and I got out of the van and waited for Lulu to grab her cane. A few years ago, Lulu had been used as a hostage during a battle between the Fearless Five and the Terrible Triad. She'd been crippled and confined to a wheelchair as a result. She hadn't been able to walk at all until Siren had zapped her with a couple thousand bolts of electricity during the battle at the observatory. As a result, Lulu's body and broken back had managed to regenerate themselves. After countless hours of physical therapy, Lulu was no longer confined to her wheelchair. She wasn't quite able to walk on her own just yet, but she'd get there someday. I admired her determination. Funny, how things could change in a heartbeat in Bigtime.

Carmen and I helped Lulu up the steps, and she punched a call box attached to one wall. A security camera swiveled over our heads, zooming in on our faces. Jasper was very particular about his security. He had to be, in his line of work.

"What's the word?" a low voice asked.

"Is it *boom-boom* again?" Carmen asked.

"No," Lulu replied. "It's not *Silent Night* either. He's changed it twice since then."

The two of them bickered back and forth a minute, trying to come up with the right code. Lulu snapped her fingers.

"I know. The word is *lucky charms*."

"Lucky charms?" I asked, not quite getting Jasper's odd sense of humor.

Lulu shrugged. "It's something new he said he was working on."

She repeated the phrase into the call box. The door buzzed open, and we stepped inside.

"Jasper?" Lulu called out when the bomber didn't appear to greet us.

"In the living room," a male voice called out from deeper in the house. "Down the hall on your right."

Lulu looked at Carmen, who shrugged. But I noticed Carmen's eyes began to glow ever so slightly. The three of us walked through the wide hallway, rounded a corner, and stopped in front of an open door.

Jasper sat on a sofa in the room in front of us. White-plaster casts covered his left leg and arm, and his face was cut, swollen, and bruised beyond belief. He looked like he'd been used as a punching bag by the Ringer—for a full ten rounds.

Jasper peered through his glasses at us, trying to focus through his half-shut black eye.

"Well, it's about time you guys got here," he said.

"Jasper, what happened to you?" Lulu asked, hobbling over to sit next to the battered man.

Carmen and I settled ourselves on some nearby chairs.

"Not what, who." Jasper picked up a half-melted bag of ice from the cushion beside him. He took off his glasses and put the ice over his black eye, wincing. "I had a visitor a couple of nights ago."

"Let me guess—Hangman," Carmen replied.

Jasper nodded. At least, he tried to. His head got about half-way down before stopping in pain. "He broke in after midnight. Crashed through one of the skylights in the bedroom. Said he was here to collect some things his employer wanted."

"Prism?" I asked.

Jasper tilted his neck a tiny bit to look at me. "You've heard of her?"

"Sort of."

"That's what we're here about," Lulu said. "We want to know everything you know about her."

"Not much. I never met her face-to-face. I don't even know her real name, but she calls herself Prism."

"Dumb name," Carmen said. "It doesn't even say what her power is."

"Dumb or not, she sent me an e-mail about a month ago wanting me to do some special work for her," Jasper said.

"What sort of special work?" Carmen asked.

Jasper just looked at her with his one good eye.

"Oh. That."

Jasper was the Bigtime's preeminent bomb maker. If you wanted something to blow up in the most impressive, spec-tacular manner possible, you went to Jasper. He did a lot of demolition work for the city's construction companies, but he also sold explosives and the like to various shady characters and greedy, desperate people who wanted to collect on their insurance policies. Jasper wasn't hard-core evil—he didn't deal with ubervillains—but he wasn't lily-white either. He was sort of like Debonair, but without the sexy body. And eyes. And hair. And lips—

Carmen elbowed me in the side. "Focus, Bella. You can think about your dreamboat later."

I rubbed my aching ribs and glared at the other woman. Psychics. Geez. Out of all the superheroes, they were the ones I hated the most. There was nothing you could do to keep them from intruding on your thoughts. Even my luck couldn't help me with that.

"What exactly did Prism want you to do?" Lulu asked. "What sort of bomb did she want?"

"That's the funny thing," Jasper said. "She didn't want a bomb. Not exactly. It was more like a consulting job. She wanted me to look at specs for some device she'd created to see if it would actually work."

Jasper was also something of a mad inventor and kept coming up with strange new ways to blow the city to smithereens.

"It wasn't a radio, was it?" Lulu asked. "Some sort of giant karaoke machine?"

The two of us exchanged nervous looks. A few months ago, Siren and Intelligal had built such a device to be the ultimate human controller—and almost enslaved the city in the process.

Jasper halfway shook his head. "No, it was more like a giant laser—the sort of device that can cut through anything—bank vaults, steel doors, iron bars, even solidium. Only an ubervillain would want something like that, which is why I didn't take the job. She offered me a nice fee, though. A very, very nice fee." His one open eye grew soft and dreamy at the thought of the money.

"Focus, Jasper. Fees aren't everything," Carmen said.

Jasper's good eye cleared. "I don't know what she planned on doing with it. She just wanted to know if it would actually work."

"What did you tell her?" Lulu asked.

Japser gave her a sly grin. "Nothing, of course. I didn't agree to accept the job. Even if I did, I would have demanded double the fee she offered me before telling her the time of day."

"Why would Prism need to steal the sapphire if she's building a laser?" Carmen asked.

"What sapphire?" Jasper asked.

"You haven't heard? About the robbery at the museum?" I asked.

He tried to hold up his plaster-covered broken arm. "I've been a little under the weather. Please, enlighten me."

I filled Jasper in on what had happened at the museum—starting with Hangman's attack and ending with the Fearless Five rescuing me. I didn't mention any of the superheroes' real names, of course. Jasper knew Carmen and Lulu were friends with the Fearless Five, but he didn't know Carmen was actually Karma Girl and that Lulu was engaged to Hermit. At least, I didn't think he did.

"I still don't understand what she wants with the sapphire, though," Carmen repeated. Her fingers twitched, as though working on an invisible puzzle no one could see or feel except her.

Lulu snorted. "Haven't you ever seen a James Bond movie? She's going to use the sapphire to increase the power or focus of the laser, maybe both. Right, Jasper?"

The bomber nodded and winced. "That could be what she wants with it. The reflective properties of something like the Star Sapphire could be used that way—to great effect if you had the proper know-how."

"What we really need to see are the specs for the laser. You wouldn't happen to have kept a copy, would you?" Lulu asked.

Jasper gave her another sly grin.

Carmen and I put our arms under Jasper's shoulders and helped him downstairs to his bomb-making lair. Lulu hobbled along behind us, her cane thumping against the steps. Jasper leaned against Carmen's shoulder and punched in a series of codes on a keypad next to the thick metal door. My eyes flicked to the center of the door, which sported a fist-shaped dent as big as my head. I didn't need Jasper to tell me that Hangman had come knocking.

The door whispered back, and we stepped inside Jasper's lab. The air smelled like rusty metal, even though a fan whirred in the back of the room. I looked around at all the wires and weird gizmos and blackened bits of metal stacked on the long worktables. I hadn't come inside the house with Lulu and Fiona when they'd gotten the bombs last time. Bombers were too close to superheroes and ubervillains for my liking.

On a normal day, the workshop would be cluttered enough, but it looked like a tornado had swept through the underground lab. Wires, springs, and tools littered the floor, along with clocks, timers, and other strange devices. Papers had been yanked off corkboards, while various technical manuals had been ripped in half and tossed aside.

Lulu let out a low whistle. "Hangman really did a number on the place, didn't he? What did he take, Jasper?"

The bomb maker sank down onto a wooden bench and scratched the side of his face, careful not to touch his swollen eye. "Nothing too important. Several explodium grenades I had lying around. He was really after the machine blueprints. Prism didn't take too kindly to me rejecting her offer. Hangman dragged me down here and demanded I show him where I'd hidden them. When I didn't give them up, he decided to tap-dance on my face. Lucky for me, Hangman set off my alarms when he busted through the skylight. Swifte showed up about three minutes later, and the police five minutes after him. Hangman split, and Swifte rushed me to the hospital."

"So you're the guy in the newspaper, the one Swifte took to the hospital." My eyes narrowed. "Wait a minute. The papers and SNN said you were attacked by muggers, not an ubervillain. Why did you lie?"

Jasper stuck a finger inside his cast and scratched his injured arm. "Because I, and my clients, like my anonymity. If I told people I was attacked by Hangman, I'd have Kelly Caleb and all the other newshounds camped out on my doorstep. Besides, it was just easier to lie. There's less paperwork to fill out."

"Since when are you dealing with Swifte?" Carmen asked, her voice high and squeaky. For some reason, she always got a little nervous whenever Swifte's name came up.

Jasper shrugged. "I see him around, and we came to an agreement. If somebody breaks into my house, he responds."

"And in return?" I asked.

Jasper pushed his glasses up his nose. "I don't sell my supplies to anyone who's going to use them within three blocks of Quicke's. Evidently, it's Swifte's favorite restaurant, and he doesn't want anybody blowing it up."

It made sense in a way. Quicke's was supposed to be neutral territory in Bigtime—both superheroes and ubervillains could eat there without fear of reprisal from each other or even the police. But I supposed it never hurt to have a little extra insurance. Swifte was probably like Fiona in the fact that he constantly had to eat to keep up his strength and superspeed. And Quicke's did have some of the best food in town. Even if it was filled to the brim with hero-villain memorabilia.

Jasper pointed to a dusty floorboard. "The blueprints are on a memory card taped to the bottom. One copy, anyway. What are you girls planning on doing with them?"

"We're going to pass the information along to the Fearless Five, of course," Carmen said in a steady voice, prying up the board and reaching down to retrieve the memory card.

I admired her smoothness. I'd never been very good at lying or hiding my emotions, but Carmen didn't even blink as she fibbed to her friend. Then again, it wasn't exactly a lie.

"Do you girls or your superhero friends need some extra firepower? Or should I even ask?" Jasper raised an eyebrow.

Lulu and Carmen exchanged a look.

"Let's see what you've got," Lulu said.

Jasper gave Carmen some directions, and she pulled all sorts of hidden bombs and explosive devices from metal safes in the walls and floors. There was even a case strapped to the ceiling that looked like an air vent.

Jasper took one of the lead boxes from Carmen and opened

it on his lap. Inside lay a black velvet case, like the kind women get jewelry in on Valentine's Day. Jasper cracked open the case, revealing a shiny silver bracelet with a variety of charms dangling off it. There was a tiny book, a high-heeled shoe, a beach umbrella, a martini glass, and other items—thirteen charms in all. All of them were cute and whimsical and exquisitely made. If I hadn't known better, I would have thought it was a hand-crafted piece from Jewel's Jewel Emporium.

"This is my latest project," he said.

"Lucky charms?" I asked, thinking of the door code.

Jasper nodded.

"I didn't know you were branching out into jewelry, Jasper." Lulu smirked. "People are going to think you're going soft."

Jasper scoffed. "Soft? Hardly. The charms have enough explodium in them to level a city block. They can be used in combination, depending on how much power you need, or one at a time for smaller jobs. Use them all and the bracelet at the same time, and you've got something that would take out most of the downtown area."

Lulu let out a low whistle.

"But wait, there's more," Jasper said, beaming over his creation. "The bracelet is voice-activated and key-coded so that only the wearer can use it."

"How many of these things do you have?" Lulu asked.

"I have a prototype, of course. But this is the only other working model I have at the moment."

Carmen and Lulu exchanged a look, and Carmen lifted the bracelet out of the velvet case.

"We'll take it," Lulu said. "But who gets it?"

Carmen's eyes glowed for a second. "I think Bella should have it," she murmured.

Carmen held out the charm bracelet to me. I didn't want to take it. I didn't need to be anywhere near any sort of explosives—not with my uncontrollable power. And I definitely didn't want to be in a situation where I'd have to use the charms and bracelet. I'd never get out of it alive. Even I wasn't that lucky.

"Trust me, Bella," Carmen said in a soft voice. "I'm getting pretty good at judging these things."

Despite my frizzing hair and itchy fingers and general nervousness, I let her fasten it on my wrist. It was actually pretty, in a *one-false-move-and-I'll-blow-your-arm-off* kind of way.

"Now, just tell me the code word or words you want to arm and trigger the explosives in the bracelet, and I'll program it for you," Jasper said, gesturing at Lulu to hand him some sort of electronic doodad that resembled a calculator.

I gingerly shook the bracelet, watching the charms jiggle back and forth. They tinkled as they brushed against each other. My power pulsed around me, sensing the new device swinging from my wrist. For a moment, I thought something very, very bad might happen, but my power fell down to its usual low hum. Still, it gave me an idea for the words Jasper needed.

"Let's go with *luck be a lady*," I said.

"Why, Bella, are we feeling *lucky* today?" Lulu quipped.

I ignored her bad pun. Lulu wouldn't be nearly so chipper if she was the one with this thing strapped to her wrist. Still, maybe Carmen was right. It might come in handy if I ran into Hangman again—or the mysterious Prism. Luck wasn't much of a power when it came to the world of superheroes and ubervillains. It was barely a blip on the radar screen, compared to all the people who could form fireballs with their bare hands, or freeze a person from head to toe, or zip through the sky like a rocket. Still, I was going to be extra, extra careful with my new piece of jewelry.

Jasper tuned something on his gizmo, then made me speak my command words again. Sapphire eyes on one of the charms—an angel's head—blinked on and off three times.

"The angel is the key," Jasper explained. "Once her eyes start blinking, you have about twenty seconds to get clear or get rid of the bomb."

"Got it."

Jasper showed me how to slip the charms on and off the silver links and told me which ones were more powerful than others. When we finished, Carmen looked at her silver watch, while Lulu grabbed her cane and headed for the stairs.

"Aren't you forgetting something?" Jasper asked.

"What?" Lulu replied. "We got information on the ubervillains, figured out more or less what they're up to, found the blueprints to their ultimate-evil device, and got Bella some brand-new, supercharged explosives. I think we're good."

Jasper cleared his throat. "Well, there is the small matter of my fee."

Ah, Jasper. Ever the businessman.

★ 18 ★

"I can't believe you gave him a million dollars for that bracelet," Carmen said ten minutes later as we headed for the van. "You didn't even *try* to negotiate with him."

"There was no point. He wasn't going to get suckered again," Lulu said. "He let Fiona buy him off with clothes last time because he has a thing for her alter ego, Fiera. He wasn't going to let me get away with that too. Besides, he still gave me a discount. We are becoming regular customers of his, whether you like it or not. The man could retire on what we've spent on explosives in the past year. Sam should just put him on retainer. It'd be cheaper in the end."

Carmen sighed. "I know, I know. I'll get Sam to write you a check tonight after work."

"Nonsense. I'm as much a part of the team as you are, even if I don't dress up in a costume. Just write another glowing feature on Yee-haw! and we'll call it even," Lulu said. "They've really done wonders for me these past few months."

Yee-haw! was a therapeutic riding program financed almost in its entirety by Lulu Lo and her illegal life of crime and computer hacking. She'd been one of the program's clients for years and was forever expounding on its virtues. In fact, getting publicity for Yee-haw! was one of Lulu's main passions in life—along with Henry, computers, and making groan-inducing puns all the time.

We left Jasper behind with plenty of aspirin and promised to check on him later. Then, Lulu and Carmen drove me home. Or at least, they started to.

Carmen sat in the driver's seat, but she didn't crank the engine. "Maybe we should rethink our plan about taking you home, Bella. If Prism is anything like Malefica, she won't stop until she's got the sapphire. She'll be sure to sic Hangman on you again if she thinks there's even the slightest chance you have it or know where it is. She might even kidnap you and try to trade you for the sapphire. Then, we'd be right back where we started."

The plan the superheroes and I had come up with to keep Hangman away from me had been to let Lulu spread the word via her shady contacts that the Fearless Five had recovered the Star Sapphire from Debonair—and for the superheroes to announce it themselves on SNN. If I didn't have the stone, then there was no reason for the villains to come after me. At least, that was the theory. You could never really tell what ubervillains were going to do.

"Why don't you guys just return the sapphire to the museum?" I said.

"Why would we want to do that?" Lulu asked. "That's just stupid."

I shook my head. "If Hangman and Prism want the sapphire to power their laser, they'll have to try to steal it from the museum again. When they do, the Fearless Five can be there ready and waiting. You guys can capture the ubervillains, keep them from taking the sapphire, and save the city all in a single night."

I might not like superheroes and ubervillains, but I sure as hell could think and plot like one.

"And what happens if the ubervillains get past us?" Carmen asked.

"You guys are the Fearless Five. Surely that won't happen."

Carmen gave me a look. "You should know by now not to take anything for granted—or to be too confident."

Truer words were never spoken, but I persisted. I didn't want to sit in the Fearless Five headquarters until they managed to capture Hangman. I'd be bored to tears. And probably have an allergic reaction to all that spandex. Besides, if I was tucked away in a supersecret superhero lair, I wouldn't be able to see Debonair again. And I wanted to.

Or did I? Did I really want to see the handsome thief? Just because we'd had a hot one-night stand didn't mean he cared about me. Or that he'd even want to see me again. He'd probably had a couple more sexual encounters since our night together. Hell, maybe even a dozen, if the rumors about him were true.

But part of me still wanted to see him. Wanted to know more about him. Wanted to know if he'd felt anything at all for me besides lust—because I'd definitely felt something for him. It wasn't love, but there was a soft spot in my heart for the thief now—even if he'd seduced his way into my good graces and bed. Plus, he kept saving my life. It was really hard to be angry with a guy when he did that.

After another ten minutes of arguing, I convinced Carmen to drive me home. I thought about pressing her into looking into Debonair's real identity, but that would be pushing it. Tomorrow. I'd ask her tomorrow. It was well into the afternoon now, and all I wanted to do was go home and pretend like everything was normal. Like I hadn't spent the last few days on the roller coaster ride of a lifetime.

Carmen drove across town and turned the van onto Lucky Way. An abundance of Cypress trees and Spanish moss flanked the wide street, swaying like strands of green-gray hair in the fall breeze. Smooth, perfect, manicured lawns led up from the road, and mansion after mansion stood tall in the quiet, subdued neighborhood. Sun bounced off the roofs of the BMWs, Aston Martins, and other pricey cars parked at the top of the winding driveways. Everything was the same as the last time I'd seen it, but the street and houses looked different to me. They looked . . . smaller somehow, less intimidating.

Carmen turned into the driveway, and the wrought iron gates swung open at her approach. I leaned forward in my seat, and the Bulluci mansion came into view. Red-tile roof, stone arches, balconies, tall, narrow windows. The house wasn't nearly as large or impressive as Sublime or Brilliance, but seeing it always gave me a sense of peace. It was home, and I was glad to be back.

Carmen parked the van in front of the house, and the three of us got out.

"No valets?" Lulu asked. "No butlers to greet us?"

"We never really had any. And none at all since Fiona and Johnny hooked up. They didn't want to take the risk of someone asking why Fiona eats the way she does," I explained, taking a key from my stained purse and sliding it into the front door, which was embossed with a giant *B*.

We stepped inside. My eyes traced over the tile floors, the high ceilings, the familiar furnishings embellished with angels and halos and wings. I let out a long breath. Home. This was where I belonged. Not in the Fearless Five headquarters. Not in Jasper's bomb lab. And definitely not in the Lair of Seduction.

"Grandfather? Where are you?" I called out.

A loud *thump* sounded, followed by some sort of banging noise and a low moan.

"What was that?" I asked.

Panic pulsed through my body, shooting my hair to new heights. Had Hangman broken into the mansion like he'd done at Jasper's brownstone? Was he in here now? Hurting my grandfather, torturing Bobby to get him to tell the ubervillain where I or even the sapphire was?

"Bella, wait—"

Carmen started to say something, but I rushed deeper into the house. My power surged. My foot hit a rug in one of the entryways and threatened to go out from under me. But I focused, willing myself not to fall, and somehow, I turned my skid into a long, smooth slide. The rug hit a doorjamb and stopped. I leapt off and kept going.

The odd noises seemed to be coming from the downstairs living room. I picked up a small wooden chair by the door, stepped inside, and pulled it over my shoulder, ready to crash it down on Hangman's basketball-sized head.

I didn't see anyone in the room, but more sounds came from the direction of the sofa. Hangman probably had my grandfather pinned down on the floor, crushing the life out of him, just like he'd tried to do to me.

Nobody was hurting my family again. Nobody. Especially not some ubervillain hell-bent on taking over Bigtime. I drew in a breath, careened around the edge of the sofa, and raised the chair up high.

And found my grandfather in a very interesting position— with a woman.

19

I stared at the tangled limbs with amazement and horror. I hadn't known Bobby was that flexible. That anyone his age was that flexible. The lady he was with was also rather bendy. In all sorts of ways.

Finding my grandfather doing the nasty with his lady friend was not what I'd expected when I'd come into the room—it was far worse. My power pulsed again, and the raised chair suffered for it. The chair didn't explode so much as I ripped it in two. The two legs I had my hands on snapped off from the rest of the frame, which plummeted to the floor. As my luck would have it, one of the legs I wasn't holding on to banged into my knee before the other one stabbed my foot. Pain exploded in my toes, and I bit back a howl.

Carmen walked into the room a couple of seconds later, followed by Lulu. I hobbled around on one foot, trying to pretend I hadn't just gotten an eyeful of bare, somewhat wrinkled flesh.

"That's what I was trying to tell you—it wasn't anything serious," Carmen whispered.

Lulu peered over the back of the sofa and tilted her head to one side. "Looks pretty serious to me. Seriously kinky."

I shooed the two of them outside and hopped back to the sofa.

"Ahem." I cleared my throat.

The two of them kept right on going like they were seventeen, instead of seventysomething.

"Ahem!"

They finally stopped what they were doing, and my grandfather looked over his shoulder at me.

"Oh, Bella! I didn't hear you come in," Bobby said, disengaging himself from the woman beneath him.

He could have been telling the truth. It was rather hard to

hear when there were legs clamped over your ears. Bobby buttoned his shirt and drew back, giving me a look at his lady friend's flushed face. I managed to keep my mouth from falling open. But just barely.

"Hello, Grace," I said in the politest voice I could muster. "It's lovely to, um, see you again."

Grace adjusted her violet angora sweater over her shoulders, smoothed down her skirt, and sat up. "You too, Bella."

Of course, I hadn't expected to see quite so much of Grace Caleb at one time, but I wasn't going to say that. It was better to pretend the last two minutes had never happened. Hell, that the last three days had never happened.

"I didn't get a chance to tell you before, but the benefit was absolutely wonderful." Grace's voice was calm and serene as ever. From her smooth, even tone, you would have thought she and my grandfather hadn't been doing anything more strenuous than playing canasta. "We raised more money than ever, which, sadly, we're going to need now to repair the museum."

"How is the museum? How many items were damaged? Was the wing completely destroyed?" I asked, ashamed that I hadn't been by the museum yet to see the destruction for myself.

"At first glance, it looked catastrophic, but the damage wasn't as bad as we feared," Grace replied, pinning her silver hair back into place. "Several of the paintings and sculptures suffered fire and smoke damage, but Arthur says they can all be repaired. Of course, the roof was completely destroyed, along with part of one wall. Everyone keeps saying how lucky we were that the whole building wasn't leveled."

Grandfather gave me a knowing look, which I ignored.

"But the community has really pitched in. Several superheroes, including Swifte, the Invisible Ingénues, Pistol Pete, and Halitosis Hal, have been working to get the museum whipped into shape so it can open back up to the public as soon as possible . . ."

Grace loved the museum almost as much as I did. She launched into a detailed account of which items had been damaged and what was being done to repair them. I didn't know if Grace was genuinely aware of what she was saying, or if she was just talking to fill the silence. She finally took a breath, and Grandfather interrupted her.

"You and Grace can chat more about the museum tomorrow. Grace is going to join us for dinner. Aren't you, darling?" Bobby pressed a kiss to her wrinkled hand.

The older woman patted her coif of silver hair. A blush painted her cheeks a delicate pink. "Well, if you insist, Bobby."

"I do insist," he said, pressing another kiss to her hand. "And Bella does too. Don't you, Bella?"

"Of course," I murmured.

We made some more polite, meaningless, let's-pretend-I-didn't-see-you-two-having-sex chitchat. Thankfully, Grace announced she had a dinner date and had to go, ending the awkward torture session. We said our goodbyes, and Bobby offered to walk her out. They started whispering to each other as soon as they left the room. A giggle followed, followed by smacking noises that sounded suspiciously like French-kissing. My grandfather, French-kissing! The thought was almost too much to bear.

I gave Bobby and Grace a few minutes to get out of sight. Then, I left the living room and went looking for Carmen and Lulu. I found them in the kitchen, sitting at the table. Lulu had her laptop out, and she was scanning through the blueprints Jasper had given us. Bobby joined us several minutes later, his silver hair mussed and his shirt unbuttoned once more.

"Grace? Grace Caleb? She's your mystery woman?" I asked my grandfather the second he stepped into the kitchen. "Why didn't you tell me?"

"Because I didn't think you'd approve," Bobby replied.

"It's not that I don't approve. I just didn't think she was your type."

From our time together planning the museum benefit, I knew that Grace Caleb was a reserved, quiet sort of woman. She drank tea and baked blueberry scones and never said a bad word about anyone. She was quiet and shy and retiring. And she never went anywhere without her angora sweater and string of pearls. Grace even wore gloves on occasion. The frilly white kind with fifty-year-old lace.

She was nothing like my grandfather, who was loud and boisterous and full of life. Bobby liked to drink, all right, but tea wasn't his beverage of choice. Try Brighton's Best whiskey. He'd rather have chocolate cake than scones, and he always said exactly what was on his mind—whether you liked it or not. Hell, Bobby still occasionally borrowed my brother's motorcycle and took it for a spin through the streets of Bigtime—in the middle of the night.

But everyone says opposites attract—and the two of them were definitely opposites. Besides, I couldn't talk. I'd done the one thing I'd sworn never to do—get romantically involved with a superhero. If, of course, you considered a one-night stand any sort of real involvement. The jury was still out on that one.

Bobby's face fell at my comment, making me feel about five inches tall. So, I added to my statement. I could never bear to see my grandfather sad or upset, especially when I was the cause of it.

"But she is a lovely woman, Grandfather. If she makes you happy, then I'm thrilled for both of you."

Bobby smiled and squeezed my hand. "She does, Bella. Very much so."

I opened my mouth to grill Bobby about how they'd met, how long they'd been together, and what her intentions were toward him.

"Hey, guys, come check this out," Lulu cut me off. "I've pulled up the blueprints Jasper gave us."

I filled Bobby in on what Jasper had told us, and we all crowded around Lulu's laptop to get a look at Prism's device. The computer hacker was right. It did look like something out of a James Bond movie—only much more sinister. The laser was about thirty feet long and resembled a bulldozer with a barrel on the end. Mirrors and power amplifiers and batteries decorated it from top to bottom. A seat in the middle of the device lay behind a control panel, and the whole cab section swiveled around so you could take aim at whatever you wanted to.

"This must be where the sapphire goes," Lulu said, pointing to an empty, rounded space on the blueprints just inside the end of the barrel that delivered the laser. "She's going to use it to increase the laser's power and its range."

"How catastrophic are we talking?" Carmen asked, her eyes fixed on the monitor.

"Let's just say if I had a choice between the laser and Bella's shiny new bracelet, I wouldn't know which one to pick," Lulu said. "This thing could do major, major damage to anything in its path. Cars, buildings, people. The heat would be so intense it would fry anyone within a foot of the beam."

"Terrific. Just terrific," Carmen muttered.

I shook my head. I'd never understood why ubervillains (and superheroes too) felt the need to create these elaborate contraptions. Gadgets, names, clothes, shoes. Simpler was always better. And why couldn't they just use their maniacal genius for good or world peace? Even if there wasn't any profit in it?

Carmen paced around the table. "All we have to do now is figure out what Prism's going to do with the laser and where she's hiding it. And that's always the hardest part, unfortunately. Just when you think you've got things worked out, something unexpected happens—which makes everything else that much worse."

Bobby looked at me. "Maybe you should go back to the Fearless Five headquarters, Bella, until this is all settled. Hangman is dangerous enough, but I really don't like the sound of this Prism person."

"I'm not going back," I said. "I've already had this conversation with Carmen. It might be days or even weeks before the superheroes figure out what the ubervillains are up to. I can't hide that long, and I don't want to. These people have upset my life enough already. I won't let them hold me hostage any longer. Don't worry. I'll be safe here with you."

"But the Fearless Five can protect you. I can't—not anymore. Not like I used to."

Bobby's green eyes clouded over, growing dark and sad and weary. Being Johnny Angel had been one of the most exhilarating times in my grandfather's life, and he still missed it.

"Don't worry, Grandfather," I said, holding up my new bracelet. "I've got plenty of protection— enough to blow most of the city to smithereens. If Hangman or Prism comes anywhere near me, they'll get a nasty surprise, one they won't recover from."

Of course, the down side was I probably wouldn't recover either. No matter how lucky I was.

In the end, I convinced the others to let me stay home. Carmen and Lulu left to go back to the F5 library to further analyze the blueprints, leaving Grandfather and me alone in the house—albeit with an open line to the superheroes. Lulu rigged up some device so that all we had to do was whisper the word *help* anywhere in the house, and the Fearless Five would get the message and come immediately.

The rest of the day passed uneventfully, though. No ubervillains crashed through the front door. No laser burned the house to the ground. No one made threatening phone calls telling me to give up the sapphire or else. All I got were the usual insistent requests from Kelly Caleb and the city's other reporters for an exclusive interview on my horrific kidnapping and heroic rescue.

Johnny also called that afternoon.

"Hi, Johnny," I said into the receiver.

"How did you know it was me?" My brother's familiar voice filled my ear.

"Caller ID, of course. Your cell phone number popped up on the screen. Besides, Grandfather said you were going to call."

"Well, I had to check up on my baby sister." Johnny turned to more serious matters. "How are you, Bella? I know the last few days must have been rough, especially for you. Do you want me to come home?"

Johnny knew how much I hated the whole superhero-ubervillain lifestyle. He'd seen the stress I was under waiting up for my father and the toll it had taken on me over the years. But instead of pretending Angel didn't exist, Johnny had gone a different route—he'd refused to take over being Angel from my father. It was the only thing the two of them had ever fought about. Like me, Johnny hadn't wanted any part of heroes and villains. At least, not until our father had been murdered. That's when my brother had suited up as Angel and gone out to track down his killers.

Now, Johnny occasionally roamed the streets as Angel, usually to watch Fiona's back when she was out being Fiera. He liked the rush of being a sometimes hero, but he wasn't obsessed with it like our father had been. I was glad Johnny wasn't going to turn Angel into a full-time hobby, but I still worried about him on the nights he did go out.

"No, don't come home," I said. "Stay. Finish up your business, and enjoy your vacation."

"Are you sure?" Johnny persisted.

"Yes, I'm sure. I'm fine now. Physically, at least."

"Why do you say that?"

I bit my lip, wishing I hadn't said anything.

"Come on, Bella," Johnny wheedled. "Tell me what's wrong. This is your big brother here."

I sighed. I'd never been good at hiding things, especially from Johnny. He knew me better than anyone. "I sort of . . . met someone."

"That's great, Bella. Although I'll have to meet him before I give him the official big brother seal of approval," Johnny joked.

"There's a problem. He's a superhero. More or less."

"Ah." Johnny's voice rang with understanding. "That complicates things, doesn't it? Especially for you."

"Doesn't it always?" I sniped.

"So, how serious is it?"

I hesitated. I wanted to tell Johnny it wasn't serious at all. That it had been a one-time lapse of judgment on my part and nothing else. But for some reason, I couldn't do that. I might be good at pretending things weren't exactly what they seemed, but I tried not to out-and-out lie to myself. "I don't know. It's too soon to tell."

"Well, superhero or not, he better treat you right. Or he'll have to answer to me," Johnny said. "And Angel."

An image of Johnny mowing down Debonair with his motorcycle flashed through my mind. My brother beating up the man I'd slept with. That was just what I needed. Not. It was definitely time to change the subject.

"So, where are you at now? Are you having fun?"

"We're having a wonderful time. We flew into Athens today. Fiona did a little sightseeing, while I met with some of our investors. Now, we're back at the hotel. We just ordered room service."

Dishes clinked and rattled in the background. "You mean Fiona ordered room service. How many meals did she get this time? Ten? Fifteen? Or everything on the menu times three?"

Johnny just laughed.

That night after dinner and a long bath, I sat at the window seat in the hall, sketch pad and charcoal pencil in hand. A cool breeze skipped through the open window, fluttering the white lace curtains and kissing my face. I stared outside at the orchard below. Moonlight streamed through the leaves and branches, making them seem as though they'd been dipped in silver. A few birds called to each other in the trees, while squirrels and rabbits chattered from their hiding places in the tall grass.

Dozens of drawings littered the cushioned seat and floor around me, but they weren't of the garden or the impressive view below. They were of him.

Debonair.

I couldn't get him out of my mind. His voice. His lips. His touch. I might not be in the Lair of Seduction anymore, but in a way, I was still his prisoner—helpless to stop thinking about him. Helpless to stop wondering where he was, what he was doing. So, I'd spent the last two hours doing sketch after sketch, as if that would help me make sense of these strange feelings I'd developed for the sexy thief.

My nose twitched. The smell of roses filled the air, and I knew he was here. Watching me.

"Hello, Debonair," I said in a quiet voice, and put down my pencil.

He stood in the shadows along one side of the hall, his eyes glowing in the darkness. My eyes traced over his muscled form from head to toe. My power flared, and I remembered all the delicious things he'd done to my body—and I'd done to his. For once, I didn't mind the static sensation. Or the fact my hair was about two feet tall.

"What are you doing here?" I asked, my heart smashing against my ribs.

He stepped closer. The moonlight hit his hair, making it gleam. The color of his eyes intensified to the bluest blue I'd ever seen. His gaze was much more powerful than an ubervillain's laser could ever be.

"I wanted to make sure you were okay. I've been looking for you for hours now."

"I was with the Fearless Five," I explained, hating myself for reassuring him. "They checked me out and made sure everything was all right. There's nothing wrong with me."

He let out a breath, as if he'd been holding it in with worry. "That's good. I'm glad you're okay."

I didn't offer up any more information, and he didn't ask me any more questions. Instead, Debonair shifted on his feet, as if unsure of himself. Gone was the cocky, self-assured thief I'd first encountered. In his place was someone I didn't quite recognize. Maybe he didn't know what to make of our night of passion any more than I did. The thought gave me hope.

His eyes fell on the drawings on the floor, and he picked up one.

"What's this?" he asked, his eyes scanning the paper.

I snatched the drawing away from him, hating the fact he'd seen it. That he knew how much he'd affected me. How much he still affected me. Even now, after everything that had happened, I wanted to reach for him. To press my lips to his. To lose myself in his embrace. Somehow, the thief had stolen away all of my reason, my logic, my sensibilities. And I liked it. More than I would have thought possible.

But my feelings didn't change the fact he was one of them—another super-something-or-other who dressed up in leather and roamed the streets. I could never be with him—not again. I could never have a relationship with someone who would eventually get himself killed. I'd gone through that heartbreak with my father. I wasn't going to go through it again. Not even for someone as sexy as Debonair.

The thief snapped his fingers, and the drawing popped out of my hand and back into his.

"That's not fair," I muttered, crossing my arms over my chest.

He gave me a sly smile, seeming a bit more like his rakish, charming self. "Whoever said life was fair?"

He studied the drawing, then picked up several more from the floor. "What's not fair is you keeping these to yourself, Bella. You have a remarkable gift. Your work should be in all the museums in Bigtime."

"Why? So somebody like you could steal it?"

He drew nearer. The silver and black rings around his irises shimmered in the faint light. "The only thing I steal, Bella, is kisses. And I find that most of those are freely given."

Just the sound of his husky voice made my fingers itch.

Suddenly, he was holding me, and we were kissing. His lips, his tongue, his touch. He overwhelmed me. I found myself kissing him as frantically as he did me. I moaned as his hands roamed over my body, igniting all sorts of hot feelings that made me want to melt into the floor—and drag him down with me.

But I couldn't stop the nagging feeling he was using me. Again.

"No," I said, breaking off the kiss and pushing him away. "I don't want to be just another couple of notches on your belt. Or sex handcuffs or whatever you use to keep track of all the women you've slept with."

"You're not another notch to me," he protested. "I don't do that sort of thing."

I barked out a laugh. "Please. You're Debonair. One of the most notorious rogues in all of Bigtime. Seducing women is what you do. You've practically made it an art form."

A sad smile curved his lips. "You don't understand, Bella. Things aren't always what they seem."

"So you don't go around kissing random women then?"

"Oh no. I do that. It's sort of part of my job." He didn't sound the least bit apologetic about it.

"And, of course, the kissing naturally leads to other things."

"Are you jealous, Bella? You have no reason to be. There's no other woman for me but you."

My heart leapt at the words, but I forced myself to be calm. He might have come here tonight to check on me, but he probably thought he could get lucky again too. I knew a thing or two about luck—all kinds of luck.

"What are you saying?" I asked, trying not to sound too eager or hopeful. "That you want to go steady or something? If so, you're out of luck."

"What about the other night?" he asked, looming over me in the darkness.

I put a hand on his chest, stopping him from coming any closer. "The other night was an aberration, nothing more. I wasn't myself, and you were. Let's just chalk it up as one big mistake. I don't date superheroes or ubervillains or anyone who wears a leather mask late at night. I've told you that before."

Debonair arched an eyebrow. "Why not? Most women enjoy that sort of thing. The mystery, the leather, the, ah, superpowers."

"You would know, wouldn't you?" I snapped.

Debonair looked away and sighed. "How can I get you to believe me when I tell you that I'm not the playboy you think I am? That I do have feelings for you?"

"Tell me who you really are."

His eyes widened. Fear and panic shimmered in the blue depths. "I can't do that. You know I can't do that."

"Why not? I won't tell anybody your real identity. I promise. Trust me. I'm good at keeping those kinds of secrets."

Fiona and the other members of the Fearless Five could testify to that. Actually, my whole family could back up my statement.

Debonair mumbled something.

"What was that?" I asked.

He stared at me. "I can't tell you who I really am because you won't feel the same way about me as you do about Debonair." Bitterness tinged his voice.

"How do you know what I'll think of the real you?"

He looked away. "I just know."

I stared at him. "I do know you, don't I? I know who you are, the real you. Do you think I'm that shallow? That I won't like you just because you're not wearing a sexy costume?"

He gave me a sad smile. "I know it. And that's the problem, Bella. I'm not who you think I am. Not really. Not at all actually. This is just a disguise, a show. Nothing else. It's not the real me, just someone I like to pretend that I am."

I wondered at his words. He sounded so alone, so forlorn, I wanted to reach out to him, to tell him it didn't matter who he was underneath all the leather, that I'd like him anyway. But I couldn't do that. I had to stick to my rules. Had to be strong. Had to resist the temptation in front of me.

Debonair pressed a kiss to the inside of my wrist. My pulse thrummed in response. Suddenly, I didn't want him to go. I wanted him to stay. With me. If only to talk. Or do nothing at all. I opened my mouth to ask him to when—

POP!

He teleported away.

Leaving me alone.

Again.

20

The next day, I'd planned to go to the museum to check on the damage. But Bobby didn't want me to go anywhere because of Hangman, and I agreed to spend one more day at home.

The doorbell rang around nine o'clock, just as Grandfather and I finished up a late breakfast of whole wheat waffles, low-fat turkey bacon, and fresh grapefruit.

"Who could that be?" I asked, nervous.

"Don't worry, Bella," Bobby said, getting to his feet. "Hangman wouldn't be so considerate as to ring the bell."

He had a point. Ubervillains didn't usually knock when they stormed into your house. Superheroes didn't either. In fact, the front gate still creaked from where Fiera had ripped it off its hinges a few months ago when she'd decided to pay us a visit in the middle of the night.

Still, I didn't let Grandfather go to the door alone. I might have been scared of Hangman, but I wasn't about to let Bobby risk his life defending me.

Bobby made his way to the front door and reached for the knob.

"Wait a minute. Aren't you even going to look out and see who is it?" I asked, coming up behind him and trying to squint through the curtains.

Bobby gave me an amused look. "You worry too much, Bella. It's not Hangman. Even if it were, I doubt a simple door would stop him."

He had another point, but I wasn't about to take any chances. So, I grabbed a tall black umbrella from the silver stand by the door and held it out like a sword, ready to shove the heavy point into someone's stomach. An umbrella wasn't a traditional weapon, but in my hands, just about anything could be deadly. After all, I was the woman who could make steel pots explode and chandeliers fall just by looking at them. Besides, if the umbrella didn't scare off Hangman, my out-to-there hair surely would.

Bobby shook his head and opened the door. To my surprise, Joanne James and Berkley Brighton stood outside.

"Bella, darling!" Joanne said, swooping on me like a perfumed, couture-clad vulture. "How are you?"

"I'm fine." I twitched my nose to keep from sneezing.

Joanne air kissed both my cheeks and stepped back. Her eyes flicked to the umbrella, then back outside. Sunlight flooded the hall where we stood, warming my toes through my thick wool socks.

My face flushed, and I stuck the umbrella back in the stand by the door. At least, I tried to. The static crackled around me. Every time I attempted to slide the umbrella back into place, the tip caught on the edge and made a loud, earsplitting clang. The third time I tried, the umbrella popped open and refused to close. Finally, I gave up and tossed the open umbrella outside. The wind picked it up and carried it farther down the driveway. I glared at the hateful thing. The umbrella could stay out there for all I cared, along with those stupid apples I hadn't been able to find.

"How are you really, Bella?" Berkley asked in a kind, concerned tone once I'd shut the door. The short businessman came over and gave me a quick hug.

"I'm really fine, Berkley. But thanks for asking." I stepped back and smiled at him. "What brings you two here?"

"Why you, of course," Joanne said, as if the answer should be obvious.

I opened my mouth, but Joanne had already gone on the offensive. She moved farther into the house like it was hers instead of ours. I looked at Grandfather. He just grinned and shrugged. Grandfather had always had a thing for strong, take-charge women. Berkley smiled too, amused by his wife's antics.

The three of us followed Joanne, who strolled into the downstairs living room. She plopped on the love seat in the corner and patted the cloud-covered cushion next to her. Berkley gracefully took that spot. He put his arm around her shoulders, and Joanne leaned back against his chest.

Grandfather took a seat on the matching couch—the same couch I'd found him on with Grace Caleb yesterday. I started to sit down, but thought better of it. Instead, I perched on the edge of the coffee table. I wasn't sitting on that couch again. At least, not until I'd had it reupholstered.

"Can I get you anything?" I asked the couple. "Coffee? Tea? Juice?"

"No, thanks," Joanne said. "We can't stay long. We have a lunch date."

"Oh? With whom?" I asked.

Joanne looked up into Berkley's face and smiled. "With each other."

She snuggled a little closer to him, and I thought back to the day I'd found them making out in the library. I hoped they weren't going to give me a repeat show. Otherwise, I'd have to have that love seat reupholstered too. Given how amorous Fiona and Johnny were, I might as well do the whole house while I was at it.

"We just wanted to come by and see how you were, Bella," Berkley replied, his blue eyes catching mine. "It couldn't have been easy for you, being caught between the Fearless Five and Hangman at the museum."

"It certainly wasn't easy for us, realizing the sapphire had been taken," Joanne added. "I'm just glad my velvet Elvis painting was locked away in the vault. Otherwise, it might have been damaged like so many of the other pieces were."

My eyes widened. With everything that had been going on, I'd completely forgotten about Berkley. And the fact he was probably wondering what had happened to his prize possession.

"I'm so, so sorry. I should have called you. The sapphire—"

Berkley waved his hand. "Don't worry. I've already had several conversations with my insurance people. Not that it matters anymore. I got a call this morning from the Fearless Five. They recovered the sapphire and plan on returning it to the museum. So, all's well that ends well."

I let out a quiet sigh of relief. Sam Striker Sloane had probably made the call. At least he'd had the sense to remember to. But there was another question that needed answering.

"Are you going to leave the gem on display?"

Berkley opened his mouth, but Joanne cut him off.

"Well, *I* think he should have it shipped back to Brilliance where it belongs," she grumbled. "Where it'll be safe."

Berkley squeezed her arm. "Now, Joanne, you know we can't do that. The whole point was to let other people see the stone and to raise money for the museum. They'll need the money now more than ever. Arthur Anders has assured me that he'll take appropriate measures to increase security. The important thing is that no one was injured. If I'd been there, I would have gladly given Hangman the sapphire to keep him from harming Bella or anyone else."

My throat closed up, and I couldn't speak. Berkley had always been so kind to me. Most men would have been yelling and screaming and demanding their property be returned immediately after the fiasco at the museum. Instead, Berkley was willing to risk the loss of the sapphire again. Of course, it didn't hurt that Berkley could afford to buy a dozen Star Sapphires. But his generosity still touched me.

"Thank you, Berkley," I said, leaning over and squeezing his hand. "I'm sure Arthur appreciates your trust and good faith. I know I do."

"No problem, Bella." Berkley cleared his throat and looked at Bobby. "Although, I have to admit my interest isn't entirely selfless. I've been thinking about adding another motorcycle to my collection—if I can talk your grandfather into building it for me."

Bobby winked. "Of course. What are friends for?"

We all laughed.

Talk turned to other things, mainly a business deal Berkley wanted to propose to Johnny when he and Fiona got back from their vacation.

While the others chatted, I stared at Berkley and Joanne. The two of them had sunk into the soft cushions on the love seat, but they didn't seem to mind. Their hands were entwined, their bodies flush against each other. They were as close as they could be and still have clothes on.

They looked so happy together, so comfortable, so in love.

It was hard to believe Joanne could care about anyone besides herself, but her affection for Berkley was real. I could see it in her eyes every time she looked at him. Sense it in the way she hovered close to him. Hear it in her voice when she said his name.

The sight made me think about Debonair. I wondered if I looked and acted the same way whenever I was around the sexy thief. And I couldn't help wishing he would gaze at me the same adoring way Berkley did at Joanne.

"Well, I'm afraid we must be going," Berkley said, interrupting my thoughts. "Like Joanne said, we do have a lunch date."

He brought her hand to his lips and placed a soft kiss on her knuckles. Joanne let out a squeaky noise that sounded suspiciously like a giggle. Joanne James, giggling? I never thought I'd live to hear that.

The two of them got to their feet. Bobby followed suit, and so did I.

At least, I tried to.

Perhaps it was all my thoughts of Debonair. Or maybe it was just time for another round of bad luck. Either way, my power pulsed. I started to get up, but my feet skidded on the shag carpet and slid out from under me. My butt plopped down on the coffee table—hard. The solid wood let out a low groan, the legs shook, and the top split down the middle.

The table collapsed and splintered into a hundred pieces. Bits of wood shot out everywhere, pinging off the walls and tinkling off the ceiling fan. I knew because I was now flat on my back, staring up at the spinning fan.

"Bella!" Bobby asked, leaning over me. "Are you all right?"

"Sure," I wheezed. "We needed to get a new table anyway."

Joanne and Berkley left soon after that. People just never stayed around after I had one of my accidents. It took me over an hour to clean up the remains of the coffee table, then another one to fix the mess I'd made cleaning that up.

By the time I'd finished, it was lunchtime, and I decided to take a much-needed break. So, I walked out to the orchard behind the house. It wasn't nearly as big as the acres of gardens out at Sublime, but I admired its quiet beauty just the same. Pear, orange, and other trees towered over me like silent giants. A faint breeze whistled through the grove, rustling the dry leaves and sending them twirling downward like tiny helicopters.

I leaned back against a pear tree and shut my eyes against the bright glow of the noon sun. Birds twittered in the branches above, while a few bugs droned in the distance. The cool air smelled of damp leaves and turned earth.

Something crawled across my hand, and I brushed away an ant without even opening my eyes. Determined to have a nice, normal, peaceful lunch, I'd brought a blanket, my sketch pad, and some picnic goodies outside to the orchard. But, of course, my luck decided to assert itself. The plastic plates shattered, splattering me, the blanket, and the surrounding grass with low-fat, sugar-free fruit salad. It really was amazing how far strawberries could bounce, especially considering the fact they weren't exactly round. My pulverized food had attracted the attention of a colony of ants. But since they seemed content to carry off pulpy bits of orange and pineapple and not swarm all over me, I left them alone.

My fingers traced over the soft, fleecy blanket. The fabric reminded me of Debonair's skin—only it wasn't as smooth and warm. For the last hour, I'd tried to concentrate on my sketches, tried to draw the beauty around me, but I kept thinking about the sexy thief and what he'd said last night. His fear that I wouldn't like the real him as much as I did Debonair.

His confession had surprised me. Most superhero and ubervillain types were cocky to the extreme, especially the villains. They thought just because they could walk on water or stride through fire or scale skyscrapers that nothing could ever hurt or touch or bother them.

But Debonair seemed to have more of a split personality than the other heroes and villains I'd encountered. On more than one occasion, he'd seemed almost unsure of himself, hesitant even. I didn't understand why. He was charming and witty, and women of all ages threw themselves at him. I didn't understand his insecurities, whatever they were.

Maybe he thought the idea of Debonair, the memory of our night together, would cloud things between us if he told me who he really was. Maybe it would. I didn't know.

But I really wanted to find out.

I checked my watch. Later. I was going to have to find out later, because I had things to do right now. I got to my feet and picked up the bits of fruit the ants hadn't carried off. While I worked, another breeze blew through the orchard, bringing something along with it this time—the umbrella I'd tossed out the door this morning. Mouth open, I watched as the umbrella bobbed up and down on the breeze like an oddly shaped kite. But that wasn't the weirdest thing. The umbrella was still open—and filled with apples. I narrowed my eyes. Apples that looked suspiciously like the ones I'd lost during the trick-or-treat incident a few days ago.

The breeze died down, and the umbrella floated to a stop at my feet, its point sticking into the ground just so.

"Well, call me Mary freaking Poppins," I muttered.

For dinner with Bobby and Grace Caleb, I chose a short, simple, emerald-colored dress that set off my caramel-colored hair and eyes, and I fastened my silver angel necklace around my throat. Jasper's bombastic bracelet hung off my right wrist. I hadn't taken it off since the bomber had given it to me. Not even when I took a shower.

There'd been no sign of Hangman or Prism, and I didn't think I was in any real danger anymore. Everyone knew the Fearless Five had the Star Sapphire and were going to return it to the museum. SNN had run a special report on the latest developments, with Kelly Caleb reading a press release from the superheroes on the evening broadcast. But the way my luck went, the second I decided I didn't need the bracelet would be the exact moment the ubervillains came after me. So I kept it on.

The doorbell rang promptly at eight. Grandfather answered it and led Grace Caleb into the downstairs living room, where I waited. Grace looked elegant in a pale lilac flowered dress that highlighted her silver hair and blue eyes. For once, she wasn't wearing a sweater. Instead, a lavender shawl wrapped around her bare shoulders, while an egg-sized amethyst hung from her throat. A matching purple handbag dangled from her arm, which was rather well muscled for a woman in her seventies.

But Grace wasn't alone.

Devlin Dash trailed into the room behind her. He wore a classic tuxedo just like Grandfather, although he kept tugging at his tie as if it was strangling him. The gleam from his round glasses made it look like there were two silver coins where his eyes should be.

"Grace," Bobby said, kissing her hand. "You are truly a vision."

Grace's eyes slid down my grandfather's body in a frank, rather hungry way that startled me. "So are you, Bobby."

He leaned in and whispered something in her ear. Grace giggled in response. I looked at Devlin, who kept yanking at his tie. He avoided my eyes. Bobby cooed more sweet nothings into Grace's eager ear.

"Ahem."

I cleared my throat, reminding them that there were other people in the room. I didn't want a repeat of yesterday's couch incident. That image, unfortunately, would be seared into my brain for many, *many* days to come.

"Hello, Bella," Grace said. "You look wonderful tonight."

"Grace. So do you. It's so nice to see you again." I wanted to add *wearing clothes*, but decided not to.

"And of course you know my grandson, Devlin," Grace said, stepping aside.

Devlin held out his hand, which I took. He started to raise it to his lips for a chaste kiss but decided against it in midflight. Devlin settled for covering my hand with his other one and squeezing it. His fingers bit into my skin, and I winced at his firm grip.

"Oh! Sorry," Devlin said in a sheepish tone. He dropped my hand as if it had burned him. "I don't know my own strength sometimes."

I grimaced and tried not to wring out my hand in front of him. I wouldn't have thought he'd have such a strong grip. Devlin didn't strike me as the athletic type. Strange. Very strange.

I didn't have time to wonder at Devlin's sudden show of machismo. Bobby offered Grace his arm and escorted her into the dining room. Devlin did the same for me.

"You look lovely, Bella," he said in a low voice. "That color really suits you."

"Thank you, Devlin. You look very handsome as well."

He surprised me again by not stuttering or stammering. For a change. And then there was the fact he complimented me at all. I'd never known Devlin to pay too much attention to women or what they were wearing. Or for women to pay much attention to him. Most of the ladies on the society circuit fawned and drooled over the suave playboys. Devlin wasn't one of them. Oh, he was handsome enough in his own right, but he didn't have the polish of a Sam Sloane or Nate Norris, or the obscene wealth of a Berkley Brighton. In Bigtime, there was rich and handsome, and then there was superrich and superhandsome. Devlin fell into the first two categories.

We entered the dining room, and Devlin pulled out my chair. I flashed back to my time with Debonair and how he'd done the exact same thing. I sat down on the seat.

And then, Devlin shoved me into the table.

It wasn't completely his fault. My luck decided to pulse at that exact moment, and the chair slid forward a foot more than it should have, pinning me against the table. The heavy wood dug into my breasts, knocking the air out of my lungs.

"Oh! Sorry!" Devlin said.

I scooted my chair back so I could actually breathe. "Don't worry about it," I wheezed.

Devlin sat across from me, his cheeks red from his latest social fiasco. Grace settled in a chair next to him, while Bobby took the one beside me.

Bobby wanted to impress Grace, so he'd had dinner catered in from Quicke's. Several elegant warming platters perched on the table, along with candles encased in hurricane lanterns and a cornucopia stuffed full of fresh fruit and fall leaves.

Bobby removed the tops from the dishes, and I stared at the exposed food in alarm. Chicken Marsala topped with a boatload of Parmesan cheese, toasted garlic bread, a Caesar salad, fried eggplant and zucchini, broiled tomatoes, three bottles of red wine, and an angel food cake topped with strawberries and chocolate frosting. It was a heart attack waiting to happen, especially for Bobby.

"Grandfather," I said in a warning tone. "You know what the doctor says about your cholesterol and blood pressure. They're both far too high for you to eat like this."

"Bah! Doctors, what do they know?" Bobby waved his hand. "Besides, we're having guests tonight, Bella. We must make a good impression on them."

Guests. My grandfather used this same excuse whenever we had company, no matter who it was. He'd once served the cable guy a three-course meal just for installing a new soccer channel. The next day, when the plumber came, he'd gotten similar treatment. The gardener, the pool guy, the electrician. Every time the doorbell rang, Bobby was waiting with food for everyone—and a substantial serving set aside for himself. Grandfather even insisted that Fiona was still company. He knew it was the only way he could get away with eating all the things he wanted to—none of which were good for him.

I was tempted to use my power to make Bobby drop his fork or even his plate on the floor, but I didn't want to embarrass him in front of Grace and Devlin. Besides, whenever I tried to use my power like that, I always ended up with egg on my face—literally. So I resisted the urge. But just barely.

Bobby clapped his hands together. "Come! Let's eat before it gets cold!"

We dug in to the hearty spread. Everything was just as wonderful as it looked. The chicken was fork-tender, the bread seasoned just so, and every bite of the cake was a little bit of heaven in my mouth. I'd have to spend two hours on the elliptical trainer tomorrow to burn off all the fat and calories, but it was worth a little sin tonight. I thought of Debonair. He would have approved of all this. Reveled in it.

Dinner was quite pleasant, especially since I didn't have to worry about floating wineglasses or other superpowered displays. Grace was as witty and charming as ever, in addition to being a good sport. She responded to my grandfather's bawdy jokes with some of her own that were even more risqué. Maybe there was a little bit of steel underneath that soft, flowery façade after all.

Devlin stayed quiet for most of the meal, as was his way, I supposed. I tried to engage him in conversation a couple of times, asking about DCQ, his business. He answered my questions in monosyllables and stared at the half-eaten food on his plate. Every once in a while, I thought I saw him sneaking glances at me, but I couldn't be sure. Besides, it wasn't like there were a lot of people around the table to look at.

An hour later, we pushed back our chairs. Grace tucked her arm into Bobby's and whispered something into his ear. It might have been a trick of the light, but I thought my grandfather blushed. And he never did that. If one of them blushed, it should have been Grace. She was the sweet old lady in the relationship. My grandfather was the former hellion.

"If you'll excuse us, children, I'm going to take Grace on a tour of the house," Bobby said. "We'll be back in ten—"

Grace put her heel into his instep.

"Make that twenty minutes," Bobby corrected. "Give or take a few. These old bones aren't quite as quick as they used to be. Arthritis, you know."

I narrowed my eyes. My grandfather hadn't looked like he was suffering from arthritis yesterday.

Grace gave me an angelic smile, as though she hadn't just crushed my grandfather's foot—and wasn't about to give him a coronary episode with her sexual skills. Maybe the older woman had a little more hellion in her than I'd given her credit for. Maybe a lot more.

The two of them moved down the hall and rounded a corner. A second later, feet pounded away, as though they were running. Probably racing toward Bobby's bedroom, I thought in a petulant mood. At least someone was going to get lucky tonight. I'd been hoping Debonair would *pop!* into the house again today, but I hadn't seen—or smelled—the sexy thief.

"They're quite a pair, aren't they?" Devlin murmured.

"Yes, they are."

"It's good to see Grams so happy."

"Grams?" I asked.

"It's my nickname for her."

"The two of you seem very close."

Devlin nodded. "My parents died in a boating accident when I was a kid. Grams took me in and raised me."

I reached over and squeezed his hand. "That must have been rough. My mother died when I was a child too. But I still had my father and grandfather, although my dad passed away earlier this year."

The pain of my mother's loss was a familiar, small, dull ache. But it hurt to think about my father. I was still so angry with him for leaving us. For trying to be a hero. For putting that before everything else, including his family.

"I remember," Devlin said. "I came to the funeral."

"Did you? I'm sorry, but I don't really remember that day."

It had passed in a painful, hazy blur of tears and sobs and sniffles.

"You never called me after that," he said in a soft voice.

"Excuse me?"

"You never called me, after the funeral."

I frowned, confused. "Was I supposed to?"

Devlin tugged at his tie. "We went to dinner a couple of days before your father died. You, um, said you'd call me later in the week."

And I remembered. We'd been finishing up the details of an art auction we'd chaired together, and we'd gone to Quicke's for dinner afterward. From what I remembered, the evening had been nice enough—until my cell phone rang. My dinner with Devlin hadn't been a couple of days before my father had died—it had been the night he'd died. The night he'd been murdered.

I'd been out with Devlin when Grandfather called, worried he couldn't find my father anywhere. For weeks after that, I'd beaten myself up—thinking I should have stayed home. Thinking I might have somehow saved my father or at least kept him

from going out as Johnny Angel. That maybe even my luck
would have kicked in and spared him.

"I'm so sorry," I said. "I completely forgot with everything
that happened."

"Forget it," Devlin said. "It was silly of me to bring it up
now."

We stood there, not quite looking at each other. I glanced at
the angel-shaped clock on the wall. We had another seventeen
minutes before Grandfather and Grace were supposed to come
back from their rendezvous. What were we supposed to talk
about until then? Even though we'd had dinner together, I barely
knew Devlin. And why would he remind me now that I was
supposed to have called him months ago? That was just weird.

Thankfully, the businessman broke the silence.

"Actually, I wanted to give you this before I forgot." Devlin
pulled a check out of the inside of his tuxedo. "Since the one at
the benefit fell to pieces."

I took the piece of paper from him. Our fingers brushed,
and a certain sort of warmth traveled up my fingertips that
had nothing to do with static electricity or bad luck. At least, I
didn't think it did. I couldn't be attracted to Devlin Dash, could
I? Uncomfortable, I turned my gaze to the check, which had
several zeroes on it.

My eyes locked on the signature. I froze, afraid my eyes
were playing tricks on me. But they weren't. Because no matter
how many times I blinked, no matter how hard I squinted, it
was still there. A big D with an illegible scrawl trailing along
behind it. I'd seen that signature only once before. On a drawing
I had smoothed out on the desk in my room.

The drawing I'd done of Debonair.

Debonair.

Who was really Devlin Dash.

★ 21 ★

I couldn't speak. Couldn't move. Couldn't even form a coherent thought. I stared at the check, my eyes not really seeing it anymore.

"Is something wrong?" Devlin asked in a concerned tone. "You look pale. Do you need to sit down?"

"No, no, I'm fine," I lied, snapping out of my daze. "I was just a little surprised by the, ah, amount of your donation. It's very generous."

Devlin shrugged. "Not really. I'm sure twenty-five thousand dollars is just pocket change compared to what you raised at the benefit."

"Oh no. Not at all. Besides, the museum will need every penny since it was damaged by that awful ubervillain."

Devlin fiddled with his glasses. "Of course. I read about that in the papers and saw it on SNN. It truly was a tragedy. I hope the police or the Fearless Five manage to catch the villain who's responsible quickly."

He'd done more than just read about it or watch it on TV. He'd been there, right alongside me. I opened my mouth to call him on it, to demand some sort of explanation, when a voice wafted down the hall.

"But why do you have to go *now*? I thought we were having a nice time," Bobby said in a somewhat petulant tone.

Our grandparents appeared. Some of Grace's hair had come loose from its sleek do, and Bobby's tie and shirt looked rumpled. I peered at him. Was that pink lipstick on his collar? My grandfather, the seducer. He was getting as bad as Debonair in his old age.

"What's going on?" I asked.

Grace held up a small cell phone. "I'm afraid I have an emergency. I need to leave immediately."

"What sort of emergency?" Devlin asked.

She looked at her grandson. "A family emergency. Kelly's sick and needs someone to come get her from work."

"What's wrong with her?" I asked. "I just saw her on the news this afternoon. She looked fine."

Kelly Caleb had also called me earlier in the day demanding an exclusive interview, along with the other newshounds. I'd refused them all.

"Nothing serious. Just a case of the flu," Grace said, her blue eyes not quite meeting mine. "But I want to go make sure she's okay. I'm a bit of a worrier, especially when it comes to Kelly. The station works her to death, and her immune system isn't what it should be."

I didn't understand why Kelly couldn't just have a cab take her home, but Grace's plea must have meant something to Devlin, because he nodded his head in understanding. The two of them said their goodbyes and left less than a minute later.

"That was really weird," I said, shaking my head and locking the door behind them. "Did you do something to upset her?"

Bobby gave me an offended look and loosened his tie the rest of the way. "Of course not. We were having a very stimulating evening, if you must know. We were having a wonderful time—until her cell phone rang."

I thought of Johnny and Fiona. When the two of them were first dating, my brother used to complain about how Fiona's cell phone would always ring at the worst possible moment. She always had to rush off to her store to take care of some emergency. Of course, there were no emergencies—not at her store anyway. The flimsy excuses had been part of her cover as Fiera, a member of the Fearless Five, and a way for her teammates to contact her if they needed her help.

I wondered if Grace was doing the same thing. Using the phone as a way of swapping supersecret messages for Devlin— or even herself. I knew Devlin was Debonair, but who on earth could Grace Caleb be masquerading as? She didn't strike me as the superhero type. Then again, neither had Devlin. And if Grace was a superhero, wouldn't she be upset her grandson was on the other side of the law? Maybe, maybe not. Maybe she was an ubervillain herself. Or maybe she just didn't know he was really Debonair. There were just too many *maybes* right now.

I pushed those thoughts away and concentrated on my current crisis. "I'm actually glad they're gone."

"Why? Don't you like Grace?" Bobby's face fell a little more.

"Grace is just fine. But there's a problem with her grandson. A big one."

We went into the kitchen. Bobby sat down and listened while I told him my theory about Devlin Debonair Dash. He glanced at the check, then at the drawing I'd retrieved from my room.

"The signature looks the same," he admitted. "But are you sure, Bella?"

I let out a long breath. "As sure as I can be right now. I'm going to get Carmen and Lulu to help me verify it in the morning."

"I see." Bobby gave me a sidelong glace. "You like him, don't you?"

"What? Of course not." I crossed my arms over my chest.

"Bah! You think these eyes are too old to see what's right in front of them. But they're not. You like this Debonair, don't you? There's no shame in it. From what I've seen and heard, he's a handsome fellow. And Devlin seemed nice enough at dinner."

I never could get anything past my grandfather. So, I nodded. "In a weird way, I do. But things could never work out between us."

"Why not?"

I looked at him. "You know why. I don't like superheroes. I'm certainly not going to date one."

"Ah, Bella. When are you going to get over this dislike, this prejudice of yours? Superheroes and ubervillains are a part of our lives. They always have been, and they always will be. You should be proud to be a part of it, not ashamed."

If there was one sore subject between my grandfather and me, this was definitely it.

"I'm not ashamed. I'm just tired of it," I snapped. "Do you

know how many nights I would lie awake and wonder if you and Dad were coming home? If I'd get up the next morning and read in the newspaper about how some ubervillains killed Johnny Angel? Do you know what that did to me? To my mother?"

"Being Johnny Angel was something I had to do. Your father understood, and so did your mother," Bobby said in a defensive tone.

"Why?" I asked, getting defensive myself. "I never understood *why* you had to do it. You didn't have any powers. You weren't even a real superhero."

Grandfather's face jerked, as though I'd slapped him. "I wasn't a superhero, no. I couldn't do fantastic things just by thinking about them. I wasn't incredible in any way at all. But I was strong and brave and smart, and I helped people." His green eyes glittered. "And that was the most important thing."

"More important than keeping yourself safe for your family?" I snapped, hot tears gathering in my eyes.

"Of course I tried to keep myself safe for you. All of you. But helping others was something I had to do. Something I needed to do to be happy with myself. Someday you'll understand," Bobby said in a gentle tone.

I turned my face away and didn't answer. Grandfather rested his hand on my shoulder. I tensed at his touch.

"Someday you will, Bella," he repeated. "Someday you'll understand why I did what I did. Why I became Johnny Angel. Your father too."

I wiped away my tears. I thought I'd cried all that I could after my father died, but the ghost of Johnny Angel just wouldn't let me be. Not even now.

Grandfather patted my shoulder. "I don't know about you, but this old man needs his rest. Goodnight, Bella."

"Goodnight," I whispered.

Grandfather went off to sneak a cigar he thought I wouldn't know about, and I slumped over the table. I let myself wallow in my misery and self-pity for a full minute before pulling myself back together.

My eyes flicked around the kitchen. Dirty dishes and plates

from dinner covered the countertops. I really should wash them tonight, especially the bowl with the remains of the Chicken Marsala. Otherwise, the stains would never come out. It was busy work, of course, but I needed something to do. Something else to think about besides Debonair and superheroes and my murdered father.

I reached for the closest dish. My power flared, and the plate slid out of my fingers, clattered off the counter, and crashed onto the floor. The dish didn't break, but pasta and sauce oozed over the tiles, as red as blood against the white floor.

Normally, I would have hurried to clean up the mess before it soaked in. Pasta sauce can be a real bitch to get out. But the more I stared at the red goop, the angrier I became. It was bad enough the men in my family felt the need to parade around in black leather, but why did they have to involve me in their schemes? I'd never asked to be part of a superhero family, and I'd certainly never asked to be cursed with an uncontrollable power, one that aggravated me at every turn.

So what if the pasta stained the damn floor? It wouldn't be any worse than all the blood I'd washed out of my father's clothes over the years. At that cheery thought, my power pulsed again, and more plates flew off the countertops, even though I was nowhere near them. Salad, breadsticks, and a carafe of wine joined the Chicken Marsala on the floor.

But I didn't care. For once in my life, I was going to do what I wanted to. And right now, I didn't feel like cleaning up.

I left the growing mess on the kitchen floor and headed for my room, determined to take a hot bath and fall into an oblivious sleep. Maybe tomorrow I'd feel more like my clean-freak self. Maybe tomorrow I could pretend everything was all right again—and not falling to pieces around me.

My bathroom branched off my bedroom and was almost as large. It featured a shower, along with a long counter topped with mirrors, and an old-fashioned claw-foot tub resting on four angel-head feet. I didn't have quite the selection of assorted body oils and exotic bath scents Debonair did, but there was more than enough to meet my needs.

I ran myself a tub full of rose-scented bubbles and sank down into the steaming water. I sighed, long and loud, and rested my head on a folded towel I'd placed on the rim. I was still sore and bruised from my run-in with Hangman, and all the bumps and falls I'd taken in the past week. Not to mention my fight with Grandfather. It was one we'd had many, many times before, but it always left me feeling drained and upset and worn out. I closed my eyes and sank a little farther into the water.

POP!

Debonair appeared on the edge of the bathtub, and I couldn't stop myself from shrieking. My power flared, and somehow, despite my towel, I banged my head against the side of the porcelain. Pain shot up the back of my skull, and my eyes rattled around in their sockets.

"Bella! Are you all right?" Debonair asked, helping me sit up.

I touched the back of my head. A bump the size of a golf ball had already formed, throbbing with every breath I took. "I'll be fine. Eventually."

Debonair's gaze was on me, hot and warm. I realized he was staring at my breasts, which had been exposed when I'd sat up. I scooted back down into the tub and scooped mounds of bubbles around me. Debonair looked amused by my attempts to hide my nakedness.

"What?" I snapped. "You'd do the same thing if the situation were reversed."

Debonair picked up a handful of bubbles and blew them off his leather gloves. "Actually, I wouldn't. I'd be trying to figure out how to get you to join me in the tub."

I thought of what we could do in the tub together, and it didn't involve a rubber ducky. Well, not the traditional kind.

"You shouldn't hide your body, Bella," he continued. "It's quite beautiful."

His words pleased me, but I still slid a little lower into the water. Me being naked anywhere near Debonair was not good. Even being in the same room with him was pushing it.

"You probably think all women are beautiful—even your grandmother."

"Everyone is beautiful in their own right. But in your case, my interest is a little more devious than it would be in my grandmothers." His eyes glowed.

I swallowed hard, trying to ignore a sudden surge that rippled through my body. "How is your grandmother, by the way?"

He frowned in confusion. "She's fine. Why do you ask?"

Because she left in such a hurry. That's what I wanted to say, but I didn't. I didn't want to confront Debonair about his real identity as Devlin Dash. Not yet. Not until I had more proof from Carmen and Lulu. There was still a small chance I was wrong, and I was too sensible to take the risk.

We sat there in silence. I kept sneaking peaks at Debonair's face, comparing it to my memory of Devlin's. It almost certainly had to be him. Same dark hair. Same nice cheekbones. Same straight nose. I couldn't tell about the eyes, though. Not with Devlin's thick glasses on his face. Who would have thought glasses would have been that good of a disguise?

"Well, I suppose I should be on my way. I'll leave you to your bath." He turned to go.

"Wait!"

I didn't want him to go. He was a superhero who'd kept his real identity from me, who'd lied to me. I should hate him, but I didn't. I just . . . couldn't. No matter how hard I tried to pretend otherwise, I was attracted to Devlin Debonair Dash. More than I'd been attracted to anyone in a long, long time. Even if he was a damn superhero.

Debonair turned to face me. "Did you want something, Bella?"

I want you. I bit back the words. I didn't need to get myself in deeper with the handsome thief. But I didn't want to be sensible tonight. Didn't want to play it safe or sane. I wanted to be kissed and held and loved, even if it was by a man whose motives I didn't understand and probably never would.

"No," I said. "But why are you leaving? You just popped in a minute ago."

He stared at me. "Because if I don't go now, I'm going to try to seduce you. And you said before you don't want that. I might be a cad on occasion, but I try to respect a lady's wishes. Every now and then, anyway."

Sure, that's what I said when I was alone and could think and be sensible about things. I wasn't so sure that's what I wanted when I was face-to-face with the most handsome man I'd ever seen—and slept with. So I made a snap decision. One I was probably going to regret in the morning. But I was sure as hell going to enjoy it now. After the day I'd had, I deserved it.

"So seduce me," I said, rising to my feet. "Who knows? I just might enjoy it."

★22★

"Don't tempt me, Bella." Debonair's voice was rough and raw with need.

"Me? Tempt you? I'd never dream of doing such a thing."

I stepped out of the tub and moved closer to him, water and bubbles sliding off my body and making another mess on the floor. The rate I was going, the whole house would be a disaster area by morning.

"Besides," I continued, "you're the one who knows all about seduction. Not me."

His gaze moved up and down my body, searing me with its heat. But he made no move to touch me. Seconds ticked by. Neither one of us so much as twitched. I barely breathed.

Debonair closed his eyes and dropped his head. Well, so much for my grand plan. Obviously, I wasn't quite the mistress of seduction I thought I was. Maybe I should get some pointers from the folks in the Slaves for Superhero Sex club. I started to turn away and cover myself with a towel. But with a low, hoarse growl, Debonair gathered me into his arms and crushed his mouth to mine.

The smell of roses washed over me, and I sighed with pleasure. Debonair pulled me tighter, driving his tongue deep into my mouth before retreating and licking my lips. He pressed kisses to my eyelids, my cheeks, my neck. His gloves disappeared with a snap of his fingers, and his hands covered my breasts. They swelled and tightened in response.

"Do you want me, Bella? Do you burn for me like I burn for you?" he whispered against my breastbone, licking his way down my body.

I writhed against him. Lost in the sensations he stirred up inside me. Urged on by the relentless pressure mounting deep between my thighs.

The feel of his leather suit against my skin drove me crazy with need. My hands clawed at it, and I wished I had the power to teleport it away with my mind. I wanted to touch him. All of him. Feel his hard body pressed up against my own. Feel him moving inside me. Just like he had before.

My power surged, and somehow the fabric of his suit ripped, right over the scarlet rose on his chest. I didn't care. I slid my hand inside the leather, stroking the coarse hair on his solid chest. Debonair shoved aside the bottles of lotions and shampoo on the counter, then picked me up and set me there.

I hooked my leg over his thigh, drawing him closer. He slid his fingers down my damp body, tangling them in the curls at the junction of my thighs. Then—

Someone knocked on the door.

"Bella? Are you okay?" Bobby's voice floated through the thick wood. "I thought I heard something fall."

Debonair kept right on with his exploration of my body, even though my grandfather was standing less than two feet away from us. His mouth teased my nipple, while his nimble fingers danced across my outer folds. My entire body quivered in response. Pleasure rippled through me, and I had to focus on answering my grandfather.

"I'm fine," I rasped out, tangling my fingers in Debonair's dark hair. "I just knocked over a couple of shampoo bottles."

"It sounded like a louder bang than that," Bobby said. "And I heard some noises coming from the kitchen earlier. Are you sure you're okay?"

"I'm fine. I'll be coming out soon," I promised, panting for air.

"Well, all right. I'm going to bed. Call me if you need me."

Muffled footsteps moved away from the door. At least I thought that's what I heard. It was sort of hard to concentrate with Debonair stroking me. I caught his head in my hands and drew his lips up to mine again. Debonair responded by slipping his fingers farther inside me, even as his teeth raked across my lower lip.

I cried out my release in his mouth. But Debonair wasn't satisfied. He kept right on stroking me, until I burned for him once more. Again and again he moved me, until I wasn't sure where I left off and he began. Finally, though, the last shudder of pleasure cascaded through my body. I slumped against his shoulder and wrapped my arms around his neck.

"Well, Bella. If that's how you're going to respond, I think I'll let you seduce me more often," Debonair said in a playful, teasing tone. His eyes sparkled in the faint light.

All I could do was look at him, still too drunk with passion and afterglow to respond. Sometimes, it felt absolutely wonderful to be completely senseless. He pressed a kiss to my temple, then grabbed a towel from a nearby rack and wrapped it around my body.

"Now, go put on some clothes. And be sure to get a heavy jacket."

"Why?" I asked, not wanting to move away from him.

He pulled back and smiled. "Because, Bella, I'm taking you out for a night on the town—Debonair style."

Twenty minutes later, a heavy gray fisherman's sweater covered my body, along with a pair of jeans and black boots with a low, sensible heel. I slid my arms into my favorite black wool pea coat and pulled a pair of fleece-lined gloves onto my hands. Debonair leaned against my dresser, nodding his approval.

"You should be warm enough in that," he said.

"I don't understand," I said. "Why are you doing this? Why do you want to take me out?"

"Because, Bella, I want to spend time with you."

He sounded sincere, but I still had a hard time believing him. He was Debonair. He could have just about any woman in Bigtime he desired. I couldn't quite believe he wanted me, with my horrible hair and thunder thighs. Or that he was actually Devlin Dash under all that blue-black leather.

"But didn't you already get what you wanted the other night when we slept together?"

He smiled. "Of course I did. Didn't you? If it wasn't satisfying enough, maybe we can try something different next time.

Like maybe handcuffs? Or whips and chains? You never did tell me the answer to that question."

I couldn't stop blushing.

"Now, come on." Debonair opened his arms wide.

I hesitated. This was not a good idea on so many levels.

"Please?" he asked, his voice quiet.

But I'd broken so many of my own rules the past few days. What was one more?

So, I stepped into his embrace and inhaled, letting his sweet, musky scent fill my lungs.

"Now, just try to relax," Debonair murmured, gathering me close. "Teleporting can be a bit disorienting. We won't go far until you're more comfortable with it."

POP!

The world dropped away. There was blackness. Wind rushed against my face, further tangling my already snarled hair. The smell of damp, turned earth filled my nose. And then—

POP!

The world righted itself, and I blinked. We stood in the orchard in the backyard underneath the pear tree where I'd had my picnic earlier today.

"Amazing," I said. "I wish I could get where I wanted to go so easily. It'd save me a ton of gas money."

Debonair laughed. The sound warmed me, despite the frosty chill in the air.

"How does your power work?" I asked, for once curious about a superhero. "Can you just teleport anywhere you want?"

Debonair shook his head. "No, I can only teleport to places I've been before. And I can only teleport objects I've seen before. Plus, I have to know their exact location when I want to teleport them to me or to some other place. Otherwise, I would have been able to bring you back to the island when you sailed out into the bay. Or find you once you were in the custody of the Fearless Five."

"I see."

"So, are you ready to try something a bit more challenging?" he asked, smiling. "And fun?"

I nodded and stepped back into his arms.

POP!

Colors and lights dazzled my eyes. People laughed. Kids lets out squeals of joy and excitement. Music trilled in the night air. And then—

POP!

We landed on the main carousel at Paradise Park. I sat on a carved white horse, gliding up and down, while Debonair perched on a black mount beside me.

"Look!"

"Over there!"

"It's Debonair!"

Our sudden appearance caused quite a stir among the other riders, especially the women. More than a few fanned themselves with their purses, even though it couldn't have been more than thirty degrees outside. One even managed to unhook her bra, write her phone number on it, and toss it his way—in under a minute. Debonair didn't pick up the bit of pink lace, but I couldn't keep from snorting. He gave me a satisfied smirk.

"Wait here. I'll be back in a minute," he said.

He bowed with a flourish, and then—

POP!

POP!

POP!

Debonair teleported all around the carousel, poofing onto every available seat. Everyone clapped and cheered at his antics. I laughed too, completely captivated by him.

The ride slowed, and Debonair teleported back to my side, standing up on the black horse and commanding everyone's attention.

"And now, ladies and gentlemen, I must bid you goodnight."

People groaned, especially the women.

Debonair raised his finger. "But . . . I am going to leave you something to remember me by."

Debonair pointed through the crowd toward a popcorn stand. A skinny man with a big nose stood inside the booth, handing out bags of the steamy, buttery confection to his customers. The vendor turned to reach for another bag, but it disappeared from sight. So did the rest of his wares. The man turned round and round in confusion, while the bags reappeared on the carousel, one for each person on the ride.

"All right!"

"Free popcorn!"

"Debonair rules!"

This time, the kids sounded the cheers, even as they stuffed kernels into their mouths. Debonair took my hand, and we teleported away to the other side of the park. A fountain populated by stone nymphs gurgled beside us.

"That was really great of you," I said, still laughing. "Although I bet the popcorn guy's not too happy that all his bags disappeared."

"Don't worry," Debonair replied. "When the vendor checks his cash register tonight, he'll find a note with a couple extra hundreds in it for his trouble."

"You mean to tell me that Debonair, superthief extraordinaire, actually pays for what he steals?"

He smiled. "Sometimes."

I thought back to the painting he'd stolen from Berkley. I opened my mouth to ask him about it, but Debonair took my hands in his.

"Now, let's take a tour of the rest of Bigtime. My Bigtime."

We teleported all over the city. Laurel Park. Quicke's. The public library. The mostly rebuilt observatory.

The cloudless sky sported a heavy blanket of stars. The bright pinpricks reminded me of a mound of sequins on one of Fiona's dresses, surrounded by oceans of black velvet fabric. A full moon bathed everything in a hazy glow, softening the glare from the neon signs of the downtown businesses. Every part of the city twinkled now, just after midnight. It was so beautiful that for once I didn't even mind all the superheroes we ran into. And there were plenty.

Granny Cane pummeled some mugger in Laurel Park. Wynter chowed down on a couple of burgers at Quicke's. And we passed Black Samba so many times I lost count. Didn't she have anything better to do than ride bus tops around town all night long? Evidently not.

But Swifte was the worst of the bunch. He lounged downtown near Jasper's brownstone when we landed there. Even though the street was dark, I could still see Swifte. His shimmering white costume announced his presence a mile away. I'd once asked Fiona if she'd designed the garment, but she strenuously denied it, claiming men should never, ever wear white. Still, I wondered. It looked exactly like the sort of over-the-top outfit she'd create.

Debonair waved to Swifte, and then we popped over to the top of the *Chronicle*. Debonair looked down and pointed. A second later, Swifte skidded to a stop in the street below. He did the same thing a minute later when we landed on the *Exposé*'s skyscraper.

"Is he following us?" I asked.

"Yeah, it's sort of a game we play." Debonair grinned. "We're always arguing over who's power is better and faster—his superspeed or my teleportation."

It seemed like a silly thing to argue about to me, but then again, I'd never professed to understand superheroes.

Debonair wrapped his arms around me. "Let's give him a run for his money, shall we?"

POP!

POP!

POP!

We teleported to other places, so fast I barely registered where we were before we were off again. Oodles o' Stuff. The front steps of the art museum. The marina. But instead of being frightened or disoriented, I found the experience exhilarating. There was something so free and wonderful about being able to go wherever you wanted, whenever you wanted. And it didn't hurt matters that my luck decided not to bother me. Oh, the static was still around me, but I didn't feel any disasters coming on.

Finally, we teleported back over to Quicke's and waited. Swifte zoomed to a stop in front of us a second later.

"Bringing up the rear, just like always," Debonair said, smiling at the masked man.

"Watching your back, just like always," Swifte retorted.

The two of them punched each other on the shoulder, shook hands, and started exchanging the latest hero-villain gossip. Swifte did most of the talking, spitting out words as fast as he could run. I guess he got around more than Debonair did. Literally.

"Are the two of you friends?" I asked during a rare moment when Swifte stopped long enough to take a breath.

I didn't know much about Swifte, but I'd never heard of him being part of a superhero team before. He was a loner, like Debonair. Swifte was one of the heroes who liked to keep the spotlight fixed on himself, but the two of them acted awfully chummy. They had to be more than casual acquaintances. Did superheroes have real friends? Or maybe their relationship was more of a professional colleague kind of thing.

"Not really," Swifte said. "I'm just always around whenever D here gets himself into trouble."

"Is that often?" I asked.

"Often enough." The superhero looked me up and down. "So this is your main squeeze, huh, Debonair? The one you keep yammering about all the time. Not bad. Not bad at all."

Debonair slung his arm around my shoulders. "Not bad? Bella is gorgeous from head to toe. Anyone who says otherwise is a fool. Besides, at least I have a main squeeze. How long has it been since you've had a date?"

Swifte grinned. "About two hours, if you count speed dating."

Debonair shook his head, then laughed.

The way they poked fun at each other reminded me of my relationship with Johnny. I would have thought they were brothers, except I knew that Debonair, Devlin Dash, was an only child.

"Well, folks, I'd love to stay and chat, but I've got a city to patrol." Swifte gave us a salute. "Later."

I blinked, and he was gone. I shook my head, trying to get

the world to slow back down to normal. Talking to Swifte was like living your life on permanent fast-forward.

"Now that we've gotten rid of motormouth, I'm going to take you somewhere really special," Debonair said. "Hold on to me, and don't let go."

I was all too happy to wrap my arms around his waist, lean my head on his shoulder, and close my eyes.

POP!

The wind whipped my hair around my face, and I opened my eyes. We stood on top of the Skyline Bridge. The enormous suspension bridge stretched over the bay and connected one side of Bigtime to the other. The mile-high platform offered a sweeping view of the nighttime skyline. The towering skyscrapers resembled slender candles from this distance, set here and there with jeweled lights. Cars zoomed over the bridge below, their headlights winking like fireflies, while the lapping water of the bay shimmered all around us, a silver carpet at the bottom of the world.

"It's amazing," I whispered.

"Isn't it?" Debonair said. "This is my favorite place in the entire city. I come up here a lot to get away from it all and just think."

Debonair snapped his fingers. Two lawn chairs appeared, along with a thick stadium blanket.

"Shall we?" he asked.

I nodded. We sat in the chairs, scooting close together, and Debonair wrapped the blanket around us. I didn't really need it, though. Just being near him was enough to keep me warm. We sat there, listening to the whistling wind and the hum of the cars below for a long time.

"So what do you think of superheroes now?" Debonair asked, his voice light and hopeful.

"What do you mean?"

"Are we all still as bad as you think we are?"

I frowned. "Wait a minute. That's what this is about? You've been teleporting me around the city because you're hoping I'll change my mind about dating a superhero?"

He gave me a shy smile. "Guilty as charged. So, is it

working? Being with a guy who can take you anywhere you want to go does have some perks, right?"

I shook my head. "It's not about having powers. That's not why I don't like superheroes."

"Then why?" Debonair asked. "What's so terrible about being a superhero?"

"Because where there are heroes, there are also villains. Villains who want to do bad things. Villains who hurt people. Who kill people."

"So, you're afraid something will happen to me?" Debonair asked. "Bella, I can promise you—"

"Don't," I snapped, my voice as cold as the solidium cables around us. "Don't you dare promise me that you won't get hurt. I've had other people make those same promises to me. And they never, ever kept them."

Memories of my father flooded my mind. His face. Smile. Laugh. Voice. All gone forever because he'd cared more about being Johnny Angel than he had about me and my brother.

I suddenly couldn't stand to be near Debonair. To be touching him. To feel him next to me. I stood up and threw off the blanket. My power flared, and the wind whistled down and tore the fabric from my fingertips. Debonair reached for it, but the blanket sailed away, floating out over the bay.

"I'm sorry about that. I'll buy you another blanket." I rubbed my aching head. "I think you should take me home. Now."

Debonair stared at me, his eyes two pools of blue against his pale face. "All right. If that's what you really want."

I nodded.

Debonair snapped his fingers, and the chairs disappeared. Then, he put his arm around me and teleported us back to my bedroom. I stepped away from him, shrugged out of my coat, and yanked off my gloves.

"Thank you for this evening. I had a nice time," I said in a stiff voice.

And I had. For a little while, I'd been able to pretend Debonair wasn't a superhero. That he was just a guy that I liked. Instead of someone I could never be with.

"Bella—" he started.

"I've had a long day, and I'm really tired. I think you should go."

Debonair reached for my hand and pressed a kiss to the inside of my wrist. I couldn't stop my pulse from speeding up at his touch, but I kept my face and eyes hard.

"As you wish," Debonair murmured, his voice sad.

Then—

POP!

He was gone.

23

After a night of fitful sleep, I headed into the city to visit the art museum the next morning. Despite Bobby's protests, I needed to get out of the house. Needed some time away to think about me and Debonair. And if we could really have a future together. Because somehow, somewhere along the way, I'd started falling for the sexy thief, blue-black leather, mask, and all.

But before I left, I cleaned up the mess I'd made in the kitchen. It wasn't pretty. The pasta and sauce had glued itself to the floor, and it took me twice as long to scrape it up than it would have last night. I'd almost finished when my luck turned against me, and I knocked over the bucket of water I'd used to mop up the pasta. I sighed and started all over again.

I showered, changed into a fitted black suit, and drove my Benz into the city. Even though it was lunchtime and downtown hummed with activity, I snagged a parking spot right outside the museum. The Bigtime Museum of Modern Art was closed for repairs, but one of the security guards waved me through.

If I hadn't known better, I would have thought there was another benefit planned. People scurried back and forth in the marble halls. But instead of fund-raiser types, most of them were construction guys, hauling supplies over to the damaged wing. Just about everybody wore a hard hat and carried tape measures, rulers, or some other sort of tool. They chattered among themselves, shouting over the steady *thwack* and *thump* of sledgehammers. The harsh chemical smell of paint and plaster filled the air, burning my nose.

I walked over to the wing that housed the museum offices. I pushed open the glass door and went inside, my heels sinking into the plush carpeting. A secretary manned the information desk out front, her multiple phones jangling in time like instruments in a symphony. I waved at her and strolled down the hall to Arthur Anders's office. I knocked on the door and cracked it open.

Arthur sat behind his desk, talking on the phone. He waved me in and finished his conversation. Then, he rose, straightened his plaid jacket, and came around the desk. Arthur gave me a friendly hug and kissed me on both cheeks. My old professor was very continental that way.

"Bella, how are you feeling?" Arthur gestured for me to sit down and took the chair opposite mine. "I was so glad to hear the Fearless Five rescued you. And so quickly."

"I'm fine. I didn't come to any real harm. Just got shaken up a bit." I didn't want to talk about my ordeal, so I switched the conversation back to the thing Arthur loved best—the museum.

"How are you holding up? How bad was the damage?"

"Not as catastrophic as it could have been. Being the location of a superhero-ubervillain battle has long been one of my greatest fears." Arthur took his glasses off and started polishing them with the edge of his jacket. "The roof was destroyed, along with one wall. Most of the items on display escaped major damage, though. We were extremely lucky in that regard."

I grimaced. There was that damn *word* again.

"We should be able to reopen in a couple of days," Arthur continued.

"So soon?"

He slipped his glasses back on. "People have been wonderful. Donations have poured in to pay to repair the damage, and all the local construction crews have been more than willing to help get the museum back into shape. We've even had some heroes come and clear out the rubble and get things back on track."

"That's wonderful," I said, grateful something was going to turn out right from all this messy drama.

"What's even more wonderful is that the Fearless Five recovered the Star Sapphire. Berkley's agreed to let us put it back on display and continue the *Whimsical Wonders* exhibit—with a bit more security, of course."

"Of course," I murmured.

Arthur's phone rang again. He moved to pick up the receiver, and I waved a silent goodbye and left his office. I'd learned what I needed to. But I still wanted to see the damage for myself, so I headed back to the new wing of the museum.

Arthur was right. It wasn't as bad as it could have been. One of the walls was gone, probably from the force of the grenade blast. Construction workers clustered around the empty space, measuring and talking about angles and structural soundness and other building terms. All the glass and rubble and debris had already been cleaned up. The roof had been replaced, as had the many spot- and footlights. All the items that had been on display were gone, though. They wouldn't be brought back in until they'd been cleaned, and everything was pristine and secure once more.

As I stared at the beefy workers, my thoughts wandered back to Debonair and what had happened between us last night.

Now that I knew—or at least thought—he was Devlin Dash, things were even more complicated. He wasn't just some guy in a sexy suit who'd seduced me. He was a real person, someone I knew. Or at least, thought I did.

I thought back, trying to remember every encounter I'd had with the awkward businessman, including our dinner together the night my father had been murdered. I'd told him the truth. I couldn't remember much of anything that had happened around the time of my father's death. Oh, I remembered ordering the appropriate flowers, picking out a casket, making sure the newspapers printed the correct obituary. But the service itself was a blur. I'd felt that way for weeks afterward, like I was just going through the motions of life, instead of actually living it.

From what I could recall, I hadn't thought of it as a date. Just a dinner between two acquaintances. We'd been working late, chairing the art auction, and had stopped by Quicke's heading to our respective homes. I wondered why Devlin thought it had been a date. And whether he actually wanted to see me now or was just hanging around because he knew he could get lucky—

My cell phone rang. I pulled it out of my purse and checked the caller ID. *Hannah Harmon.*

I frowned. What could she want? Despite working on the

benefit, we weren't exactly friends. We were just associates and barely that. Hannah had made noises after my father died about making a bid for Bulluci Industries. She's retracted her offer after Grandfather made it clear Bulluci was and always would be a family affair. Family was everything to Grandfather—and to me.

"Hello, Hannah. How are you?" I asked in my best business voice.

Family might be everything, but you should never burn bridges.

"I just wanted to call and see how you were doing." Hannah's voice was just as smooth and professional as mine. "I hope I'm not bothering you."

"Of course not."

"I heard about what happened at the museum. What a terrible tragedy."

"Yes, yes it was."

"But thank goodness you're all right. I heard the Fearless Five rescued you from Debonair."

"Yes, they did. They also recovered the Star Sapphire, from what I remember." I was purposefully vague on the details. Jasper was right. Sometimes, it was just easier to play dumb.

"From what you remember?"

"I took a rather nasty fall in the museum and hit my head quite hard. I don't really remember much of what happened." It was all part of the cover story the superheroes and I had come up with.

"But you're feeling better now?" Hannah asked.

"Oh yes. Much."

"Well, that's wonderful."

Her expressionless voice didn't quite match the good wishes coming out of her mouth. Then again, Hannah had never been overly charming to me. She wasn't one for blowing smoke up people's asses—unless she wanted something.

"Tell me, just out of curiosity, do you know what the Fearless Five are going to do with the sapphire? I imagine Berkley's rather anxious to get it back."

"Actually, I just talked with Arthur about that," I replied.

"The superheroes are going to return it to the museum so it can go back on display. They really didn't include me in their plans. You know how the Fearless Five are. They just show up, rescue you, and leave."

"I see." Hannah paused. "Well, I know you must be busy. I'll let you go."

"Thanks for calling and for your concern—"

She hung up before I finished. I frowned at the phone, puzzled by the call. Was Hannah hoping another death in the family would convince my grandfather to sell out? It wasn't happening, not unless Grandfather, Johnny, Fiona, and I all died in some terrible, fiery accident at the exact same time. Even then, our wills would ensure we left the company in the proper hands—Sam Sloane's.

I didn't have time to think about Hannah Harmon and her strange call. Not a moment after Hannah hung up, my phone rang again. *Devlin Dash*, the caller ID informed me.

My hands tightened around the phone. I thought about not answering it. For about half a second. "Hello."

"Hi, Bella. It's Devlin Dash." His voice sounded cool and smooth over the phone. He seemed much more sure of himself when we weren't actually talking face-to-face. Or when he was wearing a leather mask.

"Devlin. It's nice to hear from you." I tried to remain as calm as possible.

"I just wanted to call and say that Grams and I had a wonderful time last night. I'm sorry we had to cut it short."

I hung on to his every word, looking for hidden meanings in each and every syllable. "I'm glad the two of you enjoyed yourselves. Did Grace take care of Kelly?"

"Oh yes," Devlin said. "It turned out to be something rather minor, actually."

"Like what?" I asked, pressing for details, hoping he'd slip up and expose himself.

"Oh, nothing important. Kelly was just feeling a little tired, that's all."

"I see."

Silence hung between us. I dug through my purse, snagging

a pencil and a stray sheet of paper I'd tucked into one of the side pockets. I sat down on a nearby bench and started sketching another portrait of Debonair. Except this time, I put Devlin Dash's face on the body of the handsome thief. It fit perfectly, further convincing me of the superhero's true identity.

Devlin cleared his throat. "Anyway, I was also calling to . . . I was wondering . . . maybe . . . if you'd like to have dinner with me tonight? For the auction?" His voice wavered with every word.

I didn't respond. I wanted more information before I saw Devlin—or Debonair—again. I wanted to be ready to confront him with the truth. I didn't want our relationship to continue based on sex alone. Actually, I didn't know if I wanted it to continue at all. In short, I needed Carmen Cole's help before I saw him again.

"I'm sorry, Devlin. I can't tonight. I'm having dinner with Carmen Cole and some other friends."

"Oh."

Disappointment tinged in his voice. In a weird way, it made me happy he wanted to see me as much as I wanted to see him.

I drew in a deep breath. "But how about tomorrow night?"

"That would be fantastic!" Devlin exclaimed. "Quicke's at eight o'clock?"

"I'll see you there," I promised.

"Great! I'm looking forward to it," he said.

I thought of our encounter in the bathroom last night. The way he touched me. Held me. Made me cry out his name.

"Me too," I replied. "More than you know."

I left the museum and headed out to Sublime, Sam Sloane's mansion on the outskirts of the city. I pulled my Benz up to the front of the house and rang the buzzer. No one answered. I wasn't surprised. Sam didn't believe in having a housekeeping staff around. He thought it would be too easy for them to figure out his and the rest of the Fearless Five's secret identities. The door was locked, but I punched in the 555 access code, and it buzzed open.

I stepped inside and made my way through the enormous halls. More antiques and paintings and statues clustered in the rooms than in all of the Bigtime Museum of Modern Art. Every nook, every cranny, held another treasure. It was a wonder Debonair hadn't broken in here already. Then again, Sam's security system was extra tight—and supposedly included rockets buried in the lawn. Although the billionaire did let ordinary folks and even some school groups tour Sublime a couple of times a year. Closely supervised, of course.

I called out, but no one answered me. Again, not surprising. For all the finery and bells and whistles in his house, Sam and the others spent most of their time underground. Superheroes. They were so silly sometimes.

I made my way to the wine cellar, striding past the racks of bottled spirits. In the back corner, hidden behind a panel, was an elevator that went deep beneath Sublime. Fiona had shown me the entrance to the Fearless Five's secret headquarters a few months ago, just in case of an emergency. I'd never thought I'd use the knowledge, though. Superheroes weren't my favorite people in the world, and most of the time, I was perfectly happy pretending I didn't know any of them.

But desperate, confused people did desperate, confusing things. Like me falling for Debonair. And now asking superheroes for help in confirming his real identity.

Five minutes and a couple hundred feet later, I pulled open the door to the library. Carmen Cole and Lulu Lo waited for me inside, just as I'd asked them to when I'd called from the car. They looked like they had been or were going to be busy. Carmen wore a black crepe dress with a modest neckline and flat, ballet-style shoes. She bent over her desk in the corner, working on an enormous jigsaw puzzle—the one I'd spilled all over the place.

Lulu sat at the round table and typed away on her high-powered laptop. A cobalt blue pullover—one of my designs—covered her slim body. The fabric matched the bright streaks in her ebony hair.

Both of them looked up as I stepped inside.

Carmen smiled. "You slept with him again, didn't you?"

How did she do that? And what could I do to make her stop?

"Not exactly," I mumbled.

It was the truth, more or less. We hadn't slept together. Debonair had just wreaked wicked, wanton havoc upon my willing, eager body.

"Uh-oh, Bella got *lucky* again." Lulu snickered.

For once, I was in total agreement with Fiona. Somebody really needed to set Lulu's hair on fire so she'd quit making those awful puns. Fiona kept threatening to use her fiery super-powers to do just that to the computer hacker.

"Spill it," Carmen said. "Inquiring minds want to know."

I sat down at the massive wooden table and told them everything that had happened—editing the scene in the bathroom—and who I thought Debonair really was under all that leather.

"You're telling me that Devlin Dash, who wouldn't know what to do with a woman if she drew him a picture and climbed onto his lap to demonstrate, is actually Debonair, one of the most sought-after men in Bigtime?" Lulu asked. "The Romeo of Romeos? The Casanova of Casanovas?"

"You don't believe me?" I asked. "I brought a copy of the check and the drawing along as proof."

I laid the two items out on the table. Carmen and Lulu clustered around for a closer look.

"Well, they certainly look the same," Carmen admitted. "Lulu?"

The petite Asian woman took the drawing and the check, and put them both in a large scanner tucked away in a corner of the library. She hit a few buttons, and the machine sputtered to life. A white light appeared between the cracks on the cover.

Lulu punched more buttons, bringing up images of the signatures on the check and drawing on her computer. Then, she overlapped them.

A perfect match. Just like I'd thought.

"Bella's right. The signatures confirm it. Devlin Dash is, in fact, Debonair." Lulu shook her head. "I don't know what this town is coming to."

"What do you mean?" I asked.

"First, I find out who the Fearless Five really are, then Johnny Angel, now Debonair. Pretty soon I'll know who everybody is. And what's the fun in that?" Lulu asked, her dark eyes serious. "Half the mystique of superheroes is the whole secret-identity thing."

"Well, get Henry to put on his mask the next time the two of you are together," I sniped. "Right now, we've got work to do. I need your help, both of you. I want to know everything there is to know about Devlin Dash and Debonair."

Carmen arched an eyebrow. "Why the sudden interest, Bella? Or do I even have to ask?"

I crossed my arms over my chest. "If you must know, I have a date with Devlin tomorrow night."

"Let me guess. You're going to confront him about his real identity." Lulu shook her head. "I wouldn't do that if I were you."

"Why not? It will be so much simpler once everything's out in the open."

Carmen and Lulu exchanged a look, and the brunette reporter gave me a sad smile.

"I'm afraid that's just when it gets that much more complicated," Carmen said.

But I persisted until they agreed to help me. Carmen and Lulu tried to make me promise not to say anything to Devlin, to let him tell me that he was Debonair in his own time, but I refused. I was going to confront him whether it was the smart thing to do or not. I was tired of being sensible and calm and rational. I wanted Devlin to know I knew about his secret identity—and I wanted to find out if there was something real between us.

An hour later, Carmen and I pored through reams of paper, while Lulu pulled up file after file on her computer. I read through the bio Carmen had compiled. Devlin Dash. Age 35. Hair black, eyes a light blue. Graduated from Bigtime University with an MBA. Lots of academic and business honors. A Friend of the Bigtime Museum of Modern Art—

Lulu let out a low whistle. "I'm afraid it's not looking too good for your boy, Bella."

"Oh really? Why's that?" I asked, distracted by a photo spread of Debonair and his Lair of Seduction. I doubted there was a camera made yet that could do him justice.

"His company, DCQ Enterprises, is in deep financial trouble. According to a story in the business section of the *Exposé*, the company's chief financial officer, Nathan Nichols, was accused of embezzling several million dollars from the company coffers."

A photo of Nathan Nichols flashed up on the screen. He was a normal-looking guy with big hands and thinning hair who was confined to a wheelchair. I vaguely recalled seeing him at some of the regular society events. Like Devlin, he didn't seem to talk much.

"But nothing was ever proven, and no charges were filed against Nathan," Lulu continued. "Over the last year, Devlin's sold cars, yachts, family jewels, just about all the assets he has to keep the company afloat. His net worth barely tops two million now. Definitely subpar by Bigtime society standards. Poor guy." Lulu snickered at her bad joke.

"I remember hearing about that," I said. "That happened around the time my father died. It was the talk of the society circuit for about a week."

Most people had short attention spans in Bigtime.

"What does Devlin actually do?" Carmen asked. "What does DCQ deal in?"

Lulu scanned through more information. "Lots of real estate, restaurants, media and PR firms, art restoration—"

"Wait a minute. Art restoration?" I asked, thinking back to the room of paintings at the Lair of Seduction.

"That's what it says. One of DCQ's companies is called Amazing Art. They specialize in restoring and preserving paintings by the likes of Monet, Picasso, and others. Devlin seems to be the most heavily involved with that company. Grace Caleb runs everything else. Kelly Caleb and Kyle Quicke are the other major stockholders in DCQ, but they're not really involved in the day-to-day business decisions."

"So, Devlin really is an art lover," I murmured.

Maybe all his talk about how good my work was hadn't been just to get me into bed. The thought made me happier than I could have imagined.

Carmen flipped through the papers in her hands. "Well, he's managed to hang on to the family mansion out in Bigtime Bay at least." She looked at me. "It's about three miles east of where we picked you up in the boat. But that shouldn't come as a shock to you."

I thought of all the empty rooms I'd seen with their missing furniture. Carmen was right. It didn't surprise me. I didn't think I could be any more shocked than I had the moment I'd realized who Debonair really was.

"There's more," Lulu added. "Devlin is currently fending off a hostile takeover bid from Hannah Harmon. He's hanging on by the width of a spandex suit. And in another interesting twist, Nathan Nichols now works for Hannah as her chief financial officer."

I frowned. Hannah Harmon. That was the second time I'd heard her name today. That in and of itself wasn't unusual. Hannah loved to take over floundering businesses. If Devlin was having as much trouble as Lulu claimed, it was only natural Hannah would come sniffing around looking to make more millions. Joanne had told me the same thing at the museum benefit. Still, I didn't like coincidences.

"You don't think Hannah could be an ubervillain, do you?" I asked, thinking out loud.

"Why do you ask?" Carmen said.

I told her about Hannah's strange phone call.

Carmen's eyes glowed for half a second. They always did that whenever she was feeling psychic vibrations. Or listening to the voices in her head, as Fiona called it. "She's rich and ambitious, so she meets the basic ubervillain requirements, even if she's not on my list."

Lulu and I looked at the reporter.

"What list?" I asked.

A guilty blush spotted Carmen's cheeks, and she mumbled something.

"What was that?"

"My list of all the superheroes and ubervillains in Bigtime," Carmen said in a defensive tone. "I've been trying to figure out who's who in my spare time. It's sort of a hobby."

"You didn't tell me that, Sister Carmen," Lulu accused.

Carmen fiddled with one of her Rubik's Cubes. "Yeah, well, I figured the information could be useful someday. But I didn't want to tell Sam and the others what I was doing. You know they're all a little touchy about the secret-identity thing."

"Well, they did get stuffed into glass tubes and almost died because you inadvertently revealed their secret identities to the Terrible Triad," Lulu pointed out.

Carmen slouched farther down into her seat. Before she met Sam and became a superhero herself, Carmen used to expose the secret identities of heroes and villains for the newspaper the *Exposé*—until her boss turned out to be Malefica, the biggest, baddest ubervillain in Bigtime.

I looked through more files, stopping when I spotted a picture of Devlin standing with Grace Caleb at some society event last year.

"I want you to check up on Grace Caleb too," I said, changing the subject.

Carmen shot me a grateful look.

"Why?" Lulu asked. "She's just another old society lady. Sneeze and you'll hit half a dozen in this town."

"She's Devlin's grandmother—and she just happened to have a *family emergency* while we were having dinner last night."

Carmen rolled her eyes. "Family emergency? That's such a dead giveaway."

We sifted through the information on Grace Caleb, but couldn't come up with anything conclusive. She seemed far too interested in her afternoon teas and bridge clubs to be a superhero. Then again, I never would have dreamed Devlin Dash was Debonair.

Two hours later, I stretched my arms over my head. The motion made the charms on my silver bracelet jangle together. The three of us froze. I hadn't taken off the chain since Jasper had given it to me. I hadn't needed to use it, so, for the most part, I was able to forget I was wearing something that could obliterate me in twenty seconds. Not now, though. I slowly lowered my arm and set it on the table. Nothing happened. We all let out a breath.

"How are you liking Jasper's present?" Lulu asked, eyeing the bracelet.

"It's a bit strange knowing I could blow up myself and most of Bigtime with a couple of words, but you get used to it."

Carmen nodded. "You get used to a lot of strange things in this town."

24

By the time we'd finished checking up on Devlin and Grace, it was close to midnight. Carmen invited me to stay in one of the hundred or so guest suites upstairs, but I headed home. I'd had enough superheroes for one day, no matter how nice they were. My luck decided to be good for a change, giving me nothing but green lights, and I got home in less than twenty minutes.

Debonair didn't *pop!* inside the house to surprise me, though. I didn't know if it was because he'd gotten what he wanted last night, or if he was out being Devlin Dash. And I didn't know what I would have done if he had appeared. Probably fallen into bed with him yet again. I had precious little control where the handsome thief was concerned.

I slept late for a change and didn't get up until almost noon the next day. My luck kept pulsing around me, as if it knew I had an important day ahead. After I fried two elliptical trainers and a stationary bike, I threw in the towel on my workout and headed upstairs.

But I didn't fare any better in the kitchen. I tried to make myself a veggie special sandwich on whole-grain, calcium-fortified bread. First, the bread fell apart in my hands. Then, a tomato flew off the counter and splattered onto one of the kitchen windows. The lettuce exploded, the cheese molded the second I took it out of the refrigerator, and I snapped a knife in two when I dipped it in a jar of low-fat mayonnaise. The jagged blade missed my big toe by less than an inch.

After destroying just about everything I touched, I went back upstairs and stayed in bed sketching until it was time to get ready for my date with Devlin. I wanted to look good when I confronted my sexy, leather-wearing lover, so I took a long shower and pampered myself with all sorts of lotions and creams and other assorted beauty products. I also put mounds of conditioner in my hair in the hope that, just once, it wouldn't frizz. My nice, smooth look lasted about two minutes before my hair became sky-high once more.

Then, it was time to decide what to wear. I'd just settled on a nice pinstriped skirt and white blouse when a flash of scarlet caught my eye. I reached into the back of my closet and pulled out a crimson dress Fiona had made me for my birthday. The fabric reached the floor, but it had a deep, V-shaped neckline and high slits all around the skirt that showed off my legs. The dress was made of soft, slick, shiny satin and dotted here and there with sequins, glass beads, and bits of feathers. It also happened to be the exact same color as the teddy I'd sported in the Lair of Seduction.

I'd never worn the dress before. It was a little too loud, a little too bold and daring and revealing for me. But I was in a bold sort of mood tonight. So, I slithered into the dress, put on the reddest lipstick I owned, and grabbed a matching purse and shoes. As a final touch, I fastened my favorite silver angel charm around my throat. It went nicely with the bracelet Jasper had given me. I was getting rather used to having the bomb maker's charms dangle off my wrist. I didn't know whether that was good or bad.

I went downstairs around seven-thirty to check on Bobby. He relaxed on the couch in the living room, watching a soccer game.

"You look marvelous." Bobby whistled. "Is that a new dress?"

I turned around. "One of Fiona's creations."

"Well, it looks wonderful on you," he said.

"Why are you sitting here alone? Shouldn't you be out with Grace tonight? Or is she dropping by later?"

"No, she's not coming over tonight," Bobby said. "She had a few errands to do. We're having dinner tomorrow, though."

"Maybe it will go better than the other night."

My grandfather frowned. "We'll see."

"Well, I need to get going. I'll call you if I'm going to be late," I promised.

"Have a good time, darling." Bobby turned back to his game.

I clutched my purse, which contained the drawing of Debonair that I'd done, along with the check Devlin had written me. "Oh, it will be very interesting, to say the least."

Five minutes before eight, I stopped my silver Benz in front of Quicke's. Despite the fact that traffic crawled along and every spot on the street was taken, another vehicle decided to leave at the exact moment I turned onto the block. So I slid my car into a parking spot with no problem. Devlin stood on the sidewalk, waiting for me. He came over and held out a hand to help me out of the car. I took it, noticing how sure and capable his hands were. They looked exactly like the same hands that had driven me mad the other night.

"Here. This is for you." Devlin held out a single red rose.

"A rose. How lovely."

I sniffed it. It didn't smell nearly as wonderful as Debonair did. No rose ever could. They didn't have his faint, musky, masculine undertones.

Devlin's eyes flicked up and down my body. "You look amazing, Bella. That color really looks wonderful on you."

"So I've been told," I said, baiting him just a little.

No reaction. Not even a blink. Maybe Devlin was better at this than I thought. Or maybe I just wasn't as good.

"You look nice too. Very handsome."

And he did. For once, Devlin wore a dark blue business suit that seemed to fit just right. He'd forgone a tie, leaving his collar unbuttoned and exposing just the tiniest bit of his chest, including a patch of dark, curly hair. My power flared at the sight of him, and I had to will it to be still and not interfere.

Devlin held out his arm. "Shall we?"

I drew in a deep breath. "Let's go."

We stepped inside the restaurant, and Kyle Quicke greeted us. Like Bulluci Industries, Quicke's was very much a family business, a couple of generations strong now. It seemed like Kyle was always at the restaurant, morning, noon, and night. With his chestnut hair, light eyes, and thin physique, Kyle was cute—if a bit on the lean side.

"Devlin, my man! Good to see you!" Kyle's face broke into a grin at the sight of his cousin.

The two of them shook hands and exchanged hearty back slaps. Then, Devlin stepped aside.

"And I'm sure you know Bella Bulluci."

Kyle nodded. "Bella."

"Kyle."

He grabbed a couple of menus from underneath the podium by the front door. "Let me show you guys to your table."

We wound our way through the restaurant. All the greenery and twinkling lights for the bachelor auction had been cleared away, and the décor had reverted back to its usual superhero-and-ubervillain motif. The posters, the toys, the newspaper clippings. They beamed at me from their positions on the walls. I grimaced. Too bad.

Kyle seated us in a secluded booth at the back of the restaurant. Devlin helped me slip into my side, then took the opposite one. Kyle handed us both menus before leaving. We made small talk for a few minutes before giving the waiter our orders. Devlin opted for grilled swordfish, while I gave in to temptation and ordered four-cheese manicotti. With berry-flavored sangria and a piece of cherry pie for dessert.

"I really shouldn't be eating this," I said fifteen minutes later, eyeing the steaming mound of pasta and cheese in front of me. "I don't know why I ordered it. The carbs are going to wreck my diet."

"You don't look like you need to be on a diet."

"That's very sweet of you, but I could stand to lose a few pounds."

"Oh, be dangerous. Live a little," Devlin teased in a shy tone.

I stared at him. He was one to talk about living dangerously. Didn't he realize the danger he put himself in every time he slipped into his silly costume? Every time he broke into some museum? Every time he took something that wasn't his?

"Did I say something wrong?" Devlin asked, noticing my grimace.

"Of course not," I replied. "I'm just thinking about how many hours I'm going to have to spend on the elliptical trainer tomorrow to make up for tonight."

"There are other ways to get your exercise."

I flashed back to our time in bed together. That had certainly been a vigorous workout—*very* vigorous.

"Oh, really? What did you have in mind?" I asked in a sexy, impish voice.

Devlin almost spit out his wine. He started choking and didn't recover his breath for several seconds. If I hadn't known better, I would have bought the whole geeky, *I'm-painfully-shy-around-women* act. But I did know better. Devlin Dash could do things to a woman that she'd only dreamed about or read in romance novels.

Devlin did most of the talking during dinner, stammering through stories about Grace, Kyle, Kelly, and other far-flung members of his family. I made the appropriate noises, but I was too busy looking for hidden meanings in his words to add much to the conversation. An hour later, we finished dinner. Devlin looked positively miserable. He kept fiddling with his wineglass and rubbing his temples, as though the evening hadn't gone as he'd planned.

"Would you like to go someplace? Maybe for a walk or something?" Devlin asked.

But evidently, he wasn't miserable enough to end the evening. I didn't plan on letting him do that anyway. Not until I'd confronted him.

I stared into his eyes, blue eyes that had haunted my dreams for days. "Sure. In fact, I know the perfect place."

I asked Devlin where his car was and if he wanted to drive. The businessman claimed he had a friend drop him off. To me, it was another telltale sign he was really Debonair. Why drive when you could just teleport anywhere you wanted to?

"We'll take my car, then," I said, unlocking the Benz. "It's not that far to the marina."

Devlin looked at me strangely. "Why do you want to go to the marina this time of night?"

"I love listening to the waves and watching the moon rise over the bay. I think it's very romantic. Don't you?"

He didn't answer.

We rode in silence through the quiet streets. For once, I didn't see any superheroes out and about. No Granny Cane pummeling muggers. No Swifte racing to and fro. No Black Samba surfing on top of a city bus. After about ten minutes, I pulled to a stop in front of the entrance to the marina. Bigtime bordered the Atlantic, and the ocean cut a wide, jagged oval into the middle of the city. A man-made river flowed down the towering hill from the observatory, spilling out into the ocean and helping to form the shallow waters of Bigtime Bay.

I eased the Benz over a couple of speeds bumps and found an empty space on the street. We got out of the car and strolled toward the water's edge. Our shoes clacked on the round cobblestones that connected the street to the long boardwalk that wrapped around the bay. The tall spires of the Bigtime Maritime Museum hovered above us, along with the massive, pentagon-shaped beams that supported the Skyline Bridge. Lights from various boats bobbed up and down farther out in the bay. Chilled, I drew my scarlet wrap tighter around my shoulders.

"Here, let me." Devlin took off his jacket and draped it over my shivering shoulders.

I buried my face in the collar. Sweet roses. Of course.

We settled on an iron bench in the shadow of the Skyline Bridge and looked out over the bay. Despite my pretenses to get Devlin here, it really was a beautiful view. The moonlight made the waves seem like streams of silver coming into and going out from the sandy shore. A few gulls cried in the night sky, but the constant rush of the waves crashing on the pebbled beach muted their harsh calls.

We didn't speak for a long time.

"You know, I'm surprised you agreed to come out with me

tonight," Devlin said. "Even if I did pay for the pleasure."

"Really? Why's that?"

"I don't exactly seem like your type." He picked up a loose bit of stone and skipped it across the water.

"And what would my type be?"

He shrugged. "I don't know. Someone suave. Sophisticated. Confident. Handsome."

"You're not all of those things?" I said, trying to tease him a bit. "Because you hide it very well."

"Not really."

I was silent for a moment. "Actually, I was glad you called. I wanted to see you again."

"Really? Why?" He sounded surprised.

"Because I wanted to talk to you. To tell you that I know the truth," I said, staring him in the eyes. "To tell you that I know you're really Debonair."

★25★

Devlin stared at me. His face paled. Sweat beaded on his forehead. A bit of nervous laughter escaped his trembling lips.

"Well? What do you have to say for yourself?" I demanded.

Devlin took off his glasses and rubbed his temples.

"I could barely summon up enough courage to call you and ask you out, even though I bid on you at the auction." Devlin put his glasses back on. "I'm a total klutz when it comes to women. And you think I'm *Debonair*? Of all the superheroes in Bigtime, he's the one I'm least like."

He let out a few more nervous giggles, trying to pass off my accusation as nothing more than a joke.

"Well, that's funny," I replied in a calm voice. "Especially since I have proof that you are, in fact, Debonair."

I drew the drawing and the check out of my purse and showed them to him. "See? The two signatures match perfectly. Care to explain that?"

Devlin quit laughing. He looked at the two scraps of paper, then at me. I got the impression he wanted to teleport away. Somewhere far, far away.

I reached over and slid the glasses off his face. "You don't have to hide from me. Not anymore, Devlin Debonair Dash."

He looked at me, really looked at me, and I realized I was staring into the face of the man I'd slept with. The face of the man I'd come to care about.

Devlin tucked his glasses in his pocket. His mouth twisted. "Of course I do. I have to hide from everyone."

I thought about what Lulu had said—how finding out a superhero's real identity ruined the mystery, the fantasy, for her. Maybe Devlin thought that way too. "Why do you say that?"

He let out a harsh, self-deprecating laugh. "Because if people found out I was really Debonair, they'd be angry with me. Think I'd betrayed them in some way. That I'd lied to them all these years. They'd laugh and snicker and point their fingers, especially the women. I couldn't stand that."

"Why do you even do it?" I asked. "Why be somebody like Debonair?"

Devlin stared down at his scuffed wingtips. "I'm not like the other men on the society scene in Bigtime. I'm not that rich, at least not anymore. I'm not that handsome, and I never know the right thing to say. I can't even tell a good joke. Half the time, I forget the punch line. I've always been awkward and self-conscious, particularly around women. I've never felt like I fit in, not even in my own family. Debonair is a way for me to be everything I want to be. Suave. Smooth. Cool. Confident. Everything I'm not in real life. It's an escape from being average, boring, nerdy Devlin Dash, if only for a few hours at a time."

"I see."

And I did. I understood Devlin better than he realized. I used to dream of being Johnny Angel, and I'd seen the effect a secret identity had on people like my father. To some, it was better than the most potent drug. More desirable, more addictive, and much more harmful. At least, it had been to my family.

"I don't think people would laugh at you if they knew the truth. You're a very interesting, special man in your own right, Devlin."

He gave me a wan smile, as if he didn't really believe me.

"And your powers?" I asked, wanting to know the rest of the story. "How did you get your powers?"

Devlin looked out into the shimmering water. Memories clouded his blue eyes. "You know my grandmother, Grace, raised me. My parents died in a sailing accident when I was thirteen. What you don't know, what very few people know, is that I was with them when it happened. We were out on the bay, when a sudden storm swept up. My father tried to turn the boat back to shore, but the sail snapped. Lightning danced across the sky, coming toward the boat. I knew it was going to hit us. Right before it did, I felt this odd sort of power grow inside me. My vision grew fuzzy, hazy, almost like I was standing in a sea of fog. The next thing I knew, I was in the middle of the bay, trying not to drown. A second later, lightning struck the boat, and it exploded. They say my parents died instantly. They never found their bodies."

"But you didn't die." I squeezed his hand, willing him to go on with his story. "You survived. How?"

Devlin drew in a deep breath. "Cap'n Freebeard and his Saucy Wenches saw the explosion and came to help. They found me clinging to a piece of debris. They rescued me and kept me safe until Grams could come and get me."

Devlin watching his parents drown, discovering his power, being taken aboard Freebeard's love boat. That would have had a major impact on him. The shock, the trauma, the stress. It was the beginning of him becoming Debonair.

From his story, it sounded like Devlin had a natural, genetic mutation that gave him superpowers, unlike Carmen Cole, who'd developed hers only after being dropped into a vat of radioactive waste. Or Henry Harris, who'd been struck by lightning. Or a dozen other legends I'd heard. Devlin was more like me than I'd realized.

"I know why you were in Berkley's house that night. You were stealing the painting so you could restore it, weren't you? That's why you steal all the art you do."

He nodded. "I take the paintings, restore and preserve them, and then return them to their owners—or to the nearest museum. There's no real harm in it. I do it because I can't stand to see beautiful things wasting away. I suppose I'm an art lover, like you. I always have been."

I took a deep breath and moved on to what I really wanted to know. "I understand why you saved me from Hangman. I was in the wrong place at the wrong time. But what I don't understand is why you kept me in the Lair of Seduction. Is that standard operating procedure until your seduction techniques work? Or was there a special reason we slept together?"

"I kept you in the Lair of Seduction because I wanted to keep you safe and . . . because I wanted to spend time with you."

"But why?"

I had to know. I just had to know.

Devlin stared into my eyes. "Because I've been in love with you for a long time now, Bella."

My heart leapt up into my throat, and my stomach flipped over. "You're *what*?!"

He took my cold hand in his own. "I'm in love with you, Bella Bulluci. I have been ever since we went out all those months ago."

"But—but why? We only had dinner that one time. You barely knew me then. Or know me now. Or . . . whatever."

"I've been interested in you ever since we chaired that art exhibit out at Paradise Park."

"But that was months ago!"

"I know."

I shook my head. "But you never called or asked me out. You didn't even talk to me that much when I'd see you at events."

A wry smile twisted Devlin's face. "Like I said before, I'm not very good with women. But after that, I started watching you. Talking to you when I could. And I realized what a special person you are. How warm and kind and caring."

"But why didn't you say anything before?" I asked. "I would have gone out with you. I would have given you a chance."

"I couldn't. I was too afraid. You're so beautiful, so sophisticated, so elegant. I thought you'd just laugh at me."

With all the messes my jinx created, I knew what it felt like to be made fun of. I gripped his hand tighter. "I would never laugh at you."

He squeezed back. "I know that now, Bella. When you put yourself up for auction at the museum benefit, I decided to bid on you."

My eyebrows rose. "You spent twenty thousand dollars just to have a date with me?"

"I'd spend that much and a thousand times more."

I didn't know whether to be flattered or frightened by the fervor in his voice.

"When we had dinner earlier this year, I thought we had a wonderful time. You smiled at me and seemed interested in what I was saying. You even laughed at my jokes. Nobody ever laughs at my jokes." The smile left Devlin's face. "But you never called me afterward like you said you would."

"I was going to," I said in a soft voice. "That night after

dinner, I found out my father had been killed. Murdered, actually. I was a mess after that. It's no excuse, but I forgot all about you. Afterward . . . other stuff just kept happening."

"What other stuff?"

I grimaced. "Superhero stuff. My brother was kidnapped by ubervillains a couple months after my father was killed. It was a stressful time, to say the least."

Devlin looked puzzled. "Who kidnapped your brother? I didn't hear anything about that, and Kelly didn't mention it to me."

"It doesn't really matter," I said, glossing over the details.

We sat there for several minutes before Devlin spoke again.

"What about now, Bella? I know we haven't exactly gotten off to the best start, but I want to be with you. Do you think there's a chance you would want to be with me too?"

His voice sounded so fragile, so small, and yet so hopeful it broke my heart. Because the answer to his question was no, and it always would be.

"I don't want to get involved with a superhero," I said. "I can't, Devlin."

"Why not? I don't understand why you hate superheroes so much."

I closed my eyes, debating whether I should tell him my family secret. I supposed it was only fair, since I knew his deepest, darkest one. "Have you ever heard of Johnny Angel?"

"The guy who rides his motorcycle around town?" Devlin seemed startled by the abrupt change in conversation. "The one who wears the black leather jacket with the angel wings on the back and hangs out with the biker gangs?"

I nodded. "Well, let's just say Johnny Angel is sort of a Bulluci family tradition."

His blue eyes narrowed, but he didn't say anything.

"My father died because he was Johnny Angel," I said. "He tried to help some friends stop a couple of ubervillains, and they killed him for getting in the way."

"I'm so sorry. I didn't know."

I shrugged, used to hearing the condolences. "Not many people do."

Devlin stared at me. "You're afraid the same thing will happen to me. That Hangman or some ubervillain will kill me."

"Yes," I admitted. "I already have a bit of a soft spot for you, Devlin. I don't need—I don't want my heart to be crushed again by a superhero. And it would be if we starting seeing each other."

"But I'm not a superhero," Devlin said. "Not really."

I shook my head. "You're close enough. You go out and break into museums. Steal things from people. Teleport around the city and pick up sexy superhero awards. You even have an archenemy in Hangman." Sadness tinged my voice.

"Bella—"

He started to protest, but I put a finger to his lips, shushing him. "No, Devlin. It would never work out between us. Trust me. Please. We can't be together. Not now. Not ever."

Devlin stared at me for a long time, his eyes dark and sad. Then—

POP!

He vanished.

Just like always.

I waited for him to return. To realize my finding out his secret identity wasn't the end of the world. To tell me being a superhero wasn't that dangerous. To ask me to reconsider. To demand we be together, now and always. But he didn't.

And part of me wanted him to, no matter how I tried to pretend otherwise.

I waited half an hour before I realized he wasn't coming back. At least not tonight. Maybe not ever, given the hurt look I'd seen in his eyes.

But it was for the best. I didn't want to have a relationship with a superhero—or semisuperhero in Debonair's case. I'd spent too many nights sitting up praying my grandfather, father, and now Johnny would come home safely. I wasn't about to do that again. Not for anyone. Devlin would come to understand that in time, I hoped.

So, I wrapped his coat tighter around my chilled shoulders and headed back to my car. I was so preoccupied with my thoughts I didn't even notice the Benz was on fire until I was twenty feet away from it.

I stared in horror at the flames leaping out from underneath the hood. Why was my car on fire? I hadn't been anywhere near it for the last hour. There was no way my luck could have caused it to spontaneously combust. Even I wasn't that jinxed. At least, not usually.

I whirled around, but I didn't see anyone standing in the shadows. No superheroes, no ubervillains, no regular, old-fashioned gawkers come to check out all the commotion.

I stared at the burning car. Through the dancing orange flames, a line of fire zipped straight up the hood to the melted windshield. It looked almost like the car had been cut in two before it exploded. What could do that to a car? Especially a behemoth like my Benz? I didn't know of any ubervillains who were that powerful. Had someone new come to Bigtime?

My power pulsed. My fingers itched. My hair expanded to gravity- and conditioner-defying heights. Static energy wrapped itself around my body like a glove. Something very, very bad was about to happen.

"Ah, Bella Bulluci. Just the woman I was waiting for," a feminine voice called out.

A woman stood behind me. She wore a buttercup yellow suit that reminded me of Fiera's costume—except it was made out of shiny leather. She wore matching boots with it, sort of like galoshes young kids were always forced to endure. The bright ensemble made me grimace. I thought Fiona was bad, but yellow leather? Talk about cheesy.

A triangular-shaped prism decorated the front of her costume. A beam of light slashed across her chest, before hitting the prism and expanding into a rainbow spectrum on the other side. It was one of the weirdest insignias I'd seen. A yellow, triangle-shaped mask covered most of her face, the bottom point resting on her nose. Her bright eyes had a red tint to them.

The woman was tall, almost six feet, with auburn-colored hair that stuck up in spikes over her head. She had a decent enough figure—long legs, modest breasts, a relatively flat midsection. But her posture was ramrod-stiff. I didn't think a four-star general could have stood up any taller or straighter. She almost looked like a board someone had stuffed into a costume.

But what caught my attention most was the device in her hand. The long, slender cylinder looked like a laser pointer, except for the reddish glow burning on the end of the barrel.

And it was aimed at me.

★ 26 ★

"Who are you?" I asked, not daring to take my eyes off the laserlike device for a second. My power pulsed around me, ready to add to the impending disaster.

She smiled. "I have lots of names, but you can call me Prism. I believe Hangman might have mentioned me."

I licked my dry lips. "You're his boss, right? The one who told him to break into the museum?"

She nodded. "That's right. I want the Star Sapphire. And you're going to give it to me, Bella."

"But I don't have it. The Fearless Five do. They took it from Debonair when they rescued me. Everybody knows that."

Prism's eyes glowed red-hot for a second. "I don't believe you. You might not have the sapphire, but you know where it is and how I can get it."

I shook my head. "Trust me. I don't. I don't know anything about the sapphire."

Prism cocked her head to one side. "We'll see."

If I'd had any sense, I'd have started running. But I had a funny feeling Prism and her laser would cut me down before I took five steps. It also didn't help matters that I'd decided to wear three-inch heels tonight. Then again, I hadn't thought I'd be face-to-face with an ubervillain. Most of my dates didn't end this way. I certainly hadn't planned on this one turning out like that.

My fingers crept up to my wrist and to Jasper's bomb-laden bracelet. I thought about using it, but there was one small problem—Prism could pull the trigger on her weapon a lot faster than I could fumble with the charms, arm them, and try to throw them at her. Even then, she could still move out of the way. Or worse, stand still and take the blast. She could have superstrength for all I knew, or be impervious to explosions, like Johnny was.

My eyes slid around, hoping some superhero would see the flames and smoke from the car and come to my rescue. Debonair, Swifte, the Fearless Five, Halitosis Hal, Pistol Pete, the Invisible Ingénues, Wynter. Somebody. Anybody.

Nobody came.

"Now, Bella, enough chitchat. You're going to tell me where the sapphire is and exactly who has it." Prism waved the laser around. Smoke and flames curled up from the silver barrel. "Or else."

"Or else you're going to shoot me, right? That thing, what does it do?" I asked, stalling for time. Having seen a couple of hero-villain battles, I knew there were few things ubervillains liked better than to show off their destructive gizmos.

"My laserama? Here. Let me show you."

Prism pointed the laser at one of the curled iron streetlamps the city planners were so fond of. A red beam shot out from the barrel, cutting a straight line across the iron. The smell of burning metal filled the air. A second later, the top half of the pole slid off and crashed against the cobblestones. Bits of broken stone zipped through the air like wasps, stinging everything in site. A car alarm blared in the background.

I bit my lip to keep from screaming in horror.

Prism raised the laser to her lips and blew a bit of smoke away from the barrel. "As you can see, my laserama is quite powerful. That was its lowest setting—slow burn. Just think what it would do to that pretty face of yours. There wouldn't be enough of it left to put in a jar—much less a casket."

The sight of my father's closed coffin flashed through my mind. There hadn't been enough of him to find either. Only his Johnny Angel watch and a few of his teeth had survived Intelligal's explodium missiles.

Anger pulsed through my body, along with the usual static electricity. I grimaced. I didn't want to end up like my father. I didn't deserve it. My family had been through enough already. I wasn't going to die tonight. If I was really, really lucky.

And an exceptionally good liar.

"I told you already, I don't know where the sapphire is. The

Fearless Five have it. That's all I know, I swear." I crossed my finger over my heart.

Prism shook her head. "Not good enough."

She raised the laserama and pushed a button on the top. But I was expecting it and dove out of the way. I hit the cobblestones hard, but I kept rolling. Rolling. Rolling. Rolling. Then, I used my momentum to pull myself to my feet. My luck went along with my plan, and I did a smooth move that would have made the Bendy Brawler proud. I started to run, but I hadn't taken half a dozen steps when Prism called out.

"Stop! Or you're dead!"

I froze.

"Turn around!"

I complied. Prism stood behind me, her red lips pressed together in anger. She leveled the laserama at my chest.

"Stupid bitch. No one gets away from me. No one. If you won't tell me where the sapphire is, I'll just kill you right here, right now." Her finger started to press down on the button once more.

POP!

The smell of sweet roses permeated the air, and a dark shadow with glittering blue eyes appeared behind Prism.

"I'm sorry. But no one's killing anyone tonight," he growled.

Prism whirled around at the sound of his smooth voice. Debonair leapt at her, and they fell to the ground. The laserama slid across the cobblestones toward me, just as the Star Sapphire had all those days ago. I picked up the device—and dropped it the second my fingers came into contact with the hot metal. I blew on my hand, trying to cool it off. After a few seconds, the pain faded away. I didn't think I'd touched the device long enough to burn myself. Lucky me.

Meanwhile, Prism positioned herself atop Debonair and repeatedly punched him in the face. She must have had super-strength because every blow snapped his head back against the stones. The sight made my heart twist.

Then, I noticed something even worse. Prism's eyes. The

red glow in the depths grew brighter and brighter with every second, as though she were powering them up.

"Watch out!" I yelled. "Watch out for her eyes!"

Debonair lurched his head to one side just as rays of light shot out from Prism's eyes. The scarlet beams slammed into the stone, obliterating the spot where his face had been a moment before.

"Debonair! Let's go! Now!" I screamed. I couldn't bear to see him being hurt. Especially because of me.

POP!

Debonair teleported to my side and wrapped his hand around my waist.

A second later, the world disappeared.

Debonair, Devlin, teleported us all over the city, just as he had the night before. Quicke's, Oodles o' Stuff, the Bigtime Public Library, the top of the Skyline Bridge. The sudden flashes of colors and lights didn't upset me this time. In fact, I would have enjoyed it immensely if an ubervillain hadn't just tried to kill us.

We finally came to a stop in the Lair of Seduction. Enormous water bed, furniture, entertainment center, cozy little table in the corner. It looked exactly the same. Debonair drew his arm away and sank onto the water bed. A low groan escaped his lips. I sat down beside him. His face was red and swollen where Prism had hit him. Blood and bruises covered what I could see of his skin.

"You're hurt," I said, tipping his face up into the light, and going into full-fledged nurse mode. "Do you have any bandages? Antibiotic ointment? Any medical supplies at all?"

Debonair snapped his fingers, and everything I requested appeared. I took his arm, dragged him off the sloshing bed, and led him into the bathroom.

"Take off the mask," I commanded.

"What?"

"Take it off, Devlin. I need to see your face to patch you up. All of it."

He let out a long sigh, then slipped the blue-black leather up over his head. I made him sit down on the closed toilet seat while I cleaned the cuts and scratches on his handsome face. Luckily, none of them was very deep.

The process reminded me of all the times I'd done the same thing for my father. Blood-soaked cotton balls sticking to my hands. The harsh smell of antiseptic. Greasy ointment coating my fingers. It was all the same. As was the cold, familiar mix of fear and relief pounding through my body.

I'd almost died tonight, and Devlin along with me. And for what? So some ubervillain could try to take over the city? It was all so ridiculous. So stupid. So irrational. It made me sick to my stomach. Angry too. Why couldn't people just be content to rob and cheat and steal and lie? Why did they feel the need to dress up in costumes and try to bend everyone to their evil will? But that was Bigtime for you. Schemes and dreams. It always had been, and it always would be. I was just unlucky enough to be a part of it.

"You're very gentle," Devlin said after I'd finished pressing a butterfly bandage over a cut above his left eye. "I hardly felt a thing."

"I've had lots of practice," I muttered. "Unfortunately."

I caught a glimpse of myself in the mirror over the sink. I didn't look much better than Devlin. My dress was torn and dirty, with big smudges of oil all over it where I'd rolled across the cobblestones. A couple of scrapes slashed across my right cheek and arm where I'd hit the ground. I'd have bruises galore tomorrow, fresh ones to add to my never-ending collection.

A jangle caught my ear, and I looked down at my wrist. I might have been a wreck, but the bracelet Jasper had given me looked as good as new. None of the charms had so much as a scratch on them. I was just grateful it hadn't spontaneously exploded while I dealt with Prism.

I picked up the remaining supplies, peered into the mirror, and went to work on myself, cleaning and bandaging. When I was finished, I put the lids back on the bottles and tubes of ointment. Waste not, want not, and all that. Plus, the way my luck was running tonight, if I didn't clean up now, I'd do something clumsy later—like step on a tube and squirt petroleum jelly everywhere. Talk about a bitch to clean up.

Devlin sat there, watching me straighten things.

"Bella, I'm sorry I left you," Devlin said. "I just—I didn't know what to do. You knew my secret, you knew how I felt about you, and then you said we couldn't be together. It was . . . hard for me."

"I know," I replied. "But tonight only proves my point. We both got off with only a few scrapes and bruises, but it could have been much, much worse."

"Bella—"

"No." I shook my head. "We were lucky, that was all."

Much as it pained me to say the word.

"I'd like to think it was skill more than luck."

"No, it wasn't," I said, my voice harsh and bitter. "Trust me. I know a lot about luck—especially bad luck."

"What do you mean?"

I sat down on the edge of the bathtub. "Because that's my power. Luck."

I told him about how I could make good and bad things happen, depending on my mood and the capriciousness of my power. About my emotional flare-ups and all the chaos and explosions and disasters that went with them.

"But you can't control it?" he asked.

I shook my head. "No, I've never been able to. Not really. Every once in a while, I can focus and get something to happen the way I want. But most of the time, my power does what it wants to, when it wants to. I'm just along for the ride."

"I don't think that's right," Devlin said. "It's your power. It's part of you, not the other way around. You should be able to do anything you want to with it. You should be able to control it as you see fit."

"I don't know," I said, rubbing my head. "I don't really want to know. I just wish it would go away. Forever."

Devlin looked at me, horror in his blue eyes. "You don't mean that."

"Yes, I do. More than you can possibly imagine." I stood. "I should be getting home. Grandfather will be worried. I'm sure somebody's found my burned car by now. It'll be all over the news by morning." I grimaced. "I'll probably have your cousin Kelly Caleb camped out on my doorstep when she hears about this."

Devlin caught my hand. "It might not be safe for you to go home. Prism and Hangman could be there waiting for you. You should stay here tonight. With me."

I closed my eyes. I knew what would happen if I agreed. We'd wind up in bed together, and I'd only be more torn about my decision not to see the handsome thief again.

"No." I said. "I can't stay with you, Devlin. I'm sorry. I won't put myself through this anymore. Not even for you. Please take me home."

He argued with me about how the ubervillains might be waiting for us. He only agreed to take me home after I told him the Fearless Five were watching the house and would keep me safe. Finally, Devlin put his mask back on and teleported us just inside the front door of the Bulluci mansion. He stared into my eyes, but I scooted back out of his arms. I didn't want to tempt fate. Or myself.

"Bella? Is that you?"

Grandfather appeared at the end of the hall and rushed toward us. He pulled me into a tight hug. "Thank heavens you're all right! Chief Newman called and said they found your car on fire down by the marina. What happened?" His eyes went over my shoulder to Debonair, lurking in the shadows. "And who are you?"

Debonair stepped forward and shook my grandfather's hand. "I'm Debonair, sir. Pleased to meet you."

Bobby's green eyes took in the blue-black leather costume, the scarlet rose, the mask, the bandages over Debonair's eyes. "Are you the one who saved my granddaughter from Hangman at the museum?"

"Yes, sir."

"And he saved me again tonight." I filled Bobby in on Prism's appearance and subsequent attack.

"She seems pretty desperate to get her hands on the sapphire," Bobby mused. "That should work well for the Fearless Five and their plan to trap her."

Debonair shot me a questioning look. I shook my head.

Bobby looked back and forth between us. "Well, now that I know you're okay, Bella, I'll leave you and your friend to your own devices. This old man needs some sleep. Tomorrow, I think, is going to be a very long day."

He kissed me goodnight, then disappeared down the hall.

"What is he talking about?" Debonair asked. "What are the Fearless Five up to?"

"Come on," I said. "Let's go upstairs, and I'll tell you everything."

We ended up on the sofa in my sitting room. I explained the superheroes' plan to capture Hangman and Prism when they made another grab for the sapphire.

"The Fearless Five are going to drop off the sapphire at the museum in the morning," I said. "The museum plans to reopen tomorrow night and kick off another fund-raiser to help repair the damage done during the fight. We figure Hangman and Prism will try to steal the sapphire again after the museum closes down."

"And you're going to be there tomorrow?"

I nodded. "I want to see this thing through to the end. I want to see Hangman and Prism get carted off to prison."

"Then I'm coming too," Debonair said. "After all, I'm the reason you're in this mess."

"It's not your fault. Just my own bad luck, bad sense of timing."

Debonair took off his mask, and Devlin stared into my eyes. "Is that what you think meeting me, spending time with me, has been? A run of bad luck?"

"Of course not! I've enjoyed our time together."

Loved it, actually. But I couldn't say that to him. It would just make things harder in the end.

Before I could stop him, Devlin pulled me into his lap and

kissed me. I found myself responding, despite my promise to keep my distance.

"Let me love you, Bella. Please. Just for tonight," he murmured against my mouth.

I couldn't look away from the need in his eyes, the desire, the passion. Couldn't pretend they weren't there. Those same emotions filled me too. I'd almost died half a dozen times the past few days. I might die tomorrow night, despite the Fearless Five's assurances that everything would go smoothly.

Suddenly, I didn't want to pass up this chance, not when there were so many things that could go wrong. There would be time to be sensible later. There would be time to say goodbye to Devlin later.

Much, much later.

I climbed off his lap and got to my feet. Disappointment shimmered in his eyes. He thought I was going to tell him to leave again. I wasn't. Not tonight, anyway.

I wasn't bold and daring by nature, not like Fiona and Carmen were. But tonight, I felt like I could do anything. Try anything. Dare anything. Part of me felt like I had to. Just this once.

So I unzipped the back of the dress, peeled it down my arms, and let it crumple to the floor. Most of Fiona's gowns were so form-fitting you couldn't really wear anything under them, except for a bit of perfume. I stepped out of the ruined fabric and kicked it aside, along with my broken shoes. I stood there before him, naked, except for the angel charm around my throat and the silver bracelet dangling from my wrist.

"Stand up," I commanded.

He did as I asked. I moved toward him, careful not to actually touch his body. If I did that, I'd be a goner. So, I reached around his chest, drinking in the smell of roses that emanated from him, and unzipped the back of his costume. I tugged the leather down his arms and threw it aside. Next, I undid his boots. Devlin stepped out of them. Finally, I came to his pants. I undid the zipper, slowly, slowly, slowly, then pulled down the tight fabric.

I moved my lips along his shaft, just brushing it with the

softest, slightest touch. He stiffened and reached for me, but I evaded his grasp and finished lowering his pants. Devlin stepped out of those as well, and I drank in the sight of his naked form. He truly was a beautiful man. Toned. Muscled. And exquisitely hard just where he should be. And he was all mine. At least for tonight.

I stood up and pushed him back until his legs hit the sofa, and he sat down. I put my knees on either side of his legs, straddling him. I rested my hands on his shoulders, the only part of my body actually touching his.

"Do you want me, Devlin?" I asked, teasing him even more.

"You . . . know . . . that I . . . do," he rasped, his fingers clenching the edge of the cushions.

His eyes locked with mine. The passion shimmering in the blue depths almost frightened me, but I was too far gone to care. And I wanted him just as badly as he wanted me. Maybe even more.

"Then love me, Devlin Debonair Dash. Now," I whispered and lowered my lips to his.

I didn't have to tell him twice. I'd pushed him to the edge of his control. His tongue plunged into my mouth, hard and demanding. His hands were everywhere. My face. My hair. Breasts. Stomach. Thighs. In seconds, we were both hot and ready and eager.

Debonair popped a condom into the room and covered himself. I immediately rose up on my knees again and sank down onto his stiff shaft. I slowly began to move, sliding up and down on the hard length, riding him. His groans and cries of pleasure mixed with my own. I increased my pace, increased my rhythm, taking him a little farther in every single time.

"Bella!" he cried out my name.

I threw my head back, rose up a final time, and sank back down to the hilt of him.

The world exploded as we came together.

I slumped over his body, spent and euphoric. He nuzzled my neck, pressing sweet, soft kisses to the hollow of my throat.

"Thank you for that," he said.

"What?"

"Seducing me."

I leaned back and cradled his face in my hands. "Well, I learned from a master."

He shook his head. "No, you've far exceeded anything I've ever dreamed of. I love you, Bella."

I bit my lip and didn't respond. I couldn't. I couldn't tell him I loved him. It would only hurt that much more to let him go in the end. To walk away and never look back. Devlin's eyes grew sad when I didn't return his sentiment, but he smiled anyway.

"So what do you want to do now?" I asked, my eyes straying to the bed. It wouldn't be quite as much fun as the water bed, but it would definitely do.

An impish light appeared in his eyes. "You've had your turn, but I haven't even gotten started yet, Bella."

POP!

Suddenly, our positions were reversed. I lay on my back on the sofa, while Debonair knelt on the floor beside me. He eased my thighs apart and lowered his mouth to my molten core. I arched up off the sofa, burying my fingers in his hair.

POP!

We stood against the wall. His mouth was on my breast, his teeth scraping my hard, aching nipple. His fingers dove inside me, stroking, teasing, caressing. My head spun round and round as desire overcame me once again.

POP!

We lay on the floor, side by side. Devlin traced lazy circles around my breast with one hand, while the other explored my wet, aching folds.

"That's . . . not . . . fair . . . using your . . . superpowers," I gasped.

"But it sure is fun, isn't it?"

He continued his ministrations. I panted as sensation after sensation filled every part of my body. Pleasure. Pressure. I wanted him again. And again. And again.

Now.

POP!

We landed in the bed. I drew him down to me, and Devlin covered my body with his. As he slid into me, I found my release.

And so did he.

I awoke the next morning wrapped in Devlin's arms. It was a good place to be. Warm, safe, secure. I stared at him, watching him sleep. The early morning light streaming through the windows highlighted the sharp planes of his face. His bruises had faded to mere shadows, and the shallow cuts had sewn themselves shut overnight. Devlin must have had a bit of regeneration in him. Most superheroes and ubervillains did. It helped in their line of work.

Devlin must have felt me staring at him, because his eyes fluttered open. For a moment, he looked confused, as if he couldn't quite remember where he was or what had happened. Then, his eyes cleared, and he smiled.

"Hey there, sleepyhead," I whispered.

"Hey there, yourself." Devlin leaned in and pressed a soft kiss to my lips.

We lay there kissing for a long while, before I eased away and sat up.

"How about some breakfast?" I asked, sliding out of bed and pulling on a thick terrycloth robe with black-and-white angels embroidered on it.

Devlin sat up. The cotton sheet fell away, exposing his chest. I eyed him, thinking maybe breakfast would be better in bed.

"I'm going to go," he said, not quite looking at me. "I think it's for the best right now."

"Oh. All right."

Part of me was disappointed. But part of me understood why he was leaving. He'd told me that he loved me, and I hadn't responded. I'd hurt his feelings, but I didn't have any choice. Not if I wanted to hang on to what was left of my sanity. But still another part of me longed to say the words back to him. Because they were true.

I was in love with Devlin Debonair Dash. And I didn't want to be. I wasn't going to be a superhero's girlfriend. I'd already spent too much of my life patching up my superhero grandfather and father and brother. I didn't want to do that anymore. Didn't want to sit up nights worrying about whether Devlin was going to come home or not. I wouldn't put myself through that. Not even for him.

Because if he died, it would break my heart all over again.

But I didn't want him to leave. Not yet. Not like this. So I did the only thing I could. I let the robe fall from my body and climbed back into bed. Devlin stared at me like I was Eve offering him a ripe, juicy apple. Maybe I was. I couldn't tell Devlin that I loved him, but I could show him. In my own way.

"Are you sure you have to go?" I asked, tugging the sheet down off his wonderful body.

"Bella—" he said in a warning tone.

"Hmm?" I asked, lowering my mouth to his stiffening shaft. "What were you saying? Something about going home, I believe."

"I think I can stay . . . a little longer," he said, pulling me closer.

"Good," I murmured before covering him with my mouth once again.

After another round of passion, we lay in bed, cuddled close together. We didn't talk about last night or today or tomorrow. We just were, tangled together in easy silence. I closed my eyes and listened to Devlin's heart *thump-thump-thump* under my ear. If I'd had the power to stop time, I would have used it to preserve this single, precious, perfect moment.

Finally, though, Devlin put on his costume, promising to meet me at the museum reopening tonight. I told him the Fearless Five would have everything under control, but he insisted on being there. Just in case. His concern only made me love him that much more, and I bit my tongue to keep from telling him. Devlin pressed a kiss to my wrist and popped away.

After he left, I stayed in bed, huddled in the warm spot we'd created together. My eyes drifted over the clouds and cherubs frolicking on the ceiling, but I didn't really see the blue-and-white paintings.

I was too busy wondering if I was doing the right thing.

Maybe . . . maybe I was wrong about us not being together. Maybe Devlin and I could make it work. Maybe there was a chance for us, mask and leather and all. I loved him so much. There had to be some way we could make it work. There just had to be.

But try as I might, I couldn't think of what it could be.

Still, I went downstairs to the kitchen more cheerful and hopeful than I'd been in weeks. Bobby sat at the kitchen table, eating scrambled eggs with cheese and mustard, and reading the latest editions of the *Exposé* and the *Chronicle*.

"Someone looks happy this morning," Bobby said.

I couldn't stop the blush that crept up my cheeks, so I concentrated on pouring some juice without spilling it. "I had a nice time last night with my date."

"Ah, yes, your date." Bobby smiled and stuck his face back behind the newspaper, saving me from any more embarrassment.

Footsteps sounded in the hallway. I turned to the door, puzzled by who else could be in the house this early in the morning. Grace Caleb appeared. Her loose silver hair flowed around her shoulders, and she looked just as rumpled and satisfied as me. I froze, my glass of orange juice halfway to my lips.

Grace sashayed over to Bobby and gave him a long, lingering kiss like I wasn't even in the room.

"Ahem."

She kept right on kissing him.

"Ahem!"

The two of them broke apart.

"Hello, Grace," I said, finally taking a sip of my orange juice. The pulpy liquid tasted sweet and wet in my parched mouth.

"Hello, Bella. Did you sleep well?"

I flashed back to last night. I hadn't gotten much sleep at all, not with Devlin popping us into a variety of interesting positions. But I didn't feel tired. Not in the least.

"Oh, yes. And you?"

Grace shot Bobby a naughty grin. "Wonderful. The best sleep I've had in a long, long time."

Grandfather gave her a slow wink. I sat there and tried really, really hard to pretend that sleep was all she was talking about.

Bobby had made enough eggs for the three of us, and we relaxed around the table making small talk. After we'd finished, Grace announced she had to leave. Bobby pouted a bit, then walked her back to the *guest room* where she'd spent the night. They didn't reappear for an hour.

Since Grandfather was otherwise engaged, I drove out to Sublime to check in with the Fearless Five and plot how things would work at the museum tonight. Carmen, Sam, Chief Newman, Henry, Lulu, and I met in the library, just like always. For once, I didn't mind being part of the superheroes' inner circle.

"Everything's in place," Carmen said. "We dropped off the sapphire at the museum this morning and watched while they put it back on display. It's in the same spot as before, except with much more security."

"What do you mean, *more security*?" I asked.

Henry pulled up a schematic on his computer monitor. "Instead of the glass case the museum uses for precious items, we substituted one of our own. If the ubervillains do manage to steal the sapphire, they'll have a hard time getting to it."

I thought of Prism's laserama. "Even with her laser gun?"

"The glass isn't foolproof," Henry admitted. "Nothing ever is."

"Which is where the tracking device comes in," Lulu said. "Henry and the chief sprayed the sapphire with a clear paint that has a radioactive signature. So, even if Prism and Hangman somehow manage to steal the sapphire, escape, and get it out of the case, we'll still be able to track them down."

"It sounds like you've thought of everything," I chimed in, admiring their thoroughness.

Carmen picked up one of her Rubik's Cubes and started playing with it. "I'm still worried," she confessed, twisting the rows of colors back and forth in her hands. "I don't like the fact the museum is reopening with so much fanfare. You don't think the ubervillains will attack then, do you?"

Sam shook his head. "I wouldn't think so. Too many people around. More than likely they'll try to steal the stone after the museum closes. It'll be easier then. At least, they'll think so."

Carmen kept pacing. Sam grabbed her wrist and pulled her into his lap. He took the puzzle from her fingers and put it down on the table.

"Don't worry," he said, gathering her close to him. "Nothing bad is going to happen. We've planned this all too well, and we'll be there to make sure that nothing goes wrong. Okay?"

Carmen stared into his eyes, then pressed a kiss to his lips. "Okay."

Seeing the two of them be so gentle, so tender with each other reminded me of Devlin and how much I'd come to love him. Carmen and Sam had overcome incredible odds to be together. Why couldn't Devlin and I?

We could, I decided. We would. One way or another.

I left Sublime and went home to get ready for the reopening. Bobby had left a note in the kitchen, saying he and Grace were having dinner before going to the museum. I just smiled and shook my head. I was glad Grandfather had found someone to make him happy again. He'd been alone too long. We both had.

I picked out another one of Fiona's gowns to wear, this one a deep, dark green that accentuated the bronze color of my hair, skin, and eyes. It was made of a soft jersey material with lots of give, although the fabric still clung to my body. I twirled in front of the mirror, pleased by the effect and not the least bit self-conscious about my hips and thighs. Well, not as much as usual.

First the scarlet dress, now this one. Seducing Devlin, planning to do the same again tonight. I was ignoring my rules right and left. Not to mention my innate good taste. The next thing you knew, I'd be wearing sequins, feathers, and zebra stripes. All at once.

Maybe being around Debonair had affected me more than I'd realized. I didn't know, but I liked the feeling. I added my angel charm to the outfit, along with Jasper's bomb bracelet.

Since Prism had toasted my Benz, I called a taxi and reached the museum a little after eight. Things were already in full swing. A banner stretched over the front steps said GRAND REOPENING! COME AND JOIN THE FUN! WHIMSICAL WONDERS LIVES ON!

I entered the museum and headed for the new wing. The last time I'd seen it, the area had been full of plaster and sweaty construction guys. Now, everything looked just the same as it always did. Immaculate marble walls. Vivid paintings. Unusual statues. And the Star Sapphire sitting in the middle of the grand hall, casting its cool blue light on everything.

I worked my way through the chattering crowd, looking for one particular face. I spotted all the usual bigwigs, including Berkley Brighton and Joanne James. I even saw Jasper chatting up a woman in a corner. I waved to the bomber. His eyes landed on my bracelet, and he smiled and gave me a thumbs-up. I froze in midwave and carefully lowered my hand. I kept forgetting just how deadly my pretty bracelet was. I was just glad I hadn't had to use Jasper's creation. And if things went well tonight, I could return it to him. Maybe he'd even give Lulu some of her money back.

"Hello, beautiful. Are you here alone?" a sexy voice murmured in my ear.

I smiled and turned to find Devlin standing behind me. He looked marvelous in a black tux and his silver glasses. How could I have ever thought him awkward and clumsy and shy? I stood on my tiptoes and pressed a kiss to his cheek.

"Oh, no. I'm afraid I have a very hot date tonight," I teased.

"Maybe you'd like to go home with me instead."

I looked him up and down. "Maybe. But you'll have to give me a good reason to."

Devlin put his lips against my ear again. "How about a repeat performance of last night?"

I smiled. "That sounds like a good enough reason for me."

"I'm glad."

Devlin held out his hand, and I tucked my arm in his. The two of us wandered through the room, talking to everyone we knew. I spotted the members of the Fearless Five in among the crowd. Carmen, Sam, Henry, Lulu, Chief Newman. They'd come to the reopening tonight just in case there was the slightest hint of trouble.

More than a few eyes landed on Devlin and me, and whispers followed us around the room. We'd be the talk of the society scene by morning, as were all the new couples who hooked up in public. But I didn't care what other people thought. I loved Devlin. Now all I had to do was figure out a way to make it work between us.

Berkley and Joanne stood in the middle of the room next to the Star Sapphire, the center of attention just like always. Devlin and I strolled over to them. Hannah Harmon hovered nearby. She murmured pleasantries to the people she was talking to, but her eyes were firmly fixed on the sapphire.

"Bella! How lovely to see you again!" Joanne said, presenting her cheek for the usual air kiss.

I obliged her. "You too, Joanne. Berkley."

The older billionaire nodded at me.

My eyes went to the sapphire resting on its pedestal. The glass case didn't look any different from the one it had been under before, but I trusted the Fearless Five. Henry and Lulu knew exactly what to do when it came to gadgets—especially those designed to stop ubervillains.

By midnight I was ready for the event to end, so I could head to the security room with the Fearless Five and wait for Prism and Hangman to show up and try to steal the gem. Then, this nightmare would be over, and I could get on with my life—hopefully with Devlin.

My power flared, the first time it had acted up all day, and my feet turned of their own volition toward the sapphire. Berkley and Joanne stood next to the gem, talking with Hannah. A man in a wheelchair sat next to them, his back to me. Something about the hard set of Joanne's lips and the way she clutched Berkley's hand bothered me. She almost looked worried, and Joanne James never worried about anything.

"What's wrong?" Devlin asked.

"I don't know," I said, moving toward the sapphire.

Across the room, I saw Carmen do the same, drawn by the same bad feeling.

"I said no, Hannah." Berkley Brighton's baritone reverberated through the room. "I have no interest in what you're proposing."

"But, Berkley, think of all the power we could have," Hannah wheedled. "The money, the position, the influence."

Berkley's hand tightened around Joanne's. "I happen to be very happy with my current situation—professionally and personally. I'm sorry."

All conversation stopped. Hannah's eyes flicked around. Everyone had heard Berkley turn her down. They all stared at her, mouths slightly agape. Then, the whispers began. A few people snickered with amusement. Something red and angry sparked in the depths of her eyes at the soft sound.

"Fine, Berkley, if that's the way you want it. Nobody move!" Hannah Harmon screamed, pulling what looked like a laser pointer out of her evening bag. "This is a robbery!"

★28★

Everybody froze.

My eyes went to the device in her hands, and my mouth dropped open. It was the same laserama she'd pointed at me last night. Hannah Harmon was Prism? It didn't seem possible.

But things got even more bizarre. The man in the wheelchair sprang to his feet, kicked the contraption away, and turned to face me. I realized who he was—Nathan Nichols, the financial guru who'd bilked Devlin's company out of millions and now worked for Hannah. Nichols ripped off his tuxedo, revealing a gray spandex suit and a silver utility belt. Prism and Hangman were both here. And they were going to steal the Star Sapphire right now—no matter who got in the way.

I looked around to see where Carmen was, but she'd melted into the frightened crowd, along with the other members of the Fearless Five. So had Devlin. One moment, he was by my side, the next, he was gone.

Hannah commanded everyone's attention, holding her laserama on Berkley and Joanne.

"Why are you doing this, Hannah?" Berkley asked, his voice remarkably calm. "Surely my turning down your business and other proposals hasn't upset you this much?"

Hannah threw back her head and laughed. "Don't you understand, you fool?"

She jerked her head at Hangman. He stepped forward and ripped away the dress from her body, revealing a familiar yellow costume with a triangle on the front of it.

Joanne hissed, "You're an ubervillain!"

"Right you are, Joanne. Right you are." Hannah addressed the rest of the crowd. "My name is Prism. Learn my name, know it well, because you'll be hearing a lot more of me. Very, very soon. In a couple of hours, I'm going to be the one running this town."

Hannah, Prism, pointed her laserama up and pulled the trigger. A red beam shot out from the end of the barrel, shattering the restored glass ceiling with a tremendous roar. With one thought, people screamed and stampeded toward the exits, even as glass rained down and the alarms started blaring. The crowd rushed past me, sweeping me back, and I lost sight of the ubervillains.

I stayed in the room, looking for Grandfather. I didn't see Bobby among the panicked crowd, but I did spot Grace Caleb, half-hidden behind one of the statues. She whipped something out of her purse and snapped it down beside her leg. I squinted through the mad dash of people. It looked like a cane. A diamond-topped cane. Grace drew a mask out of her bag and slipped it over her head. Then, she draped an angora sweater across her shoulders. I recognized her at once.

My eyes threatened to pop out of my head. Grace Caleb was actually Granny Cane? The little old lady who went around Bigtime suckering thieves into mugging her? No wonder she'd had a *family emergency* the other night. I wondered if Bobby knew what Grace did when she wasn't playing bridge or drinking tea. He'd definitely approve.

Hannah continued with her rant, brandishing her laser at Berkley and Joanne. "You all think you're so clever, so smart with your little cliques and groups and inner circles. You're nothing but a bunch of phonies. I've tried to fit in. I've tried to play your little popularity games. Well, I'm sick of it. Instead of pretending to be like the rest of you, I'm going to take what I want and damn the consequences."

"People don't like you enough so you decided to become an ubervillain?" Joanne snapped. "How pathetic."

Hannah glared at the other woman. "No more pathetic than you marrying every other man in Bigtime, you tramp."

"Honey, I'm not a tramp. I'm not the one wearing yellow leather." Joanne's eyes flicked down the other woman's form. "Without the figure to pull it off."

Hannah held the laserama up to Joanne's face.

"Stop!" another voice called out.

Striker strode into the room, followed by Karma Girl, Mr.

Sage, and Hermit. Seeing the superheroes in their bright costumes reminded me of the last time I'd been here, when Hangman and Debonair had been fighting. I had the strangest sense of déjà vu.

"Come any closer, and I'll blow her away," Hannah warned, her finger hovering over the button on her weapon.

Hangman eased off to one side, giving the superheroes two targets instead of just one. Striker's eyes flicked around the room, analyzing the situation. His gaze cut to Karma Girl, who shook her head. Hermit did the same. Striker's hand twitched, as though he was signaling one of the members of the team.

Mr. Sage's eyes began to glow neon green. A moment later, something yanked down on Hannah's arm, pulling the laserama away from Joanne's face.

"What—What are you doing?" Hannah screamed. "Nobody messes with me! Nobody messes with Prism!"

Hannah raised the laserama and pressed the button.

Joanne stood in front of the ubervillain, but somehow, Berkley shoved her out of the way at the last possible moment. Joanne crashed into Mr. Sage, who caught her. The laser slammed into the billionaire's chest, and the stench of burning flesh filled the room. For an instant, Berkley's eyes flashed as scarlet as Prism's. A black, smoking hole appeared over his heart. Berkley stumbled back from the impact of the laser. He looked at his burning chest, then at Joanne. Then, he smiled once and crumpled to the floor.

Dead. I knew he was dead. No one could survive something like that. No one.

I clapped my hands over my mouth, horrified by what I'd just seen. Joanne wrenched herself free from Mr. Sage's restraining hands.

"Berkley! Berkley! No, no, nooo!" Joanne screamed, throwing herself on top of Berkley's lifeless body.

Hannah took aim at Joanne, who did something I never would have expected her to—she launched herself at the ubervillain.

Joanne might have been one of the richest women in Bigtime, but she certainly knew how to fight. She caught Prism around the ankles, and the two women hit the ground. They rolled around on the marble floor, shrieking and kicking and clawing among the shards of broken glass. Prism might have had super-strength, but it didn't faze Joanne a bit. She fought like a woman possessed—like a woman who'd just lost her husband.

The Fearless Five started forward to break up the fight, but a grenade slid across the floor and landed at Striker's feet. The sight snapped me out of my horrified daze.

"Grenade!" I screamed. "Grenade!"

Karma Girl grabbed Striker's suit and yanked him back with a strength I didn't know she had. The grenade exploded, and the room went orange, then black, then gray. The shock and fire from the blast knocked me to my knees. My power pulsed, and my feet slid out from under me just as a knifelike piece of shrapnel zipped through the space where my head had been. I landed hard on the floor. Smoke filled the air, making me cough and wheeze.

Through the billowing clouds, I felt something sticky plop onto my head. I reached up and brought my fingers back down. White foam from the sprinklers covered my whole hand. More bits sputtered through the air. I definitely had déjà vu now. And an intense desire to be somewhere other than here. I scrambled to my feet, ignoring the pain shooting through my knees and back where I'd hit the floor.

The gray haze started to clear. Hannah stood next to the sap-phire, holding the laserama against Joanne's temple and using her as a human shield against the Fearless Five. I didn't see Hangman or Grace or Bobby through the dissipating smoke.

Or Devlin. Where *was* he?

"Stay back or she dies!" Hannah screamed at the Fearless Five.

Joanne twisted and struggled in the ubervillain's grasp, mindless of the device pressed against her head. "Kill her! Kill her now, you fools!"

The superheroes froze. There was nothing they could do. If they moved an inch, Joanne would be just as dead as Berkley. From the tears streaming down her face, I didn't think Joanne would mind that much.

But Hannah had her back to me. I looked at the ubervillain, then over my shoulder. The path to the door was clear this time, with no villains standing in my way. I could slip out of the room to safety, and no one would be the wiser. No one would know I'd even been in here. No one would know I hadn't tried to save Joanne. No one but me.

I stepped back toward the door.

Joanne sobbed again and started cursing, struggling with all her might against Prism. My eyes went to Berkley's body, lying on the marble floor. If not for the smoke rising from his chest, I would have almost thought he was sleeping. But he wasn't. Berkley was dead. And Joanne would be too, if someone didn't stop Prism.

If I didn't stop Prism.

My foot hovered in midair. It would be so easy for me to put it down, turn, and run away. So, so easy. But I didn't do that. I put my foot down, but this time, I stepped toward danger instead of away from it. For once in my life, I was willingly going to get involved in a hero-villain battle.

If I could use my power to get really, really lucky, I just might be able to get the laserama away from Prism before she could use it on Joanne. If I had any sense, I'd turn and run away. If I did, though, Joanne would die.

If, if, if.

Sensing my warring emotions, my power flared to life, going from a low drone to a rising hum. My fingers itched, my hair frizzed, and I eased forward, willing my luck to work, praying it would, just this once.

Karma Girl saw me out of the corner of her eye and gave me the tiniest nod. *Go for it,* I could almost hear her whisper in my mind. *We're out of options and almost out of time.*

My hand went to my wrist, and I fingered the bracelet Jasper had given me. But there was no way I could use it in here without killing us all. So I picked up a small bronze statue shaped like a pencil from one of the pedestals. A good smack across the back of the head should be enough to distract Hannah from lasering Joanne. Then, the Fearless Five could move in and capture the ubervillain—

Beefy fingers latched on to my arm and jerked me back.

"Going somewhere?" Hangman asked, his hand tightening around my arm.

My fingers went numb, and the statue slid from my grasp, clanking against the floor. Any tighter, and he'd break my wrist with his grip. At the clanging noise, Hannah looked over her shoulder and forced Joanne to turn around so she could keep an eye on all of us at the same time.

WHACK!

Something smashed into the back of Hangman's head. He let go of my arm and staggered away. Granny Cane stood behind the ubervillain, already bringing her cane around for another blow. But Hangman recovered quickly. He grabbed the cane and swung it and Granny up, around, over his head. The ubervillain let go and sent her flying through the room. Granny hit a wall on the opposite side of the museum and slumped to the floor. Another figure darted through the smoke and foam. Grandfather. Bobby dropped to a knee beside Granny Cane's limp body. I started toward them.

"Forget the old woman! Get her! Get Bulluci!" Hannah screamed, her eyes fixed on me.

Hangman reached out—

POP!

And Debonair teleported right in front of me, protecting me from the advancing ubervillain yet again.

"Don't you dare touch her," he snarled at the taller man.

Hangman just laughed and swatted at Debonair like he was no more bothersome than a buzzing fly. But instead of teleporting out of the way, Debonair took the blow. He couldn't move, or I would have been the one getting my face smashed in.

Hangman's fist hit Debonair's nose, and the bones *snapped* and *crackled* and *popped* like cereal. Blood spewed out from his face. The blow stunned Debonair, and Hangman used the opportunity to grab his left arm. The ubervillain snapped the limb like it was a piece of brittle biscotti. Debonair groaned and slumped to the floor in agony, his face white with pain underneath all the blood.

"Debonair!" I screamed, reaching for him.

But Hangman was too quick. He grabbed me around the waist and hauled me toward the center of the room where Prism stood with Joanne. The Fearless Five started forward, but Prism pressed the laserama to Joanne's temple.

"One more move by anyone and she dies, along with Bulluci!"

The superheroes stood there. Helpless.

"Get the sapphire and get us out of here! Now!" Prism barked at her henchman.

Hangman wrenched the glass case containing the sapphire off the pedestal. He shoved it at me.

"Hold it or die," he hissed.

I didn't have much choice in the matter, so I wrapped my shaking arms around the square box as best I could. Prism snapped some sort of cable onto the utility belt around Hangman's waist and fastened it to a hidden hook in her own costume.

"Let's go," Prism commanded her henchman. "Now."

"No!"

"Stop!"

"Bella!"

Everyone started screaming and shouting and rushing forward at once. But I only had eyes for Debonair. His bloody, pain-filled face was the last thing I saw before Hangman flew us up through the museum's shattered ceiling.

PART THREE

I

♥

Debonair

★ 29 ★

Flying in Hangman's arms was nothing like teleporting around the city with Debonair. Joanne, Prism, and I hung off his belt like keys on a life-size ring, rattling and bumping and smacking together. The world zipped by in a haze of blue and white and black. The glass case felt heavy and slick in my sweaty, aching hands, but somehow I managed to hold on to it.

I wasn't even aware I was screaming until Hangman yanked on my tangled hair.

"Shut up or I'll knock out your teeth," he snarled.

Since I wanted to keep my teeth right where they were, I shut up. Joanne wasn't quite so sensible. As we soared through the cool, misty clouds, she kept punching and kicking Prism and screaming curses at the other woman. I would have helped if I hadn't been afraid of dropping the sapphire into the middle of Bigtime Bay—and following it a second later when Hangman realized what I'd done. Finally, Prism clipped the side of Joanne's temple with the laserama, and she went limp and still.

"What did you do to her?" I yelled above the rushing wind. "What did you do?"

"The bitch will be fine. I just knocked her out. Now quit talking!" Prism screamed back.

We flew for what seemed like hours, although it could have been only a few minutes. Hangman rocketed through the sky faster than any missile ever could. I had no sense of direction, only of color passing by me much, much faster than normal.

Hangman glided to a stop on top of a large yacht in the middle of the bay. He let go of me the second his booted feet touched the deck. I slumped on the slick wood, along with Joanne, who was still unconscious. My legs wouldn't have supported a feather, much less me. At the moment, I was just glad I was back on solid ground again. So to speak.

"Are we clear?" Hangman asked, unbuckling Prism from his utility belt.

Prism pulled some sort of small computer out of another pouch on Hangman's belt and starting hitting buttons. "Yes. The cops are on the scene, but they don't have a clue, like usual. No sign of the Fearless Five, but there's no way they could have tracked us here. Besides, the cloaking shield went up as soon as we touched down. We're fine."

Cloaking shield? I didn't like the sound of that. Somehow, I made my aching, shaking hands let go of the glass case, and I crawled over to Joanne. The other woman was a mess. Her hair hung in black strands around her face, which was bruised and bloody from her altercation with Prism. Her knuckles were scraped, and her perfect nails broken beyond all repair. I checked Joanne's pulse and watched her breathing. Both were strong and steady. Well, that was something to be grateful for.

My eyes flicked around, looking for a way off the yacht. But instead of a dinghy or life jacket, my gaze locked onto something far less useful—and far more horrifying.

The laser.

It sat in the middle of the deck, pointing out toward the city. It looked exactly the same as it had in the blueprints we'd gotten from Jasper—an enormous laser with a chair that swiveled around like a gun on a tank. Except for the fact the laser was bigger than a tank by itself. I didn't see how the boat could support its weight and stay above the waterline.

"Get them inside before someone sees them," Prism snapped, picking up the glass case. Her eyes gleamed with delight and triumph as she gazed at the enormous sapphire. "Mine. It's finally mine," she whispered.

"You've got the sapphire. You've got what you want. Let us go," I said, trying to reason with the ubervillain. "You killed Berkley and destroyed the museum. Again. Isn't that enough for you?"

Prism scoffed. "Hardly. That was just the opening act of this little drama. Save your breath, Bella. You won't be breathing much longer."

She turned and walked away. Hangman picked me up with one hand and Joanne with the other, like we were dumbbells. I was too shaken up to struggle with him. Prism went down a flight of stairs and through a door. Hangman followed her.

Most boats, no matter how big they look from the outside, are actually rather tiny when you go belowdecks. Not this one. It was all high ceilings, wide corridors, and massive rooms. With its gleaming brass and wood, it was one of the nicest yachts I'd ever been on. Except for the fact it belonged to a closet ubervillain.

We went down three more flights of stairs before coming to another door. Prism punched in a code on a keypad, then stuck her eye close to the machine for a retinal scan. The door slid back, and Hangman carried us inside.

Rows of computers and other equipment lined the walls, along with worktables, gadgets, gizmos, and the usual assortment of oddities. This must have been where Prism had assembled her enormous laser, one piece at a time. Windows wrapped all the way around the enormous space, offering an impressive view of the nighttime bay. The city skyline glittered in the distance, reminding me of an oasis. Or a mirage.

Hangman walked to the far side of the room, where another door stood. He leaned down and yanked it open, still carrying us. A row of metal cells lay inside, along with a few hard-looking cots. Ah, yes, the brig. What would an ubervillain lair be without some place to hold the innocent and unsuspecting heroes while the villain gave her exposition? Except, of course, Joanne and I weren't superheroes. Just unlucky victims.

Hangman slung us inside a metal cell and closed the door, locking it. Prism trailed along behind him to make sure he'd done the job right—and to gloat.

I got to my feet, ignoring the pain stabbing through my body, and lurched over to the bars. Prism regarded me with cool, calculating eyes. Even if they were glowing red orbs.

"I bet this isn't how you thought your evening would end, is it, Bella?" she sneered.

"Not quite," I admitted. "What do you plan on doing with the sapphire and that laser out there?"

Prism smiled. "Something I should have done a long time ago—destroy this city and its worthless inhabitants."

I swallowed, trying to ignore the fear that her words inspired. "And just how are you going to do that?"

Prism held up the glass case with the sapphire. "With this, of course. My laserama is quite powerful by itself. But with the Star Sapphire, it will be a weapon to truly be reckoned with. Nothing has more reflective and refractive capacity than the gem, and it will increase the power of my laser thirtyfold. In fact, the sapphire is going to be the centerpiece of my laserama. I was counting on the Fearless Five or some other superhero being kind enough to return it to the museum. I knew it would be a trap, of course, a way to lure me out into the open to try to steal it again. So I decided to strike first. With tremendous success, I'd say."

I closed my eyes. Berkley was dead, Joanne and I were kidnapped, Devlin had been injured, and Prism was about to destroy the city. Everything had gone so horribly, horribly wrong.

"By dawn, I'll bring Bigtime to its knees," Prism crowed. "I'll own this city and everything and everyone in it. Who knows? If you're lucky, I just might let you live long enough to see my plan reach its inevitable, triumphant conclusion."

"What are you going to do? Blow up something?"

She laughed again. "Of course. At least, as a demonstration of my power and determination. Being out here on the bay gives me access to any number of targets. I haven't decided yet if I'll annihilate Paradise Park or Quicke's. Maybe even Oodles o' Stuff, although I hate to destroy that particular retail outlet. Then, I plan on holding the city hostage until my demands are met."

I had to ask. "What demands?"

"One billion dollars transferred to a bank account of my choosing. A statue of me erected in the middle of the downtown district. Every street renamed after me. A public declaration by the Fearless Five on SNN acknowledging that I beat them at their own game." Prism ticked off the demands on her fingers. "You know, all the usual stuff."

"The Fearless Five will stop you," I said, hoping my voice sounded stronger than I felt. "They will. And if they don't, the other superheroes will band together. You won't get away with this. None of it."

Prism just chuckled. "That's why you and Joanne are going to make such lovely hostages. No one will dare try anything as long as I've got you two under lock and key. After all, they wouldn't want to blow up two of the richest and most beloved women in Bigtime, now would they? Especially since you seem to be on good terms with Debonair and the Fearless Five."

"You can't stay out here in the bay forever," I pointed out. "Somebody will find you eventually."

"I'm counting on it. I'm afraid when the superheroes decide to storm the yacht, there will be a horrible, tragic accident, which you and Joanne won't survive. The superheroes will think Hangman and I perished as well."

My eyes flicked to Hangman, who was leaning against the wall, listening to us. "Why?"

Prism gave me a patronizing look. "Because I can't very well retire to a nice tropical island and enjoy my victory if I'm constantly hounded by superheroes. Being an ubervillain has been fun, but I'm ready to have a little peace and quiet. The only way to do that is if everyone thinks I'm dead."

I hated to admit it, but her plan was solid. Threaten the city with the laserama, hold Joanne and me as collateral, then fake everyone's death. Well, Joanne and I wouldn't be faking, but Prism and Hangman would. It was very clever, and I couldn't think of a single way to stop it.

"You know I should really thank you, Bella. You made all of this possible."

"What do you mean?"

Prism smiled. "I've been trying for months to get my hands on the Star Sapphire, but Berkley didn't warm up to any of my advances. And then, the most wonderful thing happened—you and Joanne convinced him to put it on display at the museum."

The way she talked about Berkley made me think about the night of the bachelor auction and benefit, when Joanne had been so angry at Hannah for hitting on Berkley. Hannah hadn't been trying to steal Berkley from Joanne. She'd just wanted the gem for her laser—and had been willing to do anything to get it.

"Of course, I tried to get the sapphire before it got to the museum," Prism continued, giving Hangman a pointed look. "But some people weren't up to the task."

More memories flashed through my mind. The night Debonair broke into Brilliance, Berkley mentioned the alarms had been going off all week. It hadn't been Debonair trying to get inside, at least not those first few times. It had been Hangman, hoping to snatch the sapphire on Hannah's orders.

Another realization popped into my head.

"That's why you volunteered to help with the benefit in the first place," I accused. "You were planning to steal the sapphire all along!"

Prism smiled. "Of course. In hostile takeovers, it's smart to gather as much information as you can beforehand. It helps avoid nasty surprises. Helping with the benefit was an easy way to keep tabs on the sapphire and the security you arranged for it."

I couldn't believe I'd fallen for her scheme. I should have known Hannah had some ulterior motive. Like Joanne had said, she wasn't a nice person, just a bully with lots of money.

Prism let out another laugh. "But now, I'm afraid we're going to have to leave you and Joanne to your own devices. Come along, Hangman. It's time to finish our plan."

She walked away, followed by the tall ubervillain. The door shut behind them, and I heard the lock click home.

Let's see. I was trapped in a cell with an injured, unconscious woman, while a maniacal ubervillain held me and the city hostage. My superhero friends had no idea where I was, and the man I loved had been seriously injured. And the whole situation was largely my fault. Yep, I was batting a thousand today.

Lucky, lucky me.

★ 30 ★

I didn't dwell on my precarious predicament. I'd learned a long time ago there was no use pondering the supermesses I made. They never got cleaned up that way.

The first thing I did was see to Joanne. Hangman had been considerate enough to sling her unconscious body onto one of the cots inside the cell. The bump on her head worried me, but I couldn't do anything about that right now. I checked her pulse and breathing again. Both were still steady and strong, and the cuts and bruises on her face and hands were mostly superficial. Joanne James was made of tougher stuff than her stick figure let on. I pulled off her shoes, smoothed her hair back from her face, and put a blanket over her body, trying to make her as comfortable as possible, since it looked like we were going to be here awhile.

The second thing I did was try the cell door. It was just as solid and sturdy and steely as it looked. The bars didn't budge—not even an inch. There weren't any hinges to pop this time. I wouldn't be getting out of this cell without some serious assistance. Too bad I didn't have Fiona's superstrength to help me bust out.

I paced back and forth in the cell, trying to figure a way out of my prison. Minutes slipped by, then an hour, then another one. And still I couldn't think of a way to get out of the cell.

Frustrated, I smacked my hand against the bars. A familiar jangle sounded, and my eyes fell to the silver charm bracelet around my wrist. Then again, maybe I had something even better than superstrength—a toy from Jasper. I'd forgotten about the bomb-filled bracelet while Hangman flew us away, but I was sure going to use it now. If I could figure out how to do that without blowing Joanne and me up in the process.

"Bella?"

I turned to find Joanne sitting up on the cot. The other woman's eyes went slowly around the brig, as if she couldn't quite believe what she was seeing.

"Where are we?" Her words slurred together, her violet eyes hazy and out of focus.

"How are you feeling?" I asked, gently probing the bump on the side of Joanne's head with my fingers. It had gone down considerably since I'd checked it a few minutes ago.

"I have a headache," Joanne replied. "And my stomach hurts. What happened?"

"Don't you remember?"

She shook her head and winced. "Not really. I just remember Berkley smiling at me . . ."

I hated to be the bearer of bad news, but I filled Joanne in on everything that had happened at the museum and since Prism had knocked her out, including the ubervillain's master plan.

"She killed Berkley so she could use the sapphire to power her laser? To get money from the city?"

Joanne's eyes filled with tears. She put her head in her hands. I put my arm around her. Joanne buried her face in my shoulder and cried. Violent sobs shook her thin body, and her hot tears dripped down my shoulder and arm. The salt from them made my own cuts burn.

Joanne let herself cry for five minutes. Then, she pulled away from me and swiped the rest of the tears from her eyes. Her mascara had cascaded down her face, reminding me of some sort of black superhero mask. Joanne got to her feet, marched over to the cell bars, and started tugging on them for all she was worth.

"What are you doing?" I asked, surprised by her actions. "You're not some superhero in disguise, are you?"

"Of course not," Joanne snapped in a dark, violent tone. "I don't know about you, but I plan on getting out of here and derailing Prism's little plan. After I kill the bitch, of course. Now, are you going to sit there or are you going to get off your sorry ass and help me?"

I got off my sorry ass and went over to the bars. But instead of helping Joanne fruitlessly tug at them, I took the bracelet off my wrist and looked through the dangling silver charms.

"What the hell are you doing? Now is not the time to be admiring your jewelry, Bella."

"I'm not admiring it," I said, getting a little snappish. "And it's not really a bracelet. If you must know, each one of these charms is really an explosive—far more valuable than a bracelet right now."

Joanne's sharp eyes locked onto the bracelet. "Did Jasper make that for you?"

"Yes. Do you know him?"

"You could say that." Her mouth twisted. "He's my brother."

"Your brother?!" I screeched.

Joanne winced. "Tone it down, Bella. Your voice is getting almost as loud as your hair."

I opened my mouth to pepper her with questions, but Joanne cut me off.

"Yes, Jasper's my brother," she said. "We don't have the best relationship, which is why nobody knows we're related. He doesn't approve of my life choices, and I'm not too crazy about his."

"But—"

"I don't want to talk about it," Joanne snapped, her violet eyes hard and angry. "Can we just focus on getting out of here right now?"

Joanne James, the sister of the city's master bomber? It boggled the mind, but I decided to save my questions for later. Right now, all that mattered was the two of us escaping in more or less one piece.

"The problem is I can't remember which charm he said had the least amount of explodium in it. Even if I could remember, the explosion would probably still kill us both."

Joanne took the bracelet from my cold fingers and flipped through the charms. "Here, it's this one." She pointed to one in the shape of a small rose.

"How do you know that?"

"I just know." Joanne's mouth twisted again. "And don't worry about the explosion. We can get behind the cot. We'll be fine, trust me."

Joanne seemed to have a lot of faith in Jasper, even if they were estranged. I decided to trust her. I didn't have a lot of other options. Luck could only get you so far, and then you had to do things for yourself.

"But what are we going to do once we get out of here?" I pointed to the door at the far end of the room. "I heard them lock it. Even if we get through that door too, they'll be waiting on the other side for us. Anyway, they're bound to hear the explosion when we use the charm to blow open the cell door."

Joanne shook her head. "Not with this one. It'll make a small *pop*, but that's about it." She flipped through some more of the charms. "We can use the high-heel shoe to blast the lock on the next door. It's not much more powerful than the rose."

"And then what?"

Joanne hefted the bracelet in her bloody hands. "I'd say we arm the bracelet, toss it in the room with them, and take our chances."

"That seems like a hell of a chance to take," I said. "Jasper told me there was enough explodium in that thing to take out half the city."

"We can modify the charge a bit, but he's right. There's enough explodium here to do that—and it should be more than enough to knock out Prism and Hangman. Or just kill them. I'm okay with either of those options."

I worked it out in my mind. I couldn't remember seeing another door in the room when we'd been brought in, but surely, there had to be another way off the boat besides going back up to the deck and flying off à la Hangman.

"All right, then," I said, making up my mind. "Let's do it."

With Joanne's help, I dragged the cot away from the wall and tipped it over on its side. It wasn't much, just some metal bars with a hard pallet over them, but it was better than nothing.

As we worked, I couldn't help thinking about Devlin. He'd looked half dead the last time I'd seen him. I didn't know how badly he was hurt, and it was killing me. I could only imagine how Joanne felt, losing Berkley. I didn't think I'd be holding up half as well as she was under the circumstances.

Once we had the cot arranged to our satisfaction, Joanne took the bracelet from me. She slipped the rose charm off the silver chain and popped it into the lock like a pro.

"Where did you learn so much about explosives?" I asked. "Did Jasper teach you?"

"Not exactly."

Joanne didn't volunteer any more information, and I decided not to pry. She'd been through enough already today.

"What's the code?" Joanne said. "You have to say it out loud for the bomb to arm itself."

She knew about Jasper's code words too? Joanne was full of surprises.

I leaned down to the rose charm and said the magic words. "Luck be a lady."

Joanne raised an eyebrow, but she didn't say anything about my unusual choice. We scrambled back around the cot and crouched down behind it.

Pop!

Joanne was right. The sound was scarcely louder than someone clapping their hands together. But it was more than enough to blow the lock off the door. We waited for the smoke to clear, then stepped out of the cell and crept down to the other door. We stopped and listened, but I couldn't hear anything through the thick metal door—except for some weird sort of humming.

"What do you think that is?" Joanne asked in a hushed voice.

"Probably Prism firing up her laserama. She said she was going to own the city by dawn." I checked my angel watch. "That's a little less than an hour from now. She must be getting ready to destroy whatever her target is."

"What about the Fearless Five?" Joanne asked. "Why aren't they here yet?"

"Prism has some kind of shielding device on the yacht. Don't worry. They should find us before too long. They sprayed the sapphire with radioactive tracking paint. They're probably on their way right now. They'll save us."

Joanne's face hardened. "Like they saved Berkley?"

I couldn't think of anything to say to that.

"Call me old-fashioned, but I prefer to save myself," Joanne snapped. "Now give me your bracelet again."

I did as she asked. Joanne slipped another charm—the high-heel shoe—off the bracelet and stuffed it into the lock. I said the magic words, and we scurried back down the hallway to our cell.

Pop! Pop!

The explosion made a bit more noise than before, but not enough to draw immediate attention, because neither Prism nor Hangman came to investigate. We crept back up to the door. A bit of smoke wafted away from the obliterated lock. It reminded me of roses, the same scent Debonair trailed behind him wherever he went. My heart twisted.

We went into the workroom, but the ubervillains weren't down here anymore. I led Joanne through the halls, retracing the path the ubervillains had made. Our feet sank into the carpet. The only sounds were our labored breathing, and that faint, ominous hum. We passed what looked like a living room, and Joanne motioned for me to stop. She slid inside and picked up a fireplace poker and then a phone on top of one of the tables. My heart lifted. If she could call for help, this whole mess would be over.

Joanne made a disgusted face and slammed down the phone. "No dial tone."

So we crept on, past room after room. We went upstairs and downstairs, but we couldn't find another way off the boat—other than going back up to the main deck.

After a whispered discussion, we decided to make a break for it. We reached the door that led out to the deck. Joanne eased it open, and we stuck our heads outside. I didn't see Prism anywhere, but Hangman stood next to the laser, making notations on a large clipboard. He'd already stuck the sapphire into the machine just in front of the barrel, and it bathed the whole deck in a harsh blue glow. The machine also hummed, a low, steady drone that made it hard to think.

I scanned the deck, looking for a way off. My eyes landed on a couple of small dinghies lashed to one side. Too bad Hangman stood between us and them. There was no way we could sneak past the ubervillain without him seeing and stopping us—

The smell of roses of filled the air.

POP!

Debonair teleported in front of Hangman. The ubervillain's mouth dropped open in surprise.

"What the hell are you doing—"

That was all he got out before Debonair punched him in the face. The blow was enough to rock Hangman back on his feet, but not enough to knock him down or unconscious. It was, however, enough to make Debonair wince. He looked even worse than he had at the museum. Blood covered his face and costume, and his left arm hung at his side in a weird, twisted angle. Pain whitened his face underneath his mask, and fever and exhaustion brightened his eyes. I grimaced at the sight of the sexy thief, sickened and angry by what the ubervillains had done to the man I loved.

Hangman shook off the blow and leapt at Debonair, and the two started teleporting and flying around the deck like madmen.

POP!

Smack!

POP! POP!

Smack!

It was like standing in the middle of a sound effects machine.

"Where are they?" Debonair demanded, teleporting all around the boat, always just out of Hangman's long grasp. "Where's Bella? What have you done to her?"

In between teleports, Debonair would lash out with his one good arm and punch the ubervillain in the face or kick him with his boots. The sight warmed my heart, but it also filled me with nauseating dread. I hated seeing Debonair in danger, especially because of me.

My power pulsed, adding to my sense of unease. I realized there was something missing, or rather someone. Where was Prism?

I got my answer a second later. The ubervillain stepped out

from behind the device. She smiled, drew the laserama from her belt, and pointed it at Debonair's back. There was no time to get to her. No time to distract her or call out a warning. No time to do anything at all. Debonair was going to die just like Berkley Brighton had. Just like my father, James, had.

But somehow, I did something. I reached for my power, imagining Debonair's feet sliding out from under him, willing it to happen, praying for it to like I'd never prayed for anything before in my life.

And they did.

He took a step, and his boots skidded along the deck. Before I could warn him, Prism pushed the button on her laserama. Debonair hit the floor just as the red beam zapped through the air above his bloody chest. The laser hit one of the dinghies on the opposite side of the yacht. The wood burst into flames.

But as my bad luck would have it, Debonair smacked his head against the deck when he fell. He let out a low groan and tried to get to his feet, but Hangman was too quick for him. The ubervillain put his enormous foot on Debonair's chest, pinning him.

"Where did he come from?" Prism hissed. "How did he track us here?"

Hangman shrugged. "He must have been teleporting around the city looking for us. It's been known to happen."

Prism raised the laserama and aimed it at Debonair's chest again. "Well, this is the last time it's going to happen. Ever." Her finger hovered over the button.

"Debonair!" I screamed.

Hangman and Prism's heads whipped around to Joanne and me, still crouching inside the doorway. Joanne grabbed my arm, but I shook her off. This was exactly how my father had died—trying to fight off two ubervillains. I didn't know what I would do if Debonair met his fate. My heart couldn't take it—not again. I was going to save him—no matter what.

"Leave him alone!"

I walked to the center of the deck, where the ubervillains hovered over Debonair's crumpled from. I tried not to look at him—or at the blood pooling underneath his body. But my eyes went to his, and he had the audacity to wink at me. Wink! Even though he was facing his own death. His sly sense of humor was just one of the many things I loved about him. One of the many, many things. Which was going to make leaving him that much harder. If we somehow lived through this.

Prism's reddish eyes narrowed. "Well, well, you're more resourceful than I gave you credit for, Bulluci. How did you get out of your cell? Not that it really matters, but it's good that you're here now to see your champion die."

"I got out of my cell with this." I yanked the bracelet off my wrist and held it in my fist. "You put your laser down and step away from him right now, or I'll blow us all sky-high."

31

Prism's eyes fixed on the bracelet. "You're bluffing. That's just a bracelet, not anything else. You've been wearing it for days now."

I held it up high. "It is a bracelet. And much more. This happens to have been made by my good friend Jasper. You remember Jasper, don't you, Hangman? You almost beat him to death when you broke into his house."

Prism's eyes slid to the other ubervillain, who nodded his head in confirmation. Her eyes glowed red with anger, but she plastered a fake smile on her face and turned back to me.

"Now, Bella, there's no need to be hasty," Prism said, trying to make her voice light and pleasant. "I'm sure we can come to some sort of arrangement."

My hand tightened around the cold metal. "The only *arrangement* we're going to come to is the one where you put your laser away and let us off this boat—right now."

Prism scoffed. "You're bluffing. You're not going to set off that thing. You don't have the balls to do it."

I didn't know what to do. She was right. I didn't want to blow myself up. I didn't want to die. Not now. Not like this. Then, my eyes went back to the laser, and I thought of all the destruction Prism had wreaked—and would wreak—if somebody didn't stop her. Of all the lives she would and could destroy.

And I realized that I would die—to stop her. In that instant, I realized what my grandfather had been talking about. Why he and my father and brother really dressed up as Johnny Angel. It wasn't about getting a kick out of wearing a mask or riding around town raising hell. It was about being strong enough to take on ubervillains. Being strong enough to look out for the weak. Being strong enough to fight for those who couldn't fight for themselves.

That realization, earth-shattering as it was, wasn't enough to get me out of my present predicament, though.

"Give it up, Bella. Give me the bracelet." Prism pointed her laserama at me. "Or I'll just take it off your dead, burned body."

Debonair let out a growl and started to rise, but Hangman slammed his foot into the superhero's chest. Something snapped, and Debonair collapsed against the deck with a low, pained groan. Blood bubbled out of his mouth. The sight, the sound, of his agony sliced my heart like a paper shredder.

I didn't get a chance to answer, because Joanne chose that moment to pounce. She'd crept around behind the laser during my confrontation with Prism.

"Don't worry, Bella. I'll take care of it," Joanne said, climbing onto the side of the laserama.

"What—What are you doing? No!" Prism screamed.

But it was too late. Joanne reached into the machine and ripped the Star Sapphire from its position. But she didn't stop there. With her other hand, she swung the fireplace poker at the laser, bashing a whole section of wires and doodads and gadgets. Bits of metal spewed everywhere, tinkling against the floor as if someone were playing a piano. Joanne was stronger than she looked.

"This is for killing Berkley, you bitch!" Joanne screamed.

She kept hitting the laserama with the poker as if her life depended on it. More pieces of metal broke free, smoke spewed out, and flames started to flicker inside the device. Joanne gave it one more good whack, then climbed down. An explosion ripped through the laser, and the flames and smoke grew brighter and thicker.

Prism cursed and raced over to her precious device, followed by Hangman. Joanne dashed around the other side to me. Another explosion shook the boat as part of the machine collapsed in on itself. Blue and red sparks shot everywhere. Part of the deck began to burn, and smoke boiled out from the laser.

I dropped to my knees beside Debonair and stroked back his bloody, matted hair. He pressed a kiss to the inside of my wrist. My pulse pounded in response, even now in this time of crisis. I opened my mouth to ask him how hurt he was when something blue zoomed down from the sky and wrapped itself around my head.

Frantic, I clawed at the thing for about ten seconds before I realized it was a blanket. I unwound the soft fabric from around my face and looked at it. Unless I was mistaken, it was Debonair's stadium blanket—the same one I'd tossed off the Skyline Bridge a few days ago. That was a strange occurrence, even for me, but I covered Debonair with it.

"We've got to get off the boat," I said. "Can you teleport us away?"

Debonair shook his head. "No, I'm too weak. I wouldn't be able to get us to shore. But we can take one of the dinghies. I can row with one arm, well enough anyway. Help me up."

Joanne put her arm under Debonair's shoulder, while I did the same on the other side. We dragged the superhero over to the side of the deck to the remaining dinghy. Meanwhile, the ubervillains continued to mess with the imploding machine. I hoped it blew up in their faces—literally. I started forward to hoist the dinghy over the side and into the water. At least I tried to. The wench that lifted the boat up and over the side of the yacht was stuck, and no matter how hard I tried, I couldn't get it to move. I turned to ask Joanne for help, but she had other ideas. She picked up her poker and started back toward the ubervillains.

"Where are you going?" I asked.

Joanne jerked her head toward them. "Back to finish what I started. To kill Prism, just the way she killed Berkley."

"That's suicide. She's an ubervillain. They both are. And Prism still has her laserama."

Raw, naked pain filled Joanne's eyes. "I don't care. I just want her dead."

I grabbed her arm. "Berkley wouldn't want you to die, Joanne. He wouldn't want that for you. He saved you. He threw himself in front of that laser so you could live."

For a moment, I thought Joanne was going to shake me off and charge back toward the smoking laser. But some of the rage faded from her purple eyes, and she nodded.

"All right. What now?" she asked.

I shielded my eyes against the harsh glare of the rising sun. Sometime during the middle of all this, night had given way to dawn.

"We wait for the cavalry to arrive and hope the ubervillains leave us alone until then. Somebody had to hear those explosions and call the police. Surely, there's somebody else out here besides us."

I was right. A few boats floated in the water around the yacht, and people were already gathering on the other decks. Although they didn't look much bigger than ants, I could see them pointing and talking and gesturing. I waved my hands and jumped up and down, hoping someone would spot me.

"Help us!" I screamed, even though no one could hear me. "Please help us!"

Then, the most wonderful thing of all happened. A helicopter appeared on the horizon. A big, black, beautiful helicopter bearing the *F5* insignia. It drew closer, and I realized just how big it was. This wasn't your one- or two-seat chopper. Oh no. The thing was huge. An entire fleet of superheroes could sit inside. In fact, it looked like something the Coast Guard would use to rescue people stranded in bad weather out on the bay.

"A helicopter," I said, shaking my head. "They even have a freaking helicopter."

But now was not the time to chastise Sam Striker Sloane about his expensive equipment, especially not when one of them was going to save my sorry ass. I waved my hands, urging the Fearless Five to land the chopper on the deck so we could climb aboard and soar away to safety.

I spotted Hermit at the controls, with Mr. Sage in the copilot's seat. Striker stood in the open door, ready to hustle us inside. The chopper drew nearer to the yacht, whipping my tangled hair around my face. Suddenly, Hermit pushed the stick back, and the chopper snapped up, up, up into the blue sky.

"Where are you going? Come back! Come back!" I screamed, although the wind tore away my words before anyone could hear them.

A moment later, a grenade exploded where the helicopter

had been. Hangman and Prism had noticed the chopper too—
and were coming right at the three of us.

Joanne didn't hesitate. She ran at Prism and plowed into the
other woman as if she were a linebacker for the Bigtime Barra-
cudas football team. The two women went down on the deck.

Hangman's eyes lit on Debonair's still form, and he marched
toward the fallen superhero.

"Go, Bella! Run! Save yourself!" Debonair said as he got to
his trembling feet.

I looked around for something I could use to fend off Hang-
·man. Debonair was in no shape to stand, much less have another knock-down, drag-out fight with the ubervillain. Hangman
would kill him.

But there was nothing on the deck. Not even so much as a
loose metal pipe I could crack the ubervillain across the head
with.

So I stepped in front of Debonair. Hangman snickered. He
looked amused to see me defending the superhero. I suppose he
had a right to laugh. After all, he had at least a foot and a half
and a hundred pounds on me.

"Get out of the way, little girl. Or I'll throw you overboard,"
he snarled. "After I break every bone in your body."

"You're not going to hurt him anymore," I said, gritting my
teeth.

"We'll see about that."

Hangman reached for me. And I did something I'd never
done before—I gave in to my power.

Fully, completely, absolutely.

I let the static electricity build and build and build around
me. Then, I reached for it. A strange sensation, an odd force,
enveloped me, almost like there was an enormous hand wrapped
around me, guiding my every movement.

Hangman came at me, but I ducked out of his grasp and
kicked him in the ankles. The motion surprised the ubervillain,
and he stumbled forward, hitting his knees on the dinghy.

"You're going to pay for that, bitch," he snarled.

"Then come and make me, you bastard!"

So he did. Or tried to. Hangman stalked me around the

deck, trying to wrap his massive hands around my throat, as well as punch and kick me into next week. But somehow, just before his hand connected with my face, he'd slip and fall. Or I'd jerk out of the way at the last possible second. We did a strange dance around the deck, bobbing and weaving at each other. I felt in total control of my body and completely not at the same time. But I went with the weirdness. It was the only thing keeping me alive. Somehow, my jinx had turned into a run of good luck.

Hangman tried to punch me, but slipped and fell to his knees again. A flash of movement caught my eye, and I turned.

"Now, it's your turn to die, bitch!" Prism screamed above the roar of the hovering helicopter.

She stood over Joanne, the laserama pointed at the other woman's chest. They were too far away, and there was nothing I could do.

Prism pushed the button. A red beam shot out—

And nothing happened.

Prism pushed it again.

Nothing happened.

Joanne didn't crumple into a heap. A smoking hole didn't suddenly appear in her chest. Her eyes didn't flash red with fire as her internal organs cooked inside her body.

Instead, Joanne smiled. A big, wide, wolfish smile that showed off every one of her white teeth. Prism looked at her laser, then at the other woman. Confusion entered her reddish eyes. The laserama must have missed because Joanne sprang to her feet and started clawing at Prism again.

But I had my own problems to worry about. My power threw me to one side. Hangman's fist punched the air where I'd been a second ago. He came at me again. And again, my power pulled me out of the path of his enormous beefy fist.

"Stand still!" he snarled, white spit flying from his thick lips.

"Go to hell!" Not the best or most original of retorts, but it was all I could come up with.

Hangman and I fell into a weird sort of dance. He tried to punch and strangle and snap me in two. I dodged his seeking grasp and got in what blows I could, but they didn't really hurt the ubervillain—only his manly pride. I let my power take over my body, twisting me like a puppet. My body turned and moved in ways I hadn't even dreamed were possible. The Bendy Brawler would have had a hard time keeping up with me.

Debonair slumped against the side of the boat, too injured to do anything but cheer me on with his encouraging eyes. While I danced with Hangman, I also kept an eye on Joanne and Prism. They were engaged in their own sort of dance, although Joanne was doing far more damage than I was.

Prism got in a lucky punch. Joanne stumbled back and fell on her ass. The ubervillain used the opportunity to run over to Hangman, who was still trying to knock me into next week.

"Forget about them! Let's go! Let's go!" Prism screamed, clipping herself to Hangman's utility belt. "Fly! Fly! Fly!"

With my remarkable ability to elude him, and the Fearless Five helicopter hovering overhead, Hangman knew when he was beat. He gathered his strength, wrapped an arm around Prism, and looked up at the sky.

I watched in horror as the two ubervillains lifted off the yacht. My eyes went to the Fearless Five chopper. It was more stable than it had been when the grenade had exploded, but Hermit still struggled with the controls. They wouldn't recover in time to give chase to the ubervillains.

Prism was going to get away. The woman who'd hurt Debonair, who'd killed Berkley, was going to sail away into the sky free as a bird.

Not if I could help it.

"Luck be a lady!" I screamed as loud as I could.

The sapphires in the angel charm's eyes flashed on and off in warning. I unsnapped the clasp, reared back, and threw the bracelet with all my might. I'm not much of a thrower. I never played baseball or softball or anything like that in school. So I reached for my power, willing the small silver chain to soar higher, faster, farther. Just when I thought it was going to fall short, a gust of wind snapped up the bracelet, and it somehow hooked itself onto Hangman's utility belt.

Five seconds later, the bracelet exploded—taking Hangman

and Prism along with it. One second, the ubervillains soared in midair. The next, they disappeared in a ball of orange fire that would have made Fiona very, very proud.

"How did you do that?" Joanne asked, mouth agape as pieces of ash and other things I didn't want to think about fluttered by us on the breeze.

I just shrugged. "Sometimes, it's better to be lucky than good."

32

"If you touch me again, I'm going to take that tube and shove it where the sun doesn't shine," Joanne snapped.

I stared at the other woman, who glared at Mr. Sage. The superhero looked at me for help, but I shook my head. I wasn't about to argue with Joanne. She'd just lost her husband and helped save my life in the space of a few hours. As far as I was concerned, she could do whatever she wanted.

Joanne crossed her arms over her chest and lifted her head up high, as if she were the queen of the world, instead of covered in enough blood, grime, soot, and ash for a whole legion of firefighters.

"I'm fine," Joanne protested. "Just a little bruised and sore."

"You've got several serious cuts, not to mention that bump on the side of your head. Now hold still."

Mr. Sage dabbed some more ointment onto Joanne's face. She turned her head away and refused to look at him.

Joanne, Debonair, and I were in the sick bay at Fearless Five headquarters. Hermit and Mr. Sage had gotten the helicopter under control enough to land on the yacht. Striker and Hermit had stayed behind to help the fire and police departments handle the cleanup, while Mr. Sage and Karma Girl whisked us injured folks back to headquarters—blindfolding us, of course, so we couldn't see where we were going. Even though I knew, Joanne and Debonair didn't.

Mr. Sage had seen to Debonair first. The superhero had a broken arm, cracked ribs, a broken nose, and a major concussion. Mr. Sage gave Debonair a sedative for the pain before setting all the bones and sticking him in another room. His injuries were serious, but not life-threatening.

Then, the superhero had gone to work on Joanne and me. I

happily submitted to Mr. Sage's ministrations. He announced I had gotten through my ordeal with just a few minor cuts and bruises, mostly from all the debris flying around Prism's yacht, as well as from Jasper's bombs. Joanne was a little more banged up, but not too bad off, considering she'd gone toe-to-toe with Prism. I still couldn't quite believe she'd somehow escaped getting smoked by the laser.

"Enough!" Joanne snapped, knocking away Mr. Sage's hand. "I want to see Berkley. Where is he? Where did they take him?"

"Bigtime University Hospital," Mr. Sage said. "They pronounced him dead on arrival. I'm so sorry, Joanne."

She stared at Mr. Sage. Pain, grief, anger, and more emotions swirled in her violet eyes one right after another. "Give me some drugs or blindfold me or do whatever the hell you have to do to protect your precious anonymity, then take me to the hospital."

Mr. Sage's green eyes flicked to at me, and we both looked at Joanne.

"What are you waiting for? Now!" she snarled, her hands tightening around the metal rails of her bed.

"As you wish," Mr. Sage replied.

He went to the cabinets that lined one wall and took out a syringe and a small vial. He came back to Joanne and injected the clear liquid into the IV already pumping fluid into her arm. Mr. Sage looked at me. I nodded, and we left the room.

"She's not herself," I said. "That's why she's acting this way."

Mr. Sage looked through the glass at Joanne, who stared at the ceiling and tried not to cry as the drug took effect. Her eyelids fluttered once, then closed.

"Of course she's not herself. She just lost her husband. Because of me." Mr. Sage's voice was sad and bitter.

I put my hand on his arm. "It's not your fault. Prism was too quick for any of us to stop."

The superhero shook his head. "I should have known what she was up to—that she would steal the sapphire in front of all those people. I'm a psychic. I should have known."

"I've always thought being a psychic is sort of like being lucky—you have good days and you have bad days," I said in a soft tone.

A wry smile twisted his face. "Yeah. Unfortunately, people always seem to suffer when I have bad days."

I couldn't argue with him. I knew about bad luck and making people suffer all too well. So I didn't even try.

I left Joanne to Mr. Sage and went next door to Debonair's room. Debonair lay in the hospital bed, surrounded by clean white sheets with a dusty black mask covering the top half of his face. Mr. Sage hadn't removed it out of professional courtesy. Karma Girl sat in a nearby chair, playing with a Rubik's Cube and keeping an eye on his vital signs.

"Any change?" I asked, looking at all the beeping and chirping machines.

"No. He's still serious, but stable. He's going to pull through, Bella. Don't worry." Karma Girl's eyes glowed for half a second. "I just know he is."

My heart lifted a bit. Karma Girl was never wrong. At least to my knowledge. If she said Debonair was going to be okay, then I believed her.

I dragged another chair up to the bed and sat down. Then, I reached over and took Debonair's hand. It felt warm, almost hot. A fever was sweeping through his body, as it tried to mend all the damage that had been done to it.

Karma Girl reached up and took off her mask, morphing into Carmen Cole once more.

"Why don't you get some rest?" Carmen said in a soft voice. "You've had a hell of a night."

I shook my head. "I'm fine, just a few bumps and bruises." I sounded like Joanne now. "Besides, I want to be here when he wakes up so he can see I'm okay too."

"All right. If you need anything, just use the intercom."

I nodded. "Any word on Granny Cane?"

"Swifte showed up on the scene right after Hangman took off with you. He rushed her to the hospital. Granny Cane had a concussion and a broken wrist, but she'll be fine. Your grandfather is with her. Once the doctors give her the all-clear sign, he's going to drive out here."

I nodded. "Good."

Carmen got to her feet and left the room.

I turned back to Devlin. My eyes fixed on the cast on his left arm and the white bandages that swathed his chest. He was lucky he'd gotten off with just some broken bones. We'd all been very, very lucky today.

Everyone except Berkley. Poor Joanne. I knew what she must be going through right now. The pain, the anger, the grief, the rage. I'd experienced it all when my father had died. If Devlin had been killed instead of Berkley, I don't think I would have been able to live with myself. It made what I had to tell him that much harder.

Because I'd finally realized we couldn't be together. Before the second museum benefit, I'd been willing to try, to figure out some way to make things work. But they never would. Today had shown me that, and Berkley's death had driven it home. I'd just been fooling myself before. Because Devlin was Debonair. A suave, sexy superhero. That leather costume he wore might as well have been a bull's-eye on his back. He'd always be a target for both the uber villains and the police. I wasn't going to let my heart get caught in the cross fire when his luck finally ran out and some villain killed him. It had come so close to happening today that I still couldn't quite breathe.

I grasped Devlin's hand, leaned back in the chair, and closed my eyes. I didn't mean to fall asleep, but I must have, because I awoke to find Devlin staring at me, his blue eyes hazy from the drugs.

"Hey," he said, his voice thick.

"Hey there, yourself. How are you feeling?"

"Tired. Stiff. Sore." His eyes slowly wandered around the room. "Where are we?"

"You're safe. We're in the Fearless Five headquarters in one of the sick bays. Mr. Sage checked you out and says you're going to be fine."

I gave Devlin the lowdown on his injuries.

"And you? How are you?"

I smiled and squeezed his hand tighter. "I'm fine. Just a few bumps and bruises. I got lucky today. It seems to be something I'm good at."

Devlin tried to laugh but stopped because it hurt his ribs. "And Joanne?"

"She's fine, physically. Emotionally, she's a wreck. The Fearless Five are taking her to the hospital to see Berkley's body."

I couldn't stop the tears from filling my eyes. Berkley had been a good friend and a wonderful man. He hadn't deserved what Prism had done to him, and Joanne didn't deserve to be suffering his loss now.

"Hey, hey. None of that," Devlin said, squeezing my hand. "The ubervillains are dead, and the city is safe again. And we've got the rest of our lives to spend together. That's the most important thing."

I didn't want to do this. Not today of all days. Not when he was sick and weak and injured. But I had to. Otherwise, I'd just keep putting it off . . . and putting it off . . . and putting it off until it would be too late.

I drew in a deep breath. "No, we don't."

"What? What are you talking about?" His eyes grew wide and frantic. "Are you hurt? Is something wrong with you?"

"No, I'm fine. But we can't be together, Devlin. Not anymore." My heart cracked a little as I said the words. But I knew they were true, that it was for the best.

"Why not? I love you, Bella, and I want to spend the rest of my life showing you just how much. Don't you love me too?"

I bit my lip to keep from confessing the depth of my feelings. "I care about you. A lot. But we can't be together, Devlin. It just wouldn't work out. You're a superhero. You always will be."

"And you don't want to be with a superhero," Devlin said. "Because of what happened to your father. You're afraid I'll die just like he did. That a couple of ubervillains will corner me in a dark alley one night and kill me. It won't happen, Bella. I promise. I won't let it."

I laughed, but it wasn't a happy sound. "You won't let it?

Don't you think my father thought that very same thing? Don't you think he would have come home to us if he could?"

Devlin didn't respond.

"We almost died today—you, me, Joanne. And Berkley *did* die. I can't go through this again. I can't sit at home every night wondering whether or not you're going to come back in the morning."

Devlin looked at me. "I could always quit," he said in a low voice.

I stared at him, stunned. "Quit? Quit what? Being Debonair?"

He nodded.

I shook my head. "You couldn't do that any more than I could quit breathing. And I wouldn't want you to."

"You don't want to be with me because I'm Debonair, but you don't want me to stop being him? I don't understand, Bella. I would give it up, I would do it for you. I'd do anything for you."

The words and the love shining in Devlin's eyes filled me with hope, but I pushed it back down, smothering it with reason. It wasn't going to work out between us. We both had to accept that now.

I let out a long sigh. "I believe you. I know you would do it for me. But you'd be doing it *for me*, not for yourself. In time, you'd come to hate me for making you give up being Debonair. And I couldn't stand it if you hated me. I just couldn't."

Devlin grabbed my hand. "I would quit for you, and I wouldn't hate you for it. I could never hate you for anything. I'm not like your father, Bella. When are you going to realize that?"

A sad smile curved my lips. "The only problem is I've heard this all before. Word for word. Don't you think my mother tried to make him quit? Don't you think she begged and pleaded with him to stop putting himself in danger?" Another bitter laugh escaped my lips. "They fought about it constantly while she was still alive. Sometimes, my father would listen to her. He'd give in and put the mask and the motorcycle and the leather jacket away. For a while. A week, a month. Three months later, he'd put them back on, and the whole sad cycle would repeat itself. I don't want to go through that again. Any of it. Not again, and especially not with you."

Devlin just stared at me, his eyes more hurt and wounded than the rest of his battered, bruised body.

"I'm sorry, Devlin." I looked away. "But it's over between us."

33

Devlin tried to change my mind. He begged and pleaded and told me how much he loved me, but I didn't listen. I couldn't. I closed my eyes and ears and heart to him and held firm.

Mr. Sage made Devlin spend the rest of the day at Sublime for observation. I slept beside him in an extra bed. Around midnight, Devlin decided he felt well enough to go to the hospital to check on Granny Cane. I didn't call him on her real identity as Grace Caleb. I'd had enough superheroes and ubervillains for one day. For a lifetime.

"Come with me, Bella. Please," Devlin said, taking my hand again. "We can make this work, I know we can."

"No," I said, swallowing the lump in my throat and pulling away. "Trust me. It's better this way. It's better to end things now. Go check on Granny Cane. She needs you."

Devlin dropped my hand. Then—

POP!

He teleported away.

But this time was different. This time, I knew he wasn't coming back. Devlin was gone.

Forever.

I couldn't stop the tears from trickling down my flushed face.

Bobby came out to Sublime early the next morning to drive me home. On the ride back into the city, I told him everything that had happened after the disaster at the museum—including what Grace Caleb did late at night.

Bobby's reaction to the news that his lady friend masqueraded as a superhero surprised me, to say the least.

"Oh, I knew all about that," he said, taking a sip of his early morning espresso.

My mouth dropped open. "You knew Grace Caleb was Granny Cane? How did you figure it out?"

Bobby smiled. "Bella, when you're as old as I am, you've seen it all—especially when it comes to superheroes and uber-villains. I knew the first time Grace left in the middle of one of our dates that she was Granny Cane. Nobody walks out on Bobby Bulluci without good reason. And what better reason could there be than being a superhero?"

"Why didn't you tell me?" I asked, a bit miffed.

He shrugged. "It wasn't my secret to tell. Unlike you young folks, I'm not obsessed with finding out who everybody really is. Now, tell me about Devlin. Why wasn't he still at Sublime with you this morning? What's going on between the two of you?"

I could never hide anything from Grandfather, so I decided to tell him the truth. "We broke up," I said, looking out the window.

"Why?"

I told Bobby my reasons for ending things with Devlin Debonair Dash.

"Bah! Just because the boy's a superhero is no reason not to be with him," Bobby said, waving his hand.

"You don't understand." I looked at him. "Being Johnny Angel was always *your* choice. It was never mine. Going out, getting hurt, putting yourself in danger was always your choice, my father's choice, and now Johnny's choice. Well, I'm making a choice. And I choose not to go through all that again. Not even for Devlin."

"But you love him, don't you, Bella?" Grandfather asked, his green eyes soft and sad.

"Yes," I replied, staring out the window so he wouldn't see me cry. "But sometimes, love isn't enough. No matter how much you want it to be."

Berkley Brighton's funeral was held two days later at the Cathedral of the Angels. Practically the whole city showed up to put to rest one of its favorite sons. Berkley hadn't only been rich—he'd used his money to help others, funding scholarships, grants, and much more in Bigtime and beyond.

I sat in a pew near the front of the massive church, nestled between Grandfather and Carmen Cole. Sam sat on the other side of Carmen, while Henry, Lulu, and Chief Newman slid into the seats behind us. The inside of the church was dim and smelled faintly of incense. A white light highlighted Berkley's face, which looked calm and serene in his casket.

The service had already stretched into its third hour, with one person after another getting up to talk about Berkley and what he'd meant to them and the rest of the city. Grandfather had been among those to speak.

Another person left the stage, and I saw Abby Appleby gesture to the organist. Abby stood off to one side, partially hidden by a spray of roses. In addition to party planning, Abby also arranged funerals, and Joanne had called upon her to make sure Berkley had a proper send-off and burial. From the flowers to the casket to the order of speakers, everything had been perfect. Berkley would have approved.

Now, it was Joanne's turn to talk. She wore a simple black suit, one of my designs. Her only jewelry was her enormous diamond ring. Her face looked even thinner and paler than before, and dark circles ringed her eyes. Even her perfect makeup couldn't disguise the fact she was grieving deeply. Joanne's eyes swept over the crowd, taking in all of the people. Our gazes met for a moment, before she continued on with her perusal. Then, she leaned toward the microphone.

"Well, Berkley would certainly be pleased with the turnout today. I am. I want to thank you all for coming and paying your respects to Berkley. He was a kind, gentle, caring man. He loved me, and I loved him more than words could ever say." Joanne paused, struggling to keep her composure. "That's it. That's all I want to say. Because no amount of words will ever bring Berkley back. Nothing will. I love you, Berkley. Goodbye."

Joanne walked away from the podium. She went over to where Berkley rested and placed a kiss on his cold lips. She motioned to the pallbearers, and they closed the casket and picked it up. Abby came over to Joanne to escort her outside, but she waved the event planner away. Joanne held up her chin, slid a pair of oversized sunglasses on her pale face, and strode outside. Her steps faltered only a little.

The casket glided out the stained glass doors of the cathedral. The crowd of mourners trailed along behind, walking the three short blocks to Bigtime Cemetery. We gathered around a freshly dug hole. The brown blotch ruined the smoothness of the golden grass. The cemetery workers lowered the casket into the ground, while a minister said prayers of comfort and hope. Joanne stepped forward and threw a violet rose onto the casket just before they put the first scoop of dirt on the gleaming surface.

I looked up from the sight and locked eyes with Devlin. My breath caught in my throat as his blue gaze held mine. The minister kept saying prayers as the service continued, but I didn't hear them. All I could hear, see, think about was Devlin. He moved through the crowd until he stood next to me. I drew in his scent of sweet, musky roses. It made me a little dizzy, the way it always did.

The service continued for the better part of an hour. Once the casket was completely covered, the minister finished his prayers. People said their condolences and goodbyes to Joanne, then drifted off to their waiting limos.

To my surprise, Jasper stood at the edge of the thinning crowd, leaning on a set of crutches. Joanne spotted him about the same time I did. They stared at each other for several seconds, before Jasper gave her a sad smile. Joanne's lips quivered, and she nodded at him. Then, Jasper turned and hobbled away. Joanne watched him go, something like regret flashing in her eyes, before she turned to the next mourner, Chief Sean Newman. The chief whispered something in her ear. Joanne gave him a wan smile and moved on to the next well-wisher. The chief moved off to one side, his eyes lingering on the grieving widow.

Devlin took my elbow and led me over to a nearby bench. I let him. We sat there in silence for a long time, watching the workers erect the statue that would mark Berkley's grave.

I'd thought of nothing but Devlin these last two days, and it was all I could do to keep from throwing myself into his arms and begging him to give up being Debonair. To tell him I loved him just as much as he loved me. To plead with him never to leave my side for anything ever again.

"Can we talk?" Devlin asked in a soft voice.

I devoured him with my hungry gaze. I'd missed him so much. I still wanted him so much. But it could never happen. We could never be together. Not again.

"Of course," I said in my calmest, most sensible voice, trying to pretend we were just a couple of friends sitting on a bench together.

"I've been thinking a lot about what you said. About how you didn't want to be with a superhero. And you're right. You shouldn't have to go through all that again. Not for anybody."

I nodded, glad he could see my side of the argument.

"But we live in a city, in a world, full of superheroes and ubervillains. You're never going to be truly free of them, Bella. Never."

"I know," I replied. "But I can do everything in my power to stay away from them. That much I can do."

"I've come to a decision. I'm going to do one more thing as Debonair, then I'm going to quit stealing art—forever."

Devlin's words thrilled me, but I couldn't let him go through with his plan. I couldn't let him change that part of himself just for me. He would come to hate me for it. I knew he would.

I put my hand on his. "That's very noble of you, very sweet, Devlin. But it won't work, and you know it. There's always going to be one more thing you have to do, one more person you have to save, until one day, your luck is going to run out. And I'll be back in this cemetery again, crying over your grave, instead of Berkley's."

Devlin shook his head. "No, this is different. You'll see. I'm not giving up on us, Bella. Not now, not ever. I love you too much to let you go."

"Devlin—"

He pulled me into his arms and kissed me. And all the feelings I thought I'd buried, that I thought didn't matter, roared back to the surface. In an instant, I was kissing him just as much as he was kissing me. Maybe even more so. We broke apart, breathing hard.

Tears gathered in my eyes. "Please, Devlin. Don't make this any harder than it is already. Please."

He stroked my cheek, then leaned down and pressed a soft kiss to the inside of my wrist. "Things will work out, you'll see, Bella. Trust me. I'll be in touch soon."

For once, Devlin didn't teleport away. He walked just like everybody else, but it didn't ease my hurt any less.

34

"*You're being stupid*" Fiona announced. "*Completely, totally,* willfully, horribly, awfully stupid."

I gave her a sour look. Fiona was one to talk about being stupid. She'd had Johnny convinced she was still in love with her dead fiancé before they'd gotten together.

Fiona and I sat in the kitchen at the Bulluci mansion, along with Carmen and Lulu. Fiona and Johnny had come back from their trip a couple of days early because of everything that had been going on. I'd invited Carmen and Lulu over to join us for brunch. Johnny and Grandfather were off watching a soccer game, while the other men in our lives were all busy with their day jobs.

It had been a little over a week since I'd last seen Devlin at the cemetery. He hadn't called or even popped into the house to see me. I didn't know whether to be relieved or disappointed. Still, I checked the news on SNN every night before I went to bed and first thing when I got up in the morning—praying I'd see Debonair on there and hoping I wouldn't.

I was a mess. A confused, sad, conflicted mess, which was why I'd invited my few girlfriends over to commiserate with me. What I hadn't expected was for Fiona to berate me for my lack of faith in love.

"Stupid, stupid, stupid."

Fiona punctuated her statement by shoving a forkful of scrambled eggs into her mouth. Two empty plates sat on the table beside her, along with a pitcher of apple juice and a tub of cream cheese she'd slathered on the six bagels she'd eaten. So far. We'd only sat down to brunch fifteen minutes ago.

Carmen and Lulu looked back and forth between the two of us, amused by the whole exchange.

"Why am I being so stupid?" I asked. "It's all perfectly clear and logical to me."

"That's your problem. You're so damn *sensible* all the time," Fiona said. "Sometimes, you just have to follow your heart, Bella. No matter where it leads you. Carmen and Sam, and Lulu and Henry, are proof of that. The four of them couldn't have been more wrong for each other, but they made their relationships work. Despite my efforts to the contrary." She muttered that last part under her breath.

"Hey!" Lulu growled. "Henry and I were, are, and will always be perfect for each other. Besides, I'm not the one who beat my future husband to a bloody pulp while we were dating. That was all you, Fiona."

Fiona's eyes fixed on Lulu's blue-streaked hair, and a few sparks fluttered from her fingertips. I was very glad we had tile floors throughout the house. Otherwise, Fiona would have burned it down long ago.

"I think what Fiona and Lulu are trying to say is that it takes a lot of effort and compromise to make a relationship work, no matter how perfect you might be for the other person—or how much you love him," Carmen said, sliding a stack of pancakes to Fiona.

Fiona's eyes fixed on the food, and the sparks around her fingers snuffed out. She was easily distracted sometimes.

"I do love him, but it's never going to work. I can't ask him to give up being Debonair for me, and I don't want to be with a superhero."

Carmen put her hand on top of mine. "I know how you feel, Bella. But you have to ask yourself—do you love him enough to at least give it a chance? And isn't getting your heart broken better than never knowing if it would have worked out or not?"

The three of them went back to their brunch, but I didn't have any appetite for the high-protein, low-fat cheese-and-spinach quiche in front of me. I stabbed a bit of burned cheese and ate it without really even tasting it. Were my friends right? Should I try to make things work with Devlin, even if he was and would always be Debonair?

I thought back to all the time we'd spent together. That first confrontation in Berkley's house, meeting at the museum, our time in the Lair of Seduction, the way he held me, the way he listened to me, the way he loved me. He was a nice, mostly normal guy wrapped up in a bad-boy package. He was everything I wanted. Everything I needed.

And I knew what I had to do. I had to at least give Devlin a chance. I had to try. It was the only sensible thing to do.

Carmen looked at me, as if she knew what I'd decided. She smiled. "Go answer the phone, Bella. It's for you."

I looked at her. "But it's not even ring—"

A second later, the phone in the kitchen rang out, a loud, beeping sound.

I looked at the phone, then at Carmen. "That's just creepy."

"Tell us about it," Lulu said, taking a swig of her mimosa. "You don't see her that much. We've got to deal with that stuff all the time."

I walked over and picked up the phone. "Hello?"

"Hi, Bella. It's Arthur Anders."

"Hello, Arthur," I said in a listless voice, wondering why the curator of the Bigtime Museum of Modern Art was calling me on a Sunday morning. "What's up?"

"Bella, could I ask you to come down to the museum? I've got something I'd like to show you."

"What is it? Is something wrong with the exhibit again?" I asked, worried.

Despite the latest attack, the museum had reopened, and the *Whimsical Wonders* exhibit was still on display—minus the Star Sapphire. Joanne hadn't wanted it to be part of the show again, and I hadn't blamed her. But it would be just my luck if some other disaster befell the exhibit, now that it had already been wrecked by ubervillains twice, and the main benefactor brutally murdered.

He hesitated. "Not exactly."

Which meant there was something *seriously* wrong. Wonderful. Absolutely wonderful.

"I'll be there within an hour," I promised and hung up.

"What was that about?" Fiona asked, slathering cream cheese on another blueberry bagel.

"I'm not sure, but it didn't sound good."

"Don't worry, Bella. I think you're in for a pleasant surprise." Carmen's eyes glowed for half a second. "A very pleasant surprise."

"With my luck? I don't think so, no matter what kind of psychic vibe you're getting."

"Oh, trust her, Bella," Lulu piped up. "No matter how annoying she is, Sister Carmen and her psychic premonitions are rarely wrong."

I didn't know which I was more afraid of—my bad luck or Carmen's uncanny ability to see into the future.

35

I kept my word, leaving the girls to their brunch and arriv-
ing at the museum about an hour later.

Arthur waited inside the door for me. I was a little taken
aback by his appearance—jeans and a white polo shirt. It was
the first time I'd ever seen the curator not wearing his usual
plaid jacket.

"What is it? What's wrong?" I asked.

"Calm down, Bella. Nothing's wrong with the exhibit. In
fact, a piece has been added to it. One that I think you'll like
very much."

I frowned. "What are you talking about? We didn't get any
more donations. Not since the second ubervillain attack."

After that, I'd had to work very hard to convince people to
leave anything on display. To my surprise, Joanne had helped
me, pretty much bullying everyone else into doing what she
wanted. I still didn't understand why.

Arthur gestured for me to follow him. "I got a call this morning from the security folks saying that someone had broken in.
The weird thing was that he didn't take anything. Instead, he
left something behind for once. A drawing."

My heart started to pound. Somehow, I knew Debonair was
behind this. Devlin, Devlin, what had you done?

"Can I see it?" I asked.

"Of course. That's why I called you. The person who broke
in left a note, saying you were the one who had done the drawing, although you had nothing to do with the break-in itself."

I almost fainted, and my hair frizzed so badly I thought it
would leave my head altogether. I knew what I was going to
see even before Arthur stepped aside to show me the piece
of paper. My drawing of Debonair hung in the middle of a
wall, right next to a painting by Pandora, as though it were

the same sort of masterpiece. Somehow, all the crinkles and stains and rumples had been smoothed out of the paper, and it had been mounted and framed in silver. Even if I hadn't drawn it, I would have thought it was a breathtaking piece— or maybe that was just because I happened to be in love with the subject.

"Do you recognize it?" Arthur asked.

I swallowed. "Yes, it's something I drew a few weeks ago after the first attack on the museum."

"I see."

Arthur continued to stare at the drawing, his eyes dark and hooded. He didn't say anything, but I knew what he was thinking. That I was still an amateur artist with no real talent—and that I always would be.

"Here," I said, stepping forward. "This must be someone's idea of a practical joke. I'll take it down."

"Leave it up," he said.

"What? Why?"

The curator smiled. "We'd like to keep it on display. In fact, if you have any more work that's similar to this, we'd like to see that as well."

"You want to what?" I asked, stunned.

"We want to do an exhibit of your drawings. You have a wonderful style, Bella. You've really grown as an artist. You've finally found your passion. You should share it with others."

Arthur pointed to the drawing and began describing everything he liked about it—from the shading to the subtle shadows to the smoky detail. In short, he loved it—and wanted to see more works. Pronto.

"This is like a dream," I said in a shaky tone. My knees felt like they were going to buckle. "I can't believe you like my work, especially after that critique you gave me in college."

Arthur patted my arm. "Of course I like it. I've always liked it. You're very talented, Bella. You just needed to find a way to fully express yourself. Your work has always been good, but this—*this* is truly magnificent."

Arthur started talking to me about when I could show him more of my work, but all I could think about was Devlin.

Carmen and the others were right. We could make it work. We could make anything work. Devlin had just made one of my dreams come true. I was going to spend the rest of my life making his a reality.

The moment I left the museum, I whipped out my cell phone and called Devlin. No response. The phone just kept ringing and ringing. I called his office, his cell phone, his home out in the bay. The last line had been disconnected, but none of the other numbers worked either. Try to tell a guy you love him, and he drops off the face of the earth.

Discouraged and frustrated, I went back home. Grace and Bobby were in the living room, watching television. For once, they weren't kissing, just cuddling together. I plopped down on the love seat across from them and looked at Grace.

"Where is he?" I demanded.

"Who?" she replied, a smile curving her lips.

"Devlin. I need to talk to him. Now."

Grace waved her hand. "Oh, he's around somewhere."

"Listen up, lady. I'm in love with your grandson. Totally, completely, madly in love. I plan on telling him this as soon as possible. So you'd better tell me where he is right now. Or else I'm going to knock you into next week, even if you are a superhero. Are we clear?"

Grace looked at me, then Bobby. "Well, it's about time you came to your senses. Devlin has been worrying about you for two weeks now. Change the channel to SNN, Bobby."

"Where is he?" I asked, growing impatient with the older woman.

She pointed at the screen. "Just watch. He should be on in a few minutes."

I looked at Grace, then the television. What would Devlin be doing on SNN? The only thing the television station covered was superheroes—

The anchor was prattling on about the latest ubervillain video game releases. Suddenly, his words became clipped and hurried.

"Now, we go out to our reporter Kelly Caleb with a breaking story. Kelly, what's the situation?"

Kelly smiled into the camera, giving the audience a nice view of her trademark teeth. "Well, Jim, I'm here at the Bigtime Museum of Modern Art, where the board of directors has just made a surprising announcement regarding Debonair, one of the city's resident superheroes. Debonair, can you tell the audience what this is all about?"

Debonair's dashing face flashed onto the screen, and my pulse started to pound.

"Well, Kelly, as you know, I've been responsible for a string of art thefts in the past. I'm here today to tell you and your loyal viewers I'm turning over a new leaf. I'm no longer going to steal paintings—I'm going to help the museum restore them."

Debonair went on to describe how he pilfered paintings from people's homes in an effort to restore them before the works were lost forever. Arthur Anders came on a moment later to tell Kelly how happy the museum was to have someone of Debonair's background working to preserve these priceless works of art. He kept shooting suspicious looks at Debonair, but Arthur seemed happy enough with the arrangement. The story went on for quite a while, before Kelly had to send it back to the studio to cover Swifte rescuing a turtle from a storm drain over in Paradise Park.

Grace clicked off the television. I fell back against the sofa, stunned.

"I don't believe it," I said. "Why did he do that? Why did he agree to work for the museum?"

"Because he loves you and wants to make you happy," Grace said in a soft voice. "He's not giving up being Debonair completely. He's just making himself a little safer. For you. All because of you."

I looked at Grace and Bobby. Then, I got to my feet and rushed out the door to find Devlin and tell him how much I loved him. How much he meant to me.

I went back to the museum, but he wasn't there anymore. I cornered Kelly and demanded to know where he was, but she didn't know. Some cousin she was. Nobody did. I called all his numbers again. I didn't get an answer, but there was a message waiting for me when I tried his cell phone.

"I'm in our special place. If you love me like I love you, come and find me there. I'll be waiting. If not, well, I'll try to understand."

I hung up the phone in frustration. Our special place? We had lots of special places now. The museum, the bridge, the bench down by the marina. At least, I thought we did. Suddenly, the answer came to me, and I knew where he was.

I went down to the marina, determined to hop on board one of the tourist boats that cruised through the bay on an hourly basis. But there was no one milling around the stands where you bought tickets. I went over and banged on the ticket booth. No one answered. Finally, I spotted a sign on the door that read, CLOSED UNTIL DEC. 1 FOR MAINTENANCE AND REPAIRS.

Well, this wasn't going to stop me. I was a woman on a mission—one I was going to complete even if I had to hop in the water and swim all the way over to that damn island myself. Of course, I'd be frozen by the time I did that, but a few minutes with Devlin would be more than enough to thaw me out.

I stalked back and forth through the marina, fruitlessly searching for somebody, *anybody* with a boat that could ferry me out to the island where Devlin's mansion was. But it was cold and rainy, and the marina was deserted, except for the gulls huddling underneath the picnic awnings. I prowled up and down the dock, considering stealing a boat, but then, of course, I didn't have the keys and wouldn't be able to start any of the monstrous yachts. I didn't know anything at all about sailing, so the sailboats were out. I wasn't dumb enough to try that again.

Just when I was about to call Sam Sloane and demand to use the Fearless Five rescue boat, I spotted a shimmer of color out on the horizon. Bright lights and crazy colors and calypso sounds that could only mean one thing—Cap'n Freebeard and his Saucy Wenches were out on the bay partying, while everyone else was home where it was nice and warm.

"Hey! Hey!" I screamed and jumped up and down, waving my arms. "Over here! Over here!"

My power flared, and I reached for it. It was something I was doing more and more of these days. Something had changed about my power, my luck, ever since I'd been trapped on Prism's yacht. It wasn't as much of a jinx anymore. Oh, things still exploded and spontaneously combusted and shattered whenever I was around, but the incidents were fewer and farther between. It was as if I'd lifted the curse off myself by finally giving in to my power and accepting it. I'd even started working with Chief Newman to see if I could fully control it someday.

So, using my luck, I focused on the boat and willed it to turn in my direction. And it did. Ten minutes later, Cap'n Freebeard eased his massive party barge up to the end of the dock where I stood.

"Ahoy there, matey! What can I do for ye on this fine, salty day?" Cap'n growled, squinting even though the sun wasn't anywhere to be found.

"I need your help, please."

I explained the situation to Cap'n, telling him that I needed a ride out to Devlin's house in the middle of the bay.

"Devlin Dash, eh? He's a fine lad, a fine lad. Come aboard, missy." Freebeard beamed at me. "And join the fun."

I wouldn't say it was fun, but it certainly was something. Freebeard and his Saucy Wenches knew how to have a good time. They boogied and drank and ate seashell-shaped sandwiches nonstop—when they weren't slathering each other with coconut oil and singing sea shanties. Jimmy Buffett music played in the background. "Lovely Cruise" was the name of the song that kept repeating over and over again, along with "On a Slow Boat to China" and some tune called "Take It Back."

I stood next to the railing, tried not to get suntan lotion all over my clothes, and avoided staring at all the exposed cleavage around me. Somehow, I managed it.

After about half an hour of steady sailing, we came within sight of Devlin's mansion and island.

"That's my stop," I said to Freebeard.

The dreadlocked captain swung the wheel around. "All right, lass. Here you go."

He cruised the party barge up to the dock. I hopped off, careful to step on a steady-looking board, and waved back to the captain to tell him that I was okay. He took off his hat, waved it, then whipped the wheel back around. Two minutes later, the party barge was no more than a dot on the horizon. The thing had a powerful motor in it, much more so than it looked.

I turned toward the house. I had to pick my way carefully along the rotten dock, but as soon as my feet touched the grass, I started running. My luck held, and I fell only once. But it didn't hurt much, and I kept going.

I dashed along the lawn, through the copse of trees, ran up the steps to the house, then sprinted through the silent, dusty halls. I pounded my way back down the stairs to the Lair of Seduction and threw open the door.

Devlin waited inside. There was a table with flowers, champagne, chocolates, and more. But I only had eyes for him. He was wearing his Debonair suit, but his mask was off, exposing his beautiful, beautiful face to me.

"Bella, I—"

That was all he could get out before I swooped down on him and pressed my lips to his. I planted kisses on his cheeks, his eyelids, even the tip of his slightly crooked nose.

"I love you," I said. "I love you, Devlin Debonair Dash, and I want to make this work."

Devlin's eyes held mine. "Are you sure, Bella? Are you positive? I know you have a lot of issues regarding superheroes. Even sometimes heroes like me."

I shook my head. "What you did today with the news conference blew me away. It was more than I could have ever hoped for. I know you'll never stop being Debonair, and I don't want you to. But you came halfway, so I can come the other half. I want to be with you, Devlin. If you'll still have me."

"Always, Bella. Always."

We kissed again, and I felt Devlin nudge me back toward the bed. I happily obliged. It had been too long. A day was too long to go without him. An hour, a minute, a single second.

"You're *my* superhero," I said as he lowered me to the bed. "And that's all that matters."

★ Epilogue ★

Six weeks later

How does it feel, Bella? Joanne asked.

I clutched the glass of champagne in my hand. Tonight, I knew there was no way I was going to spill it. "Wonderful. Absolutely wonderful."

Joanne's eyes roamed over my drawings, which lined the walls of the Bigtime Museum of Modern Art. Tonight was the grand opening of my first art exhibit at the museum. All the bigwigs on the society circuit had turned out, including Carmen, Sam, Lulu, Henry, Johnny, Fiona, and Chief Newman.

"Well, your work seems to be very popular. Most of the sketches have already sold," Joanne said. A sad smile tinged her lips. "I'm glad I got my request in early."

I'd done a portrait of Berkley for her a few weeks ago. Joanne had given me three times what the drawing was worth. I hadn't wanted to take her money, but she'd insisted. I think it was her way of paying me back for hanging in there with her when we'd been kidnapped.

"How are you?" I asked, putting my hand on her arm. "I haven't seen you at many of the events lately.

Joanne shrugged. Her face looked thinner and paler than usual under her perfect makeup. "I'm getting by."

"Call me if you need anything," I said. "Even if it's just to talk."

"Of course." Joanne downed the rest of her champagne and moved off into the crowd.

Bobby and Grace appeared at my elbow. Both congratulated me on the exhibit. I congratulated the couple on their engagement, even though I still had some reservations about it. But as Bobby pointed out, there wasn't much time to waste when you were their age. Still, I was happy for them, even if Bobby had started going out at night with Grace when she dressed up as Granny Cane. He called himself Grandpa Pain and carried a supercharged Taser. That had been my idea. Somebody in this family had to be practical. I just hoped Bobby didn't give himself a heart attack with it.

An arm slid around my waist, and the world brightened.

"It's about time you got here," I said, turning to face Devlin.

"Well, I had to appear at the opening as Debonair and mingle for a few minutes," he said, blue eyes twinkling. "It is part of my contract."

"Come on," I said, taking his hand and dragging him off to a deserted corner behind a potted fern. "Let's get out of here and go home."

Home for me these days was Devlin's mansion out in the middle of the bay. Piece by piece, bit by bit, we were slowly restoring the home to its former glory, along with Devlin's company, DCQ Enterprises. The business had finally begun to recover from Nathan Nichols's corporate shenanigans. It was something else Devlin and I were rebuilding—together.

"But this is your big night," he said. "Don't you want to stay and soak up all the accolades?"

"And I'll have lots more of them. Right now, I want to spend what's left of the night with you."

"I love you, Bella."

"And I love you, Devlin. Now get us out of here. Pronto!"

"Are you sure?" he asked.

I put my arms around his neck. "I'm always sure with you. Now, take me home and seduce me. That's an order."

POP!